Dimitri's Forbidden Submissive

Ann Mayburn

Copyright © 2014 Ann Mayburn
Published by Fated Desires Publishing
All rights reserved.
ISBN-13: 978-1-62322-126-3

This book is a work of fiction. The names, characters, places, and incidents are products of the author's imagination or have been used fictitiously and are not to be construed as real. Any resemblance to persons, living or dead, actual events, locals or organizations is entirely coincidental. All rights reserved. With the exception of quotes used in reviews, this book may not be reproduced or used in whole or in part by any means existing without written permission from the author.

Dimitri's Forbidden Submissive

As the daughter of an outlaw biker, Rya DeLuca is used to living a wild life, but nothing could prepare her for the danger of falling in love with Dimitri Novikov. To Rya he's a warm, loving, sexy as hell Dom who gives her exactly the kind of bondage and discipline she craves in the bedroom, but to the rest of the world Dimitri is a feared man, a cold blooded, heartless killer who is at the top of the Russian Mafia food chain.

While her hard and Dominant Master is her perfect match in every way that matters, their love can never last longer than a few days at most. Every moment Rya spends with Dimitri puts her life in jeopardy from rival gangs and Dimitri's own family.

Dimitri will have to decide if he loves Rya enough to walk away from her in order to save her life, or if their love is worth starting a war that could change the world of the Russian mafia forever.

Chapter One

Dimitri Novikov glanced over at his friend, Moriz, then shook his head as they moved through the massive hunting lodge that was the current home to the European Delegation of Doms and their subs visiting the United States. This was the last part of their journey through the States and a few nights after the Submissive's Wish Charity Auction, one of the most elite submissive auctions in the world. Dimitri had attended the auction but left early to help his good friend Ivan set up a capture fantasy for Gia, the woman he'd won.

Moriz lowered his voice, slowed his walk to a stroll, then glanced around. "Come on, Dimitri, help me out. This girl, Rya, she is a good woman. I feel like an asshole for how things worked out, but I really like Jean. I want to give whatever it is we have together a chance."

Scratching at his neatly trimmed beard, Dimitri shook his head again. "If she's a good woman I do not want anything to do with her, and you certainly do not want her to have anything to do with me."

"Look, I know you can't be in a relationship, but that is not what I'm asking of you. I purchased Rya for the rest of the week, then we are done. So maybe she is not like the mistresses you keep, but I promise you'll like her. She enjoys being watched—she is an exhibitionist—and you love to watch so it is a good fit, especially because you won't be jealous. And did I mention that she's hot? There was a lot of competition to win her at the auction."

For a moment Dimitri considered Moriz's offer, wondering what it would be like to spend time with a woman he wasn't paying for her company. His heart ached to have someone in his life who genuinely cared for him, but the risk to her was too great. Especially with Borya, *Sovietnik* of the Sokolov *Bratva* family, in attendance. Though technically, Dimitri's family was allied with the Sokolov family, in the world of the Russian *Bratva* there were no true friends. If Dimitri paid this Rya too much attention she would be at risk of being seen as a tool to be used against him.

No, it would be better if he just left her alone.

"Moriz, I cannot."

With a disgruntled huff, Moriz stopped them in the hallway leading to the entertainment wing of the massive lodge. "Come on, there is no one else I trust with her. She's not here looking for a boyfriend. She's here looking for a BDSM experience with a strong Master, and I know you can give it to her."

"Why me? Why not Oleg or Tusya? They are both single and are decent Dominants."

"Because she rejected them."

Raising his eyebrows, Dimitri found himself intrigued despite his determination to make Moriz see sense. "What happened?"

"After she arrived and found out that Jean and I have something special she graciously offered to bow out. Rya is a very perceptive woman and even though Jean was trying to be okay with her joining us, it hurt Jean and Rya knew it and she gracefully bowed out. Rather than just send Rya home, I offered her the chance to stay here and view it as a vacation. She agreed, and that night Oleg tried to pick her up. After ten minutes of talking with him, she politely, but firmly, turned him down. Him and six other Doms that night, I might add. It was very entertaining to watch them get sent on their way one by one."

Trying to imagine the movie-star-handsome Oleg being rejected by any woman made Dimitri's lips twitch in a rare smile. "And Tusya?"

Rubbing his face, Moriz chuckled. "You know how he just likes to announce to submissives that they're going to serve him?"

"Yes, and usually they do. Something about finding out he is Russian royalty does that."

"Not Rya. She actually suggested he might enjoy the feel of her collar for the week."

Dimitri burst out laughing, imagining the stuffy and proud Tusya's reaction. "She did not."

"Oh yes, she did." Moriz grinned. "She's a switch, but she usually only tops women. When I asked her what the hell happened with Tusya she said, as calm as you please, 'You mean you don't know he longs to serve?'"

Both men laughed and two of the submissives who traveled with the delegation smiled at Dimitri and fluttered their lashes. He gave them both a considering look, the girls were fun to play with and knew he would never give them anything more than sex, but he found his mind going immediately back to this mysterious Rya. He couldn't remember the last time any woman had turned down Tusya. He had to admit he was intrigued.

Dimitri waited until the submissives were out of earshot, then said, "So you think I would do better with her?"

"Yes. Rya's fantasies revolve around threesomes and forced seduction scenarios. You're the only single Master that she has not rejected who would enjoy those things. Plus, you're a very strong Dominant and you speak English. This will work well for Rya. She's an honest woman and will tell you what she thinks, even if it's not what you want to hear. So be ready for a bit of sass."

Trying to tell himself he wasn't even considering it, Dimitri looked down at his black button down shirt, checking it for wrinkles and checked his black slacks to make sure they were clean. "What does she look like?"

As if sensing Dimitri's growing interest, Moriz smiled. "Go and see for yourself."

Frowning at the other man, Dimitri shook his head. "This is not a good idea. I cannot offer her what she needs."

"You're reading more into this than there is. All I am asking you to do is take her on for the remainder of the week. Be her Master and show her a good time. Then, at the end of the week you both go your separate ways. She will be in no danger." Moriz gave Dimitri a considering look. "If you do this for me I will owe you a favor."

Considering Moriz was a high-ranking member of the Russian political party currently in power; having him owe Dimitri a favor was worth its weight in gold, and the bastard knew it. "I am not promising anything, but I will meet the girl."

"Excellent, I will introduce..."

"No. I want to meet her on my own terms. Where is she now?"

"Last I checked, she was in the library."

"The library?"

Moriz gave him a bemused smirk. "Yes. Unlike the women you usually date, she has a brain and she enjoys reading."

Dimitri didn't attempt to defend the women he kept. It was true, he didn't select his bed partners for their minds and actually avoided entangling himself with anyone he could possibly love. But this was a unique circumstance and Moriz was right; at the end of the week they would go their separate ways, so why not indulge himself with a woman he would normally avoid. Just this once, he could pretend he was a normal man. But he was getting ahead of himself.

First, he had to see if this mysterious Rya was indeed compatible with him and if he even found her desirable and vice versa.

"If you will excuse me, I have a submissive to seduce."

Letting out a sigh of relief, Moriz nodded. "Thank you and good luck."

"I do not need luck."

Dimitri didn't like the way Moriz laughed as he moved quickly to his private rooms at the lodge, but he couldn't deny the anticipation singing through his blood. He'd never had to actually pursue a woman, and he found himself looking forward to the challenge. Because he was worth hundreds of millions of dollars, and the son of one of the most powerful Bratva *Pahkans* in Russia, all he had to do was look at a female and she'd be naked on his bed. While his body was sexually satisfied by these women, he'd never actually been in love and planned on keeping it that way.

He checked the door to his room carefully for any sign of disturbance. Paranoia had been bred into Dimitri since birth; he never did anything that would give his enemies a chance to take him out of the game. The hair he'd placed between the door and the frame was still there and the lock showed no signs of tampering. He entered his room, and a quick glance confirmed it remained undisturbed. Not that any assassins were likely to hit him here, he had too many powerful friends surrounding him, but the one moment he let his guard down could be the moment someone ended his life.

He grabbed his laptop, deciding he needed a reason to show up in the library with Rya. If she was as independent as Moriz said, she'd no doubt want to select her own Master. While he secured his room, he wondered what kind of woman she was, what she looked like, and found himself entering dangerous territory with this woman he'd never met. No, this was merely another conquest, another woman that he would spoil, fuck, and move on. He might treat her a little better because she wasn't a woman who expected to be his mistress, but he would not allow any dangerous emotions to intrude.

He was alone and would remain alone until his father died.

Shaking off those bitter thoughts, he paused outside the library and collected himself. While he would hate to lose the leverage of Moriz owing him a favor, he wouldn't pretend to be attracted to a woman just to get something out of it. His moral code might be questionable by most standards, but he would never knowingly hurt a woman. Anticipation quickened his pulse and he took a deep breath, the uncharacteristic show of nerves somehow making him feel more alive, more aware.

Some part of his mind tried to warn him that this was perilous, that he should just walk away, but he ignored that voice of caution and opened the door.

The moment he stepped into the spacious, well-appointed library with its floor to ceiling shelves and wide window looking out into the forest the only woman in the room looked up at him curiously from the e-reader in her hand.

Dimitri felt like he'd been punched in the gut when their eyes met.

She was stunning.

Maybe not in a conventional way, her figure was too curvy for the ultra-thin look most women seemed to strive for, but she was intensely feminine even in her casual clothes. Curled up in a large brown leather chair, she wore a pair of white shorts that exposed her lightly tanned legs and beautiful little bare feet. A peach t-shirt with a scooped neck clung to her large breasts and even though her dark chestnut hair was up in a high ponytail, it trailed over her breast to her waist, making him wonder what it would be like to have all that silky hair draped over his body.

With a perfect cupid's bow mouth and soft cheeks she reminded him of a doll, but when his gaze met her unusual amber gold eyes everything inside of him stilled, and for the first time in his life, he found himself struck dumb by a woman. His brain refused to operate as a deep shiver of electricity washed through his nervous system, flooding him with arousal. Everything inside of him demanded that he take her and make her his. When she spoke to him, the sweet, husky lilt of her voice made him want to growl.

"Hi."

That one simple word and the accompanying amused smile managed to break the hold she had on him.

Clearing his throat, utterly thrown off by his intense reaction, Dimitri gave her what he hoped was a charming smile. "Forgive me, I did not mean to disturb you. I did not know there was anyone here."

She shrugged. "You didn't disturb me."

He held up his laptop case like a fool, scrambling to do anything other than imagine pressing her beautiful lips to his, tasting her, smelling her, rubbing that lush body all over his. "Do you mind if I work in here? I promise will be quiet."

The smile that curved her mouth stole his breath. "Sure, no problem. I'm just reading. I hope that won't disturb you."

Her existence disturbed him. "No, it is fine."

Without even really being aware of it he moved to the other side of the room to a brown leather couch with deep green throw pillows behind a heavy wood coffee table. It was as if he could feel her gaze on his back, and he had to resist the urge to flex for her. Good god, what the hell was wrong with him? He was acting so irrationally that he briefly wondered if he'd somehow been drugged.

After unzipping his laptop case with slow, deliberate movements meant to help him focus, he set his laptop down on the coffee table and opened it up, scarcely aware of his fingers moving as he tapped in the codes to get through the multiple layers of security followed by the fingerprint scan. There were dozens of emails waiting for him, some he needed to answer right away, but he stared with unseeing eyes at his screen. It took all of his willpower not to look up, to keep from trying to see if she was looking at him. He forced himself to answer an email to one of his *avtorityet* about an issue with a shipment of guns moving through Serbia before he allowed himself to glance up.

Much to his disappointment she wasn't looking at him, instead, she went back to reading her book. While he would have liked to have caught her watching him, hoping she was interested, this allowed him to study her further. Her radiant skin had an olive cast to it and he wondered what ancestry gave her complexion that beautiful tone. The clouds parted and sunlight shone through the window, bringing out faint hints of red highlights in her dark hair. Her ears were pierced twice on each side and she wore small diamond studs in those holes. He'd never considered it before, but she had beautiful ears, small and delicate. He wondered if they were sensitive.

She glanced in his direction and a slight flush colored her cheeks as she looked quickly back down at her book. Thrown off by being caught staring, he refocused on his laptop and tried to figure out how to approach her. Something told him his usual charm wouldn't work and he found himself struggling with what to say. If his brother, Alex, could see him right now he'd be laughing his ass off. Then again, Alex would probably be telling him to get the fuck out of here and leave the girl alone and not endanger her life, to leave now before anyone noticed his fascination with her, but Dimitri couldn't. This woman had somehow enslaved him with a glance.

Chapter Two

Rya DeLuca read the same sentence of the romance novel for the eighth time as she tried to keep her eyes on the screen and off the huge Russian gentleman sitting on the other side of the room. When he'd opened the door her mouth had gone dry at the sight of a man who moved with a decidedly deadly grace despite his large size and filled out a suit like she couldn't believe. With his well-kept beard, massive shoulders, thick biceps, and a deliciously muscled ass, he was lumberjack-hot despite his obvious high quality clothing. And his eyes...god, he had the most beautiful deep-set gunmetal grey eyes she'd ever seen. Powerful, mesmerizing eyes that went well with the air of authority surrounding him.

There was no doubt in Rya's mind that this man was one hundred percent Dom, and her heart beat faster just being in the room with him.

So far, this had been one of the shittiest vacations she'd ever been on, a huge disappointment on every level. When she'd signed up for the Submissive's Wish Charity Auction she'd been overjoyed that she'd actually been selected. Her mentor at the BDSM Club she belonged to in Buffalo, New York, had been regaling Rya with stories of the Submissive's Wish Auction for as long as she'd been playing there.

At first, Rya had been excited that she'd been selected for the auction, then she had to battle her guilt about taking time off from work, but she couldn't turn a chance like this down. Rya was all about living in the moment and experiencing everything life had to offer, and the Submissive's Wish Auction was a once-in-a-lifetime opportunity.

While she highly doubted she would find her one true love, she had been more than eager for the chance to serve a Master Dominant. Only the best of the best were allowed to bid at the auction and initially she'd been thrilled when Master Moriz won her and a lovely blonde submissive named Jean.

That is, until Rya got food poisoning.

She'd spent that night in bed at the mansion where the auction had taken place, puking her guts out, and during that short time Moriz and Jean had fallen in love. Oh, the handsome Russian man didn't call it love, but Rya could see the sparkle in their eyes when Jean and Moriz looked at each other. Moriz didn't have to ask Rya to step aside; she could easily read that he wanted to focus all his attention on Jean. Even more importantly, Rya saw the pain in Jean's eyes at the thought of Rya joining them.

Moriz had put her into an opulent room of her own and gave her carte blanche use of his credit card to buy and do anything she wanted, but what Rya really wanted was to have a wild sexual experience with a good Dominant or two, and so far, they all seemed to be taken. Oh, she'd been approached by dozens of Doms, but none of them clicked with her, and since she didn't owe any of them her service, she found herself being particularly picky. Yes, she was sure she could have had a good time with them, but something in her heart told her to wait.

Since she trusted her instincts, she'd politely, and sometimes not so politely, rejected every offer from the men so far...although she wouldn't mind if the intensely sexy bull of a man she'd just caught staring at her approached her.

She considered talking to the bearded man first, but he seemed occupied with his work. For all she knew he was taken, but she hadn't noticed a ring on his finger. So he probably wasn't married, but she couldn't imagine a man as good looking as he was being single. She barely suppressed her sigh of disappointment when she realized he probably wouldn't be interested in her anyway. The majority of the submissives who belonged to members of the European Delegation were supermodel gorgeous. Thin, elegant, and stunning. Not that Rya had a problem with them, she enjoyed women of all kinds, but it was a bit intimidating. Rya had a classic hourglass figure and her boobs probably weighed more than most of the submissives she'd met.

Glancing up from her screen, still stuck on the same sentence she'd been reading since the hot lumberjack guy walked into the library, she found him watching her again with a decidedly hungry look. The immediate flood of moisture between her thighs would have been embarrassing, but the loud sigh of delight that escaped her trumped that. Utterly embarrassed by her lack of self-control, she quickly looked down back at her book and loudly cleared her throat, hoping that maybe he hadn't noticed.

When he gave a deep, rumbling chuckle she debated running out the door. Damn, this crazy shyness wasn't like her. Usually, she could hold her own in any situation, but one look from that sexy bastard and she was reduced to a blushing mess. Hell, they'd barely spoken and her nipples were pressing against her thin t-shirt in a most embarrassing manner.

She swore the sexual tension thickened in the room until she became hyperaware of her every move, afraid to look up to see if he was still watching her. Her skin felt sensitive to the slightest breeze, and she hoped that he didn't notice how she was fighting the need to squirm and press her thighs together. When she'd dressed this morning she anticipated a leisurely few hours spent reading in silence, never imaging that anyone else would be using the library what with all the sexual excess available throughout the lodge.

She wondered again if he was single.

Her curiosity battled with her unusual bout of shyness, and just as she was about to introduce herself, the door to the library opened.

Tusya, the sexy blond Russian guy who was a switch in denial of his submissive side, entered and he immediately looked for her. With his lovely auburn-haired submissive trailing behind him with a collar and leash around her neck he approached Rya and she couldn't help but grin at the slightly disgruntled look on his handsome face. They'd played poker last night and Tusya had lost to her, big time. The poor guy was obviously dying to submit to her, but for whatever reason, he was in hardcore denial. She found it funny that Moriz and the rest of Tusya's friends seemed oblivious to the fact, but then again, she often saw things other people didn't. Her mother had the same gift, and while Rya didn't quite think it was a psychic thing, she could spot a lie a mile away and was very good at reading people. Which was one of the reasons she'd kicked Tusya's ass at poker.

Part of her hadn't actually expected him to pay up on his bet, but here he was, giving her use of his submissive for two hours. Katya, the petite auburn haired submissive, had seemed eager to serve Rya, so she hadn't objected when he bet that if he won, he'd get Rya's service for two hours, and if she won she'd get Katya's service. However, she had a sneaking suspicion that Tusya would have liked to have been the one being ordered around by her instead. She might have indulged him, but he was in such denial that she really didn't have the time or the desire to dig through his bullshit to get him to admit a truth he seemed to hide, even from himself.

Tusya's pale blue eyed gaze went from Rya, then over to the man on the couch, and his full lips thinned. They exchanged a greeting in Russian, and she didn't like the way Tusya seemed to dismiss her. Not only was it rude, but it was setting a bad example in front of Katya. If her Dom didn't respect Rya, neither would she.

Clearing her throat, Rya said, "It is rather poor manners to speak in a language that not everyone in the room understands, that is, assuming your friend knows English."

Just as she intended, the verbal zing hit its target and Tusya stiffened before turning to her and tilting his head in her direction. "Forgive me for my poor manners."

It was a struggle to keep from looking at the sexy Dom across the room, to see what his reaction was to her calling out Tusya, but she didn't dare. "Forgiven."

Tusya started to speak in Russian, then switched to English. "Katya, present."

Dressed in a sheer brown summer dress shot with threads of gold, the pretty Russian woman knelt before Rya with her eyes down. Indulging herself, Rya stroked her fingers through the girl's short auburn hair, enjoying the silky strands running through her fingers. She took note of how Katya's nipples stiffened and smiled. "She is lovely."

"Thank you." Tusya said in a formal tone.

"What are her limits?"

"She has no limits."

Blinking up at the blond man, she tilted her head. "So you are trusting me not to harm her?"

His mouth opened and closed, that vulnerability entering his gaze before he nodded, once again stiff and cold. "I am."

"Then I am honored by your gift, but I would still like her to give me a safeword, please."

He studied her for a moment, then nodded. "Her safeword is Tusya." For the first time since they met a real smile curved the edges of his full lips. "Katya is trained in pleasuring a woman. She enjoys pampering beautiful women, so use her as you wish."

"I will. Thank you." She held out her hand and Tusya stared at her a moment before placing Katya's leash in it.

When he didn't move she had to hide a smile, knowing that he wished to stay, but she couldn't allow that. Truly, she had no desire to top or bottom for Tusya, and the intensity of his need made her slightly uneasy. If he was giving her Katya to play with she was going to fully indulge herself, but not with him here.

"I will return her to you in two hours."

He licked his lower lip, his gaze darting over to where the other Dom sat, no doubt silently watching them. "Are you sure? I would enjoy watching you dominate her."

She put an edge of steel into her voice, channeling that inner strength deep within her that would never submit to a man she viewed as being less than her equal in terms of dominance. "I'm sure."

He stiffened and gave her an almost regal nod. "Then I will leave you alone."

When she didn't reply the slightest tinge of regret seeped into his eyes, but he turned and left.

Wanting to sigh, but also needing to focus on the girl kneeling so prettily before her, Rya leaned forward and cupped Katya's chin. "So, sweet girl, what is it you can do for me?"

Katya licked her lips, distress filling her expression. "My English not so good."

Well, that put a wrinkle in things. Maybe she should have kept Tusya around so he could translate. Crap.

From across the room the sexy beast she'd been trying to ignore spoke. "If you like, I translate for you."

She looked up at the hot lumberjack and tried to keep her expression smooth. "And you are?"

His lips twitched into an almost smile that made her want to sigh. "My name is Dimitri. And you are...?"

"Rya DeLuca." She looked down at Katya. "Are you okay with this?"

Without asking Dimitri translated for her and she tried to ignore how utterly sexy he sounded when he spoke Russian. Katya visibly brightened and nodded. "Yes. Master Dimitri good."

Not sure what to make of that, she arched a brow when Katya turned to the Dom, speaking in Russian. He smiled at Katya, then met Rya's gaze. "She said that you can trust me, that I will not press where I am not wanted, and that she does not mind me watching. But what about you, Rya? Do you mind if I watch you with Katya?"

She licked her suddenly dry lips, wondering how the dynamics of this situation had suddenly become so complicated. Without even trying Dimitri had taken charge of the situation, yet she was still Dominant to Katya. It was as if she was both a top and a bottom at once and she found the sensation to be exhilarating. The best of both worlds.

Excitement zinged through her and she barely managed to contain her smile. Realizing he was waiting for an answer, she tried to keep her expression nonchalant as she said, "As long as you can keep your hands to yourself."

He gave that rich chuckle again that sent chills up and down her spine. "I believe I can control myself."

He stood abruptly and began to put away his laptop. "Where is your room?"

"What?"

"Katya takes great joy from serving." He frowned for a moment. "I do not know right words, but she likes to run bath, massage, give you pleasure. It would be hard to do in this room."

Her imagination suddenly ran wild with thoughts of Dimitri watching Katya pleasure her, of wondering if he had enough self-control to truly only watch, and praying that he didn't. "Good point."

She picked up her eReader and stood, absently stroking Katya's hair as Dimitri came closer. He was a big man, wide and solid. Her head came up to just below his collarbone and he smelled really, really good. Crisp and clean, reminding her somehow of the woods in winter. Up close she could see the dark grey eyes and she wanted to rub up against him in the worst way.

Trying to get her libido under control, and figure out if he had a submissive without being obvious, she said, "Would you like your girl to join you?"

The faint lines around his eyes deepened and she had a feeling he was laughing at her even though his expression remained stoic. "I do not have a girl. Do you have Master who will join, beautiful Rya?"

The way he almost growled out the R in her name made her sink deeper into the fog of lust that seemed to surround him. She wasn't surprised when her voice came out soft as a whisper as she said, "No."

"Good. If you will show way to your room, I will follow." Nodding, still caught up in gazing into his eyes, she just stood there before he cleared his throat. "If you will."

Blinking rapidly, wondering how the hell things had gotten so out of control so quickly, she moved away from him. "Follow me."

Chapter Three

Dimitri was in hell. Gorgeous, lush, ball-pounding hell.

Across the expansive black marble bathroom, his bathroom, Katya was helping Rya into the warm water of the bath she'd drawn for her temporary Mistress. He'd suggested his room after he found out that Rya had a very nice, but standard bathroom while he had a suite with a massive tub. Plus, the idea of having her here, touching his things appealed to him. He tried to tell himself that they were here merely because he knew his room was secure, but that wasn't the whole truth. They were here because he wanted Rya in his room and he wanted to keep her here. Giggles rose from behind him and he inwardly groaned. While he could hear their light laughter, he'd been asked to turn his back while Rya got into the bubble bath.

When he'd volunteered for this he envisioned watching one of his favorite things on earth, two women playing with each other. Instead he'd been tortured by being politely, but firmly, asked to avert his eyes whenever Rya was in a state of undress. It made his already unhealthy fascination with the woman grow to an almost unbearable level. He couldn't think of the last time a woman had refused him...well, anything. That was part of the appeal of only having women he paid for their companionship in his life.

If he wanted it, they did it.

Then again, he'd never felt for the kept women what he found himself feeling for Rya and that worried him. If he was a smart man, he'd distance himself from this, look at it from an objective standpoint, and get the hell away from Rya once they were done. But he already feared he'd become trapped by the lovely woman with amber eyes and a very strong will. It fascinated him to see her be so dominant with both Katya and Tusya, yet when she looked at him she somehow softened. He liked that he had that effect on her. A lot.

"You can turn around now, Dimitri," Rya said in a low, content voice. "Thank you for respecting my modesty."

There was a hint of laughter in her last words. When he turned from where he leaned against the wall, he took in the sight before him, trying to hold back his tortured groan. Rya leaned back against the edge of the large cream-colored jetted porcelain tub, surrounded by mounds of bubbles that hid her delectable body from his sight. Katya was naked, but he'd played with her before and while she was fun, she didn't hold one-tenth of the allure that Rya did. He schooled his features into the impassive mask he assumed in public and nodded to Rya.

She gave him a lazy smile, her long hair twisted up into a bun on top of her head. "Can you tell Katya that I would like her in the bath with me? And that I would like her to wash me, please, but all beneath the bubbles."

He swallowed hard, but nodded. It seemed little Rya liked to tease. "Of course."

After relaying the orders, Katya slipped into the bath with Rya, wet a wash cloth and began to work up a lather with a bar of his personal soap. While Katya had a nice, svelte little body, she did nothing for him in the face of Rya's rich sensuality. As Katya washed Rya, he liked the idea of Rya smelling like him. Even though it was a masculine fragrance, he enjoyed he thought of everyone around her knowing she'd been here, in his bathroom, smelling of his custom-blended fragrance. Katya's hands disappeared beneath the bubbles and Rya let out a soft sigh.

"Tell me about yourself, Dimitri. You're so dark and mysterious, perhaps even dangerous. What wicked things do you do?" He stiffened and immediately and the fine lines around her eyes deepened as a blush heated her already rosy cheeks. "I'm sorry, that was meant to come out as a joke."

Moriz had told him Rya was perceptive, but not many people could read him as well as she seemed to. He'd been trained to show no emotion, to give away nothing, but she'd detected his discomfort. Who was this woman? "My tale dull and boring. I find you interesting, little Rya. It is unusual name for an American, yes?"

She leaned back against the small towel placed behind her head on the edge of the tub and shrugged, her smoothly rounded shoulders briefly lifting above the bubbles. "My mother wanted to name me after my father. His name was Ryan. He passed away before I was born."

"I am sorry for your loss."

"It's okay."

He could still detect the hint of pain in her voice and it made him feel like a bastard. "I was named after my mother's brother. He passed before I was born as well."

She smiled and a dimple appeared in her cheek that he wanted to kiss. "Well, we have that in common. But don't feel bad, while I miss never knowing my dad, I had over a dozen surrogate fathers. He left me in good hands."

"What do you mean?"

Instead of answering him, her gaze grew heavy and she let out a soft moan that made his mouth dry. While they'd been speaking Katya had evidently moved up Rya's legs and he was pretty sure right now she was washing Rya's pussy. He wanted to plunge his hand beneath the warm water and find out if Rya kept her sex bare, or if she had those lovely, soft curls he so enjoyed on a woman's cunt.

Keeping himself in check was difficult, but he loved watching the way Rya's neck arched and the small gasp that escaped her. Katya seemed captivated by the American woman, not that he could blame her. There was just something about Rya that was so sensual. Still, he was curious and wanted the woman's mind on him. It was selfish, he should let her enjoy Katya's skills, but he wanted Rya's attention and did not want to share it.

"I do not understand. You had many fathers?"

"Hmmm?" She turned her head and opened her golden eyes, the heat in her gaze stroking over his face like a caress of sunlight.

"Answer me, Rya."

The edge of command in his voice seemed to reach her and she bit her lower lip before answering. "My father was a biker."

"What is that?"

Katya moved away from Rya's sex and lifted the other woman's arm from the water. "This is hard to explain to someone not familiar with American culture. My father belonged to a biker club. He was high up in their ranks, and when he was killed in a motorcycle accident, the other members of club helped my mother raise me."

Not used to being out of his element, he found himself paying more attention to what Rya was saying than the erotic visual of her being bathed. "What is a biker club?"

To his surprise her expression closed down and she gave him an apologetic smile. "Sorry, I can't talk about it. Club business."

"Of course. May I ask what your full name is?"

"Why?"

"I am curious about you. Often you can tell something about someone by their full name."

She shrugged and he marveled at her trusting nature. "Rya Marie DeLuca."

"Marie DeLuca, you are part Italian? Sicily?"

Her laughter echoed through the room and she sat forward while Katya scrubbed her back. "Among other things, yes, I'm Italian."

"What other blood do you have flowing in your veins?"

"Well, I'm fourth generation American so I have quite a bit of blood. Italian, German, French, Spanish, and even some Havasupai."

"What is Havasupai?"

"They're a Native American tribe in the US desert southwest. My grandfather on my Mom's side was full blood Havasupai."

"You are interesting woman. If you will excuse me for a moment I must attend to some business."

Leaving the room, he took out his cell phone and called one of his trusted men.

After two rings Stefan picked up. "Hello, Dimitri. How is America?"

"Good. I need you to do a background check for me."

"Of course."

"Her name is Rya Marie DeLuca. American, part of the Submissive's Wish Auction."

"Age?"

"Probably early to mid twenties, maybe between twenty three and twenty five. She is five foot three, with brown hair and hazel eyes."

"Any idea what region she is from?"

He frowned, trying to think if he could place her slight accent. "She is not from the southern United States, but other than that I do not know. Her father passed before she was born and his name was Ryan. He was part of a biker club. I want information on this club as well."

"When do you need this information?"

"As soon as possible. And this is confidential, understood?"

"Of course."

He hung up and tapped his phone against his mouth, his thoughts totally occupied by Rya. Maybe if he knew more about her his obsession with her would lessen. Yes, he was sure that once he had sex with her she would lose her appeal. But he didn't want to rush her. She deserved to have her desires attended to.

Dimitri had no idea how long he'd been standing there, staring out the window and trying to tell himself that his interest in Rya wasn't dangerous before movement from the bathroom caught his attention. Dressed only in a thick white towel, Rya smiled at him as she walked into his room with a definite sway to her hips. The sunlight made her skin glow as if she was lit from within, and he was suffused with the need to kiss her pink cheeks and fill his hands with her water-warmed breasts.

"Thank you for lending me your bath."

He took a step forward, needing to touch the damp skin of her neck with his lips. "My bath is very lucky to have such beauty in it."

Katya rubbed her cheek against Rya's shoulder like an affectionate kitten and Rya reached back, stroking her face. "I'll take Katya back to my room now."

"No." Both women startled at his stern voice, so he tried to soften his expression and reassure them. "Please, use my room."

"Why?"

He told her the truth. "I do not think you safe alone."

She smiled at him, the dimple that he wanted to kiss so badly showing up again. "I can assure you, I know how to take care of myself. Besides, who would hurt us here?"

Gritting his teeth, he wanted to tell her about Borya, how the man was responsible for running the prostitution network for the Sokolov *Bratva* and was always looking for new women, but she had no need to hear any of that. That, in and of itself, did not make Borya a bad person. After all, Dimitri was responsible for the prostitutes who worked for his family, but unlike Dimitri, Borya bought and sold women on the black market, addicting them to cheap drugs and using them in his whorehouses until they died.

With these thoughts racing through his head he tried to keep his face blank and shrugged. "There is danger everywhere."

"You're really worried about me, aren't you?"

Disconcerted by her ability to read him, he didn't bother to lie. "Yes."

Tilting her head to the side, Rya examined him from beneath her lashes. "I don't feel like it's fair to you to play without you being able to participate. I would...that is...well, Katya isn't mine to share. Do you understand?"

"I do. I will not lie, I want you, but I do not go where I am not invited."

She licked her lower lip and glanced over her shoulder at Katya, then back to Dimitri. "Ask her if she would like to stay."

He did and Katya smiled at him then said in Russian, "Does she wish for you to join us?"

When he relayed the message to Katya he was surprised by the flash of jealousy on Rya's face. "No."

Wanting to know if she was jealous because she didn't want to share Katya, or if it was because she didn't want to share him, he asked, "Do you find me not good looking?"

She laughed, the warm sound racing through his blood and landing in his heart. "Oh, Dimitri, I think you know you're extremely lumberjack-hot."

"What does that mean?"

A pretty blush painted her cheeks. He loved how easy it was for him to make her blush. "It means I find you very attractive in a…masculine way. But I think your ego already knows this."

Before he could respond, she turned and took Katya's hand, tugging her over to Dimitri's large bed. His room was done in shades of blue and silver, giving it a cool, clean feel that he enjoyed. Except there was nothing cool about watching Rya saunter across the room, her delicate golden fingers wrapped around Katya's pale ones. When she turned and smiled at Katya he found himself wanting her to smile at him, and only him, like that.

Disconcerted by his odd, possessive feelings he strode across the room and shut the curtains on the windows. True, his room was on the second floor and no one could see into it easily, but he didn't like the idea of anyone he didn't trust witnessing Rya's passion. He didn't view women as a threat because most of the women he knew enjoyed playing with other women, even loved them, but not like they loved their men.

That thought made him clench his hands into fists, digging his nails into his calloused palms. No, he would *not* think about love. It was absolutely forbidden, eliminated from his life until his father died and a deal could be struck with the top six Bratva families to ensure the safety of any woman he dared to cherish. A hard cramp gripped his gut as memories tried to surface, but he ruthlessly suppressed them. Mourning would do no good; it would not fill the hole in his heart and soul. According to his father, only revenge would do that, but Dimitri and his brother Alex wanted more than revenge for the next generation, they wanted to give them a chance at life. So he needed to quash these unusually tender feelings he had for Rya and view her as nothing more than one of his kept women.

With that thought, he turned around and swore softly.

The women had pulled the cover back, and slipped beneath the white sheets. They were two lumps beneath the cloth, indistinct shapes that he could barely make out and certainly not the fully exposed flesh he'd been hoping for. As he stared at the bed he couldn't help but laugh, and giggles answered him from beneath the sheets.

"Rya," he said in a chiding voice, "you are a naughty woman to tease a man so."

More giggles, followed by a soft moan. Shaking his head, he pulled over a comfortable padded blue chair from the small sitting area and placed it next to the bed. Not close enough that he would be intruding on them, but close enough that he could make out their shapes better. His imagination went wild as he tried to figure out what they were doing, the lack of a clear visual somehow making it more exciting. He was forced to pay attention to their sighs and sexy whimpers.

After watching for a few moments he was able to tell the difference between who was on top and who was beneath. Katya's body was more slender while Rya's lush form made his hands itch to grab her, to sink his hands into all that softness and squeeze. He loved a curvy woman and Rya was perfectly proportioned. Right now, her ass was pressed up in the air while he was pretty sure her face was buried between Katya's legs.

Dimitri loved eating pussy, loved it, and his mouth salivated as he imagined licking at Rya's cunt while she ate Katya. Judging by the sounds Katya was making, Rya was very, very good at pleasing a woman. He wondered what her technique was, and more importantly, what she liked. Katya was soon calling out for Rya to please suck her clit, to make her come, so he relayed that information.

"Rya, she is begging for you to take her clit between your pretty lips and gently suckle her. To make her come."

The movement on the bed stopped for a moment and Rya said, "I bet she is."

Leaning back in his chair, he grinned as Rya continued to torment Katya, from the sounds of it driving the other woman almost to orgasm, then pulling back. After ten minutes of this—he timed them—she finally gave the other woman the release she was craving. Katya's screams of pleasure made his cock ache. If he'd been a lesser man, he would have torn the sheet back and impaled Rya, fucking her until she was screaming like that for him.

The movements beneath the sheets slowed down and the soft cloth outlined their bodies as Rya moved up until the women were face to face. From the soft murmurs and sounds of pleasure he was pretty sure they were cuddling, something he didn't do, but right now, he wished he did. Cuddling led to tender feelings and tender feelings led to danger for any woman he touched. But Rya wasn't like most women. Maybe he could indulge in some affection with her. After all, she was a purchased submissive who knew this arrangement was for a limited time. He could use this week to pretend that he was something more than a killer, someone more than his father's son.

He could be a man, not a criminal. He could be Rya's man—the ultimate forbidden pleasure.

When the covers peeled back enough to show Rya's flushed face and her passion-glazed eyes, he studied her carefully as she said, "Dimitri, do you have a shirt I could borrow?"

Not expecting this, he nodded. "*Da.* I mean yes."

She slowly licked her lips and pushed herself up enough that he could see her upper back and the partial curve of one large breast. Katya was currently holding Rya's tit, and if he wasn't mistaken, suckling at her nipple. The sight transfixed him and he actually startled when Rya cleared her throat.

"Dimitri? A shirt please?"

He gave her an unrepentant grin and stood, allowing her to see how his hard cock pressed against his pants. She let out a soft moan, but he didn't stop to check if it was for his dick, or because of something Katya was doing to her. Going to his closet, he selected one of his white silk dress shirts. Moving back to the side of the bed, he waited, watching as best he could through the long fall of Rya's dark hair. It had come out of its loose bun during their play beneath the sheets and he loved the peaks of her creamy gold skin between the dark locks.

Rya must have sensitive breasts because Katya's sucking on them, a wet noise that was driving him crazy, seemed to have the same effect on Rya. She was rubbing her hips in slow circles and he'd bet that she was straddling Katya's leg right now, pressing her clit against the other woman's smooth flesh. Taking another step forward, so the bed hit his legs, he inhaled and the scent of their arousal made him growl.

He loved the way Rya shivered, then held out one arm, giving him a brief flash of her breast with Katya's lips sealed around the nipple, hiding its color from him.

She grabbed the shirt out of his hands. "Thanks.

Close your eyes, please."

Not used to being ordered about, but willing to indulge her, he did as she asked. The bed shifted against him and he wondered if she meant for him to stand here with his eyes closed until they were done. After what had to be at least a few minutes, small hands pressed against his chest.

"Dimitri, do you mind if I balance myself against you?"

He opened his eyes and found that Rya was right in front of him, straddling Katya's face. His cock punched against his fly and he swore a small bit of come shot out. Even when he'd been a horny teenager he'd had better control of his body, but the sight of Rya with her small hands on his chest over his heart, dressed in his shirt, unbuttoned enough to show some fantastic cleavage, yet draping around her hips enough to hide her sex from his view, had to be one of the most erotic moments of his life. He'd seen and done just about everything a man could wish for sexually, indulged in every carnal pleasure that caught his fancy, but the simple act of looking into Rya's amber gold eyes while she touched him was a remarkable thing.

He placed his hands over hers, lightly stroking her soft skin. "I do not mind. Find your pleasure, little Rya. I will hold you."

She gazed up at him and her beautifully shaped lips parted on a sigh. He wanted to kiss her, to taste Katya on her lips, to stroke his tongue against hers and discover Rya's unique flavor. Pink tinted her cheeks and she shivered as Katya did something that she liked. Slowly one of Rya's hands slid down to his waist, but he grabbed her wrist in a firm hold before she could touch him.

"No. You do not have permission."

Instead of fighting him she submitted to his hold,

leaning on him further until he had to brace his legs as she laid her head over his heart and wrapped her arms around his waist. This allowed him to see Katya's small breasts beyond the generous swell of Rya's ass, half revealed by his shirt lifting as she rode Katya's face. He caught the edge of a tattoo on one rounded cheek and wanted to lift the shirt so he could see what it was. While he was sure her tattoos were nothing like his, all of his ink was put on for marking reasons within the Bratva, it intrigued him that she would have something along the smooth curve of her lower back.

Her small hands fisted the back of his shirt, then she released him and leaned back, one of her hands going to his bicep and the other stroking his beard.

"Dimitri, I'm going to come, kiss me, please. I need you."

Looking into her eyes, he slowly leaned down and brushed his lips over hers. When she tried to immediately deepen the kiss, he pulled back and whispered against her lips. "Stay still, *malyshka*. I control our kiss."

She moaned and her hand convulsed on his bicep, making him smile before he brushed her lips with his own again. Though she trembled, she followed his command as he slowly and carefully explored her mouth, licking the taste of Katya off of her, struggling with himself to drag out Rya's pleasure. The need to own her orgasm was too great to resist.

"You will not come until I say. Yes?"

"Oh, please," she whispered into his mouth, inhaling his air and giving him hers when she exhaled.

"Are you close? Does your cunt ache?" He licked across her mouth again and she whimpered. "I think you are soaking Katya right now with your honey, but she is greedy and licks it up. Maybe she licks your clit, or sucks on it like a little cock. If I had my mouth on your sweet pussy that is what I would do. I would be gentle, then bite."

She moaned low in her throat, and as her lips parted to make that sexy sound, he slipped his tongue into her hot little mouth. He licked her, learning what aroused her, what drove her higher in her excitement until she sucked on his tongue, making him think about that pretty mouth sucking around his cock. He wrapped her long hair in his fist and tugged her head back, studying her expression, her eyes, and reading her body language to gauge how close she was.

By the strained, almost pained look she was fighting her orgasm with all she had.

That pleased him.

Greatly.

Ignoring her nails digging into his skin, welcoming the pain that helped him control his own desire, he stroked her cheek gently and said, "Come for me, *devochka moya*."

Her orgasm was quiet, not the usual screaming and moaning he was accustomed to from his women. But that didn't make it any less beautiful. In fact, he loved the way her voice sounded like a soft dove's cry, sweet and gentle, just like the woman in his arms. She shuddered against him, wrapping herself around him as she made those honeyed sounds. He rubbed a soothing hand down her back, enjoying the flex of her body beneath his fingers. While her back was smooth, no shoulder blades or knobs from her spine sticking out through skin stretched over bone, she also had surprisingly good muscle tone. His little Rya was small, but she was strong.

She made a pained sound, the whimper of an overstimulated woman having her tender pussy touched too hard, and he lifted her off of Katya in an easy move that made Rya gasp and cling to him. For a moment he held her close, let her feel his strength, let her know that he was a man capable of carrying her, before giving her a kiss on the forehead and setting her down next to Katya. She looked up at him, dazed, before drawing Katya into her arms and cuddling the other woman close.

He wanted to join them on the bed, but if he did he would not be able to resist pulling his pants down and plunging into Rya's welcoming heat.

After a few moments Rya sighed, then seemed to collect herself. She gave Katya a gentle kiss, then pushed herself up. It amused him that the glance she gave him was shy and yet flirtatious, a marked difference from the self-possessed woman that he'd seen in the library. He liked that she seemed drawn to him. Without a doubt Rya was his, but he had to tread carefully with her, to make her want him as much as he wanted her. Though they had a limited number of hours together, something he didn't want to think about, he wanted to take his time with Rya.

"Thank you for lending me your room, Dimitri." She rolled off the bed on the opposite side and stood on unsteady legs for a moment before snapping her fingers. "Katya, come."

When she began to walk to his door, still clad in only his shirt, he moved to stop her. "Where are you going?"

"I have to take Katya back to her Master." She gave the petite redhead woman a kiss and Katya beamed at her. It seemed like he wasn't the only one who was entranced with his little Rya. "Could you please tell her that she pleased me very much?"

He did and Katya smiled at him. "Tell her thank you, and that if she ever would like my service again it would be my honor."

Speaking Russian, Dimitri asked her, "Was she that good at eating pussy?"

Katya actually shivered before replying, "Oh, yes."

"Go, get your clothes and collar from the bathroom along with Rya's things."

He smirked and turned back to Rya who was watching them curiously. "She said you eat pussy very well and she would be honored to serve you again."

Rya actually blushed. "Okay."

He laughed, his mouth watering to taste her again. "Does my filthy talk arouse you?"

Turning away, she shrugged. "I don't know."

Not liking her hiding from him, he wrapped his hand in her silken hair and made her look up at him. "No hiding from me, Rya. Does it make your pussy wet and swollen when I say dirty things?"

Her pupils dilated and she nodded. "You have the sexiest voice. You could read a menu and it would make me wet."

He laughed and placed a quick kiss on her lips before releasing her. Katya was back, once again wearing her see-through brown sheath dress along with her collar and leash. He took the leash and handed it to Rya, then took Rya's clothes from Katya. He turned his back and waited until she was dressed before he stepped into her personal space. Energy arced between them strong enough that he would not have been surprised to look down and see sparks.

Rya looked up at him, then back down to the ground. "Well, thanks again."

He shook his head. "No, I am walking you to Tusya's room. That is not up for debate."

"I don't want him to be mad that you were with us, even though you weren't really *with* us."

"He will not be. I have had Katya many times with his permission. He is more her protector than her beloved."

A cold look flashed through her eyes and his soft,

smiling girl disappeared as she stood straighter and lifted her chin. "I see."

There was a knock on the door and a moment later, Ilyena, his brother's current supermodel-beautiful blonde girlfriend, and two of her friends, Betta and Dominique came in. All three were nude and covered in glittering body paint. Ilyena wrapped her arms around him and gave him a quick kiss while Betta and Dominique stood on either side of him and pressed their bodies against his.

"Hello, Master," Ilyena purred in Russian. "Alex sent us to come get you. We are playing in the dungeon and he could use a hand. There are seven of us and one of him. We need your cock."

Ilyena had been dating his brother for around three months and he knew that Alex would soon break up with the beautiful blonde. While Dimitri couldn't date women for fear of falling in love, Alex didn't have that problem. His brother was immune to loving any woman.

From his right came a soft, hurt sound and he looked up to find Rya watching him with a pained look in her eyes.

Dominique whispered, "Did we interrupt something?"

Assuming his usual cold, arrogant smile he shook his head and said in Russian, "Not at all. Go tell my brother I'll be there in a few minutes."

Betta leaned up on her tiptoes and gave him a heated kiss that he barely returned before giving him a puzzled look. "I look forward to serving you, Master."

He slapped her ass and noted how Ilyena was watching him too closely. "Go. I need to return Katya to her Master."

The three women left, and when he turned to look at Rya, he found her staring at him with an expression of complete disgust.

"What is wrong?"

"Nothing." She gripped Katya's leash hard enough that her knuckles turned white and the auburn haired submissive shook her head at him as she walked past like he'd done something wrong.

Baffled at her sudden change in mood he followed Rya as she walked through the lodge with Katya's leash in her hand. They passed several groups of people and more than one submissive asked Dimitri if he would like to play later. Every time a woman said his name, Rya would stiffen further so that by the time they reached Tusya's room, he swore her ass was clenched hard enough to crack walnuts. Frowning at her, he knocked on Tusya's door before Rya could.

A few moments later Tusya opened it and his smile turned to a frown when he spotted Dimitri. "What are you doing here?" he asked in Russian.

Rya spoke up first. "It is bad manners to use a language I don't understand."

Dimitri was surprised at the unexpected bolt of jealousy clawing at his stomach when Tusya's expression softened as he smiled at Rya. With a low growl, Dimitri moved a step forward so his hip pressed against Rya, and became angry when she quickly stepped away. Frowning, Tusya held out his hand and Rya placed the leash in it. He blatantly ignored Dimitri and said in a gentle voice to Rya, "Would you like to join us for lunch in our room?"

"No, she wouldn't," Dimitri said with a low growl.

"Actually," Rya stepped into Tusya's room and gave Dimitri a dismissive look. "I would."

"Rya," he said in a warning tone, not above beating Tusya's ass in order to get her out of his room.

She narrowed her lovely eyes at him. "Thank you

for lending me your room, but it is too far crowded for my taste."

Tusya watched this exchange with a small smirk while Katya stared at Rya as if she'd lost her mind. "Rya, I did not know they were coming."

"Like I said, it's none of my business whose throat you stick your tongue down. Now, if you'll excuse us, we're going to have lunch."

That fucking bastard Tusya shut the door in Dimitri's face, and for a moment, he was tempted to kick it down. He'd never before had to deal with a woman who cared that he had sex with other women as long as he continued to have sex with her. Monogamy was too much like a relationship and he did not do relationships, yet the hurt on Rya's face when the submissives started kissing and fondling him upset him as well.

For a long moment he stared at the closed door, then turned away and tried to figure out why the thought of going back to the dungeon and fucking beautiful women no longer appealed to him.

Chapter Four

Dimitri sat in the chair still facing the bed in his room, staring at the rumpled sheets of his bed. Stefan had texted him that he had some interesting information on Rya and now Dimitri waited for his call with his mind totally occupied by the little American submissive. He still couldn't believe she'd dismissed him like that. Then again, he was almost ashamed to admit that it had been a long, long time since he'd considered the feelings of the women he kept as company, and letting the other woman touch him after the moment he'd shared with Rya was in poor taste.

It wasn't that he didn't know how to treat a woman; he always treated his friends' submissives well. He pampered them and made sure they knew he appreciated being allowed to join them in the bedroom and dungeon. Not because he wanted to take them from his friends, though he was often a third in the bedroom with them, but because he could safely care for those women. He could give them affection without having to worry that they would be killed. He could care for them and give them pleasure without worrying that they might fall in love with him. Or at least, he tried. He'd made the mistake early on of allowing a few women to care too much, causing the breakup of relationships when the women left their men for Dimitri, only to learn that he had no interest in them on their own.

Now, he made sure to keep the boundaries firmly in place, only allowing himself to care for a few of his friend's wives and submissives. People like his friend Nico and his wife Catrin. They loved each other deeply and Dimitri never had to worry that Catrin would want anything more from him than fun and friendship. More importantly, they both knew his situation and were well aware of the consequences of his loving someone. The main reason he enjoyed being with married couples was so that he could feel cared for, even if it was just for a moment. Pathetic, he knew, but the older he got, the more the reality of his life chafed.

Swearing at himself for being a fool, he stood and began to pace, anger replacing the dangerous longing. How could such a brief amount of time with a woman he barely knew upset him this much? Why was it that she seemed like a catalyst that set his heart into motion, which made him want…more? It was bullshit, he should go join Alex and fuck the women until he passed out, but his dick didn't even twitch at the thought of seven beautiful submissives eager to please him. It was almost like they were fake, sex dolls that he would use to masturbate while Rya was a real, warm, soft woman.

He could still taste her kiss.

His phone rang and he answered it as soon as he saw Stefan's name. "What did you find out?"

"Rya Marie DeLuca, twenty-six years old from Buffalo, New York. Never married, no known criminal record, decent credit score, and well educated."

These all sounded like normal things, nothing that would have caused Stefan to say he had a surprise. "And? She sounds like a typical woman."

"She is, but her family is not."

Tired of Stefan beating around the bush, Dimitri growled out, "Get to the point."

"Rya's mother is married to the current vice-president of the Ice Demons Motorcycle Club, New York chapter."

He frowned, Rya had mentioned something about a club then closed down. "What does that mean?"

"In the United States, some of these motorcycle clubs are criminal organizations. They are like Bratva, but different. Still organized crime, but more about freedom and money than seeking social status or political control of cities."

"Are you telling me Rya is like the daughter of a Bratva lord?"

"Yes and no." Stefan sighed. "From what I was able to gather the Ice Demons MC deals mostly in drugs, with some gun running, and prostitution on the side. They own a couple of strip clubs, repair shops, and several other legitimate business, and they have alliances with other MC groups."

"Any affiliations with the Bratva?"

"Only secondary. No direct dealings that I could find, but I have not dug very deep. Their information is surprisingly secure and I would need to use one of our hackers to break into it. I did not think you would want me to possibly insult them by breaking into their system and potentially getting caught."

"No, no that would be bad. But Rya, is she involved in any criminal activities?"

"Not that I can see. Like I said, she has no arrest record and appears to be a fairly normal girl, considering she was raised in the environment of the MC. They treat their women, at least those that they marry or consider theirs, very well. Since Rya is the step-daughter of a high standing member, and also the daughter of a former member, it would be logical that she was treated well."

Taking a seat again in the chair, Dimitri stared at the spot where Rya's head had lain. "What else?"

"She has traveled quite a bit. All to vacation

destinations."

"Anything unusual? Any sign that she might be working for the Ice Demons and doing their business overseas?"

Stefan laughed. "No, I don't think so."

"How do you know?"

"Look at her social media sites. That woman loves to take pictures of everywhere she's been. She has quite an adventurous streak and has visited many places and done daring things like sky diving and swimming with sharks in a cage. I'm emailing you the links to her different social media sights, you can take a look for yourself."

"Thank you. So in your judgment you do not think she could be a spy?"

Most people would have laughed at that question, but Stefan, like Dimitri, had been born into the Bratva, so he understood the constant need for a level of precaution most would consider paranoid. "No, she is simply an unusually beautiful woman with a taste for adventure."

"Lose all the information you have on her. I want no record that she's been researched. Understood?"

"Of course."

"Thank you, Stefan."

"I hope you are enjoying yourself, Dimitri. I will see you when you get back. We will drink and you can tell me if this girl was as good in bed as she looks. She has many pictures of her in a bikini and I would love to get my hands on her. Those tits...I'd suck on them until she was sore." Stefan made a pained noise and Dimitri gritted his teeth.

Dimitri almost told him to fuck off, but that would have alerted Stefan that Rya meant more to him than a simple night of sex. While he trusted Stefan to a point, the only person he trusted with his life, and Rya's life, was Alex. "I will see you next week."

After hanging up, he sat back in the chair and tapped his lips. So Rya came from a family similar to the Bratva. He wondered if she knew about the club's criminal dealings; he would bet she did. No matter how careful people tried to be, they would eventually slip up and say something around her. If Rya had been raised among these bikers, then she would have seen or heard something that would have tipped her off. And he remembered the way she'd said 'Club business', as though just those two words would end a conversation. She was loyal, and he liked that.

More importantly, he remembered how she had spoken fondly of the men who helped raise her. If she could love them in spite their criminal dealings, maybe she could...

No. Absolutely not. He would not even think it. To do so would be torture. For years, *decades*, he'd managed to make a life for himself under the restrictions of the world he'd been born into, and while he wasn't happy, he survived. He just had to hold on a little longer, to wait for the bastard who sired him to die so they could end the bloody feud and move on.

If the old man wasn't so well-guarded, Dimitri would be tempted to kill his father himself. But if he did, he would be signing his own death warrant. He had too many people, good people within their family, who were depending on him and Alex to take over the Novikov Bratva. If he or Alex died, there would be a blood bath as the rival factions battled for supremacy, not to mention the outside families that would make war. No, he knew his lot in life, and it did not involve indulging his fascination with Rya.

Five hours later, he stood in the large foyer of the rented lodge, waiting for Alex's submissive, Ilyena, to arrive so they could take the helicopter to Boston for a party. Alex stood across the foyer speaking with the dark-skinned Nico and rough-looking Ivan, both men good friends of Dimitri's, but he waited on the other side of the room out of respect for Ivan. This morning, before he'd heard about Rya, he'd attempted to buy Ivan's submissive, which caused a problem between them. Normally, Ivan would have laughed it off, but to Dimitri's surprise, Ivan seemed serious about this girl, Gia, he had won during the Submissive's Wish Charity Auction.

The three men stopped talking and Dimitri followed their gazes to see Gia, Ilyena, and Catrin coming down the stairs. Gia was a pretty, slender woman with deeply tanned skin and long honey brown hair. Tonight, she wore something that looked like a navy blue and silver couture sari and sapphire jewelry. When her gaze met Ivan's she went from merely pretty to gorgeous as she beamed at him, her face lit from within, and Dimitri's heart constricted with jealousy. Gia looked at Ivan like the sun rose and set on his command, her love for Ivan evident in her every move. He looked similarly besotted as he ignored Alex and Nico, staring at Gia like she was the only woman in the room.

Dimitri had to look away, and tried to focus on something other than his childhood friend falling in love. Irrational anger burned through him with the knowledge that Ivan could have Gia, that he could marry the woman of his choice and have beautiful children with her while he and Alex would be alone. Dimitri made it a point to leave a woman before she could get that warm look in her eyes for him and never had a moment of regret, but right now his heart ached from emptiness. He closed his eyes and took a calming breath, locking his emotions away before he could reveal anything that would provide ammunition to be used against him.

He needed to leave, to go and stay in Boston and try to fuck Rya out of his memory.

Alex's low voice interrupted his thoughts. "Dimitri, are you all right?"

Opening his eyes, he found Alex standing in front of him with a concerned look. Though they were only half brothers, they each favored their father enough that there could be no doubt about their paternity. They both had the same dark grey eyes that ran in the Novikov family, but while Dimitri's dark hair had a hint of red in the sunlight, Alex's was deep brown with just the first threads of silver at his temples. A scar partially hidden by a goatee twisted the side of his brother's mouth, a constant visible reminder of the terrible price Alex paid for loving a woman.

Focusing on that scar, Dimitri nodded. "Yes, I am fine."

"Ilyena told me that she tried to get you to come play with us earlier, but that you were already busy with Katya and a little American woman."

Not wanting to worry his brother, he shrugged. "I had some business to take care of."

"Betta and Dominique will be there tonight, along with Polly and Svetlana. They have all expressed their hope to spend time with you."

Normally, the thought of those beauties serving him would have at least aroused Dimitri, instead, his cock didn't so much as twitch. Shit. He tried to imagine the pleasure that would come from fucking those well-trained submissives, but all he could see in his mind was Rya—his gorgeous, curvy, Rya who kissed him like he was something special.

As if his thoughts had summoned her, he watched Rya stroll into the foyer wearing a flowing purple dress that fell to just above her knees and left her arms bare. Her dark hair had been pulled back into the high ponytail she seemed to favor and silver bracelets glittered on her right wrist. His body tightened at the sight of her and his cock went from soft to hard in the space of three heartbeats. Even though she wasn't wearing an expensive couture gown or dripping with jewels like many of the women in the foyer, to him, she was the most beautiful woman here.

She turned and he noticed that the dress plunged in the front, revealing the large mounds of her breasts. His gut tightened as his gaze fastened on her cleavage. He needed to lick those curves, to tease her nipples into hardness, to watch her breasts shake while he fucked her. When she smiled at a passing Dom, Dimitri wanted to go over there and beat the other man's face in.

"Who is she?" his brother asked.

Glancing over at Alex, Dimitri did one of the things he hated most. He lied to his brother. "An American submissive that I was thinking about fucking. She ended up here single by an odd circumstance after the Submissive's Wish Auction and I find her interesting."

Alex arched a brow and Dimitri inwardly cursed at the way his brother's gaze sharpened. "Why don't you invite her along with us? I'm sure Ilyena would like to play with her. She is quite beautiful."

Remembering Rya's negative reaction to Ilyena kissing him earlier, he shook his head. "I do not think so."

"Ahh, she doesn't like women?"

"No, she likes them, but she is a switch who only bottoms to men. With Ilyena being a switch who likes to dominate women as well, I fear we might have a bit of a cat fight about who got to be on top."

Alex gave a dark chuckle. "But that is the best kind of pairing to have. I love to watch two women fight with each other for dominance then bow instantly to me."

Dimitri liked it as well, but for some reason, the thought of Alex seeing Rya naked before he did made Dimitri strangely uncomfortable, possessive even, and he was never possessive of a woman with his brother. They'd shared women easily in the past, but he wanted Rya all to himself. Every fucking inch of her amazing body belonged to him. Across the room, Rya smiled at an older silver haired woman dressed in a royal blue velvet dress who looked vaguely familiar. When he saw the four men with the older woman he recognized Mistress Angelique, an infamous Parisian Domme and her harem of men. While he didn't know Angelique personally, he knew one of her men in passing and watched with growing jealousy as they openly checked out Rya.

He wondered if Rya would be going to Boston with Mistress Angelique, but instead of heading for the fleet of waiting helicopters they moved in the direction of the dining room. His heart sank as he realized Rya would be staying behind. The sight of her lush hips swaying beneath the purple silk of her dress as she walked away was unbearable. Without thinking, he went to follow her, but Alex grabbed his arm.

"What are you doing?"

"I've decided to stay."

Looking in the direction Rya went, Dimitri turned back and gave him a concerned look. "Don't."

He jerked his arm away. "Don't what?"

"Come with us, Dimitri. Don't torture yourself like that."

Gritting his teeth, he kept his face as blank as possible. "What? I just want to fuck her and I haven't had a chance yet. We're leaving in a few days so I'm not going to miss this opportunity. You worry too much."

Alex stepped closer and said in a low voice, "Lie to others, even lie to yourself, but do not lie to me. I saw the way you looked at her. It is dangerous."

Anger filled Dimitri and he whispered back, "It is nothing."

"You look at her the way I looked at my Jessica."

Startled, Dimitri stared at his brother. Alex rarely, if ever, said the name of his dead wife. "Alex..."

His brother closed his eyes and the pain radiated off of him in almost visible waves before he regained control of himself and looked at Dimitri again, his gaze totally devoid of emotion. He shared the same deep grey eyes ringed with black that his father and brother did. Looking at Alex was like looking at himself in many ways, and his brother's pain was his pain. Dimitri had held his brother together when Alex completely lost his mind to grief for a year or so before he finally began to make peace with his wife, Jessica's, death. It had been...not good. Alex had been feral with anger and ended up staying at the family's compound in Siberia of all fucking places, isolating himself from the world as he mourned the loss of a beautiful, gentle woman who had loved him more than anything in the world.

When Alex was sure Dimitri was paying attention, he said in a low, deadly voice, "You cannot have her."

"You're overreacting." He lifted his chin. "Go, Ilyena is waiting for you."

"Come with us," Alex said with an edge of desperation in his voice.

He wanted to give in to Alex's heartfelt demand, but now that he'd seen Rya again he knew he had to have her. He said in English, "I will see you in two days. We will celebrate our last night in the United States together, then we will return home to Russia. Maybe we will get lucky and father will die, yes?"

Shaking his head, Alex didn't smile like he usually

did at the mention of their father's ill health. He gripped Dimitri's head and pulled him close before whispering, "Protect her, Dimitri. Protect her by leaving her alone or she will be taken from you forever."

Without another word Alex turned and left, giving Dimitri a glimpse of a very worried Ilyena. Dimitri took off after Rya, and as he moved through the lodge to the dining area, he tried to tell himself that he just wanted to avoid the crowd that would be in Boston, that he wanted some time to himself with the lodge half empty. Those excuses vanished like smoke in the wind as he heard the sound of Rya's laughter, and his heart thumped hard in his chest. He stepped into the dining room and found her almost immediately, as though they had some kind of connection between them that drew his gaze instantly to her.

She was sitting with Mistress Angelique at a large, round table and eating dinner, her head tilted back as she laughed at something one of Angelique's men said, exposing the perfect line of her throat. Once again his heart lurched in his chest, but he remained frozen in the doorway, unsure of how to approach her or if he still had time to turn back. She'd somehow woven a spell around him, his dark-haired siren, and when she turned around and looked at him like she could feel him watching her, he knew he was lost as his gaze met her beautiful golden hazel eyes. Her long, thick lashes framed her remarkable eyes perfectly, but he was distracted by her lips. They were warm and pink, begging for his kiss.

Tonight, she belonged to him and as he sat down and waited for her to finish her meal, he began to stalk his tempting little prey.

Chapter Five

What should have been a delicious dinner tasted like paste to Rya as she tried to enjoy her *Coq au vin* while chatting with the French Domme, Angelique, and her submissives. Rya had met them the previous evening while playing cards and had instantly clicked with Angelique. The elegant, silver haired woman was probably in her early sixties and had a stable of five men serving her ranging in age from a stud in his thirties to a fit and delicious salt and pepper haired man probably around Angelique's age. All four men were utterly devoted to the French Domme and Rya was fascinated by the dynamic of the household. Each submissive had his role and somehow they were all able to co-exist without jealousy.

Speaking of jealousy, she was pretty sure Dimitri was still sitting across the vast dining room, staring holes into her back. She didn't know what his problem was. Tusya had informed her that Dimitri never had a girlfriend; he had what amounted to a harem of submissives at his beck and call as well as a variety of couples in which he was a regular third. She'd heard of men having harems before, and if that was his kink, more power to him, but it still irritated her that she'd been so attracted to the kind of man she could never be with. Oh, Rya had no illusions that anything that happened during her time here was permanent, but it didn't mean she liked seeing a man she'd just kissed mauling three other women.

That was just plain rude.

So, even though he'd tried to catch her attention earlier, she ignored him. Some men just liked the chase; there was no fucking way she was going to be another notch in that playboy's belt. Too bad he was the only man her body was focused on now.

Her hormones had shitty taste.

Clearing her throat, Rya turned back to Angelique. "I have a favor to ask of you."

The other woman gave her a suspicious look before her face smoothed down into a polite mask. "What is it?"

"Nothing bad. There is a...man here I think you and your men should talk with. He's a switch and a very good Dom from what I hear, but for some reason, he's totally freaked out by his need to submit. I thought that maybe if he talked with you and your men he'd stress out less about it. I spoke with him today at lunch about it and he's interested, but because of some personal bullshit, something about the world he lives in never accepting him as having submissive leanings, or some misogynistic shit, he's tried to reject that part of himself for years."

Angelique pursed her lips. "But he is ready to talk about it now?"

Tossing her ponytail over her shoulder, Rya then shrugged. "I don't know if he'll ever be ready, but I kind of badgered him into it. He wanted me to top him in private but we just don't have that spark together and I really don't get off on topping men, only women. But you have such a good thing going with your guys I thought that if he talked to you and your men he might be more comfortable with himself."

Angelique lightly tapped her long, pink painted nail against the stem of her wine glass. "Why is this important to you?"

"Because...I don't know, I guess because he's making himself miserable without need. He seems like a really nice guy and life is too short to waste it trying to be something you're not. I mean, can you imagine living like that? No, he needs to learn to love himself or he'll never be able to love someone back."

"You have a very kind heart. Tell me more about this man. I may wish to speak with him."

She told Angelique about Tusya and a small weight lifted off her shoulders. He really was a nice guy once she got past his stuffy exterior and she hoped he got what he needed from Angelique. Rya was surprised Katya had been very supportive of Tusya seeking out a Mistress. She'd also learned that Katya and Tusya were more like friends with benefits than true lovers. Katya had lost her husband, who had also been her Master, two years ago and while she craved domination and enjoyed the sex, her heart wasn't into looking for love which made the commitment-phobic Tusya the perfect Dom for her.

And speaking of the perfect Dom...

Glancing over her shoulder, Rya found Dimitri still watching her. She looked away and took a sip of her wine then pretended to observe the army of helicopters out in the field behind the lodge as they took off one by one. Evidently, there was a big party going on tonight in a nearby city. Moriz had invited her and even offered to buy her a dress for the occasion, but she really didn't feel like being a fifth wheel. Oh, there were plenty of couples and single subs she could play with, but for some reason that thought just didn't appeal to her right now. If she was being honest it was because she was still hung up on that damn womanizer who'd given her one of the best orgasms of her life—with one fucking kiss.

"Rya?" Angelique said with a slight hint of laughter in her voice.

She looked over at the Domme who was watching her with an amused twinkle in her blue eyes and smiled. "Sorry. I was daydreaming."

"About a certain Russian Dom?"

"I don't know what you're talking about."

Angelique snorted, the sound somehow elegant and refined. "Do not lie to me. He has been watching you like a starving wolf looking at a tasty rabbit."

"Yeah, well, this rabbit isn't interested in becoming part of his dinner."

One of Angelique's men—Rya thought his name was Maurice—said something to Angelique in French and she caught Dimitri's name a couple times. The Domme's eyes went wide and she glanced at where Dimitri probably still sat, then back at Rya. "Yes, perhaps it is better that you stay away from that particular wolf."

"Why?"

Angelique pursed her lips, but to Rya's surprise Maurice spoke up and said in halting English. "He is Bratva. No good for you."

"Uh, what?"

Motioning Rya closer, Angelique said in a low voice, "Dimitri is a high ranking member of the Bratva, the Russian mob."

"What?" She really wanted to look over her shoulder at him now. "For real?"

"Yes. He is a dangerous man and trouble follows him. It is best you do not attract his attention. His reality is not your reality."

Which, of course, only made him all the more interesting to Rya. She'd like to have blamed it on having a biker mom and being raised by an outlaw MC club, but truth was, dangerous men just flat out did it for her. While she had a healthy respect for the law, she'd grown up surrounded by people who either skirted the edges of the rules the rest of the world had to follow or outright broke them. Hell, her own mother had served time for getting caught up in a marijuana deal gone bad and was in jail for two years when Rya was a young teenager.

But the Russian mob? That was big time crime. While Rya kept her nose out of club business as much as possible, she still heard things. What little she knew of the Russian mob was that they weren't anyone you wanted to fuck with. They were also businessmen, and they ran their criminal empires with ruthless efficiency. Despite her best intentions to ignore him, it felt as if an irresistible magnetic pull had her looking over her shoulder at Dimitri who was still watching her.

While she sat with Angelique at one of the many tables set up to serve the people staying at the lodge, Dimitri sat by himself in the far corner of the room, surrounded by the rich amber light of the setting sun coming through the large windows. He wore a tuxedo and she wondered if he was leaving for the party on one of the waiting helicopters, then scolded herself for caring.

A big, scary, rough, handsome man dressed in a tux was her personal Kryptonite, and her breath caught as she met Dimitri's gaze. She swore his eyes darkened even though she couldn't really see him well in the dim lighting. Swallowing hard, she tried to look away and break this connection between them, but her whole body tingled with awareness as he simply stared at her. Her nipples hardened beneath her silk dress and a low, throbbing need settled between her thighs.

She had no idea how long she gazed into his eyes, swept away by the crazy attraction between them, before Angelique gently squeezed her wrist. "Rya?"

Whipping her head around, she flushed and cleared her throat. "What?"

Angelique studied her, then sighed. "It's like that, is it?"

Taking another big gulp of her wine, she tried to keep the tremor out of her voice. "Like what?"

The Domme snapped her fingers twice and all of her men stood at once. "He is calling you, and you will answer. Just be aware that you, tasty little rabbit, may not survive the meeting."

"I'm not going to talk to him," she said, a protest that utterly lacked conviction.

"Yes, you are." Angelique stood and patted Rya's cheek. "I have been a Domme for a long, long time, and I can tell when there is chemistry. Go. Tempt your wolf and see if you can outrun him. At the very least, you should enjoy the chase."

Before Rya could ask her what she meant, Angelique sauntered away with her men in tow. Maurice gave Rya an exasperated look and shook his head, but he followed his Domme, leaving Rya alone at the table. She sat there, paralyzed by indecision. Part of her wanted to flee, to run away from the perilous temptation Dimitri offered, but the wild darkness that lived in the heart of her soul felt almost a…resonance with Dimitri.

She was still trying to figure out what to do when his deep, magnificent voice said, "Rya, come with me."

She looked up and found Dimitri standing next to her chair with his hand out. Before she could second guess herself, she went with her gut and placed her hand in his, letting him help her to her feet. Warmth streaked through her from where their skin touched and she tried to pretend her nipples weren't now clearly poking through the thin fabric of her dress. Even in her four inch heels he towered over her and she looked up at him, drowning in how fucking sexy he was. In a vain effort to regain control of both the situation and herself, she lifted her chin and tried to give him a cold look.

"Where's your harem?"

"Harem?"

"Yes. All of your women. I'm sure they're missing you."

"Where is Tusya? Is he missing you?"

She frowned up at him. "I have no idea where he is."

"So you do not want him?"

The urge to tell Dimitri that she'd fucked Tusya's brains out tempted her, but she had a feeling he wouldn't react well. The last thing she wanted was for Dimitri to pick a fight with him, and as odd as the thought was, she was pretty sure Dimitri felt possessive of her. It was in the way he stood, the way he looked at her, and the way he glared at any man who tried to approach her tonight from the moment he found her in the dining room.

She sighed. "No, I don't want him."

"You want me."

"Arrogant much?"

"Is not arrogant when true."

Scowling at him, she tried to pull her hand away. "I'm sorry, Dimitri, I know this may sound stupid to you, but I don't share so it would be best if we end things right now."

"You share Katya with Tusya."

"That's different."

"How?"

"It just is."

His lips twitched and she swore he was laughing at her. "Come. Let us walk."

Giving his tux a glance, trying to ignore her body's purr of approval at the way he filled it out, she said, "Aren't you going somewhere?"

"Not anymore."

"Why?"

"You will not be there. I will be where you are."

"What?"

"Come. Walk. Is too crowded here."

He tugged her after him, leading her outside. It was still warm enough that she wasn't too chilly in her sleeveless dress, but her shoes weren't really made for walking on the grass. When they stood at the top of the steps leading down to the right side of the house with the paths leading to the lake just down a small hill, she tugged her hand out of Dimitri's.

"Hold on, I need to take my shoes off." A faint smile curved his lips and she sighed up at him as she removed her heels. "You're used to getting your way, aren't you?"

For a moment he looked surprised, or at least his version of surprise which was the faintest raising of his eyebrows. "*Da*. I mean yes."

"Thought so." She almost asked him if it was okay to leave her shoes here. She highly doubted anyone would want to steal her clearance rack fifty dollar heels when most of the women around here were wearing designer footwear that cost as much as the monthly payment on her brand new SUV.

Once her feet touched the grass, she couldn't help but stop and wiggle her toes in it, delighting in the feeling. Dimitri watched her closely, like she was something new and unusual that he couldn't quite figure out. Well, that made two of them.

"What are you doing?"

"Enjoying the feeling of the grass beneath my bare feet."

"Why?"

"Because it feels good." When he tilted his head to the side and looked even more confused she couldn't help but laugh. "Come on, Dimitri, when was the last time you walked barefoot through the grass?"

He shook his head, then scooped her up into his arms.

Clinging to his jacket, she stared up at him, hoping he hadn't heard her little girly squeak of fear. "What are you doing?"

"You have small, tender feet. I do not want you hurt by hidden stone."

While she liked that he was worried about her hurting herself, she wasn't sure about being held by him like this. "Won't your harem get jealous if they see you walking off with me?"

Ignoring her, he carried her down the lawn and out to the lake. She had to admit, it was nice being cradled by a man strong enough to carry her without any complaints. Really nice. And he smelled good, like the soap Katya had used on her earlier mixed with a scent she could only identify as intensely masculine.

He took her out onto the dock to the very end where a group of padded adirondack chairs faced the water. He took a seat in one of them and adjusted her onto his lap until she was curled up in his arms like a contented kitten. Mad at herself for not putting up more of a fight, she tried to sit up, but he easily tucked her back into his arms. Her tension disappeared as she inhaled a deep breath of the smell of the lake cooling as the sun set filled her. Contentment moved through her and she took in the raw natural beauty around her while snuggling in his firm grip.

"Dimitri, what are we doing out here?"

"Appreciating the sun."

"What?"

He looked down at her and gave her a real smile. "You enjoy grass, I enjoy sun."

She realized he was much more relaxed now that they were alone. But that would make sense if he really was part of the Russian mafia. The thought of how dangerous his life must be worried her, and she wasn't sure if she liked the fact that the thought of him getting hurt made her chest ache. While her heart had always been quick to love, this attraction between them was unusual, even for her.

"Now, you ask about my harem. I do not have one."

Pushing against his chest, and once again getting nowhere, she snorted. "Yeah. Right. Dude, I was there. I saw you kiss them."

"It upset you that I kiss them after you, yes?"

Just the memory stung and she nodded. "Yes. I know I have no right..."

He squeezed her hip, cutting her off. "Rya, we do not have much time together. I would propose something to you."

Confused by rapid turn of the conversation, she frowned up at him. "What are you talking about?"

He looked down at her and gently ran the back of his knuckles over her cheek. "I would like to spend the rest of my time here with you. I want you to be my submissive. Only you."

"What about your other women? Won't they be pissed that you're not available to maul?"

He looked sad for a moment and she found herself reaching up and stroking her fingertips over his beard, surprised at how soft it was. He briefly nuzzled his face against her hand, his eyes closing before he opened them and looked down at her again. "My life is very different from yours, Rya. I cannot...I do not love any woman that I have been with. They are my kept women."

"What? Look, I'm not going to be your *kept* woman. Sorry, I don't work that way."

"I do not want that with you. Ever." He made a frustrated noise. "There are many things I wish I could share with you, but it is not safe."

A sudden understanding dawned on her. "Because you're in the Russian mob, right?"

He stiffened immediately. "How do you know

this?"

She didn't like the suspicion in his eyes, or his slightly scary look, so she quickly said, "The people that I was having dinner with told me."

"What did they say?"

Oh fuck, now he sounded really pissed. "Nothing bad. Just that you're a wolf and I'm a rabbit. Shit, that's not what I meant. Sorry, you're kind of freaking me out right now. You can be very scary, has anyone ever told you that?"

His nostrils flared and she watched him visibly calm himself. "Explain."

"The woman, Angelique, she's kind of my friend and she warned me that being with you is dangerous."

That sadness came into his eyes once again and her heart ached for him. "*Da.* Very, very dangerous. That is why I only have kept women."

"What do you mean?"

Shaking his head, he looked out to the lake and his chest rose beneath her cheek before he blew out a harsh breath. "It is best for you not to know. Would be risk otherwise. Do you understand?"

"I think I do." Actually, she understood rather well because of her upbringing, but she wasn't going to share that with him. Club business was club business...just like mafia business was probably mafia business. "Don't worry. I won't ask you to tell me anything that might make me a target."

He frowned down at her. "How do you know?"

"Know what?"

"That you would be target."

She shrugged. "Just that if someone within your family thought you'd told me family secrets that would put me in danger, right? Not hard to logic that out."

"*Da*, yes." His dark brows came down and he

looked at her in such an intense manner that she squirmed on his lap.

"Did I say something wrong?"

"No. No you say right things, which makes it hard to believe. Who are you, Rya DeLuca?"

"Just a girl from New York. Nothing special."

His gaze thawed and he smiled at her. "You are wrong. You are very special."

She wasn't usually one to blush, but his compliment warmed her from the inside out. "Thank you."

"Now, back to proposal. I would like to be your Master for the time we have together. But you will need to know I cannot show you open affection—favor—in public. It cannot be known that I care for you."

Elation filled her that this mysterious man said he cared for her, but then the rest of what he'd said filtered through her happy glow. "Are there people here who would hurt you?"

He hesitated, then nodded. "Yes."

"Then we should go somewhere else."

Once again his dark brows drew down. "It would be out of character for me."

"Why?"

"Because I rarely leave my brother's side."

"You have brothers here?"

"Right now he is in Boston, but he will be back at the lodge in two days."

"Okay, well then let's get out of here for two days."

He chuckled. "You trust me enough to leave with me, even knowing I am Bratva?"

"You might as well learn this now, Dimitri, I live my life to the fullest. I have a job that demands all of my attention so I rarely get to take vacations, but when I do, I try to experience everything I can. I've gone with my instincts my whole life, and so far, they've done a pretty good job at keeping me alive and happy. Right now, my instincts are telling me that I need to spend some time with you."

"Why?"

"Because...because life is so very fragile." Dark memories filled her and she shivered as phantom cold iced her skin.

"You are chilled." He leaned forward enough to hold her with one arm, then the other as he took his jacket off and settled it around her shoulders.

The cloth was still warm from his body, and she took in a deep breath of his smell still lingering on the material. It was such a nice gesture she didn't want to tell him that she wasn't really cold, that the shiver came from a memory rather than reality. Talking about her past was a total mood killer, and she didn't want to answer the questions he would ask right now.

"Thanks."

He began to stroke her cheek with his thumb, the touch at once arousing and comforting. "If you could go anywhere, do anything, what would it be?"

"Hmmm...well, I've put a pretty good dent in my bucket list, but if I could go anywhere and do anything right now I'd have to say I would like to go motorcycle riding along the Grand Canyon. I've heard it's stunning and my grandfather's people were from that area."

"That is natural wonder, yes? The Canyon?"

"Yeah. I've heard it's really beautiful and I love riding on a motorcycle. It's so...freeing. I can go where I want, do what I want and feel the world around me. Do you ride?"

"Yes, I can drive motorcycle. I have a Ducati Monster 696."

She didn't know that exact model, but Ducati's were wicked expensive. "Wow, nice."

"What about you? You have motorcycle?"

"Yeah. I have a Harley Davidson Softail Slim. I don't get much of a chance to ride it in the winter because it's cold as hell in Buffalo and we get a lot of snow, but if the weather's nice, you won't see me in a car if I can help it."

He gave her a swift kiss on her nose then lifted her off his lap. "I must make call. Please sit here. I will not be long."

Confused, she shrugged then sat back in the chair, cuddling into his jacket while she watched the sun set over the forest. She couldn't decide if the sky was purple or blue in the beautiful twilight. Dimitri's voice rumbled behind her as he spoke Russian during his phone call, enchanting her with how exotic the language sounded even if she had no idea what he was saying. She snuck a quick peek over her shoulder and found him staring back at the lodge. The lights were on inside and she could see people moving around behind the windows, though not as many as there had been last night. It seemed like over half of the guests at the lodge had left for the party in Boston, and she wondered who the people were that were a threat to Dimitri.

It still seemed surreal that Dimitri lived the kind of life where she could be in danger from just being seen with him. She should be more worried about it, any normal person would be, but she wasn't scared of dying. Hell, she dealt with death every day at her job as a nurse at a hospice facility outside of Buffalo. Beyond that, she'd had her own brush with mortality and knew that there was life after death.

She was drawn from her dark thoughts by Dimitri's hand rubbing her shoulder. "Rya, would you go on adventure with me?"

Blinking at him in the dim light, she stood and pulled his jacket around her. "What are you talking about?"

For a moment he hesitated, looking almost uncertain, then his usual arrogance returned. "I take you on two day adventure. Where we can be Rya and Dimitri."

"Okay."

He looked stunned. "Okay?"

She smiled up at him, remembering he wasn't used to her impulsive ways. "It sounds like fun."

"You do not want to know where? Or if you will be safe?"

"Sit down, please, I'm getting a cramp in my neck looking up at you."

With a bemused smile he sat down then pulled her back onto his lap. "I do not understand you, Rya DeLuca. You are not like any woman I have met."

"I hear that a lot."

"Why do you not fear me?"

"I'm a very good judge of character and I have a fantastic bullshit detector." He laughed and shook his head. "Fine, lie to me."

"What?"

"Go ahead. Try to lie to me. Tell me three true things and one false. I'll tell you which one is a lie."

"Is this some sort of trick?"

"No. I'm just really, really good at spotting a lie." She winked. "That's why you should never play poker against me. How do you think I won Katya's service from Tusya?"

He looked closely at her, studying her face, the nodded. "I have been trained on how to lie, so do not feel poorly if you do not know."

She had to resist the urge to roll her eyes. "Just get on with it."

"I have an army of over three thousand men that answer to me."

Holy shit. Truth.

"My father is one of the most evil men on earth."

Truth again.

"I am content being alone."

Her chest ached for him. Lie.

"If I love a woman, she will die."

Truth. Heartbreaking truth.

She swallowed hard, wondering why he chose to tell her those things. "I'm so sorry you're so lonely."

He jerked back as if she had slapped him. "How did you do that? You should have believed the part about three thousand men serving me as a lie."

"I've just always had a gift for knowing when someone is trying to lie to me."

Suddenly his face hardened and his grip on her tightened. "Who are you really? Who do you work for?"

"What?" She tried to get off his lap, but his arms held her in place. "What the hell are you talking about?"

"I have been trained by the best, Rya. It is impossible for you to read me. Tell me. Who are you really?"

"Jesus Christ! Can you be a little more paranoid? I am exactly who I say I am. A chick from Buffalo New York, who by some weird twist of fate, ended up on your lap tonight. I'm a fucking nurse, not a spy." She smacked at his hands, but he wouldn't loosen his grip. "You need to get a grip right the fuck now because you're scaring me. Again."

His head dropped and he blew out a hard breath. "Swear it."

"What?"

Looking up, he gently held her chin and stared into her eyes. "Swear that you mean me no harm."

The distrust in his expression hurt her, but even more, she felt pity that the world he lived in made him doubt everything and everyone. She rubbed her face against his hand, but didn't look away from his eyes. "Dimitri, I mean you no harm, I swear it. Until this morning I had no idea you even existed."

"How can you trust yourself alone with me? Do you have any idea of what *Bratva* means? Of the terrible things that I have done?"

"Good point." She smoothed her fingers over his forehead, down his cheeks, and over his lips. "Have you ever raped anyone?"

"No."

"Would you rape me?"

"Never."

"Would you abuse me?"

"Never."

"Would you kill me?"

"*Nyet*."

He said the last word with such vehemence that she smiled up at him. "See, I'm safe with you."

"You believe that? But you do not know."

She shrugged. "I know what I need to know. You won't hurt me."

He looked at her in wonder. "You are either incredibly naïve or very brave."

Trying to lighten the mood, she winked at him. "Or a fool."

"No. Not fool. I think you are brave."

Night had almost completely fallen around them and she looked up at him through her lashes. "So does this mean you're my Master now?"

His hand convulsed on her hip and he said in a low, raspy voice. "Yes, little Rya, I am your Master. For the next two days you belong to me and only me. You are mine."

Chapter Six

Dimitri tried to keep his elation contained as he looked down at his Rya. She stared back up at him with complete trust, something so unusual he wasn't sure what to make of it. Maybe she was foolish for believing him; maybe he was foolish for believing her, but the instincts that had kept him alive this long believed her. He knew about going with his gut and he admired Rya's self-confidence. It was so refreshing to be with a strong woman, one who truly did not fear him. His gaze dropped down to her pretty lips and he took in a deep breath, his attraction for this small woman burning him. Her lipstick had gradually worn away, revealing her naturally pink lips. They looked so soft, so tender. He wanted to defile her mouth with his own.

His cock swelled against her bottom and her pretty hazel eyes went wide. "Well, hello there."

She made him want to laugh, something he rarely did. "Hello, *zaika moya*."

"What does that mean?"

"My rabbit."

Her giggle lightened his heart. "Your rabbit?"

"Yes. You said I am a wolf hunting you and I agree. You are little, soft, and cute. I want to touch you, pet you. I want to eat my rabbit."

Her lips parted and she shifted against him, the tempting softness of her body urging him to squeeze. "Then you're my wolf? How do you say that in Russian?"

"In Russian wolf is *volk*, and my is *moy* or *moya*. So it would be *volk moy*."

"*Volk moy*," she said in her soft American accent and looked up at him with a small smile. "I like that.

You remind me of a wolf. A predator."

He didn't like to think that she feared him, even though he was indeed a predator. "But for you I do not bite, yes?"

She wiggled her lush ass against him again. "Actually, I kind of like biting."

It took a great deal of effort to not lean over right now and sink his teeth into the plump cleavage awaiting his touch. He allowed himself to slip into his dominant space, to look at Rya not only as a woman, but as a submissive, his submissive. The need to know what she liked, what she needed, filled him. He wanted to leave such an impression on her so that when she was old and gray, she would think of their time together and her heart would beat like a young girl's. The fragility of being human struck him, and he wanted to take her someplace safe, to keep her in a gilded cage so that nothing could ever harm her, but that would not work. His Rya was indeed like a wild rabbit and she would eventually find a way out and run free. And she might be much harder to capture a second time.

Stroking his finger over her cheek, loving the soft feel of her skin, he looked into her eyes and asked, "What do you need to make you climax? What kind of spice do you like in your BDSM play?"

Even in the dim twilight he could see her pupils dilate. "Everything."

He blinked in surprise. "Everything?"

"Sorry, let me collect my thoughts." She looked away and a hint of a blush colored her cheeks. "You're very distracting. I don't like burning, or cutting, or anything that would leave scars. And I absolutely cannot stand any form of breath play."

Her whole body tensed and he studied her, sensing something behind those words. When a slight tremble went through her his anger sparked in the visceral reaction. She was thinking about something that scared her, maybe even terrified her. Keeping his voice low and soothing he said, "Did something happen to you Rya?"

She muttered a few words he couldn't make out and he grasped her chin, making her look at him. The thought of anyone harming her, even someone from her past, made him want to break bones. "Tell me who hurt you, and I will make them pay."

It startled him when she laughed and gently stroked his hand still cupping her chin. "You know, you're lucky I was raised around men who considered it perfectly acceptable to break the legs of any guy who hurt my feelings."

"Tell me, Rya."

"Fine, while it's not a nice story, it's also not what you think."

He waited patiently, moving his hand from her chin and stroking her hair back from her face with a gentle touch. It surprised him to see how his hands, the same hands used to kill and do evil, could move so slowly and gently. Oh, he'd pleasured many, many women with his hands, but he'd never allowed himself the bliss of comforting a woman like this. He became fascinated by the warmth filling him, the tender feelings that he did not immediately try to reject. He had two days with Rya to pretend that he was a normal man and he was determined to enjoy every moment of the life he'd been denied before he had to return to his bleak existence.

She visibly gathered her courage then said in a tight voice, "The winter when I was twelve, right around Christmas, I was staying at my grandparent's farm in upstate New York. They had a big pond behind their house that my grandfather would smooth out so my cousins and I could go ice skating on it. I loved doing that, loved the feeling of flying through the air on my skates. That year it had been an especially warm winter and we weren't allowed to go out on the ice. I was out walking with one of their farm dogs, they always had at least three, when I spied the pond. Everyone else was inside helping grandma make cookies, or watching football, so I figured it wouldn't hurt to just play a little."

Dimitri could imagine what happened next, but he quietly waited for her to continue.

"You know how when you're a kid you feel like the rules that apply to the rest of the world don't apply to you? That you're invincible? That even gravity wouldn't dare interfere with your life?"

"*Da.*"

"Yeah, well invincible me decided that I could play on the partially frozen pond, that I would just stay near the edge where the ice was thick and slide around on my boots. I swear I was being careful, but it started to snow, really hard, and I kind of became lost in my own mind. I was imagining…"

She looked away and stiffened again, making him want to know what she wasn't saying. "What were you thinking, *zaika moya*?"

Off in the distance a bird sang its last song before night firmly took hold, and somewhere across the lake, a frog began to croak. He relished the sense of isolation he had out here with Rya, as if they were the only people for a thousand miles. "I was pretending that I was a Snow Fairy, that I was the size of a snowflake and I was dancing through the air. Unfortunately, I was heavier than a snowflake and…and I fell through."

Her last words came out in a whisper and a visible shudder ripped through her. Holding her closer, he tucked her head beneath his chin and enjoyed the way she clung to him, easily accepting the comfort he offered her. She smelled good, like vanilla and spices, and he grazed her soft hair with his lips. Touching her reassured him that she was alive, warm, and safe. He would protect her, care for her, and take the fear from her eyes.

"If I tell you something, do you promise you won't laugh? Or think I'm lying?"

"I swear."

"I died that day, Dimitri. I really did. I was trapped beneath the ice for close to twenty minutes without oxygen. When they pulled me out my heart wasn't beating. I was blue with cold."

He found himself holding her tighter, reassuring himself with her warmth that she did survive, that she was really here. "How did you survive?"

"Well, the doctors say that the hypothermia, where your body cools way down really quick, managed to somehow keep enough oxygen in my brain to keep me alive, kind of like putting my brain into hibernation."

"What do you remember?"

"I remember going in the water, and how my clothing instantly got so damn heavy. I remember not being able to breathe." She shivered hard and almost convulsively gulped in a big breath of air before letting it out in a shuddering sigh. "That's why I hate breath play, hate not being able to breathe. But that's not all I remember."

"I promise, I will never strangle or choke you. Any collar you wear will not constrict you. I swear it." He hated the pain in her voice. "Do not talk about if the memory is bad."

"Thanks." To his surprise she laughed softly. "Are you sure you want to hear the next part? You may think I'm crazy."

"I know many crazy people, you are not one of them."

"You might disagree after you hear what I have to

say, but okay. I lost consciousness, was just nothing in a vast universe of darkness. I could have been there for a few seconds, or a million years, I had no sense of time passing at all, it was just…nothing. I was nothing. Then I saw a light." She paused as if waiting for him to say something, but when he didn't she continued with more confidence in her voice. "I know it sounds like all those cheesy movies about people seeing a light at the end of a tunnel, blah blah blah bullshit, but I swear to God, I did. It was beautiful, Dimitri, the most amazing thing I've ever felt. It was like I was moving through the essence of joy, of love, of happiness. But there was someone waiting for me, someone standing between me and the light."

The hair on his arms stood up and even though he chided himself that her memories were probably just the dreams of a girl suffering oxygen deprivation, the awe in her voice held him spellbound.

"It was my Dad." Her tone choked up and she cleared her throat. "He hugged me, I felt him just as real as you are, and he told me that it wasn't time yet. That I needed to live, to enjoy everything the world has to offer. He made me promise that I would live every day of my life to the fullest because there were things I must do, people I must meet, before I passed. We all have a purpose on Earth, a calling, but we aren't just put here to learn and work, we're also put here to enjoy. That's what I try to do, to enjoy everything that the world has to offer so when I see my father again, he'll know that I lived, really, truly lived."

Stunned, Dimitri looked out over the water with unseeing eyes. Had she really died? Was it possible that a heaven he'd stopped believing in, a God he stopped acknowledging years ago was real? And if there was a God, was there also a devil? And who did his soul belong to?

Rya leaned back and ran her fingers through his hair, studying his face. "Are you okay?"

Such a compassionate woman. "I am okay."

She sighed and continued to pet him. "I'm sorry I'm such a downer. I didn't mean to kill the mood like that. My past is the ultimate cock block."

"No, it is good that I know." He placed a soft kiss on the tip of her little nose, then brushed away a few tears that wet her cheek. Laughter rumbled through him. "I am honored that you shared with me, and I do not think is a cock block."

Her bright smile lit up his world. "Thanks for believing me. Most people think I'm crazy, even if they're too polite to say it. You, Mr. Dimitri, are much nicer than you appear at first."

"Only for you, *zaika moya*."

He wanted to ask her more about it, but part of him was afraid of her answer to the question if there was a Hell. Then again, maybe Hell was that darkness she spoke of. An eternity spent in nothing. The thought made his gut churn and he wondered if God would forgive him for the men he killed. They had been bad people, all of them, yet he'd taken their lives.

"Dimitri?"

He returned his attention to her. "*Da?*"

"Don't worry, you'll go to the light."

The shock made him jerk away from her. "How do you know?"

"I'm going to assume you're asking how did I know what you were thinking. Don't worry, I'm not psychic or anything like that. I'm just used to people considering their own mortality after they hear my story. Well, at least the ones that believe me. The others I know they're thinking about how quickly they can get away from me," She shrugged. "People in our society, or at least in the States, don't like to think about death. It's kind of like if we don't think about it, then it won't happen. So far ignoring it hasn't worked out for anyone I know."

She grinned at him and he shook his head, a slow smile curving his lips. "Good point."

"Dimitri?"

The way she said his name, he enjoyed it. "What is it, *zaika moya*?"

"Would you kiss me please? I need...I need to feel alive."

"No."

"No?" She tried to hide her hurt look behind a brittle smile. "That's okay, you don't have to, I mean..."

He wrapped his fist in her hair and tugged hard enough to give her a little pain. "Shhh. I will not kiss you out here because once we start I will not stop and I do not want splinters in my knees or mosquito bites on my ass."

The hurt fled from her expression and she giggled before saying in a teasing voice, "I'm yours to do with as you wish, Master."

His world narrowed down to the woman in his arms and he made sure she was paying attention. "For two days, Rya, you are mine. But only for those two days."

A flash of hurt went through her gaze, but then she nodded and gave him a small, understanding smile. "I know. For two days you are my Master, my *volk*."

"*Da, zaika moya.*"

She traced her finger over the lapel of his tux jacket that she still wore. "Soooo...what do you plan to do with me, Master?"

"Do you like role play?"

"When it's done right, yes."

He glanced at his watch. It would take a little bit

for the helicopter to refuel and return. It might be enough time for what he had in mind. And if it wasn't he would just continue their play in the helicopter then on the plane. This beautiful, vibrant woman was his and only his. All of her smiles, all of her passion, all of her joy was for him only and he could not wait to begin to explore what it would be like to be able to care for someone like her.

Chapter Seven

Rya watched as the carpeted hallway of the lodge passed beneath her face with her long hair trailing down almost enough to drag across the floor. She gave a futile kick, but Dimitri had her firmly in a fireman's carry and she wasn't going anywhere. He'd carried her all the way from the lake, refusing to put her down. When she really started to bitch about it, worried he'd hurt his back, he simply flipped her over his shoulder, gave her a spank that made her ass burn, and continued on his way with her.

A couple times she heard people greet Dimitri as they moved through the lodge, but they didn't stop. If she didn't know he was being honest about fearing for her safety, she would think he was embarrassed to be seen with her. And she had to admit, the evil claws of jealousy had come out a few times when women greeted him in a way that left no doubt they were inviting him to their bed, even if Rya couldn't understand what they said.

Soon, Dimitri stopped, then opened a door and the next thing she knew she was flung onto his bed.

"I get your suitcase from your room. Stay here. Do not open door unless I knock twice, then three times. Like this. Understood?"

She arched a brow, but nodded. "Okay."

He hesitated. "Do not leave, Rya. Stay here. Promise?"

Wondering why he seemed so afraid that she would leave, she tried to give him a reassuring smile. "I promise."

He stared at her as if memorizing her features,

then nodded and left.

Once the door closed behind him she let out a harsh breath and flopped back on the bed, staring at the ceiling above. Wow, he was one of the most intense people she'd ever met. It seemed like every moment with him was somehow richer, clearer, like he brought her world into a hyperfocused reality that was at once exhausting and wonderful. She cuddled his coat around her and smiled as she inhaled the scent of his cologne.

Being around him was at once exhilarating and exhausting.

Well, she'd found the kind of Master she'd been hoping to meet via the Submissive's Wish Auction, but he was nothing like she thought he would be. Usually, she went for Doms who were a little more lighthearted, bringing a playful atmosphere to their scenes. Then again, while she'd had fun during that kind of BDSM play, she'd never experienced the bone-deep, soul-altering connection that her friends talked about with their Masters. It wasn't like she didn't try to make that connection, she really had given it her all, but she'd ended up parting ways with all of the Masters she'd played with back at her home club in New York. There was always something missing, some element she couldn't name that just wasn't there.

Part of her hoped she'd find that missing piece with Dimitri, while the more practical side of her mind warned her to keep her distance. But how was she supposed to distance herself from the most interesting man she'd ever met? Not only that, but Dimitri was one of the few people who had ever listened to her story about almost dying when she was a kid and believed her. He hadn't been humoring her, and she could tell that he didn't dismiss her ramblings as being bullshit. That touched her, deeply and she wondered why he'd been so...well, afraid of death. No, not afraid of dying, but what came after. Did he really believe he was such a bad man?

Was he a bad man?

Turning that thought over in her mind, she had to resist the urge to snoop through his stuff. Not that she expected to find a severed head in his suitcase or a collection of post cards made of human skin, but Dimitri was a perfect example of still waters running deep. She wanted to know what was beneath the surface of his mind but was afraid there might be monsters lurking in those depths. A bit of anxiety twisted through her stomach and she sat up, looking around the room, trying to find some hint of the personality of the man who slept here.

It was clean, neat, and if she didn't know he'd been staying here for the last few days she would have no idea that anyone actually used this room. Her own room wasn't exactly messy, but she did have some stuff thrown about, her makeup on the counter of the sink, and other small things that showed the room was being used. She wasn't sure if Dimitri was a neat freak, or if the untouched state of the room was merely the reflection of a very careful man.

Chewing her bottom lip, she made the decision to call her step-dad as soon as she could and ask him to find information on Dimitri. Rock, her step-dad, was a very smart man and he knew people, who knew people, who knew people. If anyone could get her information on her new Master it would be Rock. Not that she was really worried about Dimitri hurting her, she believed him when he said he wouldn't harm her, but she wanted to know more about why he believed he was in such constant danger.

She heard the pattern of knocks Dimitri had demonstrated a moment before the door opened, revealing Dimitri and her pink suitcase. She giggled at the sight of the big, bad, bearded man holding such a feminine article. He quickly shut the door, then put her suitcase next to it.

"You did not have many things."

She shrugged. "No. The auction instructions said I should only pack two changes of clothes. So I have this dress and my shorts and t-shirt. I guess Moriz was supposed to provide me with some, but things didn't work out that way."

"Moriz bought you at auction?"

"Yep, he won me and another girl. Unfortunately, I got food poisoning and while I was recovering, they fell for each other."

He leaned against the door with his arms crossed. "Why didn't you fight to stay with him? He is attractive man and good with women."

"Because Jean and Moriz are falling in love."

Tilting his head as if puzzled, he frowned. "But he bought you. He should honor his agreement."

She couldn't tell if he was mad at her, or Moriz. "Well, if he'd honored his agreement I wouldn't be here now, would I?"

A smile tugged at his lips. "*Da*. Good point. I am glad he is idiot." His gaze darkened and she had to resist the urge to squirm as he ever so slowly looked her over. "You are so very beautiful, Rya Marie DeLuca."

Embarrassed by the almost reverent tone he used, and how tingly it made her feel, she flushed and looked at her toes, admiring the sparkly pink pedicure she'd received before the auction. "I bet you say that to all your girls."

"Look at me."

She looked up and her heart gave a hard thud at the commanding, oh-so-very Dom look on his face. Tingles spread throughout her body, flooding her with a rush of hormones that made her want to press her thighs together. Whoa, this man was seriously potent and yummy. "None of those women matter. You...you matter."

"Why?"

He strode across the room, his big shoulders stretching the white shirt he still wore. Sweet baby Jesus, he was handsome, and she could hardly believe he was really hers, or she was really his. Men like this dated supermodels and actresses, not girls like her. Hell, she wasn't going to question it. He was sexy as hell and he obviously felt the same about her. Men loved her curves, always had, and Dimitri was hard as a rock for her.

When he reached her he slowly drew her to her feet and stroked his hands down her arms, leaving a trail of goosebumps over her skin. "You are real to me."

Confused, and more than a little turned on, she swayed closer to him. "I don't understand."

"You do not act, do not say what you think I want to hear. Honesty is something very hard to come by in my world. And I do not...I do not allow myself to touch good women like you."

"Because you're afraid they'll be hurt."

"No, because I know they will be killed." He suddenly swept her up into his arms. "But I will destroy anyone before they get near you. I can have them killed from two miles away, through a forest of trees, and across a crowded room. No one will ever harm you if I am near."

Part of her wanted to laugh at the drama of that statement, but she realized he wasn't being dramatic; he was telling the truth.

"And I'll kick the ass of any bitch who hurts you."

His surprised laugh made her giggle. He brought her closer so he could rub his nose against hers. "I cannot imagine you fighting anyone."

"Hey now. I may be small, but I know how to defend myself. My step-dad made sure of it."

"Mmmm. You fight woman naked in oil for me?"

"What?" Laughing, she shoved at his chest. "Pervert."

"I want to see my beautiful girl's body." He gently set her on her feet, then sat on the edge of the bed, leaning back on his arms and watching her with dark, glittering eyes. "Show me what is mine."

A sudden case of nerves settled over her and she cleared her throat. "Just like that?"

"*Da*. I have managed to control myself, but if I do not get to touch you soon I will rip your one dress off."

She rather liked that image and really liked how he stared at her with such open hunger. Normally, she was very self-confident about her body. She was curvy, but the men she'd dated never complained. However, Dimitri was ripped. Seriously ripped. Even in his shirt she could tell that man had a magnificent body. Would he be turned off by her belly or her big butt? Shaking her head at her own stupid self-doubts she took a deep breath and slowly let it out.

"It would be my pleasure to show you what is yours, Master."

His pleased smile gave her the confidence to turn around and slowly lift her dress over her head, revealing her pink silk panties with black lace edging. The satisfied growl he made hardened her nipples, and she looked over her shoulder at him while undoing the back of her bra. His gaze was fastened on her ass and the way he fisted the comforter on the bed showed her just how much her body was turning him on.

That and the very thick erection now pressing against his tuxedo pants.

Moving slowly, she slid her bra down her arms

then removed her panties.

He moved so quickly and quietly she wasn't aware he'd even left the bed before she felt his big, rough hands on her hips. "I like your tattoo."

She looked over her shoulder and smiled at him. "Thank you. My grandmother was into making her own lace, she supplemented her family's income with it. My tattoo is a pattern from the lace my grandmother made for my mother's wedding dress."

He rubbed his thumb over the black ink that flowed from her hips to the middle of her back, then followed it to where it ended near her tailbone. "Delicate and sweet, like you. What are these sparkles here and here? Diamonds in your skin?"

She giggled as his thumbs caressed the dimples on her lower back right before her butt. "Those are subdermal implants. Like...ummm...jewels secured beneath the skin."

"They are sexiest thing I've seen. Oh little Rya, the things I am going to do to you."

Whatever response she might have had died in her throat when he leaned forward and brushed his lips over her tattoo, then traced the pattern with his tongue. She would have stumbled but his firm grip kept her steady. The brush of his beard felt nice against her skin, much softer than she imagined and sort of tickly. Though the last thing she felt like doing right now was laughing.

She was hyperaware of every move he made, how his hands felt so rough against her and how his grip tightened as he began to kiss his way over her right butt cheek, then her left. He paused and his breath warmed her skin a moment before he placed a hard bite on her bottom. The pain zinged through her and she yelped, then moaned as he licked the throbbing skin where he'd made his mark. For some reason the idea of a man placing his bite marks on her always turned her on, but when Dimitri did it, her inner thighs grew slick from her arousal.

"Turn around," he said in a low, rough voice that made her want to throw herself on him and beg him to fuck her.

She turned, but he kept his hand lightly on her hips so he never stopped touching her. When she faced him she sucked in a hard breath at the way he was looking at her. He knelt and because of their size difference his face was level with her breasts and he was staring at them like he wanted to devour her. She had to admit, she had more than a handful with her double D cup size, and she was used to men enjoying them, but the way Dimitri growled at her made her want his lips on her—now.

Her first instinct was to press her chest to his face, but she remained still. Her body was his to play with; he would let her know what he wanted her to do. The thought was exhilarating and she shivered as he gently rubbed his lips over first her left nipple, then her right. A hard throb started between her legs and she squeezed her thighs together to try to relive the ache.

Licking her lips, she struggled to remain coherent enough to remember how to please him, how to act. Silly as it was, she wanted to impress this man who impressed the hell out of her. She wanted to leave him with wonderful memories to take back to his lonely life. While some people might think he was spinning tales full of bullshit, no one could fake the loneliness she saw in his eyes, a desperation for someone to touch him like he mattered. If someone asked her what the worst thing in the world was, she would say dying alone, and living alone came in a close second.

So, when he looked up at her, she tried to put into her gaze all the warmth she wanted him to feel, to give him what he needed. For Rya, that need to comfort others, to take care of them, to love them was part of what made up her submissive soul. She never felt as alive and complete as when she was making someone else feel good. The flare of heat in Dimitri's eyes followed by his slow smile had her reaching out and running her fingers through his hair, loving the hints of red in all that dark brown.

He sat back on his heels, his gaze going from her lips to her breasts and finally down to her sex. The gruff, almost purring sound he made as he stroked the curls she kept over her pussy made her breath catch. He stroked one finger over that little patch of hair like he was petting a cat.

"Soft, like bunny fur," he said with a slight smile. "Part your legs, *zaika moya*, let me see my cunt."

Biting her lower lip, she widened her stance and tried not to blush at his blatant appraisal, wondering if he liked pussies with full outer lips and tiny inner ones. An ex-boyfriend had once told her that her pussy looked like a peach. While she wasn't sure exactly how that worked, she tried to keep that lovely thought in mind. Growing up with the sons of bikers she'd heard more than her fair share of teenage boys talking about women's bodies in not-so-flattering terms, describing women's pussies as things like meat curtains and camel toes. They hadn't known she was listening to them, but her young mind had absorbed all those mean remarks, and it had taken her a long time to get used to the idea that her sex wasn't ugly.

Still, it was always an act of courage to expose herself to a man for the first time. As he stroked lower, caressing her waxed labia, she couldn't help the stupid litany of self-doubt. With women it was easier because, well, they had the same parts and Rya found the endless variety beautiful. More than that, it gave her a great deal of pleasure to make a woman feel beautiful, to let her know that her pussy, no matter what it looked like, was gorgeous. It always surprised Rya how many women seemed stunned at her open admiration. She loved it when she could see the shift in their expression from apprehension to near-wonder as Rya worshiped them with her tongue.

Dimitri slid his thumb easily between her outer labia and through the wetness there. That was yet another hang up she had. Was she too wet? What some guys called a sloppy pussy? Did Dimitri like the fact that she had more natural lubricant than most women? Did he...

Her thoughts splintered into a thousand pieces of light as Dimitri leaned forward and began to lick her pussy. Unlike most men who just dove right in, he took his time, lapping at her while making an almost constant low, growling noise. She shivered and clutched at his head, unable to keep her hands out of his hair. Something about holding onto him like this made her feel safe and she widened her stance further, trying to give him as much room as possible to access her with his wonderful, sinful tongue.

Jesus Christ, Dimitri had a really long tongue, and when he gently parted her swollen lips to lick at her center she trembled at the electric sparks of pleasure screaming through her body and lighting up her nervous system.

"Master," she said in a half sigh, half pleading moan.

He didn't respond, just continued to explore her sex, avoiding her clit until she was wiggling, trying to get him to touch her there.

He stopped abruptly, then stood, towering over her. "Go on the bed, on your back."

She wanted to touch him, to remove his clothes, to do something to please him but his stern gaze had her meekly complying with his demands. Shit, it was like he had some kind of mental control over her, making her obey him without thought. She lay back on the bed and watched him as he went to the closet, her body restless with sexual hunger as she waited for him. He returned with a large black bag and she couldn't help but smile at the sight of what she was pretty sure was his toy bag.

Looking up at her, he gave her that almost grin of his. "You have any body issues?"

"What?"

He frowned, then said, "I tie you up, any places would be hurt? Any injuries?"

"Oh, you mean do I have any injuries that might hurt if you tie me up. Nope." She grinned at him. "In fact, I'm pretty flexible. I do yoga."

"Good."

He pulled out two odd looking pieces of leather. They almost looked like laced up black leather restraints that would be worn over the forearms, but were much bigger. He must have seen her confusion, because he gave a soft chuckle.

"What is your safeword, little Rya."

"Cookie."

Looking up from his bag of tricks, he arched a brow. "Cookie? Like the treat?"

"Yeah. It's kind of a joke, but I'll always remember it."

"Explain."

"Well, I grew up with a bunch of boys. Most of the club members had sons, with only myself and four other girls, so trash talking was part of my life." She caught his confused frown. "Trash talking is like…when guys say things to each other that sound mean but aren't. Like—shit this is hard to explain—like if we were playing cards and you got a bad hand and complained about it, your friends would make fun of you and call you a whiner or a girl or something. Well, if someone is acting weak and whiny, we ask them if they want a cookie. Like a little kid that needs a sweet to make them feel better. Am I making any sense?"

He gave her a look that was hard for her to decipher, but nodded. "*Da.* I understand. When I spar with my friends we trade insults."

"You spar? What style? Can I spar with you sometime?"

Looking completely nonplussed, he stared at her like she'd lost her mind. "You want to spar with *me*?"

Without thinking she sat up, then crawled across the bed to him, trying to give him a mean look. "Just because I'm small doesn't mean I'm not tough."

He stared at her, then began to laugh, full-on, busting-a-rib laughing. Annoyed, she poked him in the ribs. "Don't make me hurt you."

His laughter cut off abruptly and he flattened her on her back in a lightening quick move, his weight pinning her there in the most delicious way possible. For a long moment he looked down at her, then slowly shook his head. "You are different submissive."

"In a good way or a bad way?"

"Good. I am used to more...meek? Follows orders, no talking back."

"You mean boring?" She leaned up and rubbed her lips against his, sighing when he shifted and his hard cock pressed against her thigh.

"I think you are what Americans call a brat, yes?"

Busted.

"I might have been called that once or twice."

He stroked her hair back from her face and she turned her cheek, nuzzling into his hand. "Then I will need to be strict with you."

The idea at once aroused her and scared her. It

was easier to keep things light, easy when a Master allowed her little bits of defiance. She'd only had two Masters actually force her to behave. One had been an asshole who'd turned out to be all about the chase, the taming, and the other one had been a good Master who'd moved out of her area for work. Of all the men she'd been with, those two had left their mark on her the most, and she felt a little coil of apprehension tighten her gut as she looked up at Dimitri.

He must have seen her worry, because he continued to pet her, slowly soothing her with his touch until she relaxed once again beneath him. "I like your spirit, your fire, but I will not take disrespect. I am not content to be puppet Master, to dance to your tune or play role. Being Master is what I am, how I was born. This is no game to me, Rya. And I think is no game to you. Tell me, do you push to get reaction? To see if I will take control?"

Slowly, trapped by his gunmetal gaze, she nodded. "I...it's hard to find someone strong enough to Top me so yeah, I guess I kind of test people. To see if they're strong enough to make me really submit."

The feel of his hand in her hair, the strength in his gaze made her soul settle somehow. "How many times have you truly submitted, all the way to your heart?"

"Never." She sucked in a quick gasp of air, not having meant to say that. Shit, fuck, *shit*. "I..."

"No, do not lie. I see panic, why?"

She tried to look away, but he gripped her chin and forced her to look at him. "No one wants a submissive who can't submit."

"*Nyet*, little Rya, it is not that you can't submit, it is that you have not met right Master. There is no shame in that. Some women can give themselves to anyone, while others spend all their life yearning for the man strong enough to tame their wild heart. Neither is right or wrong; is how you are made." His understanding and articulation of her most private thoughts made her stare up at him with something bordering on awe. "I do not want to tame you, I do not want to quiet the wildness that lives inside of you. I want your willing submission. I want you to come to me, to submit to me because I am Master and you are slave, because your heart tells you is right. Does it, *zaika moya*? Does your heart tell you I am your Master?"

For anyone who knew Rya, they would have been shocked as she stared up at Dimitri, for once struck absolutely speechless. All she could do was nod slowly and try to put into her gaze all that she was feeling, all the emotions that his words had brought to the surface. Who was this man who had somehow seen into her soul better than anyone she'd ever met?

"Say it, Rya, and believe it."

Looking him straight in the eye, she whispered, "My Master."

Chapter Eight

Dimitri wanted to roar with triumph as the astonishing woman beneath him handed him her heart, but he only allowed himself a small smile. "Good girl."

He stared down at her, bemused by the way she kept surprising him. Little Rya was a complex woman and he found himself constantly fascinated by a new side of her. It was as if most women were a clear crystal ball, pretty but transparent. Rya was a diamond cut into a million facets, each brilliant and beautiful, but hidden until carefully observed from just the right angle.

Right now, he was looking at a very vulnerable woman, one who had to know he could dominate her. He could already see her need to try to retake control creeping in. It was in the way she tensed slightly beneath him, as if testing his hold on her, the manner in which her gaze darted about his face, studying him. The man lucky enough to become Rya's Master would never be bored.

Pain lanced through his heart at the knowledge that it wouldn't be him, but he pushed it away. He forced away thoughts of the future, focusing on the present and this woman. Once again, the image of a wild rabbit came to mind, a creature that could be so soft and cuddly, yet boldly outrun even the fiercest of predators because they were smart. How ironic that he, a wolf, wanted to protect the little rabbit from the other predators, to keep her safe and his alone.

Before his thoughts could turn to more out of character and forbidden emotions, he pushed off of her. "Give me your left arm and your left leg."

She automatically obeyed and the motion revealed her pussy to him. Such a beautiful cunt, flushed a dusky pink, the full lips of her sex shiny with her arousal. Kissing her pussy was the softest sensation he'd ever had against his mouth. He couldn't wait to split her plump labia with his cock. All in good time. First, he needed to get her in the right headspace.

He picked up the big black leather gauntlet and first pulled her calf through, then her forearm so it was on the outside of her calf. This made her pull her leg back towards her chest as she lay on her back, opening her pussy to him. "Is okay?"

Looking a little bit apprehensive, she nodded. "Yes, Master."

"Good. Do you need a cookie?"

She giggled and some of the tension in her limbs eased. "No, Master. No cookie needed here. I trust you."

He began to tighten the laces and watched her carefully as he restricted her movements, searching for any sign of panic. While he knew not being able to breathe was a trigger for her, he wanted to make sure it wouldn't remind her of drowning if she felt restrained. The memory of her almost dying made him pause to steal a quick kiss before he finished cinching up her leg and arm. After repeating the actions with her right arm and leg, he stood back and admired her. Her legs were up and spread wide, her arms pushed upwards and held next to her calves, which opened her pussy and mounded her breasts for his pleasure.

Beautiful. All pale gold skin and dark hair, and the apricot pink of her mouth and nipples made his mouth water. She had a delicious, rich taste to her arousal, an earthy flavor that he wanted more of. It was as if the essence of sex had been distilled into her honey, a unique blend just for him. Unable to resist, he stroked the plump mound of her cunt, loving the exquisite softness. She let out a low, shuddering moan, jerking at her restraints without even being aware of it.

"Rya, look at me."

She lifted her head and her breath left her in an audible rush as he began to unbutton his shirt. He kept his body in good shape, strong enough to kill any who threatened him, hard enough to break the fist of those who dared strike out at him. Women liked his body, he'd been told this on numerous occasions, but as he slowly pulled his shirt off he watched her carefully for her reaction to his tattoos.

She pulled at her restraints and breathed out, "Holy shit," as her gaze roamed his torso.

He watched as her eyes traced over the Cyrillic writing over his heart with the two entwined roses beneath and the eight pointed stars on either shoulder. Then she looked lower and licked her lips, her expression one of hunger and lust. When her gaze returned to his face she gave him a truly wicked smile and said, "Master, you are the hottest piece of ass I've ever seen."

He shook his head, trying to hide his pleasure that she wasn't repulsed by his tattoos even though she probably had no idea what they meant, he flipped open the button of his tuxedo pants and drew them down his legs after kicking off his shoes. When he stood he watched her face as he pulled his boxer briefs down, his erection sticking out hard and throbbing from his body. She made a little whimpering moan and whispered, "Please."

"Please what, *zaika moya*?" He fisted himself, loving the raw hunger on her face, the way her sweet pussy clenched as if imagining him inside of her.

She licked her lips, her gaze totally focused on his

cock while her hands opened and closed as if she were trying to grab something. "Please, take me. Fuck me, Master."

"Such a greedy little girl," he chided softly and pulled a blindfold out of the bag.

He lay down on the bed next to her and gently lifted her head, placing the blindfold on her and pressing down to make sure the foam rings on the inside of the mask blocked her eyesight completely. Once he was sure she couldn't see him he leaned back and began to explore her body at his leisure, indulging himself in the utter softness of her form. When he gave her belly a squeeze, enjoying the give of her plump flesh, she giggled and squirmed.

"Ticklish, yes?"

She pressed her lips together to try and stop her giggles, but when he tickled along her ribs her laughter filled the room. He loved her joy, loved how it seemed to make the world feel like a better place, how it filled him and seemed to lift the gloom that constantly shrouded his heart. She was light, pure and very warm. After a bit he stopped his assault and she tried to roll on her side, little chuckles still escaping her.

"Oh no, you don't get away that easy."

He rolled her back and moved her around so he could press her legs wide, then lap at her cunt. Her cries of passion fed his ego, and he gently sucked her small clit between his lips. The harsh grunt she gave made him suspect that she was close to orgasm. He looked up, enjoying the way she abandoned herself to the pleasure. He licked around her clit, trying to find where she liked to be stroked, how she liked her pussy to be eaten. Without a doubt one of his favorite things to do was give a woman oral pleasure. Not only because he enjoyed the taste of pussy, especially Rya's pussy, but because he loved the look of complete pleasure on a woman's face when she discovered that he was very, very good at it.

Rya's arousal was so abundant she'd actually made a wet spot on the bed beneath her bottom. He used one finger to rub that silken fluid into the tight bud of her anus, enjoying her little yelp, then low groan as he worked his finger in while giving her clit feather light licks. She arched her neck and whispered his name before he sucked on her sensitive nub, keeping his touch light.

She gave a soft, shuddering sigh. "Harder, please, make me come."

"*Nyet*, you will come when my cock is inside of you."

"Shit," she whispered, then stiffened.

Grinning, he sat up, then rolled her over so she was resting on her upper chest with her ass thrust up into the air. In this position the thick lips of her sex spread enough for him to see the juicy wetness within and his cock hurt with the need to fuck her. But he wanted to give her a little spice first, to start to learn her body and what made her crazy with desire.

With her round ass in the air he couldn't help the need to turn that olive skin pink. At the first spank she moaned, deep in her throat, and she tried to raise her bottom higher. Hmmm, his little Rya liked that. Giving her left buttock a harder smack he watched how her toes curled, the way she sucked in a harsh breath. A smack to her right cheek this time, his arousal surging at the way the flesh jiggled from his spank. He loved curvy women and his *dorogaya* was absolute perfection, the ultimate in feminine beauty.

Steadily increasing the strength of his smacks he was surprised at how hard he was able to spank her before she finally cried out in pain. Giving her one more spank, he then gently grasped her bottom and licked the red skin, enjoying the heat of her abused cheek beneath his lips, knowing that the scratch of his beard on her burning skin stung. While he wasn't cruel, he did have a bit of a sadist in him and enjoyed giving submissives who enjoyed the spice of pain what they wanted.

The abundant arousal from her pussy slicked her inner thighs, begging for his tongue to clean her. Her little whimpering sounds made his balls draw up tight. He was close to losing control and fucking her like he was dying to. He wanted to envelop himself in her, to lose his mind while he sank into her wet heat. Fucking women was one of the few things that took the numbness away and made him feel alive.

Moving back a little, he began to spread her arousal around her anus with one finger while digging through his bag with his other hand. After he found the anal beads he wanted, he cupped them in his hand and pressed the sterling silver balls against the wet slit of her pussy, lubricating the metal. Rya's breath hitched and even though she couldn't see, she looked over her shoulder at him.

"Master, what is that?"

"It is nothing but pleasure."

Her pretty lips curved into a smile and she rested her head on the bed again, arching further into his touch. The trust she had in him was evident in her every move and when he replaced his finger with the first ball, pressing it against the entrance to her bottom, she tensed.

"Easy, *zaika moya*. Relax for me. Give me what I want."

She blew out a slow breath and nodded, her bottom opening enough to allow the first small ball in. Wiggling her hips, he watched as she grew accustomed to the intrusion, then began to press the next ball in. This one was slightly bigger than the first, still petite but with a little bit more substance.

By the time all four balls were in, a fine sheen of sweat on her skin made her body glow in the low light. He smiled at the sight of the purple latex rope hanging from her bottom. Maybe he would find her an anal plug that looked like a rabbit tail.

He grabbed a condom from his bag and quickly slid it on, surprised to see how his hands were shaking with need. Taking in a deep breath, he fisted himself and rubbed the head of his cock against her pussy, groaning at the sensation of her soft flesh giving way to his hard need. He was right, the feeling of those thick cunt lips on his cock was one of the best things he'd ever experienced. By now she was pleading with him in broken sentences to fuck her, to take her, to use her body.

He lined himself up with her entrance and began to push in, the tight muscles of her small sex reluctantly giving way. While he knew in theory she was little, it was an entirely different thing to feel just how snug a fit his cock was as he pushed into her. Rya let out a breathy whimper and he stroked his hand down her back and over her red bottom to soothe her as he pressed deeper. It seemed like every new inch that he fed into her set off a series of convulsions inside of her until he had to bite the inside of his cheek.

There was no fucking way he was coming when he hadn't even fully entered her yet.

When he reached her cervix he still had another inch of cock to give her, but he hesitated. Some women did not like the feeling of an erection pressing against their cervix, but he wanted to be all the way inside her, to have every centimeter of his dick inside of her that he could. Reaching around her hip, he began to circle her clit with his thumb then thrust into her. He made a strangled groan at the way her sex clamped around him.

Rya bucked against him, a small smile curving her lips before she whispered, "Fantastic."

Taking that as an encouraging sign, he began to stroke in and out of her, playing with her clit, bringing her to the edge of orgasm, then backing off. Soon she was fucking him back as best she could in her restrained position, her pussy sucking at him and continuing to quiver around his cock. He'd never felt anything like it, and the burn at the base of his spine spread despite his best efforts to hold off.

"Rya, you come for me."

Grabbing the end of the string for the anal beads he began to slowly pull them out one by one, the balls rubbing against his cock through the thin layer of skin separating her anus and her cunt. She gasped and shoved her hips back at him, the raw, amazingly sexy sounds she made as she began to climax around his dick throwing him straight into his own release. He tossed the anal beads over to the side and hammered into her, his body straining for release. With a loud roar he draped himself over her body, caging her beneath him as he thrust into her then emptied himself into her tight cunt. For a moment, he wished that there was nothing between them, but he'd never ever taken a woman without a condom and the fact that he was tempted to do so with Rya frightened him.

He pulled out of her gently then went into the bathroom, cleaning himself and the anal beads before setting them off to the side to dry. Grabbing a wash cloth, he wet it with very hot water and went back to the bedroom as quickly as he could. He set the washcloth aside for a moment and untied her. Rya was exactly as he'd left her and his cock began to fill again at the sight of her well fucked pussy. His well-fucked pussy.

She jumped at the feel of the washcloth on her

sensitive cunt, then made a little whimpering sound as he gently cleaned her.

Guilt pierced him and he quickly unbound her arms and legs. "Did I hurt you?"

She rolled over in a boneless heap and pulled the mask off, blinking up at him, then gave him a very lazy, very satisfied smile. "Hmmm?"

Chuckling, he gathered her into his arms and loved the way she snuggled against him as if she'd been made to be held by him. "You are very...small. Did I hurt you inside?"

"Nope." She gave a blissful sigh and stroked her hands over his chest. "You are *awesome*."

"Are you sure?"

"Yep. Shhhh...happy time."

He had to laugh at himself. Usually it was the woman who wanted to talk after sex, but now it was him while Rya was smiling up at him like he was her hero. He deposited her on the pillows for a moment before reaching for his pants and fishing out his phone. Checking the messages he saw that the helicopter would be here soon and that his personal assistant had acquired the things he'd requested for him.

When he looked up he found Rya dead asleep, her soft lips parted as she curled up on her side. He hated to wake her, but she needed to get dressed. They had an adventure at being normal ahead of them.

Chapter Nine

Rya turned her head and squinted at the bright sunlight streaming into her eyes. A low, dull roar filled her ears and she tried to figure out why it felt like she was vibrating. Closing her eyes and turning over, her arm came to rest on a warm, firm surface. With her mind still half-asleep she explored that surface with her fingertips, find intriguing dips and rises, then a soft trail of fur. Following that trail, her hand moved down until something hard, yet soft bumped her hand. When her fingers touched that large object in a sensual stroke, a man groaned softly.

That woke her up with a start and she blinked rapidly, trying to clear the cobwebs from her mind. She was in a small room, a bedroom of some sort, with dark brown suede walls, two odd doors, and she had a red silk duvet covering her naked body. Lying next to her, watching her with an amused grin, was the sexiest fucking lumberjack she'd ever seen and she had her hand wrapped around his very substantial cock.

Dimitri.

She blushed as sudden understanding flooded her, and she released his dick then collapsed back onto her pillow with a sigh. "Morning. Sorry about the molesting you in my sleep thing."

He chuckled. "Did you know that you sleep like dead person? Through entire helicopter ride, through limo ride you were impossible to wake. Do you even remember telling the flight attendant to piss off when she tried to wake you after we boarded the plane?"

"Nope." Yawning, she nodded and stretched out, curling her toes and extending her fingers. "When I was a baby I could sleep through a motorcycle rally.

Came in handy during college when I had a roommate who liked to have loud sex with her boyfriend. I'd sleep through the whole thing in the bunk above them."

His laughter warmed her and as her brain started to come online, she leaned up on one arm and looked around again. "Where are we?"

"We are on my plane, going on adventure."

"*Your* plane? Wait, I'm in a bed on a plane?"

"*Da*. My plane. Though this one I only rent. My personal jet I own is back in Russia. I flew over on my brother's jet."

"Um...wow." She licked her lips and made a sour face. "Does one of those doors lead to a bathroom?"

"The one on right."

"Thanks."

The fact that there was a shower on the plane gave her the opportunity to shower and brush her teeth. She didn't know how long she had until they reached their adventure, whatever that was, so she was going to take care of business while she could. After finishing, she slipped on the fluffy black robe hung on the back of the door and went back into the bedroom. Dimitri was still in bed and she smiled at him before tossing aside her robe and leaping on him.

He caught her with a surprised laugh, then rested his hands on her thighs while she straddled him. "Did you know there's a shower in there?"

"Yes, I shower earlier." He put his hands behind his head and she had to swallow hard to keep from drooling all over him at the sight of his muscles flexing. God *damn* he was hot. She wanted to just sit here and stare at him all day. But wait, she could touch him. He was her Master.

Hot damn.

Before she could lick him like a lollypop there was a knock on the door, followed by a woman's voice.

"Mr. Novikov, we'll be landing soon."

"Thank you," he replied in a loud, deep voice that made Rya tingle all over.

"No time for a quickie?" she said, hoping she didn't look too pathetic.

Rolling her on her back, Dimitri laid a seriously hot and dirty kiss on her then pulled back and smiled down at her. "I refuse to do quickie with you. You deserve to be savored, appreciated."

"I'd appreciate a quickie."

With a laugh he left the bed, giving her a very mouthwatering view of his ass. Hell, even his butt was the best ass she'd ever seen. Just a light dusting of hair and perfectly sculpted glutes. Seriously, the man could be an ass model if the crime business didn't pan out. And his thighs...thick with muscle and begging for her lips. She seriously needed to spend some time worshiping his body.

"Rya?"

She tore her gaze away from his butt and up to his face smiling back as she read the amusement that lightened his grey eyes to silver. "Get dressed. I have surprise for you."

Thirty minutes later, Rya walked down the steps of the private jet behind Dimitri and looked around with curiosity, trying to figure out where they were. The air was warm, but not hot, and the small airport was surrounded by pine trees. She'd dressed in a pair of dark jeans and brown boots coupled with a cream top that showed off her cleavage as well as perfectly fitting undergarments. She especially liked the lacy peach bra that mounded her breasts together nicely. The clothes had been provided by Dimitri and she'd been surprised that not only did he know her size, but he somehow managed to arrange to have the clothes waiting for them on the plane.

Dimitri went down the steps first and paused at the bottom, looking up at her and holding out his hand to help her down the last steps. She didn't miss the way he scanned the area, or how his face closed down into an expressionless mask. He'd warned her that he wouldn't be openly affectionate in public, but it was kind of weird, like he was a completely different person.

Dressed in a pair of faded blue jeans with a dark red t-shirt that stretched tight over his muscular build, he was at once hot as shit and dangerous, which only made him all the more arousing to Rya. And evidently, to the flight attendant as well. She'd been making flirty eyes at Dimitri, and Rya would have been pissed if Dimitri acknowledged the woman. Rya brushed back some of her hair that had blown into her face and looked up curiously at Dimitri, wondering what he was waiting for.

"Come."

He led her across the tarmac and through the airport without anyone stopping them. She gently tugged at his hand. "What about our luggage? I need my laptop."

"Do not worry. It will be at our destination."

"Um, okay. What is our destination?"

"Is surprise." He looked down at her and she wished she could see his eyes. "Trust me, *zaika moya*."

His pet name for her made her smile. "Okay, *volk moy*."

Only the slightest twitch of his lips betrayed his pleasure at her calling him her wolf. Soon they were outside of the small terminal and Dimitri scanned the area again before leading her to the left. A chunky middle aged man dressed in a nice blue polo shirt smiled as they approached and Rya's breath caught in her throat at the sight of a beautiful silver BMW touring bike parked in front of a green SUV.

"Mr. Novikov," the man said with a big smile as he approached them with his hand held out to Dimitri, "My name is Jack Barnes, I spoke with your assistant this morning and you're all set. You have quite a fun time ahead of you, sir."

Dimitri shook his hand, but when Rya went to shake the man's hand Dimitri stepped in front of her, blocking the other man from touching her. He nodded in the direction of the motorcycle. "Is mine?"

For a moment Jack looked surprised by the way Dimitri kept him from shaking hands with Rya, but then, his big salesman smile returned. "Yep, top of the line BMW K1600 GTL. She has all the bells and whistles. Perfect for what you need."

"And you have gear?"

"Sure do. If you'll follow me I have it in the back of my SUV."

Rya followed Dimitri, amused by the way he made sure to always keep her near him. It was kind of like having an overprotective bodyguard and she wondered what Dimitri thought would happen to them here...wherever the hell here was. The license plate on the SUV said 'Flagstaff Arizona' and she sucked in a quick breath, then jerked on Dimitri's arm.

"Are we going to the Grand Canyon?"

"*Da.*"

She screamed and jumped up into his arms, wrapping herself around him and peppering his face with kisses while making excited noises. Soon Dimitri's icy calm melted just the slightest bit and he gave her a small smile while he held her. "You like?"

"I love. This is the most awesomest thing anyone has ever done for me."

She gave him a kiss that left no doubt she was going to reward him for this tonight. His big hands flexed on her bottom and squeezed hard as he took charge of the kiss, licking at her lips before sliding his tongue over hers, seducing her into burying her hands in his hair as she kissed him back, her joy mixing with her passion until she was breathing heavy. When they finally came up for air she found Jack watching them with his jaw hanging open and a bright red flush on his cheeks.

Dimitri growled at the man, "Do not stare at my woman."

"What?" Jack visibly shook himself then turned and opened the back of his SUV. Inside there were two helmets, both black, and two piles of black clothes in addition to a bunch of what looked like kids soccer equipment and various little girls' toys. Clearing his throat, Jack took out the helmets and went to hand one to her, but gave them both to Dimitri instead. "They're wired with microphones so you can talk to each other."

"Good." Dimitri handed Rya her helmet. "Try on."

"One sec. Hey Jack, you wouldn't happen to have a ponytail holder in there would you?"

He blinked at her, then smiled. "I think I just might. I have four daughters so I'm finding those things everywhere. Hang on and let me check up front."

As soon as he was away from the back she stood on her tiptoes and whispered, "Stop scaring the crap out of him. You're going to give the poor guy a heart attack."

Dimitri leaned down until their noses almost touched. "No one looks at you, no one touches you but me."

She narrowed her eyes at him, but managed to surprise him by giving him a pert kiss on his nose. "You're lucky I think it's cute when you're protective. Otherwise, I'd have to grab your ear and give you a good scolding."

He lifted his glasses and stared at her in disbelief. "You know men fear me, correct? People tremble when see me? That I am dangerous man?"

Giving him a cheeky smile she fluttered her lashes at him. "Not to me you aren't. You're *volk moy*."

Before he could respond Jack returned with a hot pink scrunchie. "Sorry I couldn't find something less neon."

"That's fine." She took it, making sure not to touch Jack in order to humor Dimitri, and she began to braid her hair as she lifted her chin to the gear in back. "So what do we have there?"

Three hours later, Rya stood on the edge of the Grand Canyon, with Dimitri standing behind her and resting his head on top of hers. They'd taken off their leather jackets and the warm sun beat down on them. Instead of going to one of the tourist outlooks Dimitri had driven until they found a private place to stop and admire the view. And what a view it was. She felt...humbled as she stared down into the canyon, awed by the evidence of the vast passage of time, all the millennia it had taken for a river to flow through the land to create such magnificence. Beautiful ribbons of red and brown flowed down the canyons, each layer a page from the story of how the earth was formed.

She lightly traced her fingers over Dimitri's arms, her mind oddly drifting, just absorbing the world and enjoying the moment. His voice rumbled at her back. "Is worth the trip?"

"Oh, yeah." She looked up at him and smiled. "Did I say thank you yet?"

"Every chance you get." He placed a kiss on her forehead. "But I like. In Russia the women that are around me are....what is the English word...used to luxury. Do not see the beauty of things, only the money it took to buy."

"Spoiled?"

"*Da*, spoiled."

"Sounds like you hang around the wrong kind of women."

He stiffened, then pulled away. Rya turned away from the sight of the canyon to look at him. His expression had reverted to that cold mask again. "No, little Rya, you are wrong kind of woman for me."

That hurt, more than it should considering she'd only known him for the briefest of times. "I see."

Shaking his head, he closed the distance between them and cupped her face gently in his hands. "You are good woman. So full of life. Honorable, kind...I do not deserve you."

"You don't see yourself very clearly, do you? You're a good man, Dimitri."

Once again, she seemed to say the wrong thing and he jerked back like she'd slapped him. "No. I am not."

"What are you talking about? I mean, yeah, you're not exactly an angel, I'm sure, but you're not a bad man."

Giving her a frustrated look, he began to pace. "Bringing you here, is selfish. I should take you back."

Hurt pinged through her but she lifted her chin. "Why? I thought we were having a good time."

Instead of answering her he went to where the motorcycle was parked beneath the shade of a small cluster of juniper trees. He opened the compartment and brought out two small objects.

"Rya, come here."

Curious, and getting a little irritated by his mood swings, she walked over and stood in the shade with him. He was busy using what looked like a satellite phone, and in his other hand had her smartphone.

She frowned at her pink sparkly phone in his hand. It had been packed in a separate pocket of her suitcase which meant he'd gone through her stuff.

"Umm, what the fuck are you doing with my phone?"

He glanced at her, his expression unreadable, before handing her phone to her. "You have internet through my phone. Do a search for my name, Dimitri Cheslav Novikov."

"What?"

Instead of answering her he left her at the bike and went back to staring at the canyon while she watched him in bewilderment. With a sigh she checked her phone for missed calls, sent her mom a quick text to let her know where she was, who she was with, and that she was all right, then did a search for Dimitri's name. A bunch of stuff came up in Russian and she frowned, then clicked the first link and read the roughly translated version. It was about the Novikov crime family, starting back in the very late seventeen hundreds and going up to today. She quickly scanned through the small biographies next to each picture, her gut churning as she read tales of murder, rape, kidnapping, theft, and enough political intrigue to write a thousand books. After the fall of the Soviet Union, the Novikov family rose to the position of the top Bratva in Moscow. Since then the once powerful house had suffered from poor management, but the article hinted that things were going to change when the new leader took over as soon as Jorg Novikov died.

With her heart beating hard in her throat, she moved over to the juniper tree and slowly sat down, bracing herself against the trunk as she got to the modern day leader of the family, Jorg Novikov. Even if she didn't know it was Dimitri's father, she'd have recognized the familial resemblance right away in the picture next to his bio. They had the same eyes, similar bone structure, and the same dark hair, but there were differences. Dimitri had a stronger jaw than his father, but their resemblance chilled her to see a man who was allegedly responsible for a long list of horrendous crimes and looked so much like the man she was alone with, in the middle of nowhere.

With a shaking finger, she scrolled down and came to a picture of a man she vaguely recognized from the lodge, Alexandr Novikov, eldest son of Jorg Novikov and the *Obshchak* of the family. She opened a window and did a quick search, discovering that the *Obshchak* was one of the three men who were the most powerful people in the Novikov Bratva. The *Obshchak* was in charge of the money and dealing with the government bribes. Jorg was the *Pakhan*, the pinnacle of the pyramid, Alexandr, the *Obshchak*, was one of the second most powerful, one of two men known as 'The Two Spies'. The second was Dimitri.

She glanced up at the man in question, still standing with his back to her and his gaze focused on the canyon. With her heart in her throat she read about Dimitri, the *Sovietnik* of the Novikov family, basically the man at the right hand man of his father, the Pakhan. Or, he used to be. Almost four years ago, some kind of falling out occurred between Dimitri and his father. The website offered up a few theories, but the truth was that no one knew what happened except Dimitri and his father. Dimitri was still part of the Bratva, and still a high-ranking member, but he'd been estranged from his father for four years.

She looked over at the picture of Dimitri and her heart lurched. He was caught on camera exiting a brothel known to be owned by the Novikov family. Evidently Dimitri was in charge of the prostitution and enforcement branch of the criminal network, and was a very, very dangerous man. He was suspected of having been involved with dozens of murders and even a couple bombings. The preferred method of execution for those the Novikov family considered enemies was to skin them alive, then feed them to hogs. She'd grown up around organized crime, but nothing of this scale. This was...this was bad.

Her phone chirped and she saw that it was her mom calling. With numb fingers she held the phone to her ear. "Hi, Mom."

She was surprised to hear her step-dad "Baby girl, it's Rock."

He sounded super pissed and she swallowed hard, staring at Dimitri's back. Her heart slammed against her ribs as she realized the Dimitri she thought she knew was nothing like the Dimitri who helped run a vast criminal empire that was so brutal, so sadistic that she had trouble even wrapping her mind around it. He ran the prostitution arm of the Novikov family, for fuck's sake. A shudder of revulsion worked through her and she was *so* glad they'd used a condom.

"Hey, Rock."

"What the fuck are you doing with Dimitri Novikov? *Have you lost your goddamn mind?* Do you know who he is?"

"I...I just found out. He made me do an Internet search on him." She wondered if Dimitri could hear her and lowered her voice, "Rock, I had no idea. He seemed so nice."

"Rya, listen to me. It is not safe to be around him, do you get me? You need to get away from him as soon as possible."

"You think he'd hurt me?"

"I don't know. But I do know that the Novikov Curse will."

"What?"

"He hasn't told you about that yet?"

"I read something, but I was a little distracted. What the hell are you talking about and how do you know Dimitri?"

"I don't know him, but that's Club business."

She wanted to scream in frustration, but managed to hold it in. "Rock, what should I do? We're at the fucking Grand Canyon, alone."

"What the hell are you doing there?"

Without going into too much detail—her step-dad didn't need to know she was into BDSM and sold herself at a charity auction—she told him about Dimitri wanting to get away from everyone, how she'd mentioned that she'd love to see the Grand Canyon, how he'd flown her out there, bought a motorcycle, and basically done everything to fulfill her wish. As she spoke about it, she felt like she was talking about two different people. The Dimitri she thought she knew seemed utterly devoted to making her happy, but in his other life he fucked whores and killed people.

Rock was silent for a long time, then said in a tight voice, "I want to talk to him."

"Fuck. Rock please..."

"Baby girl, give him the phone, now."

Shit, shit, shit, shit, shit.

Screwing up her courage, she walked over to Dimitri and cleared her throat. "My step-dad wants to talk to you."

He turned and gave her a searching look, sadness flashing through his eyes before he took the phone. "Go back to the tree, Rya. This is not a conversation for you."

Part of her was tempted to tell him to fuck off, or to just get on the bike and ride off, but she couldn't leave him here. He hadn't done anything wrong—to her. Fuck, he'd tried to warn her, but she'd been too wrapped up in her romantic fantasies about him being in the Russian mafia without thinking about the cold, brutal truth of what that really meant.

With a heavy heart, she returned to the tree and sat on the hard ground, drawing up her knees and resting her forehead on them. Her emotions were all over the place, ricocheting from fear, to sadness, to anger, and surprisingly enough, to feeling pain for Dimitri. She couldn't imagine what it must have been like to have been raised by someone as ruthless as his father, to have grown up in an environment of such extreme violence. God, she was so stupid. Her idiotic optimism wanted to see the best in everyone, so she ignored the repeated warnings Dimitri had given her, and listened to her hormones and her foolish romantic heart instead.

Boots crunched in the rocks near her and she looked up, taking her phone from a silent Dimitri when he offered it. Her voice cracked as she said, "Hey, Rock, it's me."

Rock actually sounded calmer than when he'd first talked to her. "Hey, baby girl. You sound freaked out. Don't be. It's all good."

Blinking rapidly, she tried to figure out what the hell was up with Rock's sudden one-eighty. "What are you talking about? You told me...you know."

"Yeah, but trust me, Dimitri's not gonna let anything happen to you."

"But he's..." she glanced up, finding Dimitri still watching her with that cold look. "You know..."

"Yeah, I know. Better than you think. Give the man a chance to explain himself."

"Why?"

"Because he isn't going to let anything happen to you."

"Rock, you aren't making sense. And if you tell me Club business, I'm never going to bake for you again, and you know Mom can't cook for shit."

"Oh, that's just harsh." He sighed and some of the humor drained from his voice. "Look, not all bad guys are bad. Trust your heart to know the difference."

"My heart? Fuck, Rock, you sound like a crappy fortune cookie."

"Hear the man out, Rya."

She stiffened. Rock only called her by her given name when he was really serious. "Why?"

"What the fuck is it with you women and why? Just *do* it."

"Fine," she huffed.

"Love you, baby girl. Be safe."

"Thanks." She hung up and stood, crossing her arms and staring at Dimitri. "Explain."

For a long time he just looked at her, then shook his head. "I will take you home."

Her temper snapped, and she stepped forward and glared at him. "Uh-uh. You better explain some shit right now. Like how many whores have you fucked?"

A flash of pain went through his eyes before his jaw tightened. "Many."

Trying to pretend that didn't hurt, she firmed her lips. "Glad we used a condom."

"My whores are clean. I make sure and always wear condom, even for blow jobs, and they are tested weekly."

"Oh, that's right, you would know. You're their fucking pimp."

That pissed him off and she watched him struggle with his anger before the blank look came over his face again. "These women, they sell their bodies. Is *their* choice. They want to work for the Novikov Bratva because I make sure they are safe, they are not abused. The women that work for me make good money, in safe place, where *they* are in charge of what services they provide."

"Seriously? You're going to try to make this out

like you're a good guy? Helping the poor prostitutes? How noble of you."

His voice went low, real low, as he growled out, "You live in different world, different ways. Prostitution happens everywhere, women sell themselves for money, is oldest profession. *Da*, we make money off of them, but is their choice. No woman that works for Novikov Bratva is forced. I keep them safe; my men keep them safe. They work in clean places with clients that have been tested for diseases and are happy. Many are the only source of income for their family. Is hard days all over the world. If we did not protect them they would be prey to real predators who would use them, sell them on black market, addict them to cheap drugs, and do other terrible things."

She sucked in a sharp breath, not liking the world Dimitri portrayed at all. It made it hard for her to be morally offended by what he did, but personally it still hurt. "And you fuck these women?"

"Some of them."

"But why? You're...well, I thought you were such a good man." She ignored his hurt look. "At the very least, you're handsome. Why pay for what you can have for free?"

"Rya, I do not pay them for sex, I pay them to leave without loving me."

"What?"

He muttered something in a long string of Russian. "There is much I cannot tell you. Things that would put you in danger."

Hours ago she would have laughed, but after reading that website, she realized how truly out of her depth she was. "What's the Novikov Curse?"

The rage that filled him made her shrink back against the tree. He looked at her, then closed his eyes and visibly struggled for calm. "I scare you."

She considered lying, but at the moment her nails were embedded in the tree behind her like a frightened cat getting ready to climb. "You are."

"I do not want to scare you, little Rya." He held out his hand. "Please, come, I talk, but not with you being afraid of me."

She gave his hand a weary look. "Talk here."

His gaze hardened. "Is not good conversation. Many bad memories. Please, come."

Fucking hell, her stupid, soft heart always got her in trouble. With a sigh she took his hand, trying to ignore the obvious relief on his face and the little electric zing she got when they touched. He led her to the edge of the canyon and sat, pulling her down next to him. She kicked at some stray pebbles and her stomach dropped as they fell over the edge, and she imagined what would happen if she fell. As if sensing her fear, Dimitri put his hand over her hip and pulled her a little further back, next to him.

"Say what you have to say Dimitri, and get your hand off me."

His hand tightened on her hip for a moment, and her hormones took notice before he removed it. "Did you read about Curse?"

"It just said something about it, I think with your grandfather."

"*Da*, started there with that bastard." The raw anger in his words startled her and she glanced over at him, but he wasn't looking at her. "Is rule among most of the Bratva to never involve women and children in disputes."

Confused, she nodded. "Okay."

"Many, many years ago, my grandfather broke rule. He kidnapped the wife of another *Pakhan*, a leader of the Boldin Bratva. Something happened, went wrong during kidnapping, and she was killed. In retaliation, the Boldin Bratva killed my grandmother and her daughter, my great aunt. Insane with grief, my grandfather…is not good story but it resulted in the death of many young girls of the Boldin Bratva. Then my grandfather and the Boldin leader died, and my father and the leader of the Boldin Bratva met in secret, swearing to end the blood feud, both having lost so much."

"Oh my god." She placed her hand over her mouth, trying to not imagine what he meant by that. "That's terrible."

"Gets worse." He blindly reached out to her and she took his hand, squeezing it hard as the tension rolled off of him in almost visible waves, like the heatwaves off summer-sunshine-baked pavement. "One night, over thirty years ago, someone killed the Boldin leader's young wife, pregnant with their first child. Was brutal slaying and the blame was laid at my father's feet."

"Did he…do you think he did it?"

Dimitri's lips thinned. "He is evil man, but no. He loved his wife too much."

"What do you mean?"

"My father was married to my half-brother Alex's mother first. Two days after Boldin's wife was slaughtered, someone…did same to Alex's mother."

He sucked in a harsh breath, and without thinking, she moved so she could kneel next to him and hug him the best she could. The pain pouring off of him was incredible. "I'm so sorry."

"My father remarried my mother, and though he did not love her like Alex's mother, he did love her in his own way. He tried to keep her safe. For years there was uneasy truce between Novikov and Boldin families, a time during which my mother gave birth to me and my older sister." A hard shudder worked through him. "When I was eleven and my sister was fourteen, they were killed."

"Murdered?"

"I think so, but it appeared to be a random car accident, but my father did not believe it. In terrible history repeating my father ordered the deaths of the leader of the Boldin Bratva's wife and two young daughters."

She stroked his back, the shudders working through him hard enough that she was surprised his teeth weren't chattering. "He ordered me and Alex to do it, along with a handful of his assassins."

"Wait, you were only eleven! He ordered his eleven-year-old son to go kill some young girls?"

"Told you, he lost mind. His grief ate his sanity."

"Did you do it?"

He looked at her, held her gaze and slowly shook his head. "I did not, we did not. What he was ordering was no good for Bratva. But next day the women died in house fire."

"Shit." When he pulled her onto his lap and wrapped his arms around her she let him, her heart aching for him. "So that's why you won't love a woman? Ever?"

He nodded, his face buried against her hair. "When my father dies, it may be different. I...there are things I cannot tell you, but it may be different."

"That's a terrible way to live. Does your brother...is he the same way? I mean does he make sure he doesn't love a woman?"

The silence stretched out between them and she comforted him the best she could, stroking his arms, his face, his shoulders, trying to give him the compassion and empathy he'd been forced to live without for his entire life.

"Alex...is not my story to tell."

While she was curious, she'd also had about as much death and tragedy as she could take. "I understand why you would only see prostitutes, or kept women or whatever you call them, but why aren't they in danger?"

"I do not care for them. Their death would not destroy a part of me." He looked down at her and gave her a smile filled with such sadness that tears came to her eyes. "In perfect world, I would be able to court you, to win your heart. You are kind of woman I would marry."

"What?"

"Is crazy, but the moment I saw you...you are different. I felt it, here." He took her hand and placed it over his heart. "And the more I am around you, the more I fall under your spell. I find woman I could love, but cannot have her. I do not like my life right now."

"Wow, this really sucks." She blinked back tears and stroked his face. "I'm so sorry that you've had to live without love. I can't imagine what that would be like."

He closed his eyes then held her so tight she had trouble taking a breath. "If you do not know what you do not have it is bearable. Now...not so much."

She shifted in his arms so she could straddle him. "I know we only have a little bit of time together, but I would like to stay with you, if that's okay."

His brows drew down as he frowned at her. "You not want to go?"

"Look, I don't like the idea of you touching anyone, especially whores, but Dimitri, you deserve to be loved. While I understand why it can't go any further than these two days, I'd like to give you what I can."

Looking totally confused, he leaned back, his palms resting on the hard packed earth and the muscles of his thickly built body straining against his t-shirt. "Why?"

This whole situation was so weird that she

floundered when she tried to explain it to him. "Honestly? I don't have a rational explanation. I just know that everything inside of me wants to stay with you for as long as I can. You are a once-in-a-lifetime thing, Dimitri. If I don't take advantage of being with you while you're here I know I'll regret it for the rest of my life."

His shoulders flexed beneath her hands and he closed his eyes. "I do not want to hurt you, Rya. You have good heart, good soul. I am not a good man."

"Yeah, well we all have a little darkness inside of us. I'm not saying that I'm cool with whatever it is you do, but I can't deny the attraction between us. I've never wanted to jump a man's bones as badly as I want yours."

That made him open his eyes and his lips quirked. "What does that mean? Jumping bones?"

Flushing, she looked down and played with the collar of his shirt. "Just that I find you very attractive."

He gave a low, almost purring sound and sat forward, wrapping his arms around her. "And I find you delicious."

Unable to resist, she ran her fingers through his thick hair. "So, *volk moy*, are there any plans for a bed somewhere in our near future."

He nuzzled his lips against her throat, the tip of his tongue tasting her skin. "I need to be inside you, Rya."

She shivered as he began to kiss along her throat, the delicious scrape of his beard making his lips and tongue seem all the softer, driving her crazy. Something about Dimitri put her into some kind of crazy heat, like a biological imperative was sitting up and taking notice of the total Alpha male ready to take her and make her his. For a moment her heart ached at the thought that whatever it was going on between them wouldn't last, but right now, she just wanted him.

"Take me someplace where I won't have rocks or a cactus up my ass and I'm all yours to do with as you wish."

His startled laughter made her smile and as she looked down at him, at the joy that she had a feeling very few people got to see on his face and wondered if she was already falling more than a little in love with her forbidden Master.

Chapter Ten

Dimitri relished the feeling of Rya's arms around him, of her warmth pressed up against his back, and the way she'd slipped her hands beneath his jacket to rest them over his stomach. She seemed to love touching him and he had to admit, her sweet caresses aroused him to the point that he was sure the zipper of his jeans was going to leave a permanent mark on his hard cock. They were on their way to the resort he'd booked for them, and during the two and a half hour ride, they'd talked about their past.

He found himself being as open with her as he could, telling her things he thought were inconsequential, but she seemed to enjoy hearing. Rya, on the other hand, was an open book. Anything he asked her she would answer, as long as the question wasn't embarrassing. Like when he'd asked her how she lost her virginity, her mortified groan came through loud and clear over the speakers in his helmet. Of course, her reluctance only made him want to know more.

"Rya, just tell me. It cannot be that bad."

"Easy for you to say. Fine. So, I'd been dating this guy for seven months. I was in the eleventh grade and thought I was in love. You know how it is, that puppy love that seems to be all consuming?"

He answered more honestly than he'd intended. "No, I do not know. I have never been in love."

The stroking of her fingers became more soothing than erotic and she hugged him tight. "Sorry, that was insensitive of me."

"Is not your fault." He didn't like the sudden tension between them, or the reminder of the bleak world he was going to return to all too soon, but she deserved the truth. "Rya, I have no practice with how to deal with a woman I care for. This is all new to me. Is hard for me to even know how to express myself. I feel things for you that I cannot describe. The only things I know how to do well for a woman is to fuck her and spoil her."

His heart ached at the kindness in her voice as she said, "Dimitri, you don't have to try with me. Just be yourself. I like you for who you are."

She was so trusting, and it hurt him somewhere deep inside his chest when he thought of Rya having to live in his violent, cold world. "I am killer. I am thief. I am ruthless man. That is who I am."

"That's not all you are," she replied in a low voice as she continued to stroke his stomach. "You're also honorable, kind, smart, funny, and you make me feel cherished. I'd say you're doing pretty good for a first date."

Her words pleased him immensely, and he wasn't sure how to deal with the onslaught of forbidden emotions so he changed the subject. "Now why was losing your virginity embarrassing for you?

"Please don't make me tell you."

"Why? Is no big deal."

"Fine, if it's no big deal then how did you lose your virginity?"

"To a whore my father hired when I was thirteen to teach me how to fuck."

Her shocked gasp and the feel of her fingernails digging into his stomach alerted him that he probably should have kept that information to himself. They were from such different worlds; things which were normal to him were totally foreign to her. But he didn't want to lie to her. They didn't have the rest of their lives to learn about each other, only an all too limited number of hours.

The fact that she'd managed to overlook his soiled past and see beyond the darkness of his soul still astonished him. Most women would have run screaming after reading the first line about the infamous Novikov blood which flowed through his veins. More importantly, while Rya had been pissed and scared, she was either brave enough, or compassionate enough, or both to still listen to what he had to say. She amazed him, and the bone-deep craving to keep her as his own tore at him.

Her soft voice, tinged with sorrow, filled his head. "You were only thirteen? That's terrible."

He shrugged, liking the way she was stroking his stomach in a soothing gesture. "For you that may be young, but by thirteen I'd already killed my first man."

"What?"

He passed a slow moving car and let out a soft breath. "He was a bad man, Rya, a monster. I was with one of my father's *kryshas*, Levka, a man who is enforcer and protector for my father's business. One of our whores had gone missing and Levka was charged to find out what happened to her. He was very smart man, had a—what you call it— a knowing, a sixth sense about people. I do not think my father actually thought we would find anything, but we did. The whore had been kidnapped by a doctor who would take prostitutes, drug addicts, basically the dregs of society and harvest their organs to be sold on black market."

"Oh my God."

Her horrified whisper hurt his heart. "I am sorry, I did not mean to shock you."

Cursing himself for being an idiot, he gunned the motorcycle, needing to feel the speed, to escape his demons.

Rya hugged him tight. "I'm glad he's dead. I hate

that you had to kill him, but I'm glad he's dead."

He turned her words over in his mind, finding it hard to believe that Rya would wish death on anyone. "You do not think I should have turned over to authorities?"

"No. I don't know how it is in Russia, but in America, people slip through the cracks of the law all the time while others get locked up for absolute bullshit. My mom got two years for being caught driving with a bag of weed, while this drunk asshole a couple towns over did a hit-and-run with his truck on my dad. The guy in the truck totally blew a stop sign and struck my dad on his motorcycle, killing him, but because of some bullshit the drunk driver's expensive lawyer pulled out of his ass the guy got away with just a fine." She gave a laugh that wasn't at all pleasant. "But we took care of him."

He wished he could see her face right now, see if what he thought she was saying was indeed the truth. "What do you mean?"

"Sorry, can't talk about it. Club business." He couldn't help but chuckle and she made an irritated noise. "What's so funny?"

"You are very loyal to your Club. I find it amusing that you are—how you say—open book, but when it comes to them nothing is said. Maybe amusing not right word. It makes me proud that you are faithful to them."

She laughed and dipped her hands lower so they rested on the belt of his pants, her thumb stroking the line of hair that led down to his aching cock. "This is kind of surreal, you know that, don't you?"

"How so?"

"Well, since my step-dad would have cut the dick off of any biker that so much as looked at me, I've always dated citizens, I mean guys that aren't affiliated with an MC. I have to hide a big part of my life from them. They only know me as Rya, the nurse." She sighed and her fingertips pressed lightly against his shaft. "It's nice being with someone that doesn't think I'm white trash because of my family."

"What is that?"

"It's slang for people that are considered low class. Like they're garbage."

"Who calls you such things? I will make them hurt and they will never disrespect you again."

She squeezed his cock, effectively cutting off his anger and turning it to hunger. "Easy there, *volk moy*, I'm a big girl and I can handle myself. That word used to hurt me when I was a kid, but not anymore. I know who I am. I know who my people are and while they'll never be attending galas or going to the country club, they're still good people and that's what matters. At the end of the day, manners and knowing which fork to use don't mean shit, but having someone who will have your back no matter what? Who considers you family and is always there for you? That's what's important."

Emotions entirely foreign to him made his chest ache and he grappled with how to tell Rya how much her words resonated with him, and reflected his view of the Bratva. The criminal empire that he was a part of was his family, and while there were those he didn't trust, the men he surrounded himself with had proven over and over again that they were loyal to him. They were tattooed from their time in prison, many bearing visible scars, all dangerous men. Everywhere they went, people stared at them, feared them, but like Rya said, they had his back no matter what.

They rode in companionable silence, and when he saw the sign for Sedona, he said, "We will be there soon."

She bounced against his back, her earlier

enthusiasm returning. That was one of the things he liked about her, no matter what they talked about, she always managed to return to her normal state of joy. "Ohhh, I've always wanted to go to Sedona. Damn, Dimitri, you're just knocking things off my list of shit to do before I die left and right."

He tensed. "I do not like you talking of dying."

"Hey, it's okay." She gripped his cock and he clenched his teeth at the wonderful torture of her small hand. "We're alive right now and that's what matters. Live in the moment, Dimitri, because you never know how fleeting it could be."

She continued to massage him and he debated increasing their speed to reach the resort sooner, but he didn't want to endanger his precious cargo. With a soft, almost purring sound she played with him and took obvious pleasure in touching him, straining his self-control and making him desperate for her. The memory of her lush little body beneath his, her passion, and the taste of her on his tongue drove him wild.

Soon they reached the entrance to the resort and he pulled up front. The valet approached them with a smile. "Welcome, Mr. Novikov, we've been expecting you."

Rya held his hand as they walked through the foyer of the resort, decorated in the American southwest style, her beautiful eyes wide and her soft lips slightly parted as she took in the Native American artwork scattered about the foyer. "Wow, Dimitri, you don't do things half-assed."

"I do not understand."

She looked up at him with an almost shy smile that he found amusing, considering she'd been playing with his cock for the last twenty minutes. "I just mean this place is amazing."

He looked around the resort with its beige walls,

vibrant art, and luxury, then shrugged. "If it please you, it please me. Come. I have a place for us I think you like."

They made their way through the resort, following the staff member who pointed out all the amenities available to them. The only thing that caught his interest was the spa because he wanted to send Rya there. Then again, the thought of anyone but him touching her made his teeth clench. He finally understood how men could become so possessive of their women. The irony that the one woman he could never have was the one he wanted more than anything on earth was not lost on him.

They reached their private adobe villa with its view of the enormous, layered red tinged sandstone cliffs. The sun would be setting soon and he hoped his assistant had arranged the things he'd requested. They entered their suite and Rya let out a soft gasp. The staff member soon left them alone, and Dimitri watched as Rya wandered around the large space.

She slowly moved over to the seating area, a grouping of couches made of dark brown distressed leather before a fireplace tucked into the cream plaster walls. The ceiling overhead consisted of exposed wood beams and art of a style he hadn't seen before hung on the walls. Above the fireplace hung a large blanket that had geometric shapes woven into it similar to traditional Mongolian woven blankets.

He followed Rya as she went up to the second level and gave him another shy smile as she looked from the large, white silk-covered bed to him. Unzipping her jacket, she shrugged it off and threw it over the back of a nearby oversized brown leather chair. The large globes of her breasts pressed against her shirt, her hard nipples visible through the cloth.

"Dimitri, this is just amazing. Thank you."

Warmth filled him and he took off his jacket as

well before tugging at his boots. "Strip, Rya. I want you naked."

A pretty flush colored her cheeks down to her chest as she removed her clothing, revealing her lush, exquisite body to him bit by bit. Once she was nude, and he was wearing only his jeans, he slowly approached her, loving the way she froze like a rabbit watching a stalking wolf. He stopped when they were inches apart, his whole body tuned into the woman before him. Electricity seemed to arc between them and he would not have been surprised if he looked down and saw sparks. He gently brushed the hard tips of her breasts with the back of his knuckles, and smiled at the way she instantly softened to his touch.

"Are you sore from ride?"

She looked up at him and slowly shook her head.

"No, I'm sore because I want you so much." She grasped his hand and she slowly slid it down her body until his fingers rested against her mound. "I'm very, very wet for you, Master."

The need to fuck her, to cover her with his body and slide his cock into that slippery, welcoming warmth made him growl as he played with the smooth, plump folds of her cunt. "My sweet, perfect girl."

She gave him a smile that was equal parts lust and joy before he removed his fingers and gave her pussy a sharp slap. "Go up on bed and lay on your back."

While she did as he ordered, he got his black duffle bag from the closet where the staff had said it would be. As he looked through it and checked his toys, he thought of all the things he wanted to do to her, all the ways he needed to have her. He'd ordered his toys restocked with new items; he wanted nothing touching little Rya that had touched another, and was pleased to see that many of his favorite items were in there. His fingers brushed over the cool surface of a beautifully sculpted butt plug and he considered it. It wasn't huge, definitely smaller than his cock, but he liked the way the plug part had an iridescent, faceted glass jewel surrounded by smooth, rippling red and clear glass. It would look beautiful in his girl's bottom though he wanted to adorn her body with diamonds.

Pulling the plug and a set of Velcro restraints from the bag he made his way back to the bed. Rya watched him with such hunger that he had to force himself not to throw the toys away and just pounce on her. Her smooth, round limbs, the gentle rise of her belly, and her fucking amazing tits were the stuff of his hottest dreams. Combine that with her inner light and she was an irresistible woman.

He set the plug to the side, liking the way her eyes widened at the sight of it and she how she tensed slightly. "Rya, give me your hand."

She sighed softly as he kissed her palm, licking across it and sucking on each of her fingers before strapping her wrist into the restraint, then taking the other end and tucking it beneath the mattress. The Velcro would hold it in place, and keep her open to his touch. Next he took her slender ankle and secured it before moving over to the other side of the bed. As he bound her he noted the dreamy look that began to overtake her, how she watched him with increasing focus, her gaze never leaving him.

There was enough slack so she could move a few inches, but not enough to allow her to touch him unless he wished it. Later he would indulge her and allow her to explore his body, but right now, he wanted to pleasure her. After shedding his jeans he joined her on the bed, crawling up between her thighs and noting the thick layer of arousal that already coated her pink cunt. While he was tempted to lick it away, he needed to take the edge off.

He moved until he had his hands braced on either

side of her head, then curved his palms over her delicate skull. As the tip of his cock rubbed against her he let out a soft groan and resisted the urge to plunge into her. Fuck, he forgot a condom. He'd never put his bare dick on any woman's cunt before and it was torture to only allow himself to slip through her juices, to rub his cock between the split of her sex and enjoy the ball-tightening sensation of the velvet of her cunt rubbing against him. Rya moaned long and deep, wiggling her hips against him and driving him crazy.

With a muttered oath he quickly moved off of her and retrieved a condom from his bag before sheathing himself. "I will fuck you hard and fast, little Rya. You will not come. Do you understand?"

She whimpered and nodded, her body restless with her need. "Use me, Master. I'm yours."

Emotions assailed him and he quickly moved between her thighs, loving how she spread and tilted himself for him. He wanted to tell her that she was his, that she would always be his, but he couldn't do that to her. Already he feared how much it would hurt to leave her. His own agony would only be compounded by her sorrow. With a low, deep groan of pleasure he pushed into her, then bent so he could suck on her neck while he began to fuck her, giving her only a moment to adjust to his dick before taking her hard and fast like he'd promised.

Her eyes went wide and she tugged helplessly at the restraints, her back arching beneath him while he powered into her. Thanks to her dick teasing he was ready to come after only a few strokes and he didn't fight the sensation, instead allowing the explosive orgasm to overtake him. She whimpered as he shouted out and pressed into her as far as he could, filling the condom with his seed in a short, but intense climax.

"Oh God," she cried out. "Please, I'm going to come."

He swiftly pulled out and gave her pussy a hard slap. To his surprise, instead of halting her orgasm his slap pushed her over the edge and he sat back on his haunches, watching the beauty of his girl coming without anything touching her. The mounds of her breasts shook with her hard pants and her pussy contracted and released like it was sucking on a dick.

After she finished he stood and removed the condom, going to the opulent bathroom and cleaning himself before returning to Rya. She gave him an apprehensive look while he gently bathed her sex and kept silent, letting her imagination run wild with what her punishment would be. And he would punish her, then pleasure her, then punish her again. He wanted to learn what drove her wild, to give her orgasms until she was limp in his arms, then pamper her and coddle her, to do all the tender things he'd never wanted to do to one of his kept women.

Even though he knew he was only setting himself up for heartbreak, he couldn't stop the warmth in his heart that grew more intense every moment he was with his little Rya.

Chapter Eleven

Rya jerked at her bonds, the need to orgasm again a burning pain consuming the lower half of her body. To her disappointment Dimitri walked, gloriously nude and still hard, over to the closet. He dug around in his suitcase and came back with an MP3 player. She watched him fiddle with it, then put it in the dock next to the bed. A few seconds later Nine Inch Nails rendition of the song *Get Down Make Love* started to play, and her body broke out in goosebumps.

It was the perfect, hard, dirty, rough music for the way she wanted him to take her. She needed him to fuck her hard, make her ache, make her feel him between her legs, cover her in his scent and own her. Her soft whimpers were probably inaudible over the sound of the music and she was glad their hacienda was isolated from the others because the music was loud enough that she could feel it in her bones.

Dimitri prowled towards her, his gaze locked on her body, making her tremble with the intensity of his stare. He was so hot, his muscles moving beneath his skin. Better still, he was dangerous. Even if she had been unaware of who and what he was, the potential for violence came off of him in invisible waves and it made her clit throb.

Not speaking to her, he stood next to the bed and stroked his hands over her body, awakening her skin to his touch, making her crazy for him. When he slipped his fingers between her legs and stroked her clit she keened and thrust her hips into the air. With ruthless efficiency he slammed two fingers into her while stroking the little bundle of nerves that was now as hard as a pearl against his thumb.

"Come for me, my Rya," he said in a loud growl.

The orgasm burst from her like her body was no longer her own. She cried out, her vocal cords failing her as her pussy clamped down on his thrusting fingers, making her shudder. He leaned down and latched onto her left nipple, sucking it hard, then biting down. The pain mixed with the endorphins of her orgasm, drove her higher until she was begging him to stop.

He eased his fingers from her and painted her nipples with her arousal, then began to lick it off while looking at her. She'd never been with any man who liked this much eye contact, but with Dimitri she found she couldn't look away from him, couldn't free herself from his gaze. He was her wolf and she was a scared little rabbit, hoping he didn't devour her but also wishing he would. She wanted him to consume her, to make her part of him.

Once again, he slid his fingers between her legs and rubbed her clit to a fast, hard orgasm while giving her a savage smile, as if he knew he had more control of her body than she did.

Moving down the bed, he unstrapped her ankles then adjusted her legs so her feet were pressed together with her knees out, like the butterfly stretches she did for her MMA class. This opened her pussy fully to him and he smiled, his gaze possessive, almost greedy, as he looked at her sex. No one had ever been this into her before and she found herself fascinated by his every move, and the tiniest change in his expression.

His lips moved like he was saying something, but she couldn't hear him over the music. Relaxing back into the bed, she let her muscles fall loose, trying to show him in every way possible that she submitted to him, that she trusted him. He glanced up and the heat in his gaze flared, then he smiled at her and joy filled her at the depth of the emotion in his eyes.

Fuck, losing him was going to hurt.

Bad.

He must have sensed her mood change because he frowned slightly, then moved onto the bed so her ass was cradled in his hands and began to lick her.

Nothing and no one had ever pleasured her as well as Dimitri, and that included his talented mouth. He thrust his long tongue inside of her while rubbing her clit with his nose, sending a shiver through her that curled her toes. While she couldn't hear him, she could feel the vibrations of his growls against her sensitive flesh. When he bit her left labia she jerked, the pain unexpectedly strong. Then he repeated the motion on her right labia and she screamed, attempting to jerk away from his mouth, but he held her fast.

With the utmost gentleness he suckled on her aching pussy lips, laving them with his tongue and slowly turning that pain back into pleasure. Her mind grew quiet, no thoughts intruding except for the sensation of his mouth on her. Dimitri pulled her cunt wide and began to tease her clit with the tip of his tongue, drawing out an almost endless series of moans from her while Trent Reznor sang about wanting to fuck like an animal.

Something round and cool touched her anus and she tried to get her muscles to cooperate so she could look, but Dimitri picked that moment to suckle her clit and she abandoned herself to the pleasure. That roundness pushed into her ass and she spread her legs wider, wanting everything he had to give her, needing him to fill her, to take and take and take until she had nothing left to give and was blissfully drained.

A burning sensation came from her bottom and she tensed, but Dimitri began to bite on her clit and she climaxed, shouting his name over and over, torn between the sensations of his beard rubbing against her pussy and the object fully entering her butt with an almost audible pop. As she began to float in a delicious nothingness, she vaguely identified the object as a butt plug.

Dimitri lifted her limp legs, probably admiring the sight of the plug stretching her ass. It felt so odd, foreign, yet deliciously taboo.

The soft scrape of his body hair was a delicious sensation that sent shivers racing over her as he leaned over her and unstrapped her wrists. Completely limp, she could barely open her eyes and look at him after three, no, four good orgasms. He kissed her, a light stroke of his lips against hers and she sighed, breathing in the air they shared. Realizing that her hands were free, she automatically threaded her fingers through his hair and pulled him closer, accepting his tongue into her mouth and sucking on it gently. The plug in her bottom had her constantly squirming beneath him and she rubbed her pussy against his cock, her fluids making his shaft slick and wonderful to slide against.

Leaning down so he could speak into her ear, Dimitri said in a harsh voice, "Greedy girl. You want my cock in that wet cunt, don't you?"

"Please," she moaned out as he licked the sensitive skin behind her ear. "Oh god, Master, I need you."

He shuddered against her and shifted his hips so his crest pressed lightly at her entrance, then froze there. She tried to move her hips, but he wouldn't let her, pinning her body with his to the point where she couldn't draw a full breath. Tension radiated from him and he pressed just the slightest bit into her. The muscles of her pussy clamped down, trying to pull him in further, but he jerked away, saying something in Russian with a loud, angry shout.

Startled, she stared up at him and backed away a little, a trace of real fear going through her as he fisted his hands into his hair and roared at the ceiling.

Scared for real now, she almost fell off the bed in a mindless effort to distance herself from his rage.

He turned and spotted her trying to move away. With a leap a panther would envy, he jumped onto the bed and grabbed her by her hair, hauling her back on the mattress. She yelped at the rough treatment, and her body bounced on the soft surface as he threw her down. Jumping off the bed again, he shouted. "Do not fucking move."

Nodding, she froze in place while he jerked a condom on with rough hands. When he moved back onto the bed with her she flinched at his touch and he froze. Dropping his head, he took in heaving breaths, but when he looked up some of the anger had faded from his gaze.

Without another word he moved so his back was against the weathered wood headboard of the bed and hauled her onto his lap so she straddled him. He wrapped her hair around his fist, holding her captive while lifting her around the waist with his other arm until his cock was poised at her entrance. In stark contrast to the violence of his earlier movements, he gently lowered her onto his shaft, the plug inside of her rubbing the membrane separating her anus and cunt, making her feel deliciously full.

In spite of her fear, or maybe because of it, the sensation of his dick pressing through her aching pussy had Rya hovering on the edge of orgasm. He must have sensed it because he jerked her head down so he could lick her ear as he said, "Come whenever you want, *zaika moya*."

Hearing his pet name for her helped her relax and she wrapped her arms around his neck, hugging him close as she began to rise up and down on his shaft, arching her hips for maximum penetration. He was so hard, so thick, and her sex burned slightly from the invasion after his earlier hard fuck. She tried to move faster, but his superior strength kept her pace excruciatingly slow and steady.

His scent filled her and she licked at his throat, loving how he said something in Russian that sounded very sexy. Moving a little faster, he released her hair and slipped a hand between them, giving her belly a squeeze that made his cock jump inside of her before pressing his thumb to her clit. She went off like a rocket, shuddering as he continued to fuck her through the press and release of her orgasm, to fill her with him.

His grip gentled and their movements turned into a perfect give and take, moving together as one, chasing their pleasure. He pulled her back by her hair and made her look into his eyes while he fucked her. The tenderness and desperate need she saw in his gaze, mirrored her own. She tried to give him everything with her eyes, to open the window of her soul to him. An almost pained look tightened his face and he brought her mouth to his in a desperate kiss that was all bruising lips and thrusting tongue, matching the intensity of his movements inside of her.

Sweat slicked them both and she tightened on him, her body tensing in anticipation of a pleasure she was sure would change her forever. She felt so fucking good already, how could it possibly top the raw joy of having Dimitri inside of her, of tasting him, of holding him close while he filled her? His muscles turned to rock beneath her hands and she keened into his mouth as her climax rolled through her.

Jerking his lips from hers, he bit her neck hard enough that she wondered if he'd broken skin, then he began to shudder as his release merged with hers.

She felt so close to him in this moment, as if they shared the same heart, the same body, the same air, like there was nothing between them. Reveling in this amazing sense of completion she clung to him as her body slowly relaxed, sinking into him and nuzzling his chest, enjoying the feel of his body hair against her skin. Their breathing eventually slowed, but Dimitri made no move to release her, instead, continuing to hold her and pet her.

Eventually, her legs began to stiffen up and all the stress she'd put her body through started to make itself known as her endorphins wore off. Dimitri must have sensed it because he gently moved her off of his semi-hard cock, laying her down with such care that it made her whole body tingle with pleasure. He disposed of the condom, then removed the plug. She hissed in pain as it came out and he made soft, hushing noises.

He picked her up in his arms and she snuggled close while he walked across the room with her, making her feel completely safe and cared for. The cool air made goosebumps rise on her still damp skin and she looked away from Dimitri's chest. She gave a small gasp of surprise at the sight of their private deck. She took in the padded wicker furniture, the high walls on either side that kept out prying eyes, and the small infinity pool; she didn't notice the hot tub until Dimitri set her down into the water.

If she had any tension left it disappeared the moment the delicious water surrounded her because she couldn't move a single muscle. Dimitri joined her a moment later and pulled her onto his lap so her back was on his chest with his long legs beneath hers. She let out a long sigh and Dimitri chuckled.

"You feel good, little Rya?"

"Mmmm..." she stroked his arms holding her and watched the last of the sunset over the impressive sandstone cliffs. "This is perfect."

"I am glad you are pleased."

His voice was rough with emotion and she snuggled closer, if that was even possible, needing to comfort him. "Thank you, Dimitri."

"Thank you, *zaika moya*."

She laughed and looked over her shoulder at him. "For what? You're the one that made this all happen."

His face was unexpectedly serious as he said, "All this? Is nothing. You are more amazing than any of this."

His words made her yearn for something she could never have, so she tried to joke with him to lighten the mood. "More amazing than the Grand Canyon?"

"*Da*." He sighed and kissed her head. "I am sorry for scaring you."

"What?"

"I lost my temper, but it was not you I was angry with. Was me."

The memory of his rage made her tense. "Why were you so mad?"

He turned her so she straddled his lap, facing him then cupped her face in his hands. "I wanted to slide into you without condom, to feel only you."

"Well, we both have our health records and you were approved to bid at the auction so I know you're clean and I have an IUD. If you want to go bareback I'm fine with it."

He closed his eyes and hauled her to him so he could rest his face on her breasts. "You do not understand. I have never gone without condom. Never. I want things with you that I do not want with any other woman. You upset my world, little Rya.

You make me want things that would lead to your death."

The pain in his voice tore at her and she held him close, rubbing his head and trying to soothe him. "Hey, no sad thoughts, okay? We're living in the moment. If you want to take me without a condom then do it, if not, that's okay as well. I don't want to worry about tomorrow. I want to enjoy the fact that right here, right now, you're my Master and I'm your submissive."

His chest expanded against her and he blew out a harsh breath. "Are you hungry?"

Now that he mentioned it, she was starving. "Yep."

He stood up and lifted her with him, the evening chill making her shiver. Above them, the first stars had started to come out and she cursed herself for forgetting the time. "Shit. Dimitri, is my laptop still in my luggage?"

"*Da*." He looked down at her as he carried her inside and into the bathroom. "You need?"

"I...yeah, I do." She bit her lip, wondering how she could ask him for privacy without offending him. "Can I have a few minutes alone?"

"Why?"

"There's something I need to do."

He tensed. "What is it, Rya?"

The suspicion in his gaze hurt. "I just need some time alone, okay? Can you give me fifteen minutes?"

Her adoring lover slowly disappeared as the cold, hard man that helped run a criminal empire reappeared. "I will go."

Without looking back at her he grabbed a towel and quickly dried off. She grabbed one as well and followed him back into the bedroom. Coldness radiated off of him as he quickly dressed, jerking his clothes on with no expression on his face. Fuck, he must think the worst, but she couldn't tell him what she had to do. It wasn't her place or his business.

"Dimitri? Are you mad at me?"

No response, just more silence while he pulled his clothes then went for the stairs. "I will be back."

"When?"

He didn't respond, just left her with her heart aching. Shit, why was he overreacting? It wasn't like she was going to...

The loud thumps of his boots going downstairs felt like physical blows and she had to sniff back a tear. Damn it, she never got attached this quickly to any man, let alone to the point where his displeasure made her ache. She wanted to call to him, to tell him she didn't need privacy, but she couldn't. This was more important than his feelings. Still, when the downstairs door slammed she wiped a few tears away.

Double shit.

She hadn't considered how it would look to his paranoid mind. Chewing her lip, she tugged on her one change of clothes from her luggage then took her laptop over to her bed. After logging on she opened up her chat window, scrubbed the tears from her cheeks and plastered on a big, fake smile.

Chapter Twelve

Dimitri removed his boots at the front door, trying to dismiss an unfamiliar pang of guilt at spying on Rya. He was only doing what he had to do to make sure he was safe. While he doubted Rya was going to hurt him, he couldn't imagine why she wouldn't want him to see something. Whatever she had to hide was something she was either ashamed of, or something that would make him angry.

The sounds of her moving around upstairs settled, then her soft, husky voice traveled down the staircase. He moved slowly, distributing his weight to make the least amount of noise possible. Sneaking up on Rya was easy, and he paused at the bottom of the stairs where he could hear her voice and a man's voice.

Rya said, "Come on, Mark, I'm not showing you my breasts."

The man laughed, his voice coming out slightly distorted from whatever device she was speaking to him on. "Awww, come on, baby. Don't be like that. You know I think it's cute when you pout."

Dimitri crept up the stairs, his gut clenching at the openly flirting tone in the man's voice. Could Rya have someone waiting at home for her? He tried to tell himself that it didn't matter, that she was his for right now and that he had no concern about who she fucked after he left for Russia, but his gut churned with anger.

She laughed, the sound unguarded and full of genuine joy. His glut clenched at the thought of anyone making her laugh like that. He wanted to be the one to make her laugh, to make her smile. The greed for her affection burned through his blood like an addictive drug, driving him crazy.

Rya sighed with obvious exasperation. "When I get home I'm going to smack you upside your head."

The man coughed. "What if I said it's my last request?"

"No."

"Where are you, by the way, Rya?"

She was silent for a moment, then said in a soft voice. "I'm in Sedona, Arizona. You should see it, Mark, it's beautiful."

"Drove my truck through there once. Prettiest sky you've ever seen at night. Do you have someone to watch those stars with, beautiful?"

Dimitri froze, part of him wanting Rya to tell that man that yes, she had someone to watch the stars with, the other part of him fearing that she would potentially endanger them both by using his name.

After a few long seconds she sighed. "No, no I don't."

Almost at the top of the stairs, Dimitri moved as slowly as possible, but was surprised when the man said, "That's a shame. I keep hoping someone will come sweep you off your feet. If I'd met you five years ago I wouldn't have let you go."

When Dimitri lifted his head to see Rya, he found her with her back to him and her laptop open as she sat on the bed. He shifted enough to see who she was talking to and at first he couldn't make sense of the person on the screen of her laptop. It was a middle aged man, and while he'd once probably been very handsome, an obvious illness had ravaged him. He sat up in a hospital bed, a tube coming out of his nose and dark circles beneath his sunken eyes. The flesh hung off his bones and to Dimitri he almost looked like a still moving cadaver, but there was a gleam in the man's eyes as he smiled at Rya that was still full of life.

While Dimitri tried to figure out what the hell was going on, Rya hugged her knees to her chest. "That's just assuming you could catch me in the first place. You know you have no game. None of the nurses have given you a pity blow job yet."

Mark laughed. "I can't believe you won't honor a dying man's last wish." For a long moment Rya was silent and the man on the screen sighed. "Hey now, no sad face. I get enough of those around here already."

Sitting up straight, Rya nodded. "Sorry. I'm just in a mood right now."

"I'd bet you'd feel better if you gave me a blow job."

Laughing, Rya shook her head. "Pervert."

A woman's voice came from the computer. "Mark, I told you to stop talking dirty to the nurses. The last thing I want to see when I come visit you is my baby brother doing that. Yuck."

The woman that appeared on the screen next to the man smiled at the camera. She bore a striking resemblance to the sick man and Dimitri had a disconcerting image of what the man must have looked like while he was healthy. The woman winked at Rya. "How's your vacation?"

Rya waved at the screen. "Hi, Charlotte. Great, I'm having a wonderful time."

The woman on the screen gently stroked the man's shoulder. "Good. Now, you've seen that Mark is still around to annoy us, so get the hell off your computer and go vacation."

With a sigh Rya stretched out her arms. "Fine, fine. I don't have my cell phone on me, but I'll check it. Call me if you need me or email me."

They said their goodbyes and Rya slowly closed

the screen to her laptop, then began to cry in soft sobs. His heart broke for her and he sat down quietly on the stairs. He wanted to comfort her, to ask her who those people were, but he couldn't because then she'd know he was spying on her. It went without saying that she would consider that a betrayal of trust, but it made his chest ache to hear the sound of her pain.

Sneaking back downstairs as quickly as possible, he moved across the living room and opened the door, then shut it loudly. Rya's sobs immediately cut off, and a moment later, she ran down the stairs. He took one look at her red eyes and damp cheeks before opening his arms to her. With a sound that was a mixture of sorrow and relief, she threw herself at him. He swept her up and held her close before moving to the couches before the fireplace. Needing to soothe her, to somehow take away her sadness, he deposited her on the sofa before turning on the gas fire. By the time he sat down and pulled her onto his lap again her cries had gentled to hitching breaths followed by long, shuddering sighs.

Smoothing her hair back from her damp face, he hated himself for lying to her but tried to get her to open up. "What is wrong?"

"Are you mad at me?"

"What? No, no, I am not mad."

"You looked mad when you left." Her gaze searched his face. "I'm sorry, I swear I wasn't doing anything bad. It's just...well I have people that I've made promises to and I can't betray their trust. Can you understand that? And believe that I would never betray you?"

"I believe you." He stroked her cheek, brushing away a stray tear. "Why are you crying?"

Her lower lip trembled. "I...you know how I'm a nurse right?"

"*Da.*"

"Well, I'm a hospice nurse. Do you know what that means?"

He tried to remember what that word was, but couldn't think of ever having heard it during his English lessons or during his time in English speaking countries. "No. I do not know this word–hospice."

"I help people who have terminal illnesses. Basically, I help people facing death do so with the least amount of pain and the most dignity possible."

Everything clicked into place and he realized the man Rya was talking to was one of her patients. "It is hard on your heart. Being around suffering, makes you sad."

"Yeah, it does, but it also brings me peace." She shuddered and buried her face against his chest. "There is nothing worse than dying alone. Nothing. If I can be there for my patients, if I can give them the comfort they need to exit from this world with as much peace as possible…it…it's what I'm supposed to do. I know it probably doesn't make any sense, but I feel like being a hospice nurse is my calling, it is one of the reasons I'm here. Like I'm making a difference. Not a lot of people in this world get to feel that anymore, so despite the pain that is a definite part of my job, I consider myself lucky, privileged even, to help them move on. They have wonderful things ahead of them, an ending to the pain and an amazing new adventure."

He gathered her close and began to press gentle kisses on her face. "You humble me. Such a good heart with so much love to give. That is why it hurts you, because you love them."

"I do." She began to stroke his chest, almost like she was petting him. It made him feel good to know she took comfort from touching him. "When you're dying you suddenly realize what's important, and for most people, it's the connection to other people. I don't mourn for those who pass on. Yeah, I'm sad that they're no longer with us, but it's the family that's left behind to grieve that tears me up."

"I understand."

And he did, all too well. For years he'd carried the pain of the loss of his mother and older sister, a never-ending ache, a hole in his life that was never filled. With the loss of Jessica, he'd forgotten how to feel compassion for a few years. He couldn't imagine what it would be like to deal with that day after day, not only Rya's own personal pain for the patients she obviously loved, but her empathy for the family left behind.

She studied him for a moment, then nodded. "You do understand. Thank you for, well, for being you."

They stared into each other's eyes and he ached to tell her how much she meant to him, how much he cared for her, but it would be selfish of him. She needed to move on after he left, to have her own life and find some lucky bastard and marry him, and make him the happiest man on earth. Everything inside of Dimitri screamed in protest at the thought and he struggled with himself, this unusual loss of control once again making him angry with himself. Before he could get too worked up, Rya's stomach growled.

Loud.

A hot flush burned her cheeks and she pressed her hands to her stomach. "Oh my god. It sounds like I have a baby dragon in my belly."

Laughing, he gave her a swift kiss before standing. "Go. In the black suitcase with the green tag is clothes for you. Pick a dress for dinner and come back down. We go eat."

She smoothed her hands over his chest and

grinned at him. "Where did you get clothes for me from?"

He winked, wanting to keep her smiling and chase the lingering shadows from her eyes. "I am man of many resources."

"I'll say." She stood up on her tiptoes and he leaned his head down, closing the distance so she could give him a brief kiss. "I'll be right back, and thank you again, Dimitri. For listening to me and just for being you."

Dimitri sat next to Rya at the elegant bar of the restaurant within the resort. Like the rest of the place it had an American southwestern theme and the long bar was made up of some sort of pale wood that had been polished until it gleamed. A massive mirror etched with Native American designs of a more modern slant took up the entire side of the room, giving Dimitri a view of the space behind him. As much as he watched Rya, he also kept an eye on a group of middle aged men getting drunk in the corner. They kept throwing looks Rya's way, looks that he did not like one bit, though he could hardly blame them.

She was stunning.

Dressed in a flowing turquoise green dress that reached just past her knees and dipped low in the back to show the edge of her tattoo, she was the stuff of every man's fantasy. Her hair had been slicked back into a long ponytail that reached her waist and swung with her every movement, making him wish he could grab her by it and drag her back to their room, but he would fuck her raw if he wasn't careful so he was attempting to give her a body a rest by keeping her in public. The dress fastened behind her neck in a halter top and it pleased him to see evidence of his bites on her shoulders and neck, marks that clearly indicated she belonged to him. Those marks had gotten a couple double takes by people, but every time someone noticed Rya would give a mysterious, but very pleased smile and touch the one of them with a lingering caress. Most often the person would look away with a blush, but a couple times he'd caught women looking from him to Rya with open envy.

Taking a sip from her fruity martini, Rya gave him a small smile. "You keep looking at me like that and I won't be able to finish my drink."

"Do not tease, *zaika moya*. I do not have much restraint with you."

She grinned and took another sip before setting the glass down. "Where did you learn how to speak English?"

He toyed with his glass of excellent bourbon, trying to figure out how much he should tell her. "My...family is friends, maybe not friends but deals with many other families. My father's first wife came from Dubini family. Her sister was brilliant woman who spoke many languages. She was entrusted with teaching the children of other families English. That is how I met some of my best friends. We were in her class together. English is the language of business and my father was very dedicated to teaching my brother and myself everything we need to survive and make our family thrive."

"Wow. I can understand that. My step-dad got me into MMA when I was a teenager and started getting these." She gestured to her large breasts and his hands twitched with the need to fill his palms with her abundant bounty. "I thought he was crazy at the time, but my friend Tawny took them with me and it's helped keep guys in their place."

"He is smart man. You are beautiful woman, stunning. Why do you not have a man in your life?"

She sighed and her right foot began to swing. As short as she was the stools were too tall for her feet to reach the ground. "I don't know. My past relationships haven't worked out for a variety of reasons. I mean it's not like I haven't been looking, I like to date and all of that. I just haven't found anyone like you. Shit, never mind. Forget I said that. Damn vodka gets me every time."

A scarlet flush spread from her chest all the way to her ears and he leaned forward, stroking the soft skin of her exposed back. "No, I not forget. I keep this memory forever, little Rya."

When she looked over at him her gorgeous golden eyes were filled with tears. "This sucks."

He cupped her chin. "Tell me what to do in order to bring the light back to your eyes. Ask me and I will make it happen."

Her soft laugh was a reward like no other. "Really? Can you dance?"

"Of course. Though I am not traditionally well-educated, I have learned how to do many, many things well in my life."

She slipped away from him with a smile and tugged him after her to where an old fashioned jukebox sat against the far adobe wall. Rya selected a song, then took him through the archway to the patio area. A single fountain lit from within gurgled in the yard and beautiful tiles made up the floor. A desert garden enclosed the patio and he took a moment to admire the moonlit cliffs in the distance. He'd never been anywhere like the American southwest, and he found the raw beauty of the place made his spirit quiet. Usually he only felt this kind of peace out in the middle of the forest during winter, after a snowfall.

A smooth, mellow kind of music he'd never heard before came through the speakers and he absently noted people in the restaurant watching them with a smile. "What is this song?"

"It's *I Only Have Eyes for You* by the Flamingos. This was my grandparents' favorite." Rya watched him with a small smile. "Listen to the words."

He bowed to her and she giggled, then curtsied. With a well-practiced move he swung her into his arms, letting her twirl through the air with a laugh that made him feel like the luckiest man in the world, her small heels kicking. She was so petite, but such a sweet armful, and she was fun to dance with. Without even trying she followed him gracefully through the moves, almost like she knew where he was going to step before he did. The energy between them, this perfect connection, was like nothing he'd ever experienced, and he found himself drowning in the amber depths of her eyes.

Her expression went soft and she moved one hand up to let her fingers trace over his beard. She seemed to like his facial hair and he loved how the soft scruff made her shiver. He wanted to do that right now, to slip his hands beneath her dress and caress her tight nipples. They tormented him, poking out from the thin silk of her dress and begging for his lips. Not getting a raging hard-on was becoming more difficult by the second, but he didn't need to give the other couples watching them and smiling the wrong kind of show.

The song ended and they stopped, their chests pressed together as she smiled up at him. Unable to help himself, he lifted her for a kiss. As her mouth opened beneath his the group of drunk men over in the corner started to throw out ribald remarks about their kiss. Anger filled Dimitri and he was moving out of the patio area to go beat their filthy mouths shut without thought.

How fucking dare they even *look* at his woman?

"Fuck," Rya said from behind him and a moment

later she was in front of him and jumped up, lacing her hands around his neck then wrapping her legs around his waist.

He froze and looked down at her, his anger still beating through is blood. "Rya, let me go. I need to teach those *yeblans* to not talk about my woman."

She shocked him when she jerked his head back with her small fist in his hair and bit him on the side of the neck hard. He automatically grabbed her ass and she pulled back, glaring at him. In an angry whisper she said, "Fuck that shit. The last thing I want to happen is have you go to jail for killing a bunch of drunk pricks. Let it go. Take me back to our room and fuck me instead. Please, Dimitri. We have so little time together. Look around you. You're scaring people."

Two of the drunk men in the corner were laughing, but a few of them were attempting to shut their companions up, casting worried glances his way. There were other couples there and they definitely looked scared. A few had their cell phones out and he gritted his teeth, realizing his woman spoke the truth. This was not Russia. While he would get out of any legal trouble that came his way, it would waste what time he had with Rya and leave a paper trail leading back to her.

He took a deep breath and turned, still carrying her wrapped around him as they left the bar. "Do not do that again. You could be hurt stepping between men fighting. And why did you bite my neck?"

To his surprise she laughed. "My step-dad and his friends have short tempers. I've seen my Mom have to do that with Rock a couple times. She says biting his neck is like biting a pissed off horse's ear. It makes them stop and pay attention to something other than their anger."

Shaking his head, he let Rya slide down his front

when they reached the outdoors. "I see where you get your foolish bravery from."

She socked him in the arm. "Don't make fun of my mom."

Overhead, a brilliant star-filled sky stretched out over them, and he picked up their pace, wanting to get back to their room and give Rya her present. He'd ordered it last night and received a call from the hotel that it had arrived and had been placed in the safe in their suite as he'd requested. It was extravagant, but he had more money than he could spend on himself in ten lifetimes. The baubles were his way of making sure that Rya not only knew how much he valued the time she'd given him, but that she would be taken care of financially. If she sold his gifts she'd never have to work another day in her life. It gave him peace and eased his heart to know he'd provided that for her.

By the time they reached their room Rya had gone quiet and when he stole glances at her the look on her face was melancholy.

Swiping his card and opening the door, he held it for her as she walked in. "Little Rya, where is your smile? Have I made you sad?"

She shook her head and pasted on a bright, false smile. "No, I'm fine. Just having a hard time taking my own advice and living in the moment."

"Come here, *zaika moya*, and I will make sure you know nothing but me."

Chapter Thirteen

Letting out an unsteady breath, Rya devoured Dimitri with her gaze, wanting to memorize every inch of the ruggedly beautiful man watching her just as close. He was everything she'd ever wanted in a man and she was determined not to waste a moment with him. Thoughts of leaving him tried to intrude, but she pushed them back, desperate to not think of the pain ahead of her.

"Dimitri?"

"Yes?"

She flushed and looked down. The fantasy she was about to tell him had been one of her favorites for a long, long time, but she'd never found a man she trusted enough, who was kinky enough not to call her weird or suggest therapy to indulge in it.

"Would you...that is...I have this fantasy..."

He made a deep, rumbly sound that went straight to her pussy. "Tell me your secret thoughts, Rya. Tell your Master what you want."

Man, now that she'd opened her big mouth she found the words frozen in her throat. She shouldn't want these things, they were wrong and even though she knew people indulged in this role play all the time, she couldn't help feeling like a freak. Normal women didn't want things like this, she should-

Her thoughts shattered when Dimitri gripped her nipples and pinched them hard, sending painful zings of confusing pleasure through her. "Tell me."

"I want to fight you. I want you to force me to fuck you."

A slow, sensual, sexy as hell smile curved his lips. "You want to struggle, yes? For me to overpower you and hold you down? But will still have safeword. That is non-negotiable."

Mesmerized by his gunmetal eyes, she nodded. "Yes."

Increasing his pinch on her nipples, he pulled her forward by her breasts until she stood toe to toe. "How much do you want to fight? You want to slap, kick me?"

"No, I mean I might try to hit you but more like wresting."

"Would you like me to force you to orgasm?" She hesitated and he released one of her nipples, instead grabbing her ponytail and wrapping it around his fist. "Tell me, Rya, or I will tie you up and leave you in the corner all night instead of fucking you until you scream my name."

All the blood in her body seemed go to her pussy which contracted hard enough to make her moan. "I want you to overpower me, to force me to enjoy it. To take away *all* my control. I won't give in to you, you have to take it. I want to trust you but I can't just give myself to you completely. You have to earn my trust. Yes, I realize how fucked up that sounds, and it's not topping from the bottom or anything like that. I just need to know you're strong enough to protect me, okay? That I can't beat you in a fight. I've never done this with anyone before, but please don't judge me harshly."

"Harshly? Oh *dorogaya*, how can you not know that I worship you? Nothing you say will drive me away." He tilted her head back and gave her a soft, wet, hot kiss that left her whimpering. "I'm going to release you and you have to count of ten to run, *zaika moya*, then your *volk* will come hunting. *Da*?"

"*Da*, I mean yes." She sucked in a quick breath of air, her mind already sinking into her subspace.

"Fight me, curse me, tell me no, but I will take you hard and rough unless you safeword." He stepped back and began to unbutton his shirt. "Ten."

The first bit of his skin came into view and she let out a soft moan.

"Nine."

Another button, more skin and those long fingers of his moving with consummate grace.

"Eight."

She looked up, her heart pounding in her throat as she watched his expression close down, become cold, dangerous.

Fuck, she loved it when he looked evil.

"Seven."

His shirt was almost all the way unbuttoned now and she sucked in a quick gasp of air at the sight of his big cock pressing against the fabric of his pants.

"Six."

Toeing off the beautiful copper Prada heels that Dimitri had bought for her, she took a stumbling step back, her mind and body still entirely focused on him. He shrugged out of his shirt, the thick muscles of his body moving beneath his beautiful skin. The hard line between his pectoral muscles drew her gaze and she wanted to lick him there, to kiss the body that housed such a strong heart.

"Five."

Adrenaline flooded her and she finally managed to look away from Dimitri when he bent to take his boots off. With a little squeak she took a few steps back, looking around for the best way to run.

"Four."

Spinning on her heel, she darted across the room, heading for the stairs.

"Three."

She reached the edge of the couch.

"Two."

The stairs were too far away so she turned and moved so the couch was between them, balancing on the balls of her feet.

"One."

He came at her like an enraged bull, jumping onto the couch and almost grabbing her before she spun and ran. His surprised laugh rumbled behind her and before she could draw a breath he had her by her ponytail. With a hard tug that stung her scalp he drew her back to him, but she grabbed his wrist and managed to twist it to make him release her hair before sweeping his feet out from under him. The look of shock on his face was almost funny, but she didn't stick around to watch, instead running for the stairs.

She managed to reach the second step before he reached her again, this time grabbing the back of her dress. Holding onto the railing, she lunged forward and the dress ripped with a loud snarl of fabric. Her knees hit the steps with a painful thump, but most of the impact was absorbed by his arm wrapping around her waist. Her mind focused entirely on escaping him, desire and fear mixing together in her bloodstream in a way that made her fiercely aroused, but she wasn't giving up.

Shifting her weight, she managed bring her foot up between them and kicked him back, his grip loosening enough for her to scramble up a few more steps before he grabbed the edge of her ripped dress. He dragged her back to him and she tore the clasp of the halter top from around her neck, leaving him with a handful of fabric.

From behind her Dimitri snarled, "*Sic sukam sim.*"

She had no idea what that meant, but he sounded pissed. After reaching the top of the stairs she bolted to the right, intending to reach the bathroom and lock herself in. Before she got three steps he grabbed her ponytail again, but this time when he drew her to him he put her in a head lock her MMA teacher would have loved. She tried to kick him again, but he slammed her into the wall and pinned her there.

It didn't hurt, but it did limit her options for movement. She struggled against him, calling him every swear word in the book while his hard cock rubbed into her body.

"What do we have here?" Dimitri said in a threatening growl. "A little bitch who thinks she can escape me. I'm going to fuck you and there is nothing you can do about it."

He shoved his hand between her legs and tore away the pretty white silk underwear that she'd found in his bag. The whole time she kept trying to push him off, but it was like trying to move a boulder. An involuntary cry of pleasure rang out from her when his fingers slipped between her legs and stroked her slit.

"So wet for me. You like this, don't you. You want me to shove my cock in your greedy cunt."

"Fuck you," she gasped out and tried to keep from succumbing to his skilled touch.

"You protest, but your hot *pizda* sucks at my fingers."

She was going to assume he meant her pussy, which was indeed clamping down on his long, rough finger slowly pressing into her body. It was such a turn on that no matter how hard she fought him, he was still taking what he wanted from her. Letting herself slip deeper into the role, she gave a whimper and battled the urge to ride his finger that was moving slowly, so goddamn slowly, inside of her.

"Let me go you asshole!" She turned and tried to bite him, but he just pressed her harder against the wall.

He removed his finger from her pussy and fumbled with his jeans while she attempted to squirm out of his hold. Soon the hot flesh of his cock pressed against her and she froze, the wetness from the crest anointing her back. No, if he fucked her she would never be able to resist. Forcing herself to relax, she wiggled her butt back at him and smiled when he growled and slightly loosened his grip on her.

Instead of trying to push him away, she simply dropped her weight, then rolled off to the side. Once again his surprised laugh made her smile and she bolted for the bed, intending to crawl beneath it. Just as she reached the edge Dimitri picked her up and threw her onto the mattress, grabbing her ankle as she tried to scramble away. With a shriek she kicked back at him but he easily dodged her foot. Fuck, he was so strong and such a good fighter that she could give it her all and he would take it without getting hurt.

The thought made her wild and her clit throbbed while she kicked out at him again, tried to hit him, and fought him while snarling incoherent insults. The sheets twisted around their bodies and sweat slicked their skin as she continued to struggle. Dimitri managed to flip her over onto her stomach, his denim-clad legs pressing against hers, but his deliciously bare dick rubbing against her buttocks.

He made a growling sound that sent goosebumps all up and down her spine as he pressed a hand between her shoulder blades and pinned her to the soft mattress. Even though her body was getting tired, she didn't let up her struggles, incredibly turned on by Dimitri overpowering her. He placed his big thighs outside of hers and managed to get his other arm beneath her hips, raising her butt up and exposing her sex to him. The head of his dick pressed against her and she went wild, thrashing unsuccessfully until he shoved into her with a loud shout.

The moment his engorged crest hit her cervix she screamed, her orgasm detonating in her pussy as she tried to writhe in pleasure, still trapped by Dimitri's huge body pinning her. He growled again and stroked deep, riding her orgasm and drawing it out until she was making incoherent noises beneath him. He pressed in all the way until his balls slapped against her clit and she could only keen at how stuffed full of his cock she felt, how fucking good.

"*Yebanant*, your pussy is like silk." He leaned down, covering her with his body, making her arch against him, trying to get him to move. "Never felt anything better. Heaven."

She could only moan in agreement as he slowly stroked in and out, his shaft dragging deliciously over the overstretched nerve endings in her pussy. Somehow the tone of their fucking changed into love making and she moaned softly as he swept her hair to the side and began to kiss her neck while whispering things to her in Russian that she didn't understand, but still broke her heart because of the adoration in his voice. She didn't need to know the words to know that he cared about her.

He rolled them onto their sides and lifted her leg over his hip, opening her more fully to his deliberate, achingly wonderful thrusts.

"Play with your clit, *zaika moya*, come for me."

She slipped her hand between her legs while he gave her what felt like a world class hickey on the side of her neck, driving her crazy with his harsh grunts as his pace increased. When he bit her she tensed, and when he increased the strength of his bite she screamed out, coming hard as she rubbed her clit. He really began to pound into her then, rough enough that he fucked another climax out of her on the heels of the last. Unable to stand the intensity, she sank her nails into his arm around her, crying out as he pressed deep and roared her name.

She could feel the hot pulses of his release inside of her and realized he wasn't wearing a condom.

They shivered together, his dick twitching and the reflexive clamp of her pussy making him groan. After a few minutes of cuddling he began to move inside of her again and she moaned, exhaustion and pleasure battling within her. Manipulating her as if she was a doll, Dimitri shifted them so he was between her legs, looking down at her.

Their gaze locked and he didn't look away when he slipped a hand between them and circled her clit with his thumb. She strained to keep her eyes open as the pleasure built with each thrust of his dick. Shifting his hips, he adjusted his angle until he hit that sweet spot inside of her pussy that made it feel like he was stroking her clit from the inside out. A long moan escaped her and he gave her a pleased, but savage smile.

"This is my cunt, my body. Mine. Say it, Rya. Who is your Master?"

"You are." She couldn't fight the tears that flowed down her cheeks. "Oh, Dimitri, I'm going to miss you so much."

He held her close and buried his face against the side of her neck while increasing the pressure on her clit until all thoughts fled her mind except the need to come. She wrapped her hands around his shoulders and raked her nails down his back, urging him on, whispering for him to fuck her harder, faster. With a grunt he did as she begged and her cries filled the room as she clung to him, licking at his neck, biting his shoulder, moving with him as they chased their climax together.

His cock seemed to swell within her and she arched as much as she could with his bulk holding her down, crying out his name while almost blacking out as the unbelievable, exquisite pleasure from her climax roared through her.

A moment later his cries joined hers and she went limp beneath him while he filled her with his seed again. Her heart slammed against her ribs hard enough that she was sure he could feel it and he rolled just enough not to crush her, but kept his still hard length inside of her. The man wasn't human. When he finally withdrew she whimpered at the sore, delicious feeling until he pulled out all the way and the wetness of their combined release flowed out of her.

For a long moment he stayed still next to her, but she was too tired to even open her eyes. She had no idea how much time had passed, but the next thing she knew she was sitting in a warm bath in a bathtub made of some kind of creamy stone, surrounded by candles that smelled like vanilla while Dimitri washed her. A sense of wonder filled her as she turned her head to look back up at him, the warm smile he gave her making her heart thud.

"Hi," she whispered, her voice rough. "How long have I been in here?"

Smiling wider, he shook his head. "I have never met anyone who sleep as hard as you. We have been here for a while."

Turning in his arms, she gave him a soft kiss. "That was...wow."

"I do good with your fantasy, *da*?"

Rubbing her breasts over his chest, she giggled at the way his stiff cock twitched against her belly. "Are you ever not hard?"

"With you? No, I always want to fuck you." He grabbed her ass and squeezed. "You are so soft, so womanly. I look at you and all I can think about is how good it makes me feel when you orgasm."

Resting her head on his damp chest, she sighed.

"You're an incredible lover, an amazing Master, and the best man I've ever met."

His chest lifted beneath her cheek with a sigh. "Little Rya, you are...I cannot think of English word to describe how much you mean to me, how perfect you are." Sorrow tried to intrude on the moment, so she chased it away by concentrating on his body beneath her. A yawn escaped before she could stop it and his chest rumbled beneath her ear as he chuckled. "Let me dry you before you fall asleep again."

"Okay."

He helped her from the tub and she couldn't tear her gaze away from his magnificent body in the candle light. The water dripping over the well-defined sections of his muscled abdomen and down the sexy V of his lower waist drew her gaze to his hard cock. She tried to reach for him, but he captured her wrist in a hold she easily broke.

Wrapping a towel around her, he began to dry her. "You are surprisingly good at fighting me off."

She grinned while he patted her arms dry. "I told you I know how to fight."

Suddenly serious, he knelt before her and drew the towel gently across her belly. "If you ever fight for real, for your life, you must go for their eyes and throat if you can."

"What?"

He dropped the towel and took her hand in his, showing her how to make a fist in a way she wasn't familiar with, then pressed it to his throat. "Hit him here, hard as you can. You are small so they will try to overpower you with their mass. If you cannot reach them with your hand, bite them here. Or, claw their eyes out."

She stared down at him, shocked. "Dimitri, no one is going to hurt me."

A shudder wracked him and he wrapped his arms around her, pressing his wet face to her belly. "I will make sure of it."

Comforting him as best she could, she stroked his damp hair. "Really, I'll be okay. I have a great security system, a license to carry a concealed weapon, and I'm pretty good at keeping track of my surroundings."

He looked up at her. "You have gun?"

"Yep. I got a concealed permit after one of my co-workers was mugged on the way home from work."

His grip on her waist tightened. "You live in dangerous place?"

"What? No. I mean yeah. Buffalo has its share of crime, but it's pretty safe. I mean bad stuff happens to people everywhere, no matter where you live. My house is more out in the country than the city. At the moment my greatest threat is that one of my neighbor's pet goats will escape and eat my lawn."

He didn't laugh at her lame attempt at humor. "I will get you bodyguard."

She stared at him. "Are you insane? I don't need a bodyguard. Besides, my step-dad would shit a brick if I suddenly started walking around with some stranger following me."

He pressed his face against her again, his body as hard as stone with tension. "Is impossible for me not to protect you."

Grabbing his hair, she pulled his head back hard enough to make anger spark in his gaze. "Dimitri, nothing is going to happen to me. It's you I worry about. Your life is so dangerous."

"Don't you know? I am evil man. Evil men live forever. It is the good that die early. That is the bitter truth of my world."

"Oh, Dimitri." She put all her love for him into her touch her voice. "You are so good it makes my heart ache."

"Is not true, but I like who I am in your mind."

He stood and took her hand, leading her back into the bedroom. The sheets of the bed were rumpled so she straightened them as best she could before laying down. Instead of joining her, he simply stared at her for a moment before saying, "Close your eyes."

She did as he asked and the bed dipped as he joined her. When something cool touched her throat she startled and went to open her eyes, but he said in a stern voice. "Keep hands down and eyes closed."

A thrill of desire went through her at his dominant tone and she couldn't help but smile. "Why is it when you get bossy with me I find it hot, but when anyone else tries it I have the overwhelming need to put them in their place?"

His fingers touched her ear and she startled as he put an earring in her left ear, then her right. "Because you know I am your Master."

"What are you doing?"

"Hush, little Rya. Is something I have dreamed of doing. Indulge me."

A moment later something cool, a bracelet maybe, went around her left wrist, then her right.

His lips brushed against hers as he whispered, "Something to remember me by."

As she opened her eyes she held up her wrists and gasped. Two beautifully made cuffs with a swirling gold and silver pattern glittered on her wrist. She looked closer and made a choked sound. "Holy shit, Dimitri, are those diamonds?"

"*Da*. Is yellow and white diamonds. Reminds me of your eyes."

Unable to comprehend what had to be a small fortune adorning her wrists, she leapt up from the bed and raced to the bathroom, turning on the light then freezing as she got a look at the choker around her neck. Large, yellow square shaped diamonds surrounded by white baguette diamonds formed a circle around her throat, going all the way around. A sparkle from her ear caught her attention and she shoved her hair back, gasping at the exquisite yellow and white diamond earrings. They were shaped like flowers and glittered with the brilliance found only in high quality diamonds.

She wasn't sure how long she stood there, gaping at the jewelry worth more than she'd make in fifty years as a nurse, before Dimitri came up behind her, distractingly nude, and rested his head atop of hers while wrapping his arms beneath her breasts.

"You like?"

It took her a moment to find her voice. "Dimitri, I can't take these! This is crazy. Please, take it back."

He grabbed her hands before she could move to take the jewelry off and captured her gaze in the mirror. "You will take them. Please. Do this for me."

"I can't." She tried to pull her hands away but he held her tight. "This must have cost a fortune. I can't take it."

A pained look entered his gaze. "Rya, please accept my gift. I have more money than you can imagine, but no one to spend it on. Please let me give you this. It is nothing but metal and rocks. Let me show you how much you mean to me in one of the only ways I know how. I do not have the words to tell you what I feel. Please allow me to do it instead by giving you beautiful things that I hope will make you happy, to let you know that you are important to me."

"I don't need these to know how much I mean to you." Tears filled her eyes and she tried to sniff them back. "I can see it when you look at me."

He groaned softly and held her tight. "*I navsegda tebya lyublyu, Rya. Y menya ne bydet nicogoi' drygoi. Ti derjish moya temnoye serdze, moyu gryaznyu dushu. Vsyo shto moyo, tvoyo."*

"What does that mean?"

Holding her gaze, he said softly, "It means, I would do anything, give anything to keep you in my life, to make you happy, to give you everything that I have."

Swallowing hard, she let out a watery chuckle. "You know what? This really sucks."

He turned her in his arms, looking down at her with such sorrow that her already hurting heart broke for him. "I am sorry I cannot be the man that you need, Rya. Even as my selfish heart urges me to keep you, I cannot."

Lifting her face to his, she whispered, "Kiss me, then take me to bed and make love to me until the sun rises."

He did, and as dawn breached the horizon, Rya fell into an exhausted sleep, cradled in Dimitri's arms as he whispered against her neck that he loved her.

Chapter Fourteen

Dimitri stood out on the private patio off the bedroom and admired the desert sunrise. He felt alive, invigorated in a way he hadn't experienced in years. Rya still slept inside and he made a rash phone call that would undoubtedly make Alex extremely pissed off, but he had to have one more day with Rya. The thought of leaving her right now was more than he could bear.

The phone rang twice before Alex picked up. "Where are you?"

"I am still in Arizona. I've decided to stay another day."

"Dimitri," Alex's voice went low and deadly. "What are you doing?"

Anger filled him, but he tried to keep his emotions in check and his voice empty. "Nothing. I simply wish to spend another day here. It is beautiful; you would like it. Besides, once I return to Russia I won't have time to relax. I just want time away from the bullshit."

"Come back to the lodge."

The way Alex said that, like it was an order, irritated Dimitri. "No. I will be back tomorrow."

"Have you lost your mind? Do not fucking lie to me and tell me that you are staying to see the sights like some tourist. You are staying for that girl, that Rya."

He clenched his phone. "How do you know her name?"

"Please, Dimitri, spare me. I came back early last night with Ilyena and a few of the submissives were quite put off that you disappeared with some

American girl."

Dimitri's heart raced and he turned back to look at the still dimly lit bedroom where Rya slumbered among the sheets. "How bad is it?"

"It is not beyond repair, but you need to return to the lodge, with that girl, today."

The sheets on the bed were lowered enough to show the curve of Rya's lower back with her two diamond piercings in the dimples above her ass. He wanted to kiss those dimples, to put his thumbs over them while he fucked her. No, he needed just one more day with her to make their parting bearable, one more day to fill himself with her light. "We are staying another day."

Alex swore long and loud while Dimitri stood there and imagined all the ways he would have his little Rya today. "Do you not care about her at all? Think about what this could mean for her safety."

"Alex, if you could have one more day with Jessica, would you take it?"

"What?"

His brother's pained whisper made Dimitri feel like a giant ass, but he pressed on. "I have...feelings for Rya, things I have never felt for a woman before. I need one more day with her, Alex."

For a long time his brother was silent. "Do not get her killed, Dimitri. If you really feel something for her, walk away."

"I will, but not today."

"Stubborn bastard." He sighed. "I will do my best to cover you, but you must come back tomorrow. Promise me. I know how tempting it is to try and hide away with your woman, to think that if you go far enough underground no one will find you, but we both know that is not true."

The sorrow in his brother's voice hurt Dimitri. "I

understand, and thank you. I know this is not easy for you."

"No, it is not, but I will do my best to take care of things."

"Thank you."

"Go, make your memories, and know that I deeply envy you. I will see you tomorrow."

"Thank you."

After he hung up with Alex he placed a quick call to his friend and bodyguard, Luka, who was staying in the hotel. He'd kept out of sight while Dimitri was with Rya yesterday, but he was always near enough that if things went bad, Dimitri wasn't left to defend Rya on his own. Now he had plans for Luka that were more pleasure than work.

Luka answered with a yawn, "Good morning, boss."

"Good morning. Your lazy ass should be out of bed by now."

"Yeah, yeah. Not all of us have an amazingly beautiful woman in their bed. I swear you are the luckiest bastard in the universe."

Dimitri and Luka had known each other since childhood so his friend got away with remarks that he would never tolerate from other men and Dimitri granted him favors he wouldn't normally allow anyone. "So what do you think of her?"

Luka whistled, "She is exquisite. I see why you want to keep her to yourself."

"Actually, I need your help with something."

"Anything."

He outlined his plan to his friend and after he hung up he stretched out before returning to the bedroom. While Rya continued to sleep he ordered and ate breakfast, showered, dressed, and got a good chunk of his business done before she began to stir. He watched with a small smile as Rya sat up and blinked, then stretched, then flopped back into the bed and groaned. A few seconds later she sat up quickly and looked around the room. When her golden eyes found him sitting at the desk on the other side of the room they lit up with joy.

"Dimitri."

She held out her arms to him and he was up and moving across the room before he knew it, letting her sleep-warmed body snuggle into him as he held her. "Good morning, *zaika moya*."

"Morning," she mumbled against his chest, her little hands petting him. "Do we have time for a quickie before we have to catch our plane?"

"Actually, I wonder if you might want to stay another day with me?"

Apprehension momentarily tightened his muscles, he should know better than to assume that Rya would want to stay, but the idea that she wouldn't want more time with him honestly hadn't even occurred to him up until this moment.

Rya let out a squeal of delight. "Of course! But isn't your brother waiting for you? Will you get in any trouble?"

He laughed, everything inside of him loosening up instantly as he held her in his arms, basking in her obvious joy. "No, no trouble. Eat, then shower and put your riding clothes on."

"We're not staying here?"

"No. Is surprise."

Instead of questioning him she merely smiled and rubbed her nose against his. "Do you think maybe I can tempt you into a different kind of ride before we leave?"

The press of her pelvis against his left no doubt what she was offering and he smiled and nodded. "*Da*."

Rya let out a long, happy sigh as her spa attendant worked some kind of deliciously warm massage oil into her lower calves. After the ride on the back of the bike from Sedona to Phoenix, and Dimitri's ardent devotion to her pleasure, she was a little sore. She'd spent the last few hours getting a variety of treatments at the high end spa in Phoenix, Arizona that was attached to the luxury hotel where they were staying. It was super luxurious and she'd never experienced anything like the care she'd received here. Her attendants had been utterly devoted to her comfort, and she had fun sampling different types of wine while getting a pedicure. Evidently, Dimitri had gone all out because she had everything and anything she desired while the staff kissed her ass with such skill that she didn't even mind it. Dimitri was full of surprises, and as much as she loved the pampering she was currently receiving, she also wished that Dimitri was here but she couldn't imagine him sitting through a mud bath or a seaweed wrap.

Right now, she was in a lovely, serene private room in the spa painted a creamy peach being massaged by a rather handsome masseuse. The man, Luka, had dark brown hair and amazing hazel green eyes along with a body that was all hard muscle and tanned skin. She noticed that he had tattoos on his knuckles, and when he started massaging her, she found herself lost in his magic touch. Wearing the khaki pants and white polo shirt with the hotel's emblem on it, he was certainly a nice piece of eye candy, but he wasn't Dimitri, though they did have similar accents.

She wanted to ask Luka if he was Russian, but then again she really didn't want to draw any attention to Dimitri. Yes, it was slightly paranoid of her, but she knew what a risk Dimitri was taking by just being with her and she didn't want to do anything to put either of them in danger. Trying to turn her mind from those negative thoughts, she focused instead on the ride down here on the back of Dimitri's bike and how easy it had been to talk to him. They'd stopped by any roadside attraction that caught her eye and she'd bought Dimitri a black leather wrist cuff embossed with Navajo silver, turquoise, and red coral. It was such a masculine piece and the moment she saw it she knew it would be perfect for her Master.

While it wasn't the fortune in diamonds he'd showered her with, Dimitri had immediately put the cuff on with a pleased smile that made her all tingly inside.

Luka gently folded the towel covering her bottom up until it exposed the lower half of her buttocks. She sighed in delight as his oiled hands rubbed her thighs and practically melted into the table as he worked out a knot with his thumbs. After all the riding she did yesterday and today she needed this and she had to admit, it was slightly arousing to feel Luka's big, calloused hands on her, rubbing out all the tension. That was the nice thing about a professional masseuse. She could relax and enjoy the inherent sensuality of being touched without having to worry about him crossing the line.

The energy in the room shifted and right before she felt Dimitri's lips on her cheek she smelled his unique cologne. "Are you enjoying yourself, little Rya?"

Slowly opening her eyes, she smiled up at him while Luka moved down to her left calf, manipulating her limp body with ease. "Mmmm-hmmm."

He laughed and squatted down next to her. While she'd been pampered at the spa Dimitri had changed into a black t-shirt that lovingly hugged his thick shoulders and broad chest. She languidly reached out and traced her fingers over his face, enjoying the warmth that suffused his gaze as she touched him.

The men said something to each other in Russian and she leaned up enough to look from Luka, who was now rubbing her ankle, to Dimitri. "Do you two know each other?"

A smile that she could only classify as mischievous curved Dimitri's lips. "*Da*. He is friend of mine."

"That just happens to work at the spa?"

He laughed. "No, he is my present to you."

"Ummmm, what?"

His gaze darkened and her body took notice of the subtle shift in his stance that made him more...threatening. No, not threatening, more dominant. She watched as he rubbed the cuff she'd given him. "You are exhibitionist, yes?"

She flushed, all too aware of the caressing quality that Luka's touch had taken on. "Why?"

"I want to watch Luka pleasure you."

While she couldn't lie and say the thought of Dimitri watching her play with someone wasn't hot as hell, she didn't know Luka and was unsure as to what Dimitri wanted from her. "Pleasure me how?"

"I want to watch him eat your beautiful pussy, to make you come with his fingers, to watch you enjoy yourself."

The sinful temptations he offered her had Rya pressing her thighs together, all too aware of how exposed her private parts were to Luka. "Why?"

"Because...because it arouses me."

She glanced at Luka, watching them closely and motioned Dimitri forward so she could whisper in his ear, "You won't get jealous? I'll be honest with you, I want you, not him."

"No, I will not be jealous. I have known Luka many years, he is old friend and he has experience being third. He will not overstep his bounds, but he will give you pleasure. Will you do this for me, Rya?"

She couldn't help but giggle. "Well, this isn't exactly a chore. But promise me you won't let him do anything that would make you feel bad."

"Nothing bad will happen. You are mine, *zaika moya*, and I would not give the privilege of touching you to a man who does not deserve it. Luka knows his boundaries and we have shared women in the past. Sometimes he invites, sometimes I invite, but we always give the woman we share great pleasure."

Jealousy burned in her at the thought of faceless women being screwed by Dimitri. "I don't like the thought of you touching other women, so I'd rather not hear about that again, but I trust you. If you think I will enjoy this I'm willing to try."

He stood and gently pressed her head down so once again she was resting her face on the fluffy, folded towel beneath her head. "I am going to sit and watch. Relax, Rya, and give me your pleasure."

"You won't be joining us?"

She tried to keep the hurt from her voice, but evidently she didn't do that good of a job because Dimitri made a soothing noise. "I will. You think too much. Trust me, *dorogaya moya*. Let Luka care for you. He is good Master, enjoys pleasuring women and is very good at it."

"Yes, Master."

Dimitri lowered the lights until the room was bathed in a mellow amber glow and she let out a deep breath, trying to focus only on Luka's talented hands. Right now he was massaging oil into her lower back and she let out a soft moan as he expertly manipulated her. Damn, she had no idea what Luka did for Dimitri in his official capacity within the Novikov Bratva, but the man had a god given talent for massage. The men said something to each other in Russian while Luka gently ran his fingers over her subdermal implants, then he placed a gentle kiss on each diamond, sending tingles through her body.

The knowledge that Dimitri was watching them gave her pleasure a naughty edge and she arched her back slightly when Luka removed the towel so he could massage her ass. His pleased murmur made her bold and she arched further, spreading her thighs slightly. Arousal burned through her and she groaned deep in her throat and bit her lip as he began to squeeze her buttocks. Luka handled her with the self-assured touch of an experienced Dominant and she gave herself over to his manipulations. Soon his fingers began to brush over her pussy as he massaged her inner thighs and she moaned with abandon while her sex swelled beneath his glancing caress. The feathered touches were driving her crazy and she arched her back in a blatant invitation to the provocative Russian man.

Dimitri's deep voice washed over her as he said, "No orgasm until I allow it."

Her whimper was lost within the men's combined laughter and Luka tapped her hip. "Roll over to back."

She did as he ordered and gave him a lazy smile when he growled and stared at her body. Feeling reckless, aroused, and in a playful mood she arched and yawned, stretching out in a way that made Luka's jaw clench. Teasing men was fun. Luka was in his late thirties and when he smiled at her she looked at him from beneath her lashes, loving the hint of trouble in his gaze. He said something to Dimitri and her Master replied. She wanted to look over at Dimitri, to see if he was enjoying this, but she couldn't without twisting around.

Luka began to massage her arms, then her upper chest, and by the time he got to her left breast she was hungry for his touch, aching for him to play with her erect nipples. He poured some oil over her breast and both men made a pained sound as the oil dripped off of her hard peak. With a gentle touch Luka began to massage her left breast, bringing blood flow that sensitized her until she was panting and very, very turned on. At the first scrape of his finger over her nipple she cried out and Luka smiled.

"Such pretty tits, and sensitive," he whispered, "Dimitri is lucky man."

With that he began to pluck at her nipple, teasing pinches that sent a line of fire directly to her clit. By the time he was finished with her other breast she was completely ensnared by him. As his hands worked down her belly, she found herself holding her breath, tensing with anticipation at his touch on her pubic mound. He made her spread her legs until they fell off either side of the table and rested his hand gently on her lower abdomen.

Luka looked over to where Dimitri must have been sitting and said something in Russian. A moment later Dimitri said, "Luka wishes to give you g-spot orgasm. You will allow this?"

His voice was rough with lust and she would have done pretty much anything he asked or ordered at this point. "Yes, Master."

A delicious rush of anticipation tightened her pussy while Luka gave her a roguish grin. Instead of getting right to it, he began to massage her again, pinching the lips of her pussy and rubbing them together until she was fighting off her orgasm. He was very, very good at playing with her and she clawed the sheet covering the table, her head thrown back as her back arched and she tried to lift her legs to close them, but before she could move, she realized Dimitri held one leg, and Luka the other.

"Make her come," Dimitri said in a low voice while staring at where Luka continued to massage her pussy.

The sight of Dimitri watching another man finger her drove Rya crazy and she reached out, needing to touch him, needing to connect with him while Luka slipped two of his fingers into her very wet sex. Dimitri looked up at her when she clutched at his hand, then smiled. "Shhh, be easy. Enjoy."

Luka began to tap on her g-spot and she groaned deep in her throat, the amazing sensations sending sparks of raw pleasure through her, making her cry out as the tension built and built. The brush of Dimitri's beard against her pussy registered only seconds before he began to suck on her clit and she came.

Hard.

Pushing out, she screamed and soaked Luka's hand while he continued to rub that dense bundle of nerves inside of her, to pull another orgasm from her on the heels of the first. Dimitri growled against her and bit her clit. A brilliant white light flashed across her vision as the wonderful contractions of her orgasm deepened further. She bucked against them, struggled to be free of the overwhelming sensations they were unleashing in her. She struggled to draw enough breath to scream but all she could do was ride out wave after wave of a release unlike anything she'd ever experienced. Her body convulsed with the last contractions of her climax forcing a continuous stream of whimpering cries from her lips when the men finally pulled back. Two sets of hands stroked her, petting her, massaging her, helping to soothe the tremors until she could finally catch her breath.

Forcing her eyes open, she looked over at Luka, then Dimitri and smiled. "Oh, that was sooooooo good."

It took a great deal of effort to sit up, but Luka helped her and she fell against Dimitri cuddling against him and taking in deep inhalations of his cologne. "Want to make you feel good."

"What about Luka?" He whispered against her neck as he kissed the damp skin there. "Would you like to suck him off while I fuck you?"

She thrust her butt out at Luka, wiggling it at him in a taunting manner. "Do you want to see that, Master? Do you want to watch me swallow his seed?"

"I do." He wrapped his arms around her in a hug. "Does the idea arouse you, my Rya?"

A little shiver of delight moved through her at his possessive tone. "Yes, Master."

"Turn around, hands and knees."

She did as Dimitri ordered, allowing him to arrange her as he wished. The height of the massage table was perfect. He slid her legs further apart and gripped her hips before burying his face between her legs. A cry of delight escaped her and she looked up as Luka lowered his pants, revealing a delicious looking uncircumcised cock just begging for her lips. He kept the hair around his groin neatly trimmed. He wasn't as thick or long as Dimitri, but he did have an exceptionally large head and she wondered what it would feel like to have him moving inside of her.

Luka gently held her hair in one fist and brought her mouth to his cock. Dimitri licked at her pussy like it was a melting ice cream cone. She groaned in pleasure as she began to tease the extra skin around the head of Luka's dick with her lips and tongue. His rumbling growl of pleasure emboldened her and she gave herself over to pleasing this man her Master had deemed worthy of her attentions. As she began to slowly suck him into her mouth Dimitri gave her one last lick before standing. He gripped her hip with one hand, pressed his dick against her entrance with the other and began to push into her.

She sucked in a harsh breath around Luka's shaft

stretching her mouth and moaned. Whispering something in Russian, Luka began to ease in and out between her lips, fucking her with the same rhythm Dimitri moved to behind her. The sensation of her Master stretching her, filling her, satisfied Rya in a way she'd never imagined. He completed her, his body was made for hers, and the pleasure of his cock moving inside her drove her crazy. She threw her hips back at him and began to suck Luka harder, wanting them to be just as crazy with lust as she was.

Dimitri gripped her hips with both hands and began to pound her with hard, deep strokes that were a little painful, but felt so good. She ran her tongue over Luka's shaft, loving the salt of his precum and his hands in her hair. Giving herself over to them like this, allowing her mind to just drift and give over to the intense feeling of pleasing two men, was one of the best things she'd ever experienced. Oh, she'd been with more than one partner before, but never with someone she trusted as much as Dimitri. Her absolute surety that he wouldn't allow anything bad to happen to her allowed her to relax completely and live in the moment.

Reaching beneath her, Dimitri rubbed her clit, "Come for me, *zaika moya*."

Luka pulled back so his cock only grazed across her lips and she cried out, partially in longing for him to give her his cock back and partially in stunned amazement as Dimitri fucked her orgasm out of her. Her body felt as if it no longer belonged to her and her release took her by surprise, unleashing a tidal wave of hormones and endorphins that shot her straight into subspace.

As soon as she'd calmed enough to breathe, Luka shoved his cock into her mouth again and she moaned gratefully, loving how they were using her, loving that she was bringing them such pleasure.

Their grunts and growls filled the air along with the wet sound of her sucking. She reached out and fondled Luka's balls, lightly caressing them with her nails as he jerked her head back and began to fuck her mouth with abandon. Eager for his release, excited to please both Luka and Dimitri, she hummed low in her throat and Luka made a choking noise that had her eagerly sucking at him. His dick jerked in her mouth and she had one brief taste of his seed before he pulled out with a shout and came all over her mouth, cheeks and chin.

Behind her Dimitri slowed his movements, leaning over her and boxing her in with his body as he pressed his hips into her with a rolling motion that had her sighing in delight. Luka began to lick his come from her face and she moaned against his lips, sharing the taste of his seed with him while their tongues rubbed against each other. Dimitri picked up his pace and she met him thrust for thrust. She didn't care that she would probably be sore tonight, wanting only the reward of his orgasm. She continued to kiss Luka but begged Dimitri to come, to fill her up, to fuck her, take her and own her.

Luka nipped at her lower lip and she gasped as the sting translated to pleasure, rubbing her groin against Dimitri, squeezing him with her inner muscles and crying out as he smacked her ass.

He began to spank her with each thrust and she was soon begging for her release, her bottom on fire and her pussy aching with the need to come.

"Please, Master, please may I come?"

"No."

She cried out in despair, her sweaty body shaking as Dimitri seemed to swell inside of her. He pulled her up so her back was pressed to his front and through half-open eyes she watched Luka stroke himself as he looked to where Dimitri's cock was going in and out of her body. Dimitri growled out something in Russian and Luka reached out, manipulating Rya's clit while Dimitri slammed into her.

The need to orgasm suffused her and her whole body seemed at once numb and on fire. Luka caressed her clit and she couldn't help but wonder if Dimitri felt the other man's fingers toying with her, if Luka was grazing Dimitri's cock as he slammed into her. That thought was so dirty, so erotic that she was helpless as her climax exploded within her. She screamed out Dimitri's name and he shoved himself as far in her as he could get, whispering her name against her neck as his dick jumped inside of her, the warmth of his come filling her. Luka continued to stroke her and she tried to get away from his fingers, but Dimitri held her still.

"Come again, little Rya."

Her breath left her body in a hard rush as Luka leaned forward and began to lick her clit. Without a doubt Dimitri felt the other man's tongue and his cock twitched inside of her, driving her crazy. Luka had heavenly soft lips and when he began to suckle her clit she tightened around Dimitri until he swore softly, then came with a hard rush that left her close to blacking out.

Everything went fuzzy around her and she almost tumbled out of Dimitri's arms before Luka caught her with a laugh. They'd completely drained her of every ounce of energy and she was as limp as a noodle as they laid her on the table, then began to rub her down with what felt like towels. Luka gave her a gentle kiss at some point that she didn't have the strength to return and by the time Dimitri told her to go to sleep she was already well on her way out.

Chapter Fifteen

Rya fidgeted in the luxurious seat on the private jet and watched an increasingly agitated Dimitri pacing the cabin. After her massage yesterday they'd spent the day holed up in their room at the resort in Phoenix, eating, talking, and making love until the early morning hours. It had been *the* best night of her life and so bittersweet she'd found herself fighting off tears. It was so unfair that she'd finally met her perfect man, but that loving him would be a death sentence. Part of her kept hoping Dimitri would ask her to come back to Russia with him, or that he would want to stay in the States, but he never said anything. By the time she fell asleep she knew this would be their last time together.

Dimitri's shout of anger snapped her back to the present. He was nearly yelling, growling out a continuous stream of Russian as he talked to someone on the phone. They'd had a lovely, if melancholy, morning together, basking in each other's presence before boarding the plane. She wore a white dress with emerald accents that Dimitri had given her that made her feel very feminine. It was long and flowing, with an empire waist embroidered with daisies. She also wore the earrings he'd bought her, but kept the wrist cuffs and collar safely packed away in her bag. The neckline was low, displaying a considerable amount of cleavage which Dimitri seemed to love, but right now she was invisible to him.

With a final shout he threw his phone against the bulkhead and stood there with his shoulders heaving and his hands clenched into fists.

She was afraid to move, or even breathe as she

watched him struggle to get ahold of himself.

After some very long, tense moments he finally turned around. The fear she saw on his face made her own skyrocket. "What's wrong? What happened?"

For a long moment he just stared at her, then visibly shook himself. "We have problem."

"Dimitri, you're scaring me."

He moved to her and knelt before her, gripping her hands in his and searching her face before he spoke. "My absence, and yours, has been noted. My brother, Alex, returned from Boston yesterday and one of our friends informed him that a man associated with a rival Bratva of ours was asking about you."

"Oh, fuck," she whispered.

"That was my brother, Alex that I was speaking to." His grip on her hands tightened to the point of pain. "He has plan for taking suspicion from you, but I do not want to do it. Will hurt you too much."

Confused and getting more scared by the second, she tried to still the trembling in her voice. "What does he want to do?"

Closing his eyes, Dimitri rested his head against their entwined hands. "I must show that I have no feelings for you, that you are nothing to me more than any of my *nochnaja babochka*, my whores. But that is not worst."

Her heart beat thudded in her ears. "What else, Dimitri?"

"I need to fuck another woman in public, and you another man while I'm watching."

"What?" The thought of Dimitri being with any woman, touching any woman the way he touched her, made Rya physically ill even though she knew he would have lovers after her. Then the second part of his statement registered and she shoved him away. "No way. That is totally fucked up."

His voice came out hoarse as he said, "Rya, you are in danger. I cannot tell you how great it is. Please believe me, I do not want this. It will take everything I have not to kill man who touch you."

"Can't I just leave?"

"*Nyet*. You will still be under suspicion. If they think they have slightest leverage against me with you...you will be used as pawn."

She jerked her hands away from him and covered her face, not wanting him to see how much his words hurt. "Please, Dimitri, don't make me do this."

"*Zaika moya*, if there was any way to not I would do it. I would kill for you."

"So I'm just supposed to fuck some guy while you watch? Submit to him, let him do everything to me that I did with you while you fuck some bitch in front of me? How the fuck am I supposed to hide my tears?" The last words came out in a scream and she tried to shove him away but he wouldn't move. "The thought of another woman touching you makes me want to fucking kill you and her!"

Agony cut deep lines in his face as he stared up at her. "I will not let stranger touch you. Is not stranger, is man I trust to pleasure you."

"Will Luka be there?"

"No. Alex will be with you."

"Your *brother*?" Her voice rose to an unpleasant screech on the last word. "Are you fucking kidding me? That is just so wrong on so many levels."

"No, is not wrong. Is right." His voice firmed and he gripped her hands again, ignoring her struggles. "He is only man I trust with you. The only one. He will do what needs done, but will not go further."

"And who are you going to fuck? What whore do I have to watch kiss you, and touch you, and love you?"

"No. Never love. Rya, you are only woman who ever gave me love." He brushed the tears from her face with a pained sound. "Ilyena, Alex's submissive, will be with me."

"I hate you," she shouted and tried to smack his hands away. "Don't touch me."

"Rya, please..."

She kicked him away and stood, moving to the other side of the cabin. "No, I don't want to hear a fucking word out of your mouth, Dimitri. Just stay the hell away from me. I can't believe you're asking me to do this."

"*Zaika moya*, I would spare you this if I could. Please believe me. You knew dangers of being with me. I am trying to protect you only way I can."

"By fucking someone else and making me watch? No, not just making me watch, making me watch while pretending we have nothing *and* screwing your brother." She gave a bitter laugh and moved as far away from him in the cabin as possible. "Well, that will be easier than I thought, because right now I loathe you."

His expression tensed and he stood. "Do not say that."

"Fuck you, Dimitri. I can't even look at you without picturing you fucking someone else and it makes me sick. I thought...well, it doesn't matter what I thought. Leave me alone." Her voice broke on the last words and she took a deep breath, trying to hide her tears.

He nodded and moved to the back of the plane, sitting in his chair and watching her with that cold mask of his in place. She stumbled to the chair as far away from him as possible and turned it around so she didn't have to look at him. Covering her mouth, she tried to muffle her sobs. She knew leaving him would hurt, but she thought they would be able to do it on different terms than this. As foolish and illogical as it was, she was falling in love with Dimitri and the thought of watching the man she loved with another woman was torture.

Memories of him kissing and being pawed at by those three submissives raced through her head. She curled into a ball of misery, wishing she was home and had never met Dimitri, and most of all, wishing she could really hate him like she said.

They rode back to the lodge in separate cars. Tusya and Katya met her at the entrance to the lodge. Dusk had fallen and the lights of the mansion burned behind them. Tusya looked handsome as ever with his carefully styled blond hair and superb bone structure, but she felt nothing for him as he helped her from the SUV. Katya gave her a hug and a brief kiss as Rya watched Tusya speak in Russian to the men with her luggage.

He came back over to her side and swept her up into his arms, burying his face against her neck as he said, "Act happy to see me. You will be coming to my room. Your room has been bugged."

For a moment she just froze, then she wrapped her arms around his neck and whispered back, "What the hell is going on?"

"Inside, I will explain. Now, look happy to see us."

He let her slide down his body and she was pretty sure his hard cock was happy to see her, but she managed to plaster on a smile as she gave him a brief kiss. Because she didn't want any man touching her right now, she laced her fingers with Katya and held her hand before giving her a much warmer kiss than the one she bestowed on Tusya. Today Katya wore a pair of dark jeans that fit her perfectly with a soft mint green silk blouse. Though she gave Rya a bright smile, she couldn't hide the worry in her eyes.

They took Rya through the lodge, but before they could reach the wing of the lodge where Tusya had his room, a tall man with dark hair and thick lips stepped into their path. He wore a pair of tan pants with a white dress shirt, but everything about him screamed thug. Rya gave him a quick glance before turning back to Tusya. She was shocked to see the quiet, gentle Russian Master she knew had disappeared, replaced by a cold, menacing man as he glared with open malice at the man blocking their path.

The dark haired man stared at Rya until Tusya stepped in front of her, slightly to the side. "My submissive is not available to you, Borya."

Rya caught a glimpse of the man's hands as he gestured in her direction. He had some kind of odd tattoos across his knuckles and where his shirt pulled up she could see more tattoos. There was even one on his neck of a dagger going through his flesh. Despite the nice clothes, his demeanor screamed thug. Borya had dark brown eyes, and when they locked on her she felt like he could see into her soul.

The man said something in Russian and Tusya replied. They argued for a few minutes, and whatever they were saying was scaring Katya. Her hand trembled in Rya's grasp and she pulled the girl into her embrace, giving Katya a kiss on the cheek while trying to soothe her. The men abruptly stopped arguing and watched her with Katya. For a moment Borya examined her and she couldn't help glaring back at him. Borya shrugged and moved out of the way after a few more words with Tusya.

Snapping his fingers at them, Tusya led the women into his room. Once the door was shut he began to say something in Russian that didn't sound complimentary. Her bags were delivered a moment later. Once they were alone again in Tusya's sumptuous gold and green suite on the second floor of the lodge she let go of Katya's hand and moved to

Tusya.

"What the hell is going on?"

He ran his hand through his hair, but Katya came to his side and wrapped her arms around him, laying her head against his chest, obviously comforting the man.

Blowing out a harsh breath, Tusya hugged the small woman back and looked at Rya. "It would have been better if you stayed with me."

Of that she had no doubt, but she wasn't sure why he thought that. "Tusya, who bugged my room? How do you know it's bugged?"

"Do you know what the *Bratva* is?"

"Yes. And before you ask, I did an internet search on Dimitri so I know about his family."

"You know he is a powerful man in the Novikov Bratva, yes?"

"I do. Who was that guy who stopped us in the hallway? Is he in the Bratva?"

"Yes. A rival family to the Novikov. Borya is high rank. One phone call and it would bring you big trouble." He took a seat in one of the gold velvet chairs near the fireplace. "Sit. Katya, please get coffee for us."

After giving both Rya and Tusya a worried look, she left.

Tusya turned to her, his deep blue gaze intent on her. "You are in danger. That man, Borya, is an enforcer for another Bratva, a bad one where they have no respect for women."

"Wait, why is Dimitri traveling with an enemy? If they are rivals, why are they both here?"

"Is political, like everything else. Important, powerful men and women are part of the European delegation. There is much...bonding that goes on during BDSM play and Dimitri would be a fool to allow the other Bratvas an advantage like this trip without him being here to solidify his own allegiances."

"This is so fucked up."

Tusya gave a hard laugh. "Welcome to my world."

Fear skated down her spine and she clenched her hands together in her lap. "That Borya guy, is he…is he going to try to hurt me?"

"We do not think so, but he is curious. You disappeared with Dimitri. He wants to know who you are and why Dimitri took you. It is out of character for Dimitri to do anything without his brother and Borya has been keeping tabs on your lover."

"He's not my lover anymore," she said in a tight voice.

"He never was. Dimitri does not do love, Rya." His voice softened and he sat back in his chair, crossing his leg. "He only has whores he uses."

"I know." His callous words made her inexplicably defend Dimitri, but she was still angry with him. "What do you have to do with all of this? Whose side are you on?"

"I am merely trying to help you."

That might be true, but he was obviously holding a lot more back. "Bullshit. Why would you help me? Why are you really doing this? Don't lie to me, Tusya. We both know I can read you."

He glared at her. "You do not trust me."

"I don't trust anyone."

Her voice thickened on the last word and Tusya watched her with a considering expression. "You really like Dimitri, don't you?"

"No."

His smile was chiding. "Do not lie to me, Rya. You wear your heart on your sleeve. No wonder Dimitri is so worried. He actually asked for my help. Do you know how unusual that is? He will owe me a favor."

"What?"

"Borya will not suspect me of being an ally of the Novikov family. I am Russian royalty and do not mix with the likes of the Bratva. It would sully my family name and there is no love lost between myself and Dimitri."

She chewed on her lower lip, trying to figure out what was going on. "So I'm supposed to pretend that I'm your submissive?"

"Unfortunately, no. Dimitri has threatened to destroy me if I fuck you." Tusya slowly shook his head. "If I did not know it was impossible I would say he cares for you."

The words made tears gather in her eyes, but she tried to pretend they didn't affect her. "Well, you're wrong."

Shaking his head again, Tusya stood and walked over to her chair before kneeling before it. "You know he cannot love you? You know every moment you are with him you will be in danger?"

"I know about the Novikov Curse," she said through stiff lips, not liking how close he was and inching away.

He placed a hand on her leg and she smacked it away. Instead of being angry he appeared genuinely sad. "I had hoped that maybe you would be able to play with Katya and I, but Dimitri was once again right. You will not suffer my touch."

"I'm sorry, Tusya, but I just don't feel that way towards you. In the brief time I've known you I feel like we could be friends, but that spark isn't there."

"For you, it isn't," he said in a soft voice. "You are the only one to ever guess my needs."

It took her a moment to realize he was talking about his desire to submit. "Did you talk to Angelique?"

"I did and it was very...enlightening, but unfortunately does not solve my problem."

"Why don't you find a Mistress to play with in private? I know tons of switches. Hell, I'm one and there's nothing wrong with it."

He shook his head. "That is not how it works in my world. While yes, there are submissive men, my culture is very masculine. A man is expected to be a man at all times. My family tolerates my kink because it is a powerful thing to be a Master. But if I wore the collar…no, it would not end well."

Pulled out of her own worries for a moment she brushed his hair back from his forehead. "Maybe you could find another switch, a woman who will be your Mistress in private and your sub in public?"

Shrugging, he stood again. "Maybe. But right now we must worry about keeping you alive."

There was an elaborate knock on the door, and when Tusya opened it, a large, intimidating man with dark hair flecked with silver at the temples, a perfect goatee that framed a nice mouth and wearing a perfectly tailored black suit entered carrying a tray of coffee. Something about him was familiar and she looked closer at his face. He had a jagged scar going down one cheek to his jaw, and as she examined his face, she saw traces of Dimitri there. Then her gaze lifted to the same gunmetal grey eyes and she knew right away this was Dimitri's brother.

Well, it looked like being unfairly handsome ran in the family.

Tusya took the tray and set it down before closing the door. The two men conversed in Russia while Rya stared at him, but they ignored her. After a few minutes of conversation Tusya nodded and turned to Rya. "This is Alexandr Novikov. He wishes to speak with you."

"I know who that asshole is." Glaring at Alex, she stood and crossed her arms. "You can turn around and get the fuck out right now. There is no way on earth I'm letting you touch me."

Tusya stared at her like she'd lost her mind, but Alex merely lifted one brow in a cool expression of amusement that made her grit her teeth. He said something to Tusya in Russian and he left with Katya, closing the door, trapping her with Alex. Panic filled her and she slowly backed up when he walked towards her. Even in a suit the man radiated menace. It gave her chills to see just how cold his gaze was.

"Stay away from me."

He stopped advancing on her and nodded. "Please, have some coffee."

"Fuck you. It's probably drugged."

His lips twitched, but he merely shrugged and went about making his own cup. "If I wanted to drug you I wouldn't have to do it with food and drink. I could merely shoot you with a dart the moment I walked into the room."

The casual way he said that frightened her; she wished she had a gun right now. "You need to leave."

Bringing the coffee cup to his lips, he took a sip and sighed. "I will not hurt you, Rya. Please. Let us talk. Sit."

She'd backed up to the window and jumped slightly at the sensation of the cool glass against the back of her arms. "I have nothing to say to you."

"Fine, then you will listen." He sat with an elegant grace and stared at her. It was disconcerting to see someone who looked so much like Dimitri watching her. The same dominant vibes rolled off of him as his brother, but where Dimitri watched her with heat, Alex's gaze was icy. "My brother loves you and he is terrified that you will be hurt."

"Bullshit."

"Dimitri says you are good at reading lies. Am I lying, Rya?"

She bit her lower lip and studied him. "I...no, I

don't think so."

"So, we know that Dimitri loves you. I admit, I'm baffled by how quickly he fell for you, but that seems to be how it works for the men in my family." Deep, crushing pain filled his face for a moment before it vanished like snow melting on a warm day. "He tried to protect you the best he could, but your activities drew the interest of the spies we have traveling with us in the European Delegation and now we must do damage control."

She stared at him, a bit creeped out by the way he could sit so still, almost like a statue. "I'm not fucking you, Alex."

"I accept that, but we will have to do something." He sighed and his expression thawed somewhat. "You must sell them on wanting me, Rya. Even if I disgust you, we must make them believe that you are of no value to them, that there is nothing between you and Dimitri."

"How? How the hell am I supposed to pretend I want your touch when the thought makes me ill." She angrily wiped away a tear. "How can you say he loves me when he'd let his brother fuck me."

Alex abruptly stood and stalked across the room towards her. If Dimitri was a wolf Alex was a tiger and her poor little rabbit heart raced as she was caught in the gaze of a predator. "Do not question his feelings for you. He is beside himself with worry. I have never seen him like this and we have been through *terrible* things together."

He stopped just out of reach, and she had to crane her neck to look up into his eyes as he loomed over her. She shoved at his chest but he didn't move; his body was solid muscle beneath her palms. "Back off."

"I must show you something since you do not seem to understand the level of danger you are in."

Baffled, she watched as he unbuttoned his white

dress shirt, revealing a body built just as fine as Dimitri's but a bit leaner. She looked up to his face but he wasn't watching her with anything even close to lust. Instead that immense, roaring pain was back in his eyes. After shrugging out of his jacket he took his shirt off and stepped back.

She looked all over his body, stunned by the number of scars covering him. The men in the MC club had lots of battle wounds, and she'd heard plenty of stories about how they got them so she was able to catalog his scars. Bullet wounds, what looked like stabbing scars, a burn on his ribs, and various other injuries marked his body. She looked up from his stomach, absently noting he had an excellent six pack and sexy V, then up his chest.

Alex touched a beautiful tattoo over his heart. There was something written in Cyrillic and below the writing a rose in full bloom with its stem intertwined with another rose, this one still just a bud. "Did Dimitri tell you about my Jessica?"

Frowning, she shook her head. "No."

His entire body sagged and she was afraid he was going to fall to his knees before he stood straight again. He looked out the window instead of at her. "Five years ago, I met an American girl while I was...working in Ireland. She was beautiful, so full of light and love despite her harsh upbringing in the American foster care system. And smart, so smart. We would play chess after her shift ended until dawn at the pub where she worked and I rarely won. We quickly fell in love and I thought I could hide her, keep her safe. I married her and we lived together for three months before..."

"You don't have to tell me. I can guess what happened."

"We had just found out she was pregnant." His voice broke and she took a step closer to him, wanting to comfort him, but he jerked away. "I tried to protect her, even forged a deal with the Boldin family behind my father's back. I did everything I could to keep her safe. Everything. I would have sold my soul if the Devil would have bought it, but none of that saved my Jessica and our baby."

This time she didn't hesitate to hug him, merely wrapping her arms around his stiff frame, the pain radiating from him. "Oh, Alex, I'm so sorry for your loss. What happened? How did they find you?"

He gave a harsh laugh but his hands were gentle as he rubbed her shoulders. "My brother said you would listen, that I would want to tell you, but I did not believe him. Are you some kind of sorceress?"

"No, just a good listener." She felt him hesitantly hug her back and his tension lessened just the slightest bit.

"My father came to visit, somehow he'd found out about her. He wouldn't...he wouldn't give her his protection. He said that she was too gentle to be my wife, too fragile." Anger entered Alex's voice and his grip on her tightened. "Two weeks later Jessica died when her car exploded, instantly killing her and our child. They were vaporized by the intensity of the blast. I lost the only woman I could ever love. I was away, in Russia, cleaning up a huge mess my father had made when it happened. We did not even get to celebrate our baby properly. She would have made an excellent mother and I would have done everything I could to be the man both of them needed. When she died, my heart died with her."

He shook in her arms and tears slipped down her cheeks as her heart hurt. "I'm so sorry for your loss."

"Do not cry for me, *dorogaya*. I am responsible for her death and I will burn in hell for it."

"No you..."

He gripped her by the shoulders and pushed her

back so he could squat down and look her in the eye. "I tell you this so you understand why Dimitri is asking you to do something that hurts you so much. He loves you, but we cannot protect you. It is best if you vanish from our lives, but that cannot happen until our enemies are sure you mean nothing to us."

"That's a terrible way to live," she whispered. "Would you really rather have never met Jessica?"

He was still for a long moment, his heartbeat thundering beneath her ear as he stroked her hair. "No. But I should have left her before they found her. If I had, my child would still be alive today."

Abruptly he stepped away from her. "Rya, I need to take you to the public dungeon soon. What can I do to make it easier for you?"

She couldn't even look at him, her shame warring with her anger. "I don't think I can do this. If I see Dimitri with another woman...I love him. God help me but I do."

An anguished sound escaped her and Alex cursed softly before kneeling in front of her. "The woman he will be with, Ilyena, she does not mean anything to him beyond a friend, does that help?"

She shook her head, keeping her eyes closed as if that could block him out. "It will break me. I know it. Anyone who is watching me will see how much he means to me."

"Then we will take away your sight. Blindfold you. Would that be better?"

He was so earnest in his attempts to comfort her that she tried to think about this objectively. When she opened her eyes her gaze went to the memorial to his wife and child etched into his skin. It was one thing to read about and hear the stories of their loss, quite another to see the physical proof of Alex's broken heart. She couldn't do that to Dimitri, and well...shit...she really didn't want to die anytime soon.

"It would."

"How much do you think you can tolerate from me?" He gently ran his hands over her arms, causing chills to skate over her skin. "Where can I touch you?"

Embarrassed by her body's reaction she tried to step away but he griped her arms. "I don't know. How much do you need? What do you need? What are you going to do?"

He stood and picked her up, carrying her to the chair and sitting with her on his lap. She squirmed uncomfortably, not liking being this close to him. "Rya, it must look real, like you are enjoying my attentions."

"Fuck. Alex, I can't do this."

"Yes, you can." His serious expression lightened a bit and he put his hand beneath her chin, forcing her to meet his gaze. A small smile curved his lips, making her aware of just how handsome he was. "Am I that ugly?"

She sighed. Damn Novikov charisma. "No, you're not."

Something in his face, his body language changed and he began to stroke her throat, sending more of those uncomfortable chills through her. "I am a very good Master, Rya. I know how to get into a submissive's mind, how to give her what she wants. Know that I can give you vast amounts of pleasure. But I will do nothing that you do not want."

Mesmerized by his long fingers on her throat, she closed her eyes and tried to ignore how her body was slowly warming to him. "Dimitri will hate me."

"No, *dorogaya*, he will not. I am here with his permission because he trusts me to treat you right."

She gave a shaky laugh. "You know this is messed up, right?"

"Shhh, let me touch you. Let your body get used to

me. Just feel."

The command in his voice was the only thing keeping her from bolting from the chair when he began to caress her collarbone.

"Such soft skin, so pretty. I see why he loves to touch you. What does he call you? Ah yes, *zaika moya*, his rabbit. You are very brave, Rya, and I admire that in you."

Her reply was lost as he began to toy with the edges of her dress, light caresses that made her pussy grow wet, needy. The conflict she felt over his touch only seemed to heighten her arousal in a perverse way, to fan her excitement into flames. She tried to argue with herself that she didn't like it, that he wasn't turning her on, but when his knuckles brushed her hard nipple she couldn't stifle the moan that escaped her. Alex knew how to touch a woman for maximum effect and he used that knowledge on her with consummate skill.

His cock hardened beneath her and she had the nearly hysterical thought that both he and Dimitri had gotten lucky in the big dick lottery. Making a soft, soothing sound he shifted her slightly and stroked down her belly to her hip. She couldn't move, feeling like her body belonged to someone else as he slowly gathered her dress up, the fabric scraping over her thighs.

She tried to pretend it was Dimitri, but Alex's touch was different; she was all too aware of how fucked up it was that she was liking this.

When her panties came into view he made a pleased sound. "Very pretty."

His words seemed to snap her out of the trance he was putting her in and she started to push off of him, but his arm locked around her. "No, you will stay and take the pleasure I will give you. Relax, little Rya. I will take care of you."

The rough tone of his words mixed with her crazy fantasies about being forced, and she sucked in a harsh breath when his strong hand opened her thighs, moving one of her legs so her toes barely grazed the ground. His rough growl at the sight of her sex still covered by her panties made her pussy ache, and she battled her shame as she arched into his palm cupping her mound.

"Such a good girl. You love to please, don't you? Such a hot, wet little pussy. You have soaked through the fabric. It pleases me very much."

She buried her face against his chest, squeezing her eyes shut as he played with her over the silk, his long finger tracing along the slit of her sex. The hair on his chest tickled her face and she whimpered when he gently pulled her panties to the side, exposing her to his gaze. His cock twitched beneath her bottom and he let out a low growl.

"Beautiful, and so wet."

His thumb split her sex and she gasped as he began to rub her clit. Almost against her will she rocked into his touch, her breath coming in ragged pants as she clutched at him, whimpering as he quickly worked her up to almost the point of orgasm. As she hovered on the edge he pulled his hand back, then moved her panties back in place before patting her mound.

"Please," she whispered, hating herself for asking but needing the relief.

"Look at me."

It took a great deal of effort to open her eyes and look up at him. When she did she gasped at the heat in his gaze and the absolute lust emanating from him. His lips curved into a small smile and she watched in fascination as he slowly sucked her glistening juices from his thumb.

"Do you want me to make you come?"

She nodded, her cheeks burning but her traitorous body craved release.

"Say it."

The hard dominance in his voice undid her. "Please, Sir, make me come."

"How?"

"With your fingers."

"Not my mouth?"

"Ummm, not yet."

He made a warm noise. "Perhaps I will convince you to let my mouth pleasure you."

Before she could object, he began to play with her slit again, grazing his finger over her clit while he stared into her eyes. It was so odd to see that gunmetal a cool color when she was used to seeing Dimitri's hot liquid silver desire warming her from within.

Alex slid one finger into her and she arched up into his touch, her body tensing. "Spoiled girl. Stay still. You will not come without permission."

She nodded her understanding, unable to look away as he ever so slowly stroked his finger in and out. "Nice, tight *pizda*. Like wet velvet. Would feel good around my cock."

Blushing furiously, she tried to close her eyes as he began to drive her towards her orgasm. He chuckled and leaned down to whisper against the sensitive skin of her ear. "Closing your eyes will only make it worse. You will think about what it looks like to have your pussy on my lap, my fingers shiny with your arousal. How you've dripped down onto my pants and how delicious you look. Let me lick your pussy, little Rya. Let me suck on your clit."

Her clit throbbed as he slowly rubbed his thumb there. "Alex..."

"What is it?"

"I can't think when you do that."

"Do not think, feel. Know that I'm imagining fucking you with my tongue like this."

She rubbed up against his hand, "You don't fight fair."

"All is fair in love and war, innocent Rya."

Before she could protest he had her on the coffee table with her ass on the edge and her legs around his shoulders. He didn't even look up, just began to lick at her pussy with long, sexy as hell growls. She closed her eyes and threaded her fingers through his hair, wondering if Dimitri would be aroused by watching his brother eat her out. Knowing her Master, the answer was probably yes. And if she was being honest with herself, Alex had some amazing oral skills.

He spread her legs wide and she keened softly at the sensation of his thick tongue moving inside of her. Chills raced down her spine and she dropped her hips down, trying to rub herself against his face. He backed away enough to bite her inner thigh, leaving a nice bruise she was sure, before returning his mouth to her pussy with a gentle touch that made her toes curl. He reached up with one hand and began to toy with her nipple while flicking the tip of his tongue over her clit.

"Please, may I come?"

He made a pleased sound and looked up. "I want to watch you."

Alex stood and hauled her up into his arms like she weighed nothing. Apprehension filled her as they approached the bed and Alex stopped walking. "Why are you scared?"

"I...well, I won't have sex with you Alex. I'm sorry."

His gaze thawed the slightest bit, "You care for him? You really do?"

"Yes." She thumped his shoulder. "If it wasn't for Dimitri I wouldn't touch you."

He actually looked hurt. "I see. Would it help to talk to him?"

"What do you mean?"

"I can call him and you can talk to him on my phone. It is secure, I assure you."

"Really? You would do that for me?"

His gaze softened further and the smile he gave her was actually genuine. "Yes, I would do that for you."

Before she could protest he had Dimitri on the phone. After briefly saying something in Russian Alex handed his phone to her. As soon as she had is she said, "*Volk moy*?"

"Yes, *zaika moya*, it is your wolf."

At the sound of his voice she let out a little pained noise. "This is fucked up."

His voice was thick, deep as he said, "I wish I could spare you this, but I will do whatever it takes to keep you alive. Please, help me protect you. Let my brother bring you pleasure. Those people will know if you are faking. That cannot happen. So you have my permission to do everything but fuck. Only my cock goes in your pussy or ass. Am I clear?"

"Yes."

"Yes what?"

The dominance came through loud and clear in his tone and she melted against Alex. "Yes, Master."

"Good. I am proud of you, little Rya. I know this hurts you and I swear I will make it up to you. Survive this and I will find a way to make you safe in my life. It will be hard, and take time, but I will make it happen. Nothing will keep me from making you mine."

She sucked in a harsh gasp of air, anger burning through her and mixing with her lust and guilt until she was trembling. "I'm scared."

"Do not be. Alex is good man. Let him please you.

I swear I will not feel anger, or anything but pride. You are my woman, you are strong. You will do this and I will reward you for it. I meant it, Rya. If we can get through this anything is possible. Just give me chance to make things as safe for you as I can. If something happened to you, I would not be well. People would die. Many people. Please, help me keep you safe and please do not hate me so much."

"Dimitri, I don't really hate you…and I'll try."

"Such a good girl. Now relax, enjoy. Know that tonight you will be the only woman in the universe to me. No matter what is going on around me, it will be you owning my heart."

"You suck," she whispered, hating the tears thickening her voice.

"This is a bad and dangerous situation I put you in. I allowed my greed for your love result in danger for you. Is unacceptable and I am working hard to secure a future for you free from threat. You have my permission to enjoy everything this situation has to offer. I will always be close enough to keep you safe. Believe me. Trust me to be your Master."

She startled when Alex firmly grasped her breast, then rubbed his thumb over the tip. A soft moan escaped her before she could catch herself and Dimitri chuckled. "That's it, give in to his touch. Feel him, my little Rya, and know that he is only enjoying you because he has my permission, but the ultimate call is yours. I will not force you to endure any man's touch that you find deplorable. Do you understand?"

"I do, and no, he's not deplorable." She gave Alex a shy glance and was startled at the sight of his pleased smile. "Though he is an insufferable asshole. I don't know how you can stand him."

Alex gaped at her while Dimitri roared with laughter. "I would give much to see his face right now. You, my girl, are very wicked. Now give phone to Alex and be aware that I will give him my blessing to punish you if he so chooses. Do not worry, you will enjoy it, and I will love watching you come undone."

Feeling numb, she handed Alex the phone and watched his gaze narrow before he spoke with Dimitri in Russian. After he hung up he gave her a grim look that perversely made her aroused. Damn, she always loved a pissed off Dom.

"So, little Rya," Alex purred, "You will allow my touch."

"Yes? No? Shit, I don't know." She rubbed her face, trying to clear away what was probably some really smeared mascara. Alex needed to understand the boundaries between them in order for her to do this. "Okay...well see, if I had met you first and you were single I would have thought you were hot. But I met Dimitri first and I belong to him. He's my Master."

He laid her out on the bed, smoothing her hair around her head and generally just touching her gently. "I understand, Rya. But you need to understand that I would never hurt him. My love for my brother is without question, and I've never tried to take anyone or anything away from Dimitri. That is not to say I don't want you, if you were mine I would spend years—decades—learning your body, taking care of you. But you are not, so instead, I can at least have the satisfaction of watching you orgasm. You are one of those women who make certain men, men like myself and my brother, wish to care for you. So soft, so delicate, I want to protect you. My only solace for my unusually strong protective feelings for you is that whatever I feel for you, Dimitri feels it a thousand times more. I know my place, Ms. DeLuca, and it is not as the owner of your heart. However, right now, my brother has given me the honor of playing with you, so I plan to make you climax, hard. I want to feel your slippery cunt on my face and lick you from the little bud of your asshole all the way to your clit. I may not have you, but I will have your pleasure."

With a slight tremble she tried to ignore how her hand was by his cock as he curled up onto his side, facing her while lowering his hand back to between her legs. "Oh God."

"That's it, Rya, feel me. Feel my heat against you, the brush of my breath, my fingers deep inside your body. You are so wet, yet tight. It must drive my brother crazy to fuck you. No wonder he doesn't want anyone else to experience you. Men would kill to fuck a pussy like this."

He began to thumb her clit and she flexed her hand, loving how he froze as her fingers brushed his cock. His dick jumped against her knuckles and she shifted her hand, curving her palm lightly around him. Alex lightly pressed his cock against her palm and his chest expanded as he took a deep breath. When she squeezed again he pressed into her hand harder. His gaze bore down into hers, making her aware of how much bigger than her he was. And those eyes, god, it was like having Dimitri here watching her in an odd way. Together they played with each other, though Rya kept above Alex's clothes. There was no way he'd come from her touching him like this, but it must have felt good because he was beginning to sweat and a feral smile curved his lips.

"Rya, we will do as little or as much as you want. I know you said no sex, but I've already had my mouth on your pretty cunt and I would love to have your mouth on my cock." He groaned as she began to work on his zipper, then traced his dick through the small opening. Evidently Alex went commando, because she felt only hot, hard flesh beneath the pads of her fingers. Oh dear, she was pretty sure Alex shaved his pelvis. Curious, she unzipped him further and stroked her fingers over his pelvis while his cock brushed her wrist.

"Perfect, *dorogaya*. You have no idea how good you feel. Your skin is indescribably smooth, it feels amazing, and I can still taste you on my lips."

The fact that she was calling the shots helped her to be bold, to further bury her guilt beneath pleasure. Dimitri got her into this mess, and for whatever reason, he wanted her to hook up with his brother. His hot brother. Oh man, this was so messed up, but Alex felt so good that her willpower was weakening by the moment. And if he kept talking dirty to her she was going to come without anything more than the press of her thighs.

"Do you like to be flogged?"

Blinking at him, she tried to process his words, but all she could really focus on was how much she wanted his mouth on her. Shame mixed with her need and her lower lip quivered, but she nodded. She was really going to do this. There was no doubt of it now so she might as well make the best of the situation that she could.

He ran his fingers through her hair, gripping her lightly. "I will flog you, tease your lovely breasts, and stroke that beautiful pussy. May I lick it?"

She bit her lower lip, then said in a hesitant voice, "As long as you promise me Dimitri is okay with this."

If she thought the mention of his brother would make Alex back off, she was very wrong. If anything, his gaze darkened further. It was as if her caring for his brother turned him on. "He wants you to have pleasure, Rya, wants me to give you everything I can. You are so loyal to him, is beautiful. Makes the fact that your body is made for sin all that much better. Men see you and they think of what it would be like to be blessed enough to touch you, not knowing that you feel better than they could ever imagine. I want to fuck you, hard."

"No sex," she blurted out. "And I want to be blindfolded and have earplugs."

He studied her for a long moment, a flash of regret in his gaze before he nodded. "Done."

"Where…where will we be doing this?"

"The small dungeon by the game room. It will be mostly our friends, Dimitri is rather possessive of you."

She couldn't help laughing. "Possessive of me? He's letting you do everything but screw me, Alex."

To her surprise he cupped her sex again, grinding his heel against her mound. "If he wasn't possessive of you I would be buried up to my balls in your hot little cunt right now. There is no way I would have been able to resist you from the moment you hugged me and pressed those big tits against me. If you had not been his I would be marking every inch of your body with my seed."

Her heart thundered and it was a struggle to hold his gaze. The best her stunned mind could come up with was, "Oh."

When he took her hand and wrapped it around his dick, she didn't object, instead squeezing him and exploring his cock, watching his gaze darken to that familiar deep grey that made her heart ache. He began to stroke her clit again and she panted while watching him, her emotions so out of control that she couldn't even begin to process the situation. Alex rubbed his nose against hers as he thrust up into her hand with a steady rock of his hips, like he was fucking her fist.

"I would dig my legs into the mattress and push into you as far as I can, filling you until you shatter around me, your cunt milking my cock. Dimitri tells me you allow him into you with no condom. I remember what that feels like. The only woman I've ever fucked without a condom was my wife. I know how special you are to him and I envy him. But no matter how much I may want to fuck you, it will never happen." Pausing, he removed her hand from his throbbing shaft. His touch gentled and he gave her that smile again. "So yes, Dimitri is possessive of you."

That thought brought tears to her eyes again and she curled up on his lap, wanting his comfort. He seemed to sense it and removed his hand from between her legs, hugging her to him. "Please don't let me see him with another woman. I can't deal with it."

"I will make sure you see and hear nothing."

"Thank you."

He placed a gentle kiss on her forehead. "If you can get through this you will be able to spend the night with Dimitri before we leave tomorrow morning. That is if it is something that you want."

"How? I thought we weren't supposed to be seen with each other."

"We have friends who will help hide it. Just keep that in mind. If you can get through the next few hours and convince our enemies, you will be rewarded by being in the arms of the man you love."

She detected some jealousy in his tone and looked up at him, searching his face. "Are you okay with this?"

He gave her a startled look. "What?"

"Well, I mean this has got to be kind of awkward for you as well."

His laughter vibrated against her and he gently moved her off his lap and onto her feet. "Touching a beautiful woman? Bringing her pleasure? Hopefully making her pussy melt on my tongue? No, is no hardship."

Licking her lips, she swallowed hard and nodded. "Okay. So how are we going to do this?"

Chapter Sixteen

Alex knocked on the dor of a room down the hall from his. A moment later a very pretty, curvy blonde-haired woman around Rya's height opened it with a smile. She wore her hair in loose ringlets that flowed over the shoulders of her pink t-shirt and a pair of artfully distressed jeans hugged her legs. The smell of food drifted into the corridor while she held the door open.

"Alex, Rya, please come in."

Rya glanced around the suite and took note of the deep burgundy and gold décor before returning her attention to the woman. Alex had told her that the blonde—her name was Catrin—would be helping her get ready for this evening, and that Catrin could be trusted. Although what Catrin could possibly do to make this any easier for Rya other than getting her shit faced drunk she had no idea.

Catrin turned and gave Rya an unexpected hug and said in surprisingly good English, "Rya, it's so nice to meet you. Dimitri has told me all about you."

The guilt and anger that churned Rya's stomach surged and she stiffened in the other woman's arms. "Thank you."

Catrin gave her a searching look, then turned to Alex. "I'll take it from here."

"Thank you, Catrin."

Alex gave Rya an uncomfortably heated look before he left her alone with the curvy blonde. As Rya looked her over she couldn't help the pang of hurt that filled her. Catrin had the legs of a pinup girl. Jealousy chose that moment to remind her that Dimitri had either fucked, or possibly would be fucking this woman tonight. She tried to dismiss those catty thoughts, reminding herself that she'd just had Alex's cock in her hand, and that she was still wet.

She was such a hypocrite.

Could this day get any shittier?

With a smile Catrin gestured towards the small four-person table near the window laden down with food. "Come, let us eat."

Rya followed her over to the table and took in the assortment of tiny sandwiches and sweets, but shook her head. "I'm sorry, but I'm not very hungry."

Sighing softly, Catrin sat in the chair nearest to Rya and took her hand. "This is incredibly awkward and difficult for you, isn't it?"

"What could possibly be awkward about having the brother of the man I lo-like screw me while Dimitri fucks some woman?"

"I understand." Catrin gave her hand a sympathetic squeeze. "Would it help if I told you Dimitri is miserable? That I've never seen him this upset?"

In a petty way, it did feel better, but she shook her head and gently extracted her hand from Catrin's. "I'm sure he's real torn up about screwing one of his whores."

Anger tightened Catrin's angelic features. "You do not understand, do you?"

Rya gave a bitter laugh and crossed her arms, hugging herself. "Understand? I don't understand any of this. I'm so fucking confused and scared I'm two steps away from locking myself in a closet."

Catrin filled a glass with what looked like champagne and shoved it at her. "Drink."

"I really…"

"I said, drink."

The command in Catrin's tone made Rya blink,

but she took a sip, then another. "There, happy?"

"No, this situation is not ideal for any of us. I love Dimitri, he's one of my husband's best friends, and it hurts me to see him in so much pain. I know you don't understand, but please believe me when I say, in all of the time I've known Dimitri he's never given a shit about a woman other than for physical release or friendship. Never love...until you."

After taking another gulp of champagne Rya shook her head. "Are you involved...I mean do you know about his family?"

"Yes, I'm well aware of his family. My husband is part of another...family."

"Really?"

"Oh yes, but we are not here to discuss that. I need to help you be as comfortable with this as possible, because not only do I feel badly that you are in this situation, but because I need to protect Dimitri. He has helped my husband in many ways over the years and I owe him."

"So you're supposed to give me a pep talk or something?"

Catrin sighed and refilled Rya's glass. "Something like that."

She hesitated to ask, but she needed to know. "Where is Dimitri right now?"

"With my husband, Nico, and probably Alex." Catrin picked up a sandwich and nibbled on it while studying Rya. "He wanted to come see you but he's being watched too closely."

The champagne soured in Rya's stomach and she shifted in her chair. "What do you mean watched?"

"The less you know, the better. This thing that we will be doing tonight? Please believe me when I say it hurts Dimitri badly to have to make you do this." She chewed her lower lip before setting her sandwich back down. "Which brings me to a point I know you will not like."

"I don't like any of this, so just spit it out."

"Dimitri is having an issue...rising to the occasion."

"What?"

Catrin flushed and looked down at the table, playing with the edge of the plate. "It will be difficult for him to pretend to be unaffected by you if he is unable to perform."

"You mean he's having a problem getting a hard-on?"

"Yes." Catrin sighed and met her gaze again. "It will be easier for him if you can find pleasure in what Alex will be doing to you."

Smacking her hand against her forehead, Rya leaned back in her chair. "Wait, let me get this right. I need to get off on Dimitri's brother fucking around with me so he can get hard and fuck another woman?"

"Well, not exactly. He will not have sex with anyone else, only a blow job."

"How fucking saintly of him," Rya spat out while her heart ached at the thought of Dimitri pleasuring himself as some faceless bitch sucked his dick.

Catrin leaned forward and said in a soft, angry voice, "This is not easy for him. Do you think he wants anyone else to touch you? The very idea of upsetting you has sent him into a rage. I have never seen him so distraught. Dimitri never shows deep emotion. He wants to be with you and it is killing him that he cannot. I do not know how much experience you've had with Doms, but Dimitri is very, very possessive of you. He has never been possessive of a woman in his life, but you...with you he almost beat the shit out of Alex before my husband and a few of our friends managed to hold him back."

Bracing her arms on the table, Rya rested her face

in her hands. "What am I supposed to do?"

Catrin reached out and gently rubbed her back. "Well, you have some options. I can only give them to you and let you decide what you want."

Sucking in a deep breath, Rya nodded and sat up straight. "What are they?"

Shifting uncomfortably, Catrin took a deep breath and said, "This does not have to be unpleasant for you. I understand that emotionally this will be painful, but physically it can be enjoyable if you can separate yourself from it. Have you thought of maybe a blindfold so you do not have to see anything? That might make it easier."

"Actually, I have. And ear plugs."

"Good, that is good. Trust me when I say you can rest assured that Alex will do everything he can to make this as enjoyable for you as possible. Not because he wants you—well, not only because—but for his brother. The only person that Alex loves in this world is Dimitri and he will move mountains to make his brother happy." Catrin gestured to Rya's champagne and waited until she'd taken a drink before continuing. "Forgive me for being blunt, but have you been with multiple partners before?"

Flushing, Rya nodded. "I...uh, yeah."

"And you are an experienced submissive?"

"Yes."

"Good, that will make it easier. If you are open to it, I would like my husband to join you and Alex."

Staring at the other woman, Rya drained the last of her champagne. "Say what?"

Catrin frowned at her. "I do not share Nico easily, and I will not allow him to have sex with you, but I know that I can trust you not to try to steal him from me or become emotionally attached. Correct?"

"Well, yes, of course. I don't want to sound like an ungrateful bitch, but why the hell would you offer that?"

"This entire plan hinges on Dimitri showing he does not favor you. He must sell the idea that you mean nothing to him, when in fact you mean everything. Alex will dominate you, but if you are willing, Nico and I will 'unexpectedly' arrive." She clenched her jaw and Rya noticed for the first time that Catrin's hands were shaking slightly. "He will come over to Alex and ask to play with you."

Feeling like a self-absorbed jerk while watching Catrin's obvious discomfort at the thought, she reached out and took the other woman's hand. "You don't have to do this."

Catrin met her gaze, and slowly shook her head with tears welling in her eyes. "I do. You don't understand what it's like in their world, Rya, what will happen to you if they decide you can be used against Dimitri. I had a friend who was kidnapped when we were teenagers. She was the daughter of a Russian political figure and was taken by a Bratva that wanted him to do some favors for them, favors he couldn't do no matter how hard he tried. They did terrible things to her and took pictures of it. She was eventually sent to a whore house where a 'doctor' cut her ovaries out with no pain medication. That is the preferred form of contraception for the pimps of that Bratva, and they wouldn't waste resources on anesthesia. Instead she was shot up with cheap street drugs. When my friend was finally found two months later she'd been raped by hundreds of men, was addicted to heroin and riddled with STDs. Her mind was...gone. I saw her once after they found her and she was broken, utterly and completely. If you're in danger from the kind of men that did this to my friend, I will do anything I can to protect you, just like Dimitri."

Stunned, Rya could only stare at the pretty woman

who'd seen so much pain. Her stomach cramped up at the thought of someone doing that to her. Dimitri had some fucking shit to answer for. Fear sank into her gut and her voice trembled, "I'm so sorry."

"Enough about that." Gathering herself, Catrin sat up straight and patted Rya's hand. "Now, let's eat and then we can try on some outfits. We are close to the same size so I have some things you may like that I know will drive Dimitri crazy."

"Don't you mean Alex?"

"Well, maybe that too." Catrin gave her a small smile. "Would it help if I told you Dimitri is a huge voyeur? That the sight of you having pleasure with other men will make him mad with lust?"

Memories of Dimitri watching Luka touch her made her flush. "I thought you said he's possessive of me?"

"Oh, he is. He would never let anyone he doesn't trust touch you." She winked. "But he trusts Alex because, well he's Alex. Dimitri knows his brother would never betray him, and he trusts Nico because he knows that my husband loves me unconditionally. This may be hard for you to understand, but sharing women among my husband and his close friends, it is like the ultimate honor, a bonding experience that draws them together like brothers. That is not to say I let my husband fuck their women, at least not without me there, but this sharing of women is not unusual among the people we associate with in the BDSM scene."

"And you're sure you're okay with this?"

Catrin gave her a considering look, then sighed. "At first, no. I will admit the thought of watching Nico with some stranger made me very angry, but now that I have met you and I know you will not become emotionally attached to my husband, yes. I will confess, I am a bit of a voyeur as well, and since we are so physically similar other than the color of our hair, it will be erotic for me to watch you with him."

"You know how weird this is, right?" Rya picked up a sandwich, took a bite then chased it down with more champagne, her appetite returning as Catrin's words settled into her mind.

Laughing, Catrin topped off Rya's glass. "I like you and I can see why Dimitri likes you. There is something very...honest and refreshing about you. I wish things were different."

Heaving out a sigh, Rya nodded. "Me too. I'd be willing to risk my life to be with Dimitri, but after talking to Alex I couldn't put Dimitri through the pain and guilt if something did happen to me."

Catrin licked her lips and hesitated, then leaned forward. "This is strictly between you and me, okay?"

"Okay."

"Dimitri and Alex are working very hard to change things. There is much...negotiations going on behind the scenes, but nothing can be done until their father passes, that evil bastard."

"I don't understand."

Catrin made a frustrated noise. "I cannot tell you, if I could I would, but just know that someday things may be different."

The champagne was buzzing through Rya now, numbing her frazzled nerves and helping her to mellow out. "Different how?"

Sighing, Catrin stood and stretched. "That does not matter right now. If we don't get through this evening and convince those watching that you are merely an American submissive here to experience the BDSM scene, then the future will not matter because you won't be around long enough to see it."

"That's reassuring," Rya muttered before finishing off her sandwich. "What do you need me to do?"

Giving her a dazzling smile, Catrin fluttered her lashes, "Can I dress you up?"

Rya's light dinner threatened to come up as she stared at Alex. He'd changed from his suit into a pair of black leather pants that fit his muscular frame like a glove, a black mesh shirt with a black latex neckline that laced up the front, and a pair of black leather gloves that she found disturbingly erotic. Focusing on those gloves, she noted how he had rather elegant, long fingers and shame mixed with arousal had her swallowing and tearing her eyes away from his hands.

"We match," she said in a voice that she intended to come out strong and sassy, but instead came out obviously wary.

Trying not to fidget and drawing on her training to get her through this, Rya forced herself to relax and stand with her hands at her sides, her legs shoulder-width apart, and her chin held high with her shoulders back and her tits out. And her tits were indeed out, fully exposed by the series of leather straps connected by silver o-rings going across her body. They covered nothing and seemed to somehow make her more exposed than being totally naked. She wore a pair of tiny black satin panties, but she knew those would soon be gone and only two thin black leather straps on either side of her labia would highlight her sex.

Catrin had, in a thoroughly uninhibited manner, admired Rya's pussy and picked this outfit to show off her 'beautiful *pizda*'. By the time they'd reached Catrin's immense closet—the woman would need her own plane to ship back all the clothes she brought with her—Rya was feeling pretty tipsy and actually found flirting with the other woman to be rather fun...and arousing. Something about Catrin appealed to Rya, and the women had shared more than one hot look as they helped each other get dressed. At any other time, Rya would have been tempted to play with the lovely Russian woman, but even Catrin's abundant sex appeal couldn't make what was about to happen disappear from Rya's thoughts for long.

And, now, she stood before Alex with Catrin at her back, trying to keep her anxiety from showing.

Alex stepped forward, closing the space between them, but stopping when she took an involuntary step back. Her long hair was pulled back in a thick braid and she whimpered when Alex reached out and grabbed her by her braid, bringing her closer to him. Holding her head back, he slowly, deliberately looked down her body and she tried to pretend that her nipples weren't getting hard from his soft growl of approval. Guilt pierced her and she tried to look away, but she liked the way he was looking at her with such appreciation.

"You did very well, Catrin," he said in a soft, almost inaudible voice.

"Thank you, Master Alex," Catrin said and came up behind Rya, giving her a soft kiss on the shoulder. "I need to go find Nico. We'll meet you in the playroom in a little bit."

Alex looked away from Rya's breasts to Catrin. "You have discussed Nico with Rya, yes?"

"I have."

Looking back to Rya, he brought up his free hand and gently stroked her jaw. "You are in agreement with playing with Nico?"

"I'm not in agreement with any of this, but yes, I don't mind if Catrin's husband touches me. I trust her and she wouldn't marry and love an asshole."

Catrin giggled, then cleared her throat when Alex shot her a hard look. "Yes. I will be off. Don't worry, Rya, they will take good care of you. It was very nice meeting you and if things were different, I would love to play with you as well. You have the most beautiful pussy."

Flushing, Rya gave the other woman a teasing smile as Alex relaxed his hold on her braid. She'd downed three glasses of champagne and was feeling pretty good. Putting a little bit of dominance in her voice and in her demeanor, she caught Catrin's gaze. "I bet you have a very pretty pussy as well. You want to show it to me, don't you, Catrin. You want to spread your legs and let me touch you, slip my fingers inside of you, and stroke your stiff clit. I'd take my time learning you, understanding what you need, then I'd make you climax until you beg me to stop."

Catrin's gaze went hot and she said something in a soft torrent of Russian that made Alex laugh. He responded in Russian, then she left with one last longing look at Rya. Alone again with Alex, Rya's nerves returned and she went to take a step away, but he wouldn't let her.

With a soft, calming touch Alex returned to stroking her face and neck with his gloved hand. "Such a sexy little tease. Are you ready?"

"No." She swallowed hard. "I'm fucking terrified and pissed."

"Why?"

"Oh, I don't know. The Russian mob may or may not want to put a hit on me, I'm about to trust a man I hardly know to play with me in front of a bunch of strangers, and somewhere right now the guy I'm falling for is probably fucking some bitch. What could possibly be wrong?"

Alex grabbed her braid again and jerked her head back so she was looking at him. "First, do not worry about anyone harming you. I will not let that happen. Second, I regret that you do indeed not know me but I can assure you that I will bring you nothing but pleasure. Third, those women with Dimitri are not bitches. They are friends who are helping him protect his woman. Understood?"

She tried to fight her tears, but failed. "Yeah, fine, great. Whatever."

He studied her, his eyes growing darker by the moment. "I have something that would help you get through this."

"What?"

"An aphrodisiac."

That made her blink in surprise. "There's no such thing."

"Oh, little Rya, I assure you that there is." He took a small vial out of the pocket of his leather pants.

Eyeing it, she shook her head. "I don't do drugs."

"It is not a drug. It is an herbal extract that will help your desire. You are correct that it is not a true aphrodisiac, it will not make desire appear where there is none, but it will immensely heighten your arousal."

Despite herself, she was curious. "How?"

He traced the cool glass down her cheek and over her chest until he circled her left nipple. "It will make things very, very intense for you."

That didn't sound so bad. In fact, she could use intense right now, something to get her out of her own head. This was going to happen whether she liked it or not so she might as well get some pleasure from it. Originally her idea had been to get drunk, but even she knew that drunk BDSM was a really bad idea.

"But it won't make me high or anything, right?"

"No. It has no affect on your ability to think."

She searched his face and saw the truth of his words. "Okay."

He released her braid. "We are going to have so much fun."

A confusing pulse of lust went through her at his guttural tone and she watched as he unscrewed the top. He tipped the bottle and a thick, almost honey-like substance dripped onto the index finger of his other gloved hand. Watching her intently, he spread the glistening substance on her mouth. It smelled faintly like vanilla and when he stroked some on her tongue it had a sweet, pleasant taste. She nipped at his leather covered finger, then sucked the oil off. Her lips were warming and it felt good to gently bite him. When he made a rough, moaning noise she released him and licked her lips before looking down and admiring his cock pressing against his leather pants. Saints have mercy, the Novikov men were almost unfairly sexual. They reduced her to a mess of hormones with no effort.

Next, he applied it to her nipples, and by the time he finished, her mouth was tingling. She licked her lips and gave a soft, pleased gasp at how sensitive they were. She shifted as her sex clenched down and a rush of wetness slicked her labia.

Kneeling before her, Alex looked at the little satin panties covering her sex. Without preamble, he tore her panties away and tossed them to the side, his gaze focused on the juncture of her thighs. Desire crushed her resistance and she shifted, pressing her legs together to try to sooth the building ache.

"You have such a beautiful cunt," he murmured. "And the outfit Catrin picked out for you makes your already plump pussy pout like a mouth begging for my kiss. Is wonderfully dirty."

"Please," she whispered.

She held her breath, wondering if he would lick her there, and found herself wanting it. The oil he'd spread on her nipples was sensitizing them and they began to ache, to tingle like they'd been clamped. She stared down at Alex, his focus on her sex making her wetter. Thoughts of Dimitri began to intrude but she banished them, struggling to live in the moment. Alex leaned forward and gently brushed his lips over her mound, then she felt his warm, moist breath on her skin making her moan softly.

He took an audible breath, then let out a little rumbling sound that was incredibly sexy. The tip of his tongue gently brushed her clit and she sucked in a harsh breath, arousal making her legs weak. Making a soft, soothing noise he began to kiss the curls over her sex, and steal an occasional lick at her clit. Before long she buried her hands in his hair and he slowly backed her up until they hit the edge of the sofa.

"Brace yourself," he said in a low voice before he began to eat her sex in a ravenous manner.

Rya cried out and held onto the back of the sofa, sagging slightly before Alex stood with a low growl. He picked her up and set her on the sofa, hauling her butt to the very edge before kneeling between her thighs again. Then he looked up at her and began to slowly, ever so slowly, lick her sex. She wanted to look away from his eyes, from the intimacy of watching him enjoy her body, but she couldn't. He wouldn't let her.

With the tightening of her orgasm, she grabbed his head and pressed his face to her needy flesh. He had the balls to chuckle, but she forgave him for being an asshole when he began to suck her clit. For a moment he lifted his face from between her legs, "I want to eat your come. Give it to me."

Any argument she might have had at his commanding tone died a quick death when he began to play with her pussy, thrusting two fingers into her and hooking them so they rubbed her g-spot. A hard shiver raced through her legs and she fisted her hands in his hair, riding his mouth, his fingers, then screamed out her orgasm. He growled against her and she gave a startled yelp when he nipped her clit. It felt good though, especially when he began to gently caress her pussy with his lips, avoiding her clit and making her feel decadent with pleasure.

He finally lifted his face from her and gave her a slow, sexy smile. "Was good?"

Giggling, she nodded and stretched, still feeling very aroused. Her nipples tingled intensely now, and her lips were so sensitive. She couldn't stop touching them. Each caress made her nerves sing. "Was excellent."

He took the little vial and spilled it over the top of her sex, the sensation of the liquid slowly spreading over her labia unbearably arousing. When she fidgeted his gaze flashed up to hers and she sucked in a breath at the strength and control she saw there. All their personal bullshit aside, he was a Master and she was a submissive and the need to please him stirred from deep within.

"Stay still," he said in a firm, no nonsense tone and she nodded.

He capped the vial and placed it back in his pocket before he began to massage the oil into the lips of her sex with his strong fingers, the sight of the black leather against the pink of her pussy doing strange things to her insides. The oil seemed to react quicker on her sex and she let out a little shuddering moan as he pinched her labia, forcing her clit to pop out. He leaned forward and his hot breath on her exposed bundle of nerves felt amazingly good, but she needed more. Wanted more. Had to have some relief for the fire building in her body.

Alex's mouth hovered her sex while he rolled her outer labia and massaged her clit. "You feel it now. The heat growing inside, the need to come."

"Yes."

Standing quickly, he gripped her jaw. "Yes, what?"

"Yes, Sir."

His gaze darkened and he gave her a cold, cruel

smile. "Are you ready to play with me, little Rya? To see the pleasure I can offer you?"

She swallowed hard, then nodded. "Please."

The muscles of his jaw worked as he stiffened. "You are so tempting, such a soft, delicious treat. I almost hate my brother for denying me the pleasure of sinking my cock into your little pussy. But I will tell you this. When I fuck my girl tonight it will be your tight *pizda* that I'm thinking about."

He released her abruptly and she had to try to keep from squirming, from pressing her thighs together to alleviate the burning ache growing in her body. She felt like she'd endured hours of orgasm denial and this arousal had a similar feel to it, an almost desperate edge. When Alex brushed the tips of his fingers over her turgid nipples she cried out.

"I'm going to blindfold you and put the earplugs in now. Are you ready?"

All she could do was rub against his light strokes and whimper. With a rather evil smile he lightened his touch further until she was leaning into him, silently begging him to touch her, to caress her, to make the burning need go away. Passion sensitized her skin and her thinking mind slowly shut down, leaving her libido in control. Alex had lied to her, this was an aphrodisiac that fucked with her head. It didn't make her high, but it made her go into something akin to a human version of heat.

She was growing desperate to be fucked.

He held her breasts in his hands and squeezed, making her groan. "So tempting."

Stepping back he took a black silk blindfold from his pocket and quickly secured it around her head. Much like the one Dimitri had used on her, this one completely blocked her sight and left her in darkness. When Alex resumed playing with her nipples she gasped as the already intense sensation seemed to double, making her shift and squirm in an effort to soothe the ache.

"What is your safeword?"

"Cookie," she said with a moan that would have been funny if she wasn't horny enough to hump a pillow.

"Excellent. I will not stop until I hear that word. Tonight I will be flogging you, and finger fucking you, and eating your sweet cunt. Is this all right?"

"Please," she whimpered as his thigh pressed between her legs, making her straddle the hard, leather covered surface of his thigh.

He leaned down, the scent of him filling her as he whispered in her ear, "You want to press your clit against my thigh, don't you. I can feel how hot your pussy is, how slick with your arousal. But you will not orgasm. You are only allowed to orgasm when I pull twice on your braid. Understood?"

She nodded and moaned while rocking herself on his leg, the feeling too good to stop.

A moment later he put one of the earplugs in, then whispered in her other ear, "Do not hesitate to use your safeword. The oil will make you more...willing to endure pain for your pleasure than usual and I would hate to damage such beautiful skin and gentle heart."

He placed the other earplug in and she was suddenly alone in her body, with only the sound of her moans, her harsh breaths, and the pounding of her heart keeping her company. Deprived of her sight and hearing, everything intensified and she grasped onto Alex, running her hands over his body. While he wasn't as built as Dimitri, he was still a solid man and she was turned on enough to enjoy every second of touching him. Shit, she had no idea what that oil was but it was like hours, no *days* of foreplay in a bottle.

He cupped her chin and she felt the faintest brush of his goatee against her lips, then his mouth moving softly over hers. She licked her lower lip and he did it again, letting his lips drag over hers, coaxing her into an easy, decadent kiss. Being blind and deaf she strained with her other senses and she took a small taste of Alex before he tilted his head and deepened the kiss, tempting her tongue into his mouth then sucking on it. She'd never had anyone do that for her before and it felt really good. Especially considering the way the oil made her mouth tingle like it was another sexual hot spot on her body. Abruptly Alex pulled away, and when she put her hand out to find him, she touched his chest and could feel his heart slamming against her palm.

Alex grasped her hand and led her through the house, stopping to carry her down the stairs. He set her down and her feet touched cool, wood floors. With her hand in his, he slowly guided her through the house. As she imagined the people watching them she got a perverse thrill at the idea of them staring at her, their eyes on her hard nipples and seeing the wet proof of her desire slicking her inner thighs. After what seemed like hours, but was probably only minutes, Alex stopped. She took a deep breath, scenting perfume, sweat and sex, the familiar smells of pleasure that she associated with BDSM.

Before she could draw another breath, Alex took her hands and gently pulled her forward, then placed her hands on something. Holding her wrists, he let her explore the smooth surface. It felt like maybe wood and it had one small hole, then to the right of that a large hole, then to the right of that another small hole. He traced her fingers up and around the shape and as he brought her hands back down to the holes again she realized it was the stockade she'd glimpsed earlier in the lower level playroom. Her breath sped up as she realized Alex was going to put her in the stockade and have his wicked way with her.

Almost as soon as that thought came to mind she felt her hands being placed through the small holes, then her head through the large one. Alex adjusted the stockade until it was at a good height for her with her neck resting on the comfortably padded surface of the hole. There was a small rest for her head and she turned her cheek, laying her cheek against the small, padded surface. The stockade lowered a bit more so that she stood with her legs braced and her back curved enough that her butt stuck out. She tried to imagine what she looked like, and as soon as she did, she thought of Dimitri and her heart ached. Because of the aphrodisiac, her lust raged on, but she had to grit her teeth to hold back a moan that had nothing to do with pleasure and everything to do with pain.

She'd always been a semi-monogamous woman. She didn't want to see her man pleasuring another woman, and she was very possessive of a man she considered hers, so the thought of Dimitri watching his brother touch her shamed her, yet also turned her on while the thought of Dimitri touching some faceless bitch made anger clench in her gut. Alex, or at least she assumed it was Alex because of the leather-gloved hands, ran a soothing hand over her bottom and she tensed beneath his touch. Slowly, with firm strokes, he massaged her lower back until she marginally relaxed and her chaotic thoughts slowed.

Someone touched the side of her face and a moment later one of the ear buds was removed.

"Hello, *zaika moya*."

"Dimitri?" She whispered, straining to turn and look at him even though she was bound and blindfolded.

"Shhhh. I will be here, watching you, keeping you safe." His lips brushed her ear as he whispered, "I cannot touch another woman, the thought is abhorrent to me. I have pretended that I am not feeling well enough to participate, but I will sit alone and watch you take your pleasure. Alex says you feel guilt, there is no reason. It does not matter who touches you, you are mine, Rya. Now I must go, but I will be nearby, protecting you always."

He placed the earplug back in and she bit her lower lip, trying to hold back the tears of relief that wet her blindfold. The knowledge that he wasn't going to be with another woman sent and almost staggering amount of relief through her and she sucked in a deep breath as someone stroked her back, running their fingers over the lace tattoo with a soothing touch. She wondered where Dimitri was right now and tried to imagine how she looked to him, bound and spread out while Alex touched her. A forbidden frisson of desire moved through her and she moaned softly.

The floral scent of a woman's perfume filled her senses a moment before soft, feminine hands began to caress her face. That womanly touch helped her relax further so that by the time Alex moved away from behind her she was once again falling back into the moment. The woman touching her had long nails that sent delightful shivers through Rya as she gently stroked her face.

When the first fall of the flogger hit Rya's ass she startled and tried to imagine what kind of a flogger it was. It didn't feel like leather, but she wasn't sure. With sight and sound taken away her perception seemed distorted somehow. The woman began to stroke Rya's lips and she opened her mouth, capturing the feminine finger and sucking on it. Breasts pressed against her face and she turned her head to them, still sucking on that delicate finger. The mystery woman cushioned Rya's head on her generous chest and she let out a soft sigh as the flogger continued to warm up her back and ass, the strikes heavier now with more weight behind them.

She tried to imagine how she looked, her body moving with the flogger, her breasts swaying, her skin slowly growing pink, then red, her lips wrapped around some woman's finger and her face nestled against her breasts. The woman removed her finger from Rya's mouth and guided her breast to Rya's tingling lips. She eagerly teased the nipple offered to her, sucking lightly on the tip. It surprised her that while she couldn't hear the woman's moan, but she could feel it vibrating in her body.

Rya loved giving pleasure, loved making someone feel good, so that moan only added to her own increasing arousal. She spread her legs wider and tilted her ass up, offering Alex her pussy, silently asking him to touch her there. A moment later the falls of the flogger hit her sex and she cried out, stiffening at that heady combination of pleasure and pain. The hits came faster and she drew the other woman's nipple deep into her mouth, sucking at it with strong pulls, then biting down. Her ass stung, her thighs hurt, but none of that was as painful as her overly swollen sex.

The woman left her and Rya made a noise of protest before a distinctly masculine scent filled her nose. A man's strong hands cupped her face and she tensed, unsure about this development. He gently pressed his thumb into her mouth and she slowly sucked him in, crying out around his flesh when Alex's leather covered hands began to gently caress her burning ass.

The plug in one of her ears was removed for a moment and she recognized Catrin's voice as she said, "Rya, my husband, Nico, is touching you. Would you please suck his cock for me? I want to see your beautiful lips wrapped around him."

"Yes," Rya whispered, overcome by the eroticism of Catrin wanting Rya to pleasure her husband.

There was something really, really kinky about that and it made her moan when she could hear the man's deep chuckle as he said, "Catrin, go play with her breasts. I know you're dying to touch them."

The earplug was put back in, and once again, she was left alone in her head, but her body was overwhelmed with sensations. Alex continued to stroke her ass and thighs, giving her a spank every now and then that had her moaning around Nico's thumb. At the first touch of Catrin's mouth on her nipple Rya trembled. Then Alex began to rub her clit and she cried out as every nerve in her body was screaming with pleasure.

Two sharp tugs came from her braid and she thrust her ass back against Alex, begging for his touch to help her come. Alex, bless his evil heart, must have gotten the message because he rubbed her clit in hard circles that swiftly threw her over the edge into an intense, but brief orgasm. Instead of taking the edge off of her lust she only burned hotter, writhing as Catrin pinched and sucked at her nipples. Nico removed his thumb then something silky smooth and hard brushed against her lips.

She eagerly opened her mouth and moaned in appreciation at the taste of Nico's skin as he slowly slid his thick dick between her lips. Catrin's attention to her breasts increased and when Alex slipped a leather-covered finger into her pussy Rya lost herself in sensation. She no longer existed as Rya, but instead became their toy, their body to use as they wished. The thought was intensely liberating and a strange peacefulness settled over her. Right here, right now, she was nothing but a creature of desire and she sucked eagerly at Nico's dick, wanting to please not only him, but Catrin. She had given Rya a great honor in allowing her to touch her husband, and Rya wanted to make both of them happy with her efforts. She opened her throat and tried to take more of Nico into her mouth, but because of the stockade she could do nothing but moan and lick at his length. When he pulled out so just the tip was in her mouth she got a delightful taste of his precum and stuck her tongue into the slit at the crest of his cock, trying to coax more out.

Alex's big hands gripped her ass and tilted her butt up further until she was arched into an almost u shape with her sex fully exposed. His mouth sealed over her pussy and she groaned, trying to ride his face. He gave her ass a brisk slap and she shuddered. Beneath her Catrin continued to torment her nipples, sending so many good sensations through her she was pretty sure she was going to pass out at some point. Even though so many people were playing with her, Rya's mind kept going back to Dimitri and the fact that he was watching her. That, more than anything else, kept her hovering on the edge of orgasm.

With long, deep thrusts Nico began to fuck her mouth and she eagerly encouraged him, licking at his shaft and wishing her hands were free so she could play with his balls. Alex began to lash at her clit with his tongue and she cried out, trembling as her body geared up for another orgasm. All of this was all too intense, too overwhelming and she struggled to hold back. Soon she was begging Alex to let her come, her words garbled by Nico's dick in her mouth, making it all the more arousing.

When he gave her braid those two tugs she didn't just come, she exploded. Nico pulled out from between her lips and she screamed while Alex sucked on her clit as hard as Catrin was sucking on her nipples. The climax roared through her, her pussy pulsing, needing something to grip onto but achingly empty with each hard clench and release. Another climax burst on the heels of the first, making her legs weak. As her knees gave out she moaned when a man's arm caught her around the waist, holding her for Alex's greedy mouth. He continued to lick and suck at her, but thankfully, didn't touch her overly sensitive clit.

Fuck, that man had a talented mouth.

He finally gave her one last, lingering stroke with his tongue before he rose behind her. His hard cock pressed against her ass through his leather pants and he gripped her hips, rubbing his erection against her while the other man continued to hold her up. If he released her, she knew she would crumple as her entire body was one big, humming ball of satisfaction. The stockade lifted and she was limp when someone gently pulled her from it. Two sets of male hands helped lift her until she found herself cradled against a man's chest. Rubbing her cheek against it, she was sure it was Alex by the feel of the mesh and the scent of his cologne mixed with his sweat.

The world shifted and swayed as he carried her, but she really didn't pay any attention or care. Right now, her mind floated, the wonderful disconnect of subspace taking to her to a place outside of her body, a blissful darkness where she was cradled in warmth and contentment. She had no idea how much time passed, it had become irrelevant in the darkness, but eventually, she was placed on something soft. The earplugs were removed and then the blindfold. Instead of opening her eyes right away she continued to drift, the sound of two men speaking in Russian barely registering. Her mind slowly began to rise from the darkness and she became aware of her body again, of the aches and lingering pleasures of her mortal form.

It took her a bit to realize the room had fallen silent, and when she finally opened her eyes she found Dimitri looking down at her and she began to cry.

Chapter Seventeen

Dimitri's heart broke all over again as Rya's tarnished gold eyes focused on him, then glistened with tears. Shame at what he'd put her through filled him and he knelt next to the bed, wanting to touch her but not daring to. He brought nothing but pain to her life when all he wanted to do was fill it with love. At the sight of her tears he stood and backed away, feeling filthy and hating himself for the events that had taken place. It had been exquisite torture to watch other people touch her while he had to remain sitting in his chair, pretending he was ill so he could avoid the need to betray Rya. The knowledge that Rya would be hurt by him touching another woman made it impossible for him to go through with the original plan and he could only hope that the spies observing him didn't detect anything unusual.

Watching her being pleasured by his brother, Nico, and Catrin while pretending to remain unaffected had been one of the best and worst moments of his life. He'd hated that she was being forced to do this, but at the same time, the sight of her arousal turned him on immensely. It had taken all of his willpower to not join them and add his touch to the others, to have his cock between his woman's pouty lips, to use his flogger on her rounded ass, to shove his dick into her wet heat. By the time they'd finished he'd been close to snapping, the need to exert his claim over Rya filling him on a primal level until he wanted to tear Alex away from his woman.

Both Catrin and Alex tried to keep from him how much Rya hated doing this, but he'd seen it in his brother's eyes and urged him to use the aphrodisiac. He wouldn't blame Rya for despising him for this, but he could only hope it had worked. Dimitri had done his part, pretending to be unaffected by the sight of Rya being touched even as jealousy like he'd never known urged him to go over there and fuck her, to claim her as his, to let her know that while she might find pleasure in another's touch she belonged to him. He'd never, ever been jealous of Alex touching a submissive they'd shared before and he wasn't sure how to deal with the emotions now churning in his gut.

Rya's lower lip trembled and she whispered, "I'm so sorry."

"No, *zaika moya*, do not be sorry." He stood with his fists clenched, fighting with everything he had not to go to her.

"Please don't hate me."

"What?" He stared at her, his heart tearing in two as she curled into a protective ball. "How could I hate you? I hate me for doing this to you."

She shook her head and grabbed one of the pillows off his bed, hugging it to her chest. "I didn't want to like it and now you won't even touch me."

That broke his indecision and he moved swiftly to her side, lying next to her and pulling her into his arms. He buried his face against her neck and held her tight, detesting the trembling going through her body as she cried in harsh sobs. Never before had he despised himself like he did now. Even when he'd killed people he hadn't felt this kind of guilt eating at him. Rya was such a beautiful, gentle soul and he'd soiled her with the filth that clung to him.

"Forgive me," he whispered and held her closer, trying to absorb his pain. "Forgive me."

"Oh, Dimitri," she tried to turn in his arms but he wouldn't let her, unable to face her like the coward he was. "I'm sorry I liked it."

"What?"

Her voice came out broken as she said, "I'm sorry I climaxed."

Unable to understand why she felt bad, he flipped her over so he could look down at her. "Why would you be sorry? I am bastard that made you do it. Alex told me how it hurt you, and I wish to God I did not have to make you do that. I should be begging you for mercy."

She reached up to touch his face and he grabbed her hand. "If you're not mad at me, why can't I touch you?"

He placed her hand over his heart. "I am dirty, Rya. Filthy with sin and I do not want to taint you."

The softness in her gaze undid him and he sucked in a harsh breath, fighting the intense emotions bombarding him. After living a lifetime filled with absolute control, with the cold isolation that he surrounded his heart with, he was ill equipped to handle her tenderness and his shame only deepened. He didn't release her hand over his heart, but he couldn't take the forgiveness he saw on her face. He had to make her understand how unworthy he was.

"Rya, I am bad for you. I make you do things you hate, make you endure things that hurt you. I do not deserve you."

"Yeah, well, you don't get to decide if I deserve you or not. I'm pissed at you, but I don't hate you, I hate the situation that we're in." She sighed and gently caressed her fingers over his heart. "And I don't want to waste what little time we have left together on bullshit like this. Right now I need you to take care of me, Dimitri. Please."

He sucked in a harsh breath, taken aback by her lack of revulsion. Gathering himself, he shoved his darkness aside, trying to focus only on her light. He cupped her face and drew her close, rubbing his lips over hers. With all his heart he wished he was better with words and had the courage to tell her the truth. "*Ya lyublyu tyebya fsyem syertsem.*"

She softened beneath him, the tension leaving her body. "What does that mean?"

He wanted to tell her that he was falling in love with her, but that would only bring her more heart ache, so instead he said, "That you are the most beautiful woman in the world."

After brushing his lips over hers he lifted himself from her. "Come."

He took her into the bathroom and they showered together. Rya let him pamper her, allowed him to wash her, and cosset her in every way possible. He loved caring for her like this; it filled an empty spot in his heart that she so readily submitted to his touch. While he might not have the words to tell her how he felt, he certainly had the touch. Thoughts of his brother licking her pussy, of Nico fucking her mouth intruded but he focused only on Rya, and the inexpressible joy of having her in his arms. She was so small, so soft and feminine, it was no wonder Alex had quickly become so protective of her.

After meeting with Rya, Alex had been strangely quiet. When he finally spoke it was to tell Dimitri that he had a true treasure with Rya, that she was something special. He almost believed that his brother wanted Rya for his own, but then Alex began to talk about Jessica, something he never did, and how Rya reminded him of his dead wife. They were nothing alike physically. Jessica had been a svelte, stunning woman with deep auburn hair and milk-white skin; she reminded Dimitri of a fairy princess. Alex said they had the same unconditional love and kind heart, along with a core of strength that humbled him. The sorrow that filled his brother while he spoke about his dead wife reminded Dimitri how essential this ruse was even though he wished with all of his heart that he could spare Rya this pain.

Rya sighed softly while Dimitri dried her off and he hissed as he saw the welts rising along her ass and thighs. "He hurt you?"

"What?" She looked over her shoulder and smiled. "Nah, that's not bad. I've had much worse."

Unable to resist his need to soothe her, he kissed each abrasion, each discoloration of her golden skin. By the time he reached her thighs she was shifting restlessly against him. He thought she would have been worn out from her earlier sexual excess, but the flush in her cheeks and the hardness of her nipples told him a different story. Licking his way across her hip, he slowly kissed across the slight curve of her belly, delighting in her feminine shape. He loved her softness, loved the give of her flesh beneath his lips. But what he loved most of all was the way she threaded her fingers through his hair and whispered his name.

"Thank you for not being with another woman," she said in a choked voice.

He glanced up at her before returning his mouth to worshiping her body. "I do not want another woman. You have ruined me, Rya. I look at them and all that I can see is that they are not you."

"Oh, Dimitri." She threaded her fingers through his hair, sending tingles racing through his body. "I only want you, but thank you for trying to make this as good for me as possible."

The memory of his brother licking at her pussy sent an unexpected bolt of possessive anger through Dimitri. This was his woman, at least for the next few hours, and he hated the thought of anyone touching her after he left for Russia. The very idea made him savage and he shoved her back against the wall before lifting her and wrapping her legs around his waist.

Her gaze went soft and heavy as she smiled at him. "Hello, Master."

"My little Rya," he whispered against her lips before kissing her. "Who do you belong to?"

"You, Master."

He gripped his cock with one hand and laced his other beneath her bottom before lowering her onto his shaft. "And I belong to you."

She cried out softly as he entered her, but kept her gaze on his face. Working himself into her slowly, he groaned at the velvet grip of her bare pussy on him. Her body was perfection, made for him, designed to give him everything he needed. Without a doubt he was addicted to her and as he slid into her he let out a soul-deep groan at the sensation of coming home. Though he was not a spiritual man and was sure God had turned his back on him long ago, he could not help but think that as he entered her body she entered his soul, bringing light to his darkness.

Moving slowly at first, then faster, he drove into her, claiming her, possessing her, wanting her to feel every inch of him. Her first orgasm caught him by surprise and he had to bite his inner cheek to keep from joining her as she climaxed in his arms. The feel of her little nipples scraping against his chest, of her cunt contracting around him, was exquisite torture.

Once she stilled, she gave him a lazy, completely satisfied smile. "You're an amazing lover."

He smiled and carried her into the bedroom, his cock pressing into her with each of his steps. "It is you, *zaika moya*. Never have I felt anything like being inside of you."

After laying her on her back, he suckled her nipples while fucking her to her next orgasm, biting down hard when she peaked and making her scream. Then he rolled them over so she was on top and when she came again, her breasts thrust out, her head thrown back with all her glorious dark hair trailing over his thighs, he joined her and swore his balls were turned inside out by the time he finished emptying himself into her soft sheath.

Leaning over her, their bodies still joined, he stroked her cheek. "If I make Russia safe for you, would you come to me?"

Her lovely golden eyes filled with tears and she nodded. "I would come to you even if it wasn't safe."

How he could at once feel like his heart was breaking and healing he did not understand, but at Rya's words he became more determined than ever to end the feud and start a new life for both himself and his brother. Unfortunately, he had no idea how much time that would take. As long as his father was still around to potentially fuck things up he couldn't take the risk of bringing Rya with him, but Dimitri could begin working on solidifying the alliances that would keep her safe.

"Rya, I do not know how long it will be before is safe for you." He wanted to tell her that she belonged to him, that he would wait forever for her, but he couldn't expect her to wait for him. "If you find happiness with other, I will understand."

The tips of her fingers caressed his cheek, trailing over his beard as she examined his face. "Do you have any idea how long I would have to wait for?"

"Until my father die."

"Why? What's so important about his death?"

Slipping from her body, he sighed and rolled them over so she was draped over him. The softness of her full curves cushioning him was heaven on earth. "He is...insane."

She raised her eyebrows. "Okay. Insane how?"

"He is on medication for—what is word in English—for believing things that are not real are real. He sees enemies where there are none, thinks there are plots against him if he goes off his medication."

"Sounds like he's psychotic."

"I do not know if is right word, but when he is not on his medication he has done terrible things."

"Like what?"

Shaking his head, he closed his eyes and blew out a harsh breath. "Terrible. Fortunately he has been good with his medication for last four years, but before that there was an episode where someone switch his pills, make him take fake pills. Before my father was stopped he...I cannot talk about it, but was bad. Right now, he is very sick and not expected to live more than another year."

Rya made a soothing noise and began to stroke his chest, running her finger along the deep divide between his pectoral muscles. "What's he sick with?"

"He is old man, in his nineties, and he has several types of cancers."

"Oh, Dimitri, I'm so sorry."

Opening his eyes, he looked up at her. "Do not feel sorry. He is monster."

"Yes, but he's still your father."

Not liking the pang of guilt and sorrow mixing with his anger, he shook his head. "Do not give him sympathy."

"I'm not sad for him, Dimitri, I'm sad for you."

"Rya..." he tried to think of how to explain just how evil his father is, but right now he didn't want to burden her with the history of his family.

She leaned down and kissed him, a soft, gentle stroke of her lips that made his cock start to fill with blood again. While he'd always had good recovery time, and enjoyed sex, it was like fulfilling a physical need akin to eating if he was hungry. With Rya, he was constantly starving, and he wanted to gorge himself on her affection.

"I'll wait for you," she whispered against his lips.

"Will not be forever," he whispered back. "But will take time. If you find someone else to love, I will understand. I will hate him for all eternity, but I will understand."

She nipped his lower lip hard enough to sting. "As if anyone could replace you. I don't think you understand how deeply you've embedded yourself in my heart. I'll wait for you, but if you find someone else please let me know."

"There is no one else for me, Rya. You are my woman. Mine." The last word came out with a growl and she giggled.

"You're mine too, Dimitri. *Volk moy.*"

They made love three more times and by the time dawn started to break over the horizon he was physically and emotionally exhausted. Rya slept in his arms, having passed out after their last round of sex, and he stared down at her, trying to memorize every inch of her. Everything about her, from her golden skin to her tiny fingers, was perfect. Dressed in his shirt, she cuddled against him and slept like an innocent. Without a doubt she'd ruined him for all other women and he desperately tried to think of a way to bring her home with him now, but he would not risk her life.

He loved her too much.

With great reluctance he removed himself from her arms and his chest felt like someone had kicked him as she rolled over in her sleep and reached for him. It felt like he was dying as he got dressed and gathered his things, like he'd been poisoned and it was eating away at his body inch by inch. As he stood staring at Rya's sleeping form he wondered if this was how Alex felt, and how his brother possibly managed to maintain his sanity. At least Dimitri would know

Rya was out there, somewhere in the world, alive, waiting for him. He wanted to hit something, to destroy the opulent room around him at the thought of someone else earning her love, but at the same time he didn't want her to be alone.

    He debated saying goodbye to her, but if he saw her crying it would only make things worse. Better for a clean break. With that in mind, he quietly left the room and resumed his cold, ruthless mask, slipping back into the darkness that lived inside of him. The thought of never seeing her again was too painful, and as he made his way to where the helicopter idled—ready to take him, his brother, and Ilyena to the private jet waiting for them—he started to make a list of the things he would need to start on once he returned home. He didn't care if he had to fight a thousand wars, or kill the Devil himself, he was going to move heaven and earth to bring Rya back to Russia to be with him where she belonged.

Chapter Eighteen

Eleven weeks later

Rya stiffened as someone leaned over and said, "Wow, that's a great tattoo."

She glared at her friend, Tawny, a platinum blonde with mile long legs and the mouth of a trucker. Tawny was Rya's best friend and was even wilder than Rya, a true brat of a submissive. Last year, Tawny landed the cover of *Playboy's Biker Babes* edition and had spent the last six months doing a PR tour for the magazine. Normally, guys would be mobbing the beautiful blonde, but Tawny's dad was the Ice Demons' Secretary and he was very, very protective of his daughter which explained the group of Ice Demons club members playing pool on the other side of the room while keeping an eye on the women.

Rya hadn't wanted to come to the bar, she would have been perfectly happy spending another night at home, but Tawny wasn't having it. Instead she'd been dragged out by her friends who were determined to make her happy. She couldn't tell her girls about Dimitri, couldn't tell anyone, so they didn't understand why she wanted to stay home on a Friday night.

Oh, she probably could have spoken with Tawny about it, but she didn't want to endanger her friend. One of the first things she'd done when she returned home from the lodge was read everything she could about the Russian Bratva. What she learned scared the shit out of her to the point where she didn't even talk to Rock about it. He seemed happy that Rya had forgotten about Dimitri and didn't bring him up either. Thank God he hadn't said anything to her mother about it. Rya's mom was a fierce biker chick to the bone. If she thought someone was threatening her baby she was apt to go grab a gun and take care of them herself. It was better for everyone involved if Rya just pretended everything was normal and she wasn't pining day and night for her Russian wolf.

So now, here she sat in a too-loud club in downtown Buffalo, wearing her backless silver mini-dress, listening to crappy top 40 remix music, with a bunch of drunk people who were getting on her nerves.

She looked over her shoulder at the guy, a cute enough man in his early twenties with a nice, polite college boy smile, and said in a cool voice, "Thanks."

"I've never seen a wolf that realistic before. And the design around it is really cool."

"Her mom did it," Tawny piped up, ignoring Rya's glare.

The blond guy moved around to the side, his arm resting on the bar behind Rya, way too close for her comfort. "Wow, you're mom's a tattoo artist?"

Hoping he would get the hint, she merely said, "Yep," and continued to pretend to watch the dance floor.

Rya had gotten the tattoo a week after she'd returned from the lodge. It was a full back piece of the head of a wolf, beautifully rendered and done with such detail that it looked more like a painting than a tattoo. Rya's mother had managed to get the exact color of Dimitri's eyes down, and whenever Rya looked at the tattoo in the mirror she found Dimitri's wolf looking back at her. She admitted to herself that it was somewhat masochistic to constantly torture herself by wearing what amounted to his brand on her body, but it also comforted her, like he was always with her. Rya's mom had also included a traditional Russian folk art pattern around the wolf, framing it and giving the image depth.

A week after she'd gotten the tattoo she'd received an email from Dimitri asking how she was doing. She'd honestly wondered if she would ever hear from him again so his email had both elated her and depressed her, but she eagerly wrote him back and Dimitri became her pen pal, in a weird way. While she wished she could talk to him, he said it wasn't safe and she believed him.

She had an almost—no, there was no 'almost' about it—she had a stalker-level obsession with him. Every night she did an internet search for his name, dreading finding out that he'd been hurt but eager for any information she could get. The sight of his face always sent a stab of pain through her heart, but she could stare at his picture for hours and almost feel his hands on her. Unfortunately, her constant searching for his name also showed her pictures of him at various social events with an endless series of stunning women on his arm, and he swore he never had sex with them. Oh, he talked about how much he missed her, said the loveliest things about how much she meant to him, and she knew he had to keep up the appearance of his playboy ways, but fucking hell the thought of him with another woman hurt to the point where she'd been determined to go out tonight and find some faceless guy to try and ease the sting with a night of meaningless sex.

Too bad her heart wasn't on board with that plan.

The blond guy leaned down and took an audible sniff. "You smell really good. What are you wearing?"

She shrugged, because in truth, she had no idea what she was wearing. Two weeks ago she'd mentioned to Dimitri that his shirt no longer smelled like him, which led to her confessing that she slept in his shirt every night. A few days later, a mysterious package was delivered to her house and contained a bottle of unmarked cologne and five bars of soap. As soon as she smelled it she began to cry, because it was the scent that Dimitri wore. She was tempted to lift her wrist to her nose right now so she could take a sniff of his cologne.

The guy trying to hit on her just wasn't taking a hint as he leaned closer to whisper in her ear, "So what's your name?"

A deep, growly male voice said from her right, "Her name is none of your fucking business. Now move your ass before I move it for you."

Rya rolled her eyes and Tawny smirked as Gears, one of the Ice Demons club members, threw a proprietary arm around Rya's waist and tugged her to him. He was a good looking man in his early thirties with long, sun-kissed light brown hair held back in a leather thong and a wicked smile that promised nothing but trouble. She'd been friends with Gears since she was a little kid and was used to his overprotective ways, although right now, she actually appreciated it. Tawny liked to say Gears had a black belt in cock blocking when it came to Rya and she had to agree.

The wanna-be stud paled a bit and stepped back. "Sorry, man, didn't know she was taken."

As the guy moved quickly away, Rya tried to shrug Gears' arm off her shoulder. "Thanks, but you can let me go now."

He looked down at her and gave her a slow smile while rubbing her bare back with his thumb. "You really want that, babe?"

While Tawny watched them with an interested look, Rya nodded. "Hands to yourself."

He removed his arm, but as he did, his fingers caressed her back. The considering look he gave her made Rya uncomfortable and she looked away from him and back to Tawny who was now openly gawking. Since Rya had returned from the Submissive's Wish Auction, Gears had made it no secret that he was openly stalking her, and oddly enough, her step-dad seemed okay with it. Three months ago Rya might have been interested, but when Gears touched her, there were no tingles, and when she looked into his eyes she felt no heat.

It was official. Dimitri had ruined her for any other man.

Fucker.

Gears wandered back over to the pool table where he was hanging out with his buddies and Rya let out a sigh. "Shit."

Tawny shook her head and took a sip from her margarita. "I don't know why you keep turning him down. He really likes you. I know he's not a Dom, but the potential is there."

Rya shrugged and glanced at her watch. It was just after eleven, which meant it was just after eight a.m. in Russia. Usually she didn't email Dimitri this late at night, but holy shit she missed him. It had been a cruddy week at work, two of her favorite patients had passed, and he seemed to know how to make her feel better when no one else could. Not that she let him know how bummed out she was, he had enough shit going on without her troubles added to it.

Though he didn't tell her a lot about his world, he did tell her enough to keep her awake at night. Little hints of things not going right, of dangerous times, then last month when she'd read an online newspaper article about him being involved in a fight, complete with pictures of his battered face, she'd cried. God, she'd always hated women that seemed to cry over everything, yet with Dimitri, her emotions were so intense she needed some kind of outlet for them; since she couldn't fuck his brains out, tears seemed to be her only release.

She glanced over at Gears, trying to talk herself into an attraction to him, but it just didn't work. Gears was a good guy, and sexy, but he wasn't a Dom, and he just didn't do it for her.

Tawny leaned forward. "When are you going to tell me about whoever it is you're obsessing over."

Blinking rapidly, Rya tried to give her friend a blank look. "I have no idea what you're talking about."

"Ever since you came back from the Submissive's Wish Auction you've been distant, not you." Tawny sighed and patted her knee. "I'm worried about you, kid. Did you lose your heart to someone? I know the Dom who bought you ended up with someone else and you played with random people, but it sure seems like someone made an impression on you."

"I..." Shit, she wanted to pour her heart out to her friend, to tell her what was going on, but she couldn't. "I'm just tired, okay? Had a shitty week at work. Mark and Edith passed away."

Tawny immediately grabbed her in a hug and Rya felt like total pond scum for using her work as an excuse. "Oh, honey, I'm sorry."

"It's okay." Giving her friend a quick squeeze she stood and grabbed her jacket and purse. "I'm going to head out, okay? I have a funeral to go to tomorrow."

Tawny nodded and scanned the dance floor. "I'll go find Marci and Jill. Take care of yourself and call me if you need me. You know I'm always up for cookie dough therapy."

She kissed Tawny on the cheek and slipped her leather jacket on. "Thanks, sweetie."

Hoping she could duck out without Gears noticing, she made it almost all the way to her Jeep Liberty before boots crunched in the snow behind her. "Wait up, babe. Don't like you walking out on your own."

Her breath frosted the air as she turned and gave Gears an irritated look. "I'm sure I'll be fine walking myself out."

He glanced down at her silver high heels and grinned. "Not in those shoes."

Hitting the alarm for her Jeep, she opened the door then froze when Gears suddenly wrapped his arms around her. She pushed at him, her heart racing. "What the hell are you doing?"

In the odd lighting of the parking lot he studied her face. "When are you gonna give me a chance to take that sadness out of your eyes?"

She didn't want to admit how nice it felt to be held by a man, even if it wasn't the man that she wanted. "Gears, are you drunk?"

With a gentle touch he smoothed her hair back from her cheek. "You know I've had my eye on you for years, Rya."

"I...Gears I don't think of you like that."

"I know." He sighed and cupped her chin. "Just think about this."

He leaned down and kissed her, a soft, surprisingly gentle kiss that felt good even if it didn't make her blood burn. He coaxed her lips open and she found herself kissing him back, trying to feel something other than mild arousal. When Gears pulled away he surprised her again by placing a soft kiss on her forehead and stepping back.

"Just think about it, Rya."

Unable to form a coherent sentence, she got in her SUV and drove home on auto-pilot, her mind spinning around Gears' kiss. She missed dating, missed having someone to hold and be held by. But no matter how hard she tried, she couldn't see Gears as anything other than a friend. And if she did date him, it would not only feel like cheating on Dimitri, as stupid as that sounded considering she wasn't even sure if she would ever see him again. It would also be unfair to Gears. He was a good guy who deserved a woman who thought the he was the shit.

As she pulled into the gravel driveway of her two-story farm house she'd inherited from her grandparents on her dad's side, her mind and heart were heavy. Was this how the rest of her life was going to be? Alone and running from men who could give her what Dimitri couldn't? She sighed heavily and opened her car door, sliding out and taking careful steps in her heels through the snow. Though she'd shoveled the walkway earlier, another inch or so had fallen while she was in the club.

The porch lights made the snow sparkle and as she took careful steps her wandering mind noticed that someone else had been walking through her front yard. Quickly looking up, she didn't see anyone, but a feeling of unease went through her. She lived out in the sticks so it wasn't like someone would have randomly come to her house. Maybe her step-dad had stopped by…although why would he walk around her house like these tracks did?

Digging out her phone from her purse, she quickly called her mom.

"Hey, baby, what's up?" Her mom said after two rings.

"Hi Mom. Um, did Rock stop by my house or send one of the boys by?"

"No, why?"

"I'm sure it's nothing, but there's foot prints around my house. Big ones."

Her mom bellowed for Rock and a second later he came on the phone. "What's up baby girl?"

Moving quickly, she began to mince her way through the snow and back to her car. "I'm sure it's nothing, but I think someone was at my house."

His voice came out intense and deep as he said, "Get in your car and go, now."

"Rock?"

In the background she could hear her mom yelling at a couple of the guys to get off their asses. "Just get in your car and come to the club house. Got me?"

"Okay. I..."

Someone grabbed her from behind and she screamed, her phone flying out of her hand as she was dragged into her house. Panic suffused her and she bit at the gloved hand clamped against her mouth, then cried out when she was thrown up against the wall of her foyer, the edge of her coat rack digging painfully into her shoulder. The light in her living room was on, giving her enough illumination to see the harsh features of an older man she didn't recognize.

His face was heavily lined and he was maybe in his fifties. When his thin lips pulled back in a snarl she noticed he was missing a tooth, but he was physically huge and the look he was giving her was chillingly blank. "You struggle, I hurt."

With that he dropped her on the ground, then planted his big foot in the middle of her chest and stepped on her, pinning her to the wood floor hard enough that she had trouble breathing. When she struggled, he stepped down harder until she was afraid he might break her ribs. Panting, she stared up as he pulled out a phone and took a picture of her. Unable to draw a deep breath, her vision started to go spotty before he removed his foot and lifted her up. He spoke into his phone, and when she heard Russian she knew she was in deep fucking shit.

Trying to think of a way out of this, to survive long enough for her step-dad to reach her, she stared up at him. "What are you doing? Who are you?"

He ignored her and took her through her house, heading for the back door. She knew if he got her outside she was fucked, so she tried to fight him, attempting to kick him and hit him. Making an annoyed sound he lifted her by her throat and slammed her against the wall again. She cried out at the pain, her voice coming out pinched by his tight hold. As she looked into his face the memory of Catrin's story about her friend flew through her mind and she lost it.

Reaching out, she did what Dimitri had told her to do and clawed at his eyes. He yelled in pain as she felt something wet and disgusting beneath the fingers of her left hand, but her right hand only scratched his face. His fingers on her neck loosened and she kicked out at him, catching him in the knee with her high heel.

She scrambled away and clawed herself upright, lunging for a large butcher knife drying next to her sink. A moment later his hands were on her. As he spun her around she slashed at him with the knife, catching him across the throat and down his collar bone before he threw her hard enough that her head slammed against the cupboards beneath her sink and she had trouble focusing. The man was making a weird, garbled sound and holding his hands to his throat. She could see the damage she'd done to one of his eyes and blood spurted between his fingers with each beat of his heart. She managed to slice a major artery, but he wasn't down yet. As he fumbled with his jacket she tried to crawl away, but her arms weren't working right.

A scream caught in her throat as he shot at her, but his aim went high and the plates drying in the rack above her head exploded in a shower of broken pottery. Another shot rang out, then another and another, bullets slamming through her kitchen one after another before the man fell to his knees. She watched in horror as he raised the gun at her face but when he pulled the trigger it just clicked. A look of rage contorted his features and he slumped to the floor, his blood spreading around him in a thick pool.

Out of thoroughly ingrained habit, the nurse in her noted the blood loss and calculated it, but all she could really think about was the blood touching her, how the pool was spreading closer and closer to where she lay, paralyzed by fear and shock. A high pitched whine rang in her head and she started to shake. Her arms and legs felt numb, but when she attempted to push herself upright she found that she could hold her weight. Eyes locked on the blood, she pressed back into the corner and drew her legs up, whimpering as it closed in on her.

As it crept forward she heard voices, shouts, but couldn't look up. If the blood touched her she would die. She knew it.

Someone called her name but she couldn't tear her eyes away from the liquid, so dark in the moonlight coming through the kitchen windows. Just before it touched her someone picked her up and she snapped. Screaming and trying to wiggle free she fought the arms holding her with wild shrieks tearing at her abused throat. The familiar scent of her step-dad, motorcycle oil, cigarette smoke, and his cologne filled her nose, overpowering the stink of blood. He crushed her to his chest then sprinted to the living room, laying her on her yellow floral couch.

His lips moved and she blinked up at him, trying to figure out what he was saying. Panic filled his bearded face and as the ringing in her ears died down she realized he was saying her name.

"She's in shock," Terror, another one of the MC members, said when he crouched down next to her. He was an older guy, in his late sixties, who had been a medic in Vietnam and was now a nurse at a local hospital. In addition, he handled the Club's medical emergencies that couldn't be taken to a hospital without questions being asked. Moving slowly, he stroked her hair back from her face. "Rya? Baby girl, you with me? Do you know who I am?"

"Terror," she whispered, then began to shake so hard that her teeth chattered together.

"Baby girl, I gotta know, you hurt?"

"Hit...hit my head. He stepped on me. Choked me, hurt me." She let out a wailing moan that made all the men in the room flinch.

Rock shoved Terror out of the way and lifted her into his arms. "I got you. You're safe."

At that she burst into tears and clung to her stepdad. "I-I have to tell Dimitri. They f-found m-me."

Rock started to swear and held her closer. "What are you talkin' about?"

"Th-that man spoke Russian." She took a deep breath and curled into a tighter ball. "I need Dimitri. You have to call him for me, please, Rock. I need him."

Rock began to bark out orders, but she didn't pay attention anymore, just kept asking over and over for Dimitri before she gave in to the pain throbbing through her skull and everything went dark.

Chapter Nineteen

Dimitri took a sip of his coffee and watched as Petrov Dubini gave his wife, Vera, a kiss while she served them a small tray of breakfast sweets. To the outside observer they looked like a typical, if rich, couple in their early sixties. Vera still possessed the pale beauty that had once won her the Miss Russia crown while Petrov was as fit and charismatic as ever. His dark eyes warmed ever so slightly as he looked up at his wife and gave her a small smile. Only the faintest hint of silver peppered his dark hair and goatee. Dimitri counted himself lucky to be one of the few people in this world who got to see Petrov Dubini, leader of the Dubini Bratva, smile. Then again, he'd known Petrov since he was a child and considered the man more of a father than his own flesh and blood. One of Petrov's sisters was Alex's mother. Dimitri had no blood ties to the man other than being the half-brother of his nephew, but Petrov never treated Dimitri any different than Alex. To Petrov, Dimitri was as much a member of his family as Alex.

Which was why Dimitri was here talking to Petrov instead of the dying monster who'd sired him back on his family's ancestral estate. Dimitri's father kept trying to get him to come visit, but he never wanted to return to that place where the old man had entombed himself. Too many bad memories. At one time, the massive ancestral summer and winter mansions on the Novikov estate outside of Moscow had been filled with the love and light of his mother and sister, but when they died darkness had taken over. As long as his father was there, Dimitri would continue to avoid those places.

Petrov watched his wife leave and close the door to his study behind her. They were seated near the window on the third level of Petrov's townhome, a room that had the feeling of being lived in, filled with books and mementoes. The leather chairs where they sat were comfortably broken in, and the table where their coffee cooled was slightly scarred here and there from use. This wasn't a room for presentation, but rather for family and Dimitri appreciated that Petrov allowed him into his inner sanctum like this.

Studying Dimitri, Petrov steepled his fingers and tapped his chin. Today the man wore a dark grey sweater with the arms rolled up. "So you and Alex have managed to secure an alliance with the top eight Bratvas in Moscow."

"We have," Dimitri acknowledged, trying to hide his pleasure at the feat. It hadn't been easy, especially with keeping the knowledge from his father, but the Novikov Bratva was solidifying its role for when Dimitri's father passed. That included forging new friendships and breaking the old, toxic alliances.

For a long moment Petrov was silent, then he gave Dimitri a small smile that made Dimitri's pride swell. "You and Alex have done very, very well, Dimitri. And more importantly, you did it without my help or your father's. That says a lot about a man."

"Thank you." He tried to keep his face as blank as possible as he held Petrov's gaze. "I am honored you consider us among your friends."

The corner of Petrov's mouth twitched. "While I wish I could have convinced you and Alex to leave your Bratva to join mine, I am honored to consider you my family. You will always have a place in my heart and my home."

Dimitri couldn't suppress a sigh of relief. Petrov could have easily refused an alliance, the Dubini Bratva was one of the four most powerful in the world, while the Novikov Bratva had suffered from years of corruption and weak leadership. Dimitri and Alex had done what they could to mitigate the damage, but their father had surrounded himself with powerful friends who were loyal to the death and very narrow-minded. It had become a delicate balancing act between saving the Novikov Bratva and not angering their father.

But over the past four years, after Jessica's death, Alex and Dimitri had begun to build their own inner sanctum of men and women who were loyal to them. When Dimitri's father passed one of two things would happen: either Alex would assume the role of the Novikov *Pakhan*, or Dimitri and Alex would split off from the family and form their own Bratva. With the alliances they'd formed and the additional support of the Dubini Bratva, that dream was becoming reality. Even if their father disowned them in a fit of mad rage, they would still survive and those loyal to them would be under Alex and Dimitri's protection.

Petrov gave him a rare smile and saluted Dimitri with his coffee cup. "Well done, Dimitri. You have exceeded my expectations and grown from a boy into a man I am proud to call a friend."

This rare emotional display from Petrov made Dimitri's chest burn. "I could not have done it without you."

Petrov took a sip of his coffee, then set it down with a sigh. "Once, long ago, your father was my good man. I wish you could have known him before the loss of his wives. He was a different man, someone I was proud to call a friend. How is he?"

Dimitri had often heard this, but since he'd grown up with the monster he could only shrug. "Still breathing last time I saw him. Evidently the deal he made with the devil is still in effect."

Shaking his head, Petrov sat back in his chair. "I

do not understand why he hasn't named Alex as his heir yet."

"You say that like my father is a sane man. Who knows why he does anything."

"Do not discount him. While he may indeed be crazy, he is also very crafty."

There was a knock on the door, and a moment later, Vera opened it with a concerned expression. "Forgive me for interrupting, but Dimitri, Alex called and asked that you turn your phone on and check your messages."

Schooling his features into a polite mask he nodded to Vera. "I will, thank you."

Petrov stilled and exchanged a look with Dimitri. They both knew Alex wouldn't interrupt this meeting without a good reason. Adrenalin began to rush into his veins and his senses sharpened as he geared himself up for dealing with whatever shit had hit the fan.

"Pardon me, Petrov."

Without waiting for the other man to reply, he stood and pulled his phone out. As soon as he turned it on his heart clenched at the sight of the last three incoming calls from 'Rock', Rya's step-father. He'd given the man his and Alex's private numbers just in case anything happened to Rya and she needed him. The sight of the man calling three times in the last ten minutes made his blood rush in his ears.

"Dimitri?"

He looked up at Petrov and whatever the older man read on his face had him standing and shifting into full on Bratva lord mode. "I will explain. One moment."

Taking a deep breath, he hit the button to return Rock's call and waited for the international call to go through. Staring out the window Dimitri said a fervent prayer over and over again to a God that had long ago turned his back on Dimitri long ago that Rya was all right. As the phone rang he was vaguely aware of Petrov moving across the room to his desk.

After two rings Rock picked up and said in his gravelly voice, "We got problems."

"Rya? Is all right?"

"Yeah. She's banged up but she survived."

With his heart in his throat Dimitri said in a low voice, "Is connection secure?"

"My boys are jamming on my end and they say they we're good."

"What happened?"

"Coupla hours ago, someone tried to kidnap Rya, a Russian guy with Thieves in Law tats all over him."

Rage, pure, unadulterated fury roared through him and he barely kept his voice calm as he said, "How bad is she hurt?"

"She's banged up. Has a mild concussion, some bruised ribs, and her voice is rough from being choked, but she's okay. We got her locked up tight in a safe house right now. But I need to know what the fuck is going on and who I have to kill for hurting my girl."

"You question man?"

"Can't question a dead man. Rya killed him. But we got pictures of his tats for you to look at."

He closed his eyes and tried to ignore the pain streaking through him. "Send them to me."

"Hold on."

Dimitri looked up and found Petrov watching him with a concerned look. He held up his hand and motioned the older man over as the images began to come through on his phone. "Someone tried to kidnap my woman."

It didn't surprise him in the least that Petrov wasn't shocked that Dimitri had a woman. He knew Alex confided in his uncle and he would have told

Petrov about Rya. Alex was as concerned about Rya's safety as Dimitri. His brother seemed determined to keep Rya safe, as if that could somehow make up for the death of his own wife. Ever since that night back at the lodge when Alex played with Rya, he seemed almost as obsessed with his *zaika moya* as Dimitri. He wondered about the depth of Alex's feelings for Rya, but that was a concern for another day. Right now, he had to worry about who had found Rya, and whoever *he* needed to kill.

As the pictures came through, he and Petrov examined them closely. The tattoos on the corpse revealed a man who had spent fourteen years in the Russian prison system, a killer for hire and a high ranking member of a Bratva, though they couldn't tell which one. As the tattoos spelled out the man's life Dimitri's blood began to boil. Whoever hired this man to get Rya had sent an animal after her.

Petrov looked up, his gaze cold with anger. "I recognize him. That is Vitenka, a freelance assassin and a sadistic bastard. He works for anyone who can afford his fees. Your woman is very lucky he did not manage to take her. Her bodyguards deserve a raise."

Dimitri didn't think he'd ever been as furious as he was at this moment and even speaking was difficult. "She had no bodyguards. She killed him."

The shocked look on Petrov's face would have been comical if Dimitri wasn't hovering on the edge of a homicidal rage. He lifted the phone back to his ear and said in English. "He was contract killer."

Rock swore loud and long before he said, "What the fuck kind of shit did you get my baby girl into? You swore that no one would know she'd been with you, that she would be safe."

Shame filled him and he took a deep breath. "I did everything I could to keep her safe. Everything, even if it killed me to leave her."

"Yeah, well you obviously fucked up somewhere and someone figured out where she lived."

It suddenly hit Dimitri that he had indeed fucked up. He'd sent Rya a package with his personally mixed cologne in it. The scent was made especially for him by a high end parfumier in Moscow and if someone was paying attention, which they obviously were, they would have noted the shipment. Fuck, he'd been so wrapped up in forging these alliances strong enough to protect Rya when he brought her to Russia that he'd gotten sloppy with his own personal shit.

Closing his eyes, he centered himself and cleared his mind of everything, using his training and experience to calm himself. Rya was in danger, and while he had no doubt her family and MC would do everything they could to keep her safe, she was his woman and he would die for her. Despite the terrible circumstances, a spark of joy burned in his chest.

"I am coming for her."

"The *hell* you are," Rock growled. "I told your brother the same damn thing."

"She is not his woman."

Rock laughed, and it wasn't a nice sound. "Look, I don't give a fuck who fancies himself her man, neither of you are taking her anywhere."

Dimitri frowned, wondering if he needed to have a talk with Alex about who Rya belonged to. It was one thing for his brother to help him protect her, but at the end of the day Rya was his. While he felt guilt that his relationship with her was obviously bringing up painful memories for Alex, he would never share her with his brother again. *No one*, not even her family, was going to keep him from Rya. "Do not try to keep me from my woman. Rya is mine. *My* woman and I will be coming for her. I will die to keep her safe, but she is coming with me."

"No fucking way, Dimitri!"

A woman's voice came from the background and Dimitri's heart leapt into his throat as he heard Rya say, "Is that Dimitri? My Dimitri?"

Rock tried to placate her and tell her it wasn't, but his woman was having none of that. After a minute of berating Rock, Rya's beautiful voice, slightly rougher than usual, came through the phone, "Dimitri?"

"Zaika moya." He spoke softly, not wanting to frighten her. "I am so sorry."

She gave a harsh, broken laugh that sliced through his soul. "I told you I could take care of myself."

"You did good, very good. I am proud. You did exactly as you should have."

The soft, pained noise she made had his anger rising again. "I need you."

That settled it. "I coming for you, Rya. Hold on, *dorogaya moya*, I will come for you."

Her voice trembled as she said, "Dimitri, I'm scared."

"No, no fear, my Rya."

"I can't wait to see you." She gave a sharp jagged laugh. "How fucked up is that? I'm glad someone tried to kidnap me because that means I get to see you again."

"You do more than see me. You come home with me. *Da*?"

"You want me to come back to Russia with you?"

"I cannot shield you in America. You come home with me. I would want to die protecting you than live without you."

She began to cry and a moment later Rock's voice came over the phone. "You are not taking her to Russia with you."

"Is not up for discussion. I am coming for Rya. I do not want you as enemy, but no one stands between me and my woman."

"You want a war with me? I..."

"Enough," Dimitri shouted. "You are upsetting her and I do not have time to argue. They will come for her again and again, putting you, your family, your people at risk. I can keep her safe."

Rock was silent, but Dimitri could hear Rya in the background stating adamantly that she was going with Dimitri and if she had to cut the throat of every motherfucker who stood in her way she would. God, he loved her.

"You gonna treat her right?"

When Rock said that he sounded less like a pissed off man and more like a worried father, allowing Dimitri to let go of some of his anger. "I marry her if she would have me. I tried to keep her safe, did everything I could, but it not enough. They know her now. If I take her to Russia with me they will not bother you. I will send out word that you are under my protection."

Rock laughed, "And I'll send out word you're under my protection."

"I will send a bodyguard loyal to me for Rya. He will arrive before me and will help keep her safe. I need to get paperwork for Rya, but will be there tomorrow. I must go now."

"We'll keep her safe for you, but Dimitri, if you get her killed you better hope you die as well because if you don't, I'll be coming for you."

That made him smile. "She is lucky to have good father. Get her ready. Pack suitcases, can ship rest of what she wants."

"Hey, Dimitri, you wouldn't happen to be called 'the wolf' would you?"

Confused, he nodded. "Yes, I am Rya's wolf."

"That's what I thought. We'll be waiting to hear from you."

Dimitri hung up and took a deep breath, then turned to face Petrov who was sitting behind his desk, busy typing on his computer. "You know about Rya, don't you?"

Without looking up, Petrov nodded. "And just like your foolish brother you did not bother to ask me for protection for the woman you love."

"What?"

Petrov flicked an irritated glance his way. "When will you understand that you are not alone? That you have friends who will help you protect your woman?"

He gaped at Petrov. "But it puts your family in danger."

"My family is always in danger, it is the world we live in. I know of your negotiations with the Boldin Bratva, and I know that four years ago you helped to rescue two of the daughters of the Boldin Bratva from your father."

Stunned, Dimitri sat down before he fell down. "How?"

"Who do you think Alex took them to in order to hide them? Who do you think managed to get two fifteen-year-old Russian girls into the United States under assumed names without anyone being the wiser? Beautiful twin girls who'd just survived a kidnapping at that? I had help. While your father was torturing you to find out where they were, we were putting the girls on a plane for the US. My only regret is that we did not find you sooner."

A weight lifted from his soul. "They are alive?"

"Yes, alive and well, living with relatives of mine, waiting for your father to die and the new power structures to come into place before they can return to their family. This feud between the Boldin and Novikov Bratvas is bad for everyone. Our women, our children have always been off limits, everyone knows this." He gave Dimitri a steady look. "If you and Alex had not sought peace, I would have helped bring your Bratva down for the threat presented to my family.

Alex was stupid to believe that hiding his woman would keep her safe, that they could disappear together and lead a normal life under assumed names in some insignificant Irish village. He should have come to me. I would have helped him, but I will help you, because keeping you and Alex in charge of the Novikov Bratva is very important. You are good men who do evil deeds and that is hard to find."

His mind flashed back to four years ago. Their father had been acting especially irrational, but Dimitri and Alex had been so preoccupied with helping Alex to leave the world of the Bratva and vanish with Jessica that they hadn't paid as much attention as they should have. While things were going badly back in Russia, Dimitri had been busy setting up new identities for his sister-in-law and brother, immersed in trying to provide them such deep cover that no one would ever find them and Alex had been consumed with completing his last hit for the Novikov Bratva.

While many people thought a man named Maks was the Novikov's ultimate hitman, it was actually Alex who was the best assassin Dimitri had ever met. Both men had been too distracted to give much credence to the increasing rumors from home that their father was doing crazy shit until it was too late. At the time, they hadn't realized their father's medication was being tampered with, sending him into a psychotic episode.

They only found out how bad things had gotten when the head of the Boldin Bratva contacted them and begged for the return of his daughters. Alex and Dimitri had found them, thankfully unharmed, and managed to free them but they had to kill some of their father's men in the process. While Alex fled with the girls, Dimitri's father had Dimitri taken to a small house on the outskirts of Moscow where he was tortured before one of the men loyal to Dimitri managed to rescue him and hide him while he recovered. A month later, once again taking his meds, Dimitri's father had been apologetic about the 'misunderstanding' but it was already too late. Jessica was dead and Dimitri would carry the scars from his torture for the rest of his life. Whatever small amount of loyalty to his father he had left vanished, and together with Alex, they began to plan their father's downfall.

It did his heart good to know the girls were doing well, but he had no idea how deeply Petrov had been involved. "Why did you help?"

"Because it was not only the right thing to do, it was necessary to keep a war from starting." Petrov looked up from his computer. "There are those who would benefit from such a war between Bratvas. A war would weaken everyone, leaving them vulnerable to the carrion feeders who would move in to take over territory. It almost started when your father kidnapped the Boldin girls, but whoever talked your father into doing that was not counting on you and Alex being honorable men. But, did you ever wonder who whispered into your father's ear the poisoned words that made him take those children? Or who switched out his pills?"

"Of course, but we could never find out who did it." Stunned, Dimitri stared at Petrov. "Why do you tell me this now?"

Petrov held his gaze. "Because you finally have someone to fight for, Dimitri. You finally know what it is like to love someone more than you love yourself. This Rya, she is your weakness but also your greatest strength. You will be ruthless for her. You will destroy anyone who threatens her, but you will also seek a peaceful resolution to conflicts." Petrov leaned back in his chair and laced his hands over his chest. "Sun

Tzu said, *'In the practical art of war, the best thing of all is to take the enemy's country whole and intact; to shatter and destroy it is not so good.'* If you have someone you love, someone you have children with, you will work hard to leave them a legacy that is strong, solid. If you are alone and consider only yourself, only of the present, then destroying everything around you will not matter as long as you have your hollow victory. That is your father's problem. He only wants the victory, or in his case, the vengeance, not a future."

Before Dimitri could respond his phone rang and Alex's name appeared on the screen. Still watching Petrov, he answered it. "Hello, Alex."

"I have the documents needed to bring Rya back home with us and our jet is getting prepped as we speak."

Dimitri tried to keep calm at the possessive tone in his brother's voice, trying to tell himself that he was imagining it. "You will stay here. I will get Rya."

Anger replaced the tension in Alex's tone. "No, I'm coming with you."

He was tempted to tell Alex to fuck off, but now was not the time or place for an argument so he tried to keep his tone even as he said, "I need you to stay here and get everything ready for her arrival. I need you to make sure *my* woman is as safe as possible."

If he had any questions about Alex's feelings for Rya, his brother's next statement cleared it up. "If you're bringing her into our family she is *our* woman."

"Listen to me very clearly, Alex. Rya is my woman. If you cannot understand that I will not allow you around her."

Alex swore softly, then sighed. "I understand. Forgive me. She reminds me of Jessica, but she is not. I promise you I will not step over the line with

Rya, but I do care about her and it is bringing back many bad memories for me. Please, let me help you keep her alive. You are my brother, Dimitri, and the thought of you suffering like I have is abhorrent to me. I want you and Rya to have the long, happy life together that I almost had and I will do whatever I can to make that happen for you. I will not lie, Rya is very beautiful, but she is yours and I understand that. I would never do anything to try to come between you, but I will do everything in my power to keep both of you safe."

Gentling his tone, all too aware of Petrov listening, Dimitri said, "I understand. I'm going to get what I need for the trip, while I do that I need you to contact Maks and send him to protect Rya until I can get there. He's in New York, correct?"

"Yes. I'll pull him off his assignment."

"Thank you."

Petrov spoke up. "Tell Alex to call me in an hour. You can have my place in the same building that Ivan is living in with his fiancée. It will help Rya adjust to have another American woman she can talk with, and Gia is lonely. It will do her good to have a friend from her native country. Consider it my early wedding present."

Startled, Dimitri looked up at Petrov. "Are you sure? It might be dangerous to have Rya near Ivan and Gia."

Petrov nodded. "Rya has my protection, and having both of you living near Ivan will send a strong message. Besides, you know I designed the security for the building and it is safer than a fortress."

"Thank you." Dimitri spoke into his phone to Alex. "Did you hear that?"

Sounding stunned, Alex replied. "I did."

"Good. I need to go. You know what to do?"

"Yes. Be careful, Dimitri. I'll try to hide this from

Father as much as possible, but someone will tell him eventually."

Swearing softly, Dimitri stood. "I know, but it doesn't matter anymore. My life is Rya's now, and I will keep her safe at any cost."

Chapter Twenty

Rya sat in the largest communal area of the Ice Demons Club house and tried to keep from fidgeting beneath the combined stares of Maks, the bodyguard Dimitri sent, and Gears, her self-appointed bodyguard who was none too happy with her. When he'd found out about Rya's involvement with Dimitri he'd flipped out and had to be dragged out of the club house while Terror took care of her injuries. Then her mom found out that her daughter had hooked up with a Russian mobster, and she made Gears' fit look like a toddler's tantrum. If Rya hadn't been so hurt she was pretty sure her mom would have locked her up in the basement of the club house for getting involved with the Russian mafia. Hell, her mom had almost tried to kick Maks' ass when he showed up last night, but fortunately for Maks, Rock held her back.

Oddly enough, out of everyone, Rock seemed the most supportive of Rya's decision to go back to Russia with Dimitri. She felt bad because her mom was super pissed at Rock, but at the same time she appreciated that he wasn't trying to guilt her into staying. When she asked why he was being so cool he simply said that she was her mother's daughter, and that when a woman like that fell in love with a man, neither heaven nor hell was going to get in her way. Though he also added that if Dimitri hurt Rya he'd end up at the bottom of Niagara Falls.

Tawny sat on the couch with Rya stuck to her side since last night. She'd also been super pissed that Rya hadn't told her what was going on, but she understood. Like Rya, Tawny had been raised in a less than law abiding environment and knew how to keep her mouth shut. While Tawny might look like every man's walking California blonde wet dream, she was a bad ass bitch in her own right and hadn't been shocked that Rya killed her attacker. In fact, she high-fived Rya when she found out, helping dispel the last of Rya's guilt. As Tawny put it, Rya did the world a favor and simply took out the trash.

Leaning closer, Tawny's gaze cut to the side of the room where Maks stood then back at Rya with a definite gleam of desire. "Are all Russian men so fucking hot? I think my panties are soaked."

"From what I've seen, yes."

"Motherfucker," Tawny giggled. "I'm so coming to visit you."

Maks was ridiculously handsome with short reddish blond hair and the sharp bone structure of a supermodel combined with a serious don't-fuck-with-me vibe. He wore a pair of black cargo pants and a tight black thermal shirt which highlighted his muscular physique. He didn't bother to put on a jacket to hide his shoulder holster, and Rya wondered what kind of weapons he had hidden elsewhere on his person. Though his English was excellent, he barely had an accent, he hadn't said much to Rya other than to introduce himself. She liked him immediately, and not just because he was hot. Maks treated her and the rest of the women at the club with the utmost respect while pretty much ignoring all the men glaring at him.

While it wasn't unusual to see scantily clad women in the club house, Rya had no delusions about the slut butts who hung around the club and serviced the members in any way they wanted, it wasn't the club sluts that were currently hanging out. Nope. Right now, the old ladies and female relatives of the members tried to casually pretend they weren't all staring at the mysterious Russian bodyguard. Not that Rya could blame them, even in her mentally and physically fucked up state she had to admit Maks was a fine piece of eye candy.

Dimitri was supposed to be arriving soon, his plane had landed an hour ago, and Rya was beyond nervous. First, because she was about to take a huge step in her life and leave her home and family to go to Russia; second, because said family was waiting to meet Dimitri; third, because she looked like shit. She'd barely had any sleep, her shoulder was bruised from where she connected with the edge of her coat rack, and her throat was discolored from where the man had choked her in addition to her tender ribs. Thankfully, her mom and some other women from the club had gone to her house and packed up her things for her, and Rock was taking care of the cleanup. It hurt her heart to think of her grandmother's kitchen tainted by the violence and death and she hoped Rock was able to restore it, even if she would probably never live there again.

Sitting next to Rya on one of the big black leather couches on the far side of the room, Tawny leaned in and whispered, "Does that guy even blink? I mean he's got that whole scary bodyguard thing down pat, and those green eyes, yummy."

Rya glanced at Maks, then looked away again, unnerved by his unwavering stare. It wasn't sexual, but it was dominant and predatory, two things she found hot. The fact that she had to keep herself from ogling the eye candy Dimitri sent to guard her made Rya feel an unwelcome pang of guilt. Then she glanced over at Gears watching her with an equally unwavering stare and her guilt deepened. She'd underestimated how much he really liked her and it hurt her to see the look of betrayal in his eyes.

Trying to lighten the mood, Rya whispered back, "What I'm wondering is does he ever pee or is he wearing a catheter?"

Tawny snorted and glanced at Maks, then back to Rya. "If he does he'll have an audience. I'm about to go drill a peep hole in the wall of the bathroom. Then again, that wall probably already looks like Swiss cheese from the other bitches perving all over him."

One of the said perving bitches, Karen, sauntered over to Maks with a beer. The woman had pulled down her already low cut shirt even more so the very edges of her nipples were visible. She slid up next to Maks and her pouty red painted lips curved into a smile as she rubbed her tits all over his arm. Maks didn't even look at her, just said something in a voice too low to be heard that had Karen taking off in a huff with the beer still in her hand.

Shaking her head, Rya fiddled with the edge of her faded, baggy purple Led Zeppelin t-shirt. She'd been tempted to get all dressed up for Dimitri, but no matter what she put on she still looked like the victim of a beat-down and her ribs and throat were still bruised. A memory of the man who'd tried to kidnap her flashed through her mind, and she struggled to take a deep breath, phantom fingers tightening around her neck, cutting off her air. Tawny reached out and gently took Rya's hand, her cornflower blue eyes searching Rya's face.

"You okay?"

"Yeah." She sucked in a deep breath, trying to ignore the pain in her ribs. "Yeah, I'm good. Just...you know."

Tawny did indeed know. When she was fifteen she'd almost been date raped then punched and kicked repeatedly at a party by her college boyfriend who'd slipped a drug into her beer. Thankfully, a friend managed to put a stop to it and get her out of there, but Tawny looked even worse than Rya afterwards. Said college boyfriend ended up in the hospital two days later after a vicious beating. Rya knew Tawny was the one who put him there with a baseball bat, though he wouldn't say what happened. While Rya and Tawny received more than their fair share of bullying as kids because of their biker family, it was nice to be surrounded by people who knew the meaning of vengeance and how to make it happen.

Tawny looked down at her platinum Rolex, a gift from another ex-boyfriend, and sighed. "Your man should be here soon. I'm still fucking pissed you didn't tell me about him."

"I couldn't tell you, honey."

Looking a little guilty, Tawny met Rya's gaze then looked away. "Well, if I had known about him I wouldn't have encouraged Gears so much."

It took a lot to not look at the man in question staring at them from across the room, but Rya managed to keep her eyes on Tawny. "What did you do?"

Tawny fiddled with a strand of her hair, a sure sign she was stressing out, then shrugged. "I thought I was helping. I mean I've never seen you get all starry-eyed over anyone and Gears has had a crush on you forever. When your dad gave Gears the okay to try and date you I might've told him that you kinda like him."

"What the fuck, Tawny?" Rya said in a low voice, a flush heating her skin. "I totally don't feel that way about him."

"I know, I know." Tawny wound her hair around her finger and darted a glance over at Gears, then Maks, then Rya. "You always watch out for me so I was trying to watch out for you for once. Gears is a good guy and he'd treat you like gold. You deserve someone who worships you."

Rya went to rub her face, but stopped before she could touch her bruised cheek. "You need to go set shit straight with Gears."

"I will, I'm so...Holy fucking shit! Either your man just came in or I'm in instant lust with my future sexy lumberjack husband."

Men's voices came from behind them and at the first sound of Dimitri's voice Rya's heart raced so hard she was afraid she might stroke out. Her whole body froze and she began to tremble. Tawny was still staring behind Rya's shoulder and she could only watch her friend as Tawny's eyes grew bigger, and bigger.

Before he even spoke, Rya could feel Dimitri behind her like a shower of burning sparks falling onto her skin.

"*Zaika moya*," he said in a low, deep rumble that vibrated through her bones and straight into her heart.

He knelt next to her on the couch and when she turned to look at him the rest of the world vanished. While Maks was handsome in a way that could land him on the cover of magazines, Dimitri had a masculine beauty that stole her heart. She met his gaze and anger mixed with tenderness in his eyes as he looked at the bruises on her neck. Tears rolled down her cheeks as her emotions totally overwhelmed her.

Dimitri wore a black leather jacket over a fitted white dress shirt that showcased his amazing muscles. As he moved she caught a glimpse of a gun holster, but that just made her feel safe rather than scared. If she'd had her gun last night she might have avoided all that bullshit. But it had been too big for her club purse so she'd left it at home. Tension filled her and she trembled as Dimitri examined her with anguish in his eyes. They stared at each other and she was vaguely aware of people talking around them, but it didn't matter. He had the most beautiful eyes, and when he ran his thumb over her lips the invisible strings holding her in place snapped.

She launched herself at him, wrapping her arms around his neck and her legs around his waist, clinging to him while she cried. The big muscles of his body shifted against her as he stood and held her to him. His scent filled her and she buried her face against his warm neck, breathing him in while he whispered to her in Russian. This was where she was meant to be, in his arms. The hard, coiled knot of anxiety inside of her slowly loosened and she shivered when he brushed his lips against her ear, still whispering to her in Russian while gently rubbing her back with one hand. She had no idea how long they stood like that, but her mother's voice penetrated the happy fog enveloping them.

"Rya Marie DeLuca!"

Dimitri started to put her down, but she clamped her legs around his hips and lifted her head to give her mom a defiant look.

Kim, her mom, stood next to Rock looking every inch the biker babe. Rya favored her Italian Mom in her coloring, but where Rya was short and curvy, her mom was tall and lean. Dressed in a tight black t-shirt that showed off her still rocking body, her mom's full sleeve tattoos were on display and her deep brown eyes were filled with displeasure as she glared at Dimitri. Putting her hands on her hips, she lifted her chin in Rya's direction.

"Are you responsible for my daughter getting the shit beat out of her?" The traces of Brooklyn in her mom's accent started to come through and Rya winced. That was not a good sign.

Rock sighed and grabbed Kim by the upper arm. "Let's take this in the back."

Dimitri followed Rock and Kim with Rya still in his arms, she whispered into his ear, "I missed you so much."

"Never again," he said back in a low, rumbling voice. "I will never leave you again, Rya. You come back to Russia with me?"

"I haven't changed my mind. I missed you so damn bad. You have no idea."

"I was pathetic," he whispered back. "Constantly thinking of you, wondering where you were, stressing over not being able to protect you. And missing you so much. Never again. You wanted me, you have me and I will not let you go. My woman, Rya, *mine*. Believe it."

They reached Rock's office and Dimitri turned, giving a trailing Maks a nod while the stoic bodyguard stationed himself at the entrance to the hall leading to the office section of the clubhouse. Gears and a half-dozen other men from the club lingered near the hallway, all in their most badass-dangerous-man mode, but with Dimitri's arms around her she felt safer than she had in ages. He was so warm, so big, and—thank you, God—he was here.

Once they were in her step-dad's office Dimitri gently pried Rya from his body and placed her behind him. Rock's office was cluttered with biker crap, motorcycle parts, and a huge flag with the Ice Demons logo on it over the back wall, blocking out the window. Before she could move Dimitri stepped forward and blocked her view of Rock and her mom.

She tried to step around him, but Dimitri placed a hand on her belly, keeping her behind him. "Kim, we talked on phone yesterday and I understand your anger with me. But believe that I would die to keep your daughter safe. She is most important thing in my world."

Rya's heart melted when Dimitri looked back at her and his expressionless mask softened for a moment before returning his attention to her mother.

Kim started to take a step forward, but Rock grabbed her and pulled her back to his side. Not wanting Dimitri to face her mother's wrath alone, she slipped her hand into his and moved to his side. It was nice that he wanted to protect her, but she wasn't the kind of woman who hid behind her man.

With a sigh Rock wrapped his arms around her mom. "Sweetheart, you know Rya's mind is already made up on this, and Dimitri is right, he'll be able to protect her better than we can."

"Mom," Rya met her mother's furious glare and saw the fear beneath it. "I'll be okay."

"Fuck. That. Shit. You think I don't know who Dimitri Novikov is? That I don't know about all the fucked up shit he's into? He's a goddamn criminal."

Rya took a step forward, pulling against Dimitri's hand as he tried to keep her in place. "You will not talk about my man like that. I know about all the fucked up shit he's into, but I also know about all the fucked up shit Rock's into. And don't forget, mother, the way you've lived your life hasn't exactly been on the right side of the law. I seem to recall having to live with grandma and grandpa while you spent some time in jail."

Kim's chin trembled and Rya felt like a bitch for upsetting her. "All I ever wanted was for you to have a good life, a safe life, honey, to not get caught up in all this bullshit. To have a man that you didn't have to worry about ending up in prison or shot."

"I know, mom, I do. You've given me a great life, and more importantly, you've raised me to think for myself and stand up for what I believe in. Well, I believe in Dimitri."

"You barely know him," her mom whispered while Rock ran a soothing hand through Kim's still-dark hair. "And look what happened to you."

"And you only knew my dad for a week before you

two took off for Vegas on his bike. I'm not going into this blind. Yeah, what happened to me is messed up, but bad shit happens every day. It's the way of the world."

Kim started to cry and Rock rubbed her back in a soothing manner. "But Russia? That's so far away."

Dimitri spoke up, "You will be able to see Rya whenever you want. I will send my jet for you and arrange travel documents."

Kim glared at him. "What about if she wants to come home?"

"As long as she has bodyguard, yes, she can come home to visit."

Rock blew out a harsh breath and looked at Rya. "You sure you want to go with him?"

"I'm sure."

Dimitri looked down at Rya and said in a gentle voice, "We must go. I will leave you alone to say goodbye."

She didn't want him to leave, not even for a second, but her mom looked like she was about to lose it so she nodded. "I'll be right out."

Dimitri placed a gentle, heartfelt kiss on her forehead before exiting the room and shutting the door behind him.

Before Rya could move her mom was hugging her hard enough to make her ribs hurt. "Ow."

Easing her hold, Kim leaned back so she was looking Rya in the eye. "You don't have to go, you can stay here and we'll keep you safe."

"Mom, even if my being here wouldn't put you in danger, I want to go with Dimitri." She sighed and brushed a tear off her mom's cheek. "I've been miserable without him."

"Are you-"

Before her mom could finish her sentence the sound of men shouting came from the hallway and

Rock pushed past them, slamming open the door with Rya and Kim on his heels.

When Rya saw Gears pressed up against the wall with Dimitri's hand around his throat, and Maks with his gun pointed at Terror who had a gun to Dimitri's head, she flipped out.

Shoving past her mom, she ignored everyone yelling at her to stay away and stepped between Dimitri and Terror, putting herself right in the line of fire. "What the hell are you doing holding a gun to my man's head? What the *fuck* is wrong with you?"

To her surprise Maks laughed while Terror ignored her and aimed higher so he'd miss her but still have a chance at hitting Dimitri. "Tell him to drop Gears."

She remained pressed up against Dimitri's side, but turned her head and examined his furious expression. "Dimitri, what is going on? Please let Gears go."

Without looking away from Gears Dimitri said, "He tried to stop me from taking you, said you are his woman."

Sighing, she reached up and gently gripped Dimitri's wrist. "I'm your woman, Dimitri, and he knows it."

After Dimitri released Gears the other man snarled, "No fucking way, Rya. You belong here with me, with your family."

Dimitri growled, but out of the corner of her eye she noticed Terror and Maks lowering their guns. With a sigh she turned to Gears. "No, I belong with Dimitri."

"I kissed her last night and she loved it," Gears said with a sneer.

Dimitri lunged for Gears but before they could touch, Terror and Rock grabbed Gears while Maks grabbed Dimitri. "I'll kill you for touching what is mine."

"She's *not* yours," Gears shouted and almost succeeded in breaking free from Rock and Terror's hold.

"Stop it!" she shouted loud enough to hurt her throat and sore ribs. "Just fucking stop it. I am his, Gears."

"Bullshit." When he looked at Rya she sucked in a breath at the pain in his gaze. "I know you, Rya. I've been your friend since before you could talk. We'd be good together."

Shaking her head, she took a step back and looked over at Dimitri. His gaze flashed to her and she hated the hurt she saw there. Fuck, she had allowed Gears to kiss her, and even though she was pretty sure Dimitri had done a lot more with other women while they were apart, it still hurt him. Wanting to erase the doubt she saw in his eyes and let Gears know once and for all that she would never return his affection she began to slowly pull the back of her shirt up.

"What are you doing?" Dimitri said in a low growl.

She reached beneath her shirt and undid her bra strap. "Mom, can you help me lift the back of my shirt please?"

Giving Rya a stunned look, her mom said, "He's the wolf, isn't he? Damn it, I should have recognized his eyes."

Lifting her hair to the side, Rya stood still while her mom eased her shirt up in the back enough to fully expose the tattoo while still keeping her breasts covered. Dimitri sucked in an audible breath while Rya looked over at Gears. "I belong to him. He's my wolf."

Kim let the shirt drop, and the moment she did, Dimitri moved around to Rya's front and knelt before her. Because of his size even on his knees they were almost eye level. Slipping his hands beneath her shirt, he gently refastened her bra. Goosebumps erupted down her spine at his fleeting touch. Damn, her body was starved for him and even here, with everyone watching them, she had to resist the urge to jump his bones. He gently cupped her face and stroked the apple of her cheeks. The tenderness in his gaze, the pride and joy made her smile even as Gears started to swear, then walked away. Part of her felt bad that she'd caused her friend so much pain, but Dimitri's pleasure more than made up for it.

"You carry my mark, yes?"

She placed her hands on his muscled neck, rubbing his neatly trimmed beard with her thumbs. "Yes."

He rested his head on her chest and let out a deep groan, the tension leaving him while she cradled his head to her heart. The missing pieces of her life fell back into place and she let out a shuddering sigh, the never-ending background ache of her soul dissipating as he once again filled her life. Rubbing her face against his soft hair, she took a deep breath of his scent and her nipples hardened.

Finally he pulled away and gave her a smile that melted her heart. "Are you ready, *zaika moya*?"

"I am, *volk moy*."

Rya had no idea how much time had passed. Terror had made her take a pain pill and a sleeping pill before she left the clubhouse to help her during her flight. She remembered vaguely that Dimitri had said they were staying with a friend of his while they waited for her travel documents to come through, but after that, she'd fallen into an exhausted sleep. If someone had told her last week that she'd spend the first hours of their time back together passed out instead of screwing Dimitri until she couldn't walk, she would have said they were crazy, but as Dimitri's voice gently roused her from a deep sleep all she could do was yawn.

When she stretched, a bolt of discomfort penetrated the drugged fog that was lifting from her mind, and she slowly opened her eyes, trying to make sense of what she was seeing. She was in a car, in the backseat with Dimitri, and the sun was setting in the distance. They were traveling down a road lined by palm and oddly shaped pine trees. There was no snow on the ground, and the soil she could see was sandy. Sitting up straighter she looked over at Dimitri.

"Where are we?"

He handed her a water bottle. "Drink."

Eagerly draining it, she handed it back to him and rubbed her face. "So where are we?"

"In South Carolina." He studied her face and pulled her closer to his side. "We will stay with friends of mine before returning to Russia."

"South Carolina? Wow."

Right now, she could care less where they were as long as Dimitri was at her side. Oh yeah, she had it bad for him. While they were apart she wasn't sure if her memory of how good it felt to be with him could be trusted, but now, with their bodies pressed together, she realized he felt even better than she remembered. Her libido began to awaken and she licked her lower lip.

Making a soft groaning noise, Dimitri stroked the side of her face, his fingers feather light over her bruised neck. "How much you hurt?"

"It's not that bad."

The muscles of his jaw clenched, but the icy look in his gaze relaxed marginally. "I will protect you. I am sorry I failed you."

"Dimitri, you did everything you could to keep me safe." She sighed and ran her fingers through his hair, unable to stop touching him. "Shit happens."

They were silent as Maks continued to drive them down the narrow road flanked by massive homes on either side. Every once in a while the green vegetation would part enough for her to see a glimpse of the ocean. She wished it was warm enough to go swimming, but then again she didn't really want anyone to see her bruises.

"Hey, Dimitri, do your friends that we're staying with know what happened? I mean um, are they part of your...lifestyle?"

"They know you were attacked. Ivan, he is old friend from Russia and was born into a powerful Bratva. His fiancée, Gia, is American like you. They met at Submissive's Wish Auction."

"No shit. Do you think I know her?"

"I do not know. She is tanned, little taller than you, slender with round bottom. Pretty with light brown hair and brown eyes."

She tried to think of the women she knew from the auction, but shook her head. "I'm not sure if I've met her. Is she nice?"

"Yes, she is nice." He hesitated and gave her a weary look. "She does not like me."

"Why?"

"I tried to buy her from Ivan."

"What? At the auction?" She tried to move away from Dimitri. "But you were with me after the auction."

"*Da*, but not for first day. I helped Ivan fulfill capture fantasy for Gia and..." He shrugged. "She was fun to play with so I wanted to buy her. I did not know that she was not escort, that auction was not for prostitutes."

"Hold up. You thought we were hookers? You thought *I* was a hooker?"

The last word came out in a screech and from the

front seat Maks coughed. Dimitri glared at the back of Maks' head and sighed. "No. Ivan explained to me. I never thought you were a prostitute, Rya."

"And this Gia, the woman you tried to buy, is going to be at the house?"

"*Da.*"

Her stomach sank. "Oh."

"No, do not look sad. Ivan and Gia, they love each other and are getting married. Ivan does not share his woman usually, at least not with other men. Besides, I have you and you are only woman I want. Ever."

"Okay."

She turned and looked out the window, trying to blink back tears. Shit, she knew she was going to run into women Dimitri had sex with pretty much everywhere she went with him, but it still stung. Unease filled her as she thought about being basically trapped in Russia with him, at his mercy, surrounded by his whores. If he decided he wanted to have sex with another woman, or he grew bored with her, she was screwed, and not in a good way.

"Rya, what is wrong?"

"Nothing."

"Rya, please, honest with me. I cannot fix if I do not know."

Looking over at him, she sighed. He was right, if she wasn't honest with him about her feelings he would never know what was bothering her. She'd never been one of those women who enjoyed playing games, and she wasn't about to start now. Not with so much at stake.

"What if you get bored with me, Dimitri? What if you want to have sex with other women? I'll tell you right now that I won't share you. It just about killed me when I thought I had to at the lodge and I don't think I can handle it. If you aren't sure you can be monogamous, please let me know now and we'll figure something out, okay?"

Instead of being angry, he shook his head and said in a whisper soft voice, "Rya, I do not want other woman. This, what we have, is special. No one has ever made me feel like you do. There is not woman in the world who can compete with you for my heart. It belongs to you. Only you."

"Oh." Her tension eased and she looked up at him through her lashes. "I feel the same."

He gave her one of his rare smiles, "Now, if you want to play with other woman, that is fine. I love watching you Top a woman, love watching you ride her face and make her your slave. Love to taste her pussy on your mouth."

Maks made a pained noise and said something in Russian. Dimitri reached forward, smacking the other man in the back of his head while he replied in Russian with an angry growl. Instead of being offended Maks laughed and shook his head. She frowned at them both, wondering if Dimitri could hook her up with a Russian tutor. That brought to mind all the questions she had for him about where they were going, what she would be doing, but she didn't want to talk about it in front of Maks. Dimitri obviously trusted him, but to her he was a stranger.

Speaking of trusting someone, "Do Ivan and Gia know about us? About what happened to me or do I need to pretend I was in a car accident or something?"

"Ivan knows and Gia...well, she is learning more about Ivan and his family. It is hard for her to understand. Unlike you who grew up with people that live outside the law, Gia was raised by—what did Rock call it—by civilians."

"Wow, she must have been pretty surprised when Ivan threw that bomb at her."

"Bomb? I do not understand."

"Sorry, American slang. It means he gave her a big surprise."

"Yes, big surprise, but Gia is strong woman. She adapted."

They pulled up to a massive, four story beachfront mansion done in a style that reminded Rya of a Spanish villa. The courtyard out front had a beautiful brick mosaic and a set of broad stairs led to the second level entrance of the home. A red Porsche was parked out front along with a black Range Rover. The home screamed money, big money, and a bolt of apprehension went through her. Normally she wasn't intimidated by anything or anyone, but this place looked like it belonged to the top one percent of the top one percent.

Dimitri got out of the sedan and helped her out while a pair of men in black pants and navy blue polo shirts came out of the lower level of the house. They were both built, intimidating men with short dark hair and purposeful strides. The one on the right had visible tattoos all over his hands and arms and fear tightened Rya's stomach. Though they weren't the same as the guy who'd assaulted her, an irrational anxiety still made her stiffen up. Maks and Dimitri both seemed to notice and she quickly found herself pulled to Dimitri's side while Maks stood in front of her.

The two men froze, then Dimitri spoke in Russian and they nodded. The man with the tattoos looked over at her and his face tightened in anger. He said something to Dimitri and whatever Dimitri said back made him relax. Maks gestured to the luggage and the men took it, bringing it into the house. The front door to the second level opened and a big, really big, man with a buzz cut in a black t-shirt and khaki shorts that exposed his well-muscled legs stepped out. He didn't seem bothered by the temperature which had to be in the sixties and he turned, offering his hand to a beautifully exotic woman.

With her long honey blonde hair in a ponytail and wearing a jade green silk dress that showed off her lean figure, the woman who had to be Gia smiled at them in welcome. Together the odd couple made their way down the stairs holding hands and Rya relaxed as she took in their obvious love for each other. A small, jealous part of her wondered what Gia had done with Dimitri, the blushing glance Gia gave him hinted at something, but the way Gia looked at her fiancé let Rya know Gia's heart belonged to the scary man gently holding her hand.

When they came closer, Rya was surprised to see a definitely interested look come into Gia's eyes as she examined Rya. She had to admit the other woman was beautiful and when Gia gave her a shy smile with bit of heat to it Rya felt an answering rush of desire. Unused to such a strong reaction to a stranger, and in such a messed up situation, she glanced up at Dimitri to find him watching her with amusement, then over to Ivan. The other man had the most amazing teal blue eyes, totally at odds with his strong, scarred face. When he stared at her she felt horribly exposed.

Ivan held his hand out to Dimitri, "Welcome to our home."

While the men shook hands Gia gave Rya a kiss on either cheek, her small hands lightly resting on Rya's shoulders. "It's so nice to meet you, Rya."

"Thank you for letting Dimitri and I stay with you."

Gia gave Dimitri a narrow-eyed look, then returned her attention to Rya. "I just about shit my pants when I heard about you."

A giggle escaped her at the elegant, classy woman

swearing. "Why's that?"

"Because he's such a manwhore...er..." Gia flushed while Ivan gave her a stern look. "Sorry, that was uncalled for."

"Is all right," Dimitri said in a mellow tone. "Before Rya, I did not understand what it meant to love."

Rya's heart did a hard thud as she smiled up at him. The sincerity of his words made her want to throw him down on the ground and kiss him.

Ivan laughed and shook his head. "Come. You have had a long trip. We will let you freshen up then have dinner."

With a smile Gia looped her arm through Rya's. "So, Ivan tells me you're a nurse. What kind? I have an aunt who was a labor and delivery nurse for thirty years before she retired."

"I'm a hospice nurse."

They made their way into the large home while Gia chatted with Rya, putting her at ease in the opulent surroundings. Their room was on the third level and Gia and Ivan left them at the door after letting them know dinner would be ready in a couple hours and to take their time getting settled in. Placing his hand on her lower back, Dimitri led her into their bedroom and she let out a soft gasp of pleasure.

The room had white painted walls with exposed wood vaulted ceilings and a deck that led out to a private patio looking out over the ocean. A black wrought iron chandelier in keeping with the Spanish feel of the room's décor provided a warm golden light. The large, modern bed with its cream and white quilt looked inviting. A small seating area divided the large room and pretty floral artwork done in red, orange, and gold tones decorated the walls. Their luggage already sat near what she assumed was a closet and a bouquet of lilies tied with a red silk ribbon lay on the bed.

Dimitri came up behind her and wrapped his arms around her. "I have missed you so much."

It was like he'd flipped a switch inside of her, her need for him, for his touch, for his body moving inside of her, sensitizing her skin and her pussy swell. "I missed you too, Dimitri."

His long, calloused fingers stroked her hair back so he could duck down and gently lick her bruises. "I need to care for you, Rya. Please let me."

"Anything, Dimitri. I'm yours."

Chapter Twenty-One

Dimitri smoothed his hands over Rya's hips, holding back a growl as he thought about that assassin putting his hands on her and how close he'd come to losing his beloved.

"Dimitri," she said with a soft sigh and turned in his arms. "I need you. I've been so lonely without you."

Her golden eyes reminded him of molten metal, and his whole body buzzed with the amazing energy that only came when he was around his woman. She looked up at him with such trust he felt as if he could conquer the world for her, and bring the stars down from the sky and hand them over to her. He understood now what Petrov meant about loving a woman making him a better man. When he had her in his arms all he wanted to do was make sure her life was only filled with joy, to provide the best future for her that he possibly could.

Moving slowly, he helped her take her t-shirt off, the sight of the bruises on her delicate ribs sending white hot anger rocketing through him. She was so delicate she could have easily been killed, taken away from him. Overwhelmed with the need to soothe her pain he lowered himself to his knees and began to tenderly kiss her bruises.

"Do they hurt, *zaika moya*?"

Her voice came out husky with desire as she sighed. "Dimitri, nothing hurts while you're touching me. Well, except for my pussy. It aches. Maybe you should kiss that."

He smiled against her skin and reached around to her back, unsnapping her black bra and removing it before sitting back on his heels and staring at her breasts. Large, full, tipped with rosy red nipples, she had the best tits he'd ever seen. Filling his palms with her abundance, he placed a chaste kiss first on one nipple, then the other, and laughed softly as Rya whimpered.

"What is wrong?"

She shifted, her thighs pressing together. "Please don't tease me."

Rubbing his lips over her left nipple, he growled softly. "I try to go slow for you. I do not want to rush and hurt you."

She gripped his hair in her hand hard enough to hurt and tilted his face up to hers. A glimpse of her dominant side shone through as she snarled, "Fuck me."

Jerking his head from her grasp he growled at her. "Take your pants off and bend over the bed."

His dick ached when she did as he demanded, her small smile of triumph making him chuckle. His little sub thought she might top from the bottom, but that would not happen. He would always be her Dominant, her Master, and it was time to make her remember that. As soon as she was bent over as instructed he moved up behind her and slid his cock over her rounded ass while brushing her hair over to the side. The sight of his mark, his wolf staring at him from her back filled him with pride even as the bruises marking her delicate skin made his inner animal snarl with rage. He'd promised himself he wouldn't frighten Rya, so he focused instead on the tattoo, proud that no one who saw her would question who she belonged to.

Leaning over her he licked across the tattoo, enjoying the way she shivered and thrust her ass back at him. "I like this. Why you get?"

Her movements stilled and she let out a soft sigh

as he continued to lick her. "I wanted something to always remember you by. To always have you with me because it hurt so much to be alone."

"Rya," he whispered, his heart aching for her. "You are mine. I will never leave you alone again."

"Promise?"

"I promise."

Dimitri had originally intended to torment her and make her pay for her attempt to order him around, but that no longer mattered. He needed to be inside of her, needed to reaffirm their connection. In their time apart, he'd thought about taking a kept woman or playing with other couples, but he couldn't because they weren't his Rya. He kept Ilyena around for a while to take to events and parties, but they never did anything more than kiss for the camera. She was still getting over her breakup with Alex, and even though he knew Ilyena didn't love his brother, she missed him. So, Dimitri and Ilyena were miserable together, each missing someone else. It helped that he'd been working twelve-hour days, seven days a week doing everything he could to secure Rya's future.

But that was the past. In the wonderful present his *zaika moya* was finally in his arms again.

Reaching around her waist, he caressed the swollen curve of her mound and delighted in the silky arousal coating the lips of her sex. He wanted to ask her if anyone had touched her body while they were apart, but now was not the time. While it made him a selfish bastard, he really hoped she hadn't been with anyone else. Just the thought of her kissing Gears made every territorial, protective instinct in him roar to the surface.

Thrusting two fingers into her heat he found her deliciously wet and so fucking tight. She arched into his touch and let out a soft moan that wrapped around soul. This was *his* woman and he would never let her go.

He pumped his fingers in and out of her tight sheath, his dick throbbing with his need to get inside of her. "You like?"

"I love."

Before he met Rya he couldn't imagine smiling during sex. She made not only his body feel good, but his mind as well. Moving back the slightest bit he placed a kiss on each of the diamond subdermal implants in the dimples above her round ass. Those little twinkling gems were so incredibly sexy, and he rubbed them gently with his thumbs before lining up his cock with her opening. The mouth of her pussy contracted against him like her cunt was trying to draw him in.

With the first push into her he threw his head back as white hot pleasure sizzled along his spine. Her wet, velvet heat gripped his cock and he groaned at how tight she was. Her pussy resisted Dimitri, and he braced his feet as he entered her. Using one arm to hold himself above her, he reached around to play with her breasts while he continued to push into her until he was all the way in and Rya was whispering his name. Staying like that, he toyed with her nipples while trying to get control of himself. She was injured so he had to be careful when all he wanted to do was pound into her.

That became nearly impossible when she began to shift beneath him as much as she could, rubbing her ass against him while her pussy sucked at his cock.

"Please, Master, please."

She sounded so sweet when she begged, so he began to move, sliding in and out of her slick cunt, the scent of her arousal filling his nose.

"Play with your clit, little Rya. Give me your pleasure. I want it all. Come for me."

She reached beneath herself and shuddered, the

vibrations teasing his cock while he adjusted his angle. It only took a few more thrusts before she climaxed beneath him, her cries filling him with pride that he'd given his girl such enjoyment. He was sure her pussy was made just for him because he soon had her building to another orgasm, her body tightening around him while he fucked her harder now. Pushing all the way up, he gripped her hips and looked at his mark on her back, the evidence of his possession an aphrodisiac all its own. Anyone who looked at her would know she belonged to him, and he growled out his pleasure.

"Mine."

"Yours," she moaned, throwing her hips back into him. "*Volk moy.*"

He loved it when she spoke Russian to him and rewarded her by reaching around her hip to meet her fingers as they caressed her clit. Every stroke was a battle with his need to orgasm and the desire to give her another release before he let go. They rubbed her slippery little clit together and she went up on her tip toes, grinding her cunt into his thrusts with shameless abandon. He loved how she sought her pleasure, how she didn't hold back or hesitate to give as well as she received. The lovely dip of her waist, the round curve of her ass, her abundance of dark hair and the beautiful gold of her skin all seduced him further into her thrall.

As much as he owned her, she owned him as well.

Pumping into her hard enough that his balls slapped against her clit where her fingers still rubbed he tried to freeze this moment into his mind, to capture forever what had to be one of the most perfect times of his life. Words of devotion tumbled from his lips in Russian as he confessed his love for her, his fear of losing her, and how he could never let her go, how he wanted her to be his wife, to tie her to him for all of eternity.

With a sharp cry she came again, shouting his name while her pussy rippled around him. Finally letting go, he fucked her savagely, his body dictating his moves while his mind melted away to nothing but bliss. The orgasm ripped through him, making every muscle in his body tense while he roared out his pleasure, his eyes tightly shut and his body jerking against hers. His Rya, his woman, his love.

He collapsed on her and she let out a pained yelp. He immediately rolled over to his side with a curse. "Did I hurt you?"

"Just my ribs," she panted, her hair sticking to her sweaty face. "Fuck. I thought you couldn't possibly be as good as I remembered, but you're better."

Still concerned about her injuries, he gently picked her up from the bed, loving how she cuddled into him with a happy sigh. "I clean you."

The bathroom was as well-appointed as the rest of the home and he didn't release Rya until they were in the white and blue tiled shower stall, its skylights showing the deepening blue sky overhead. Even in direct sunlight, Rya was so beautiful he couldn't keep his eyes or his hands off of her. With the water falling over her she looked delicious and he couldn't resist touching her, arousing her all over again so he could pick her up and fuck her against the wall of the shower, keeping his strokes gentle and making sure his hand was behind her back, protecting her still bruised body from the hard wall. This time he looked into her eyes as he took her and the connection between them left his mind and heart reeling. He had no idea sex could be this good, that the simple act of taking his woman could arouse him in a way even the kinkiest of acts with other women never did. With Rya, he was not trying to fill a hole in his heart because she was already there, already a part of him in a way he'd been craving his whole life.

His release seared through him, filling Rya with his seed as he held himself carefully off of her, trying to protect her injuries.

Moving very slowly, he removed them both from the shower and they dried each other off with lingering touches. Dimitri dropped to his knees before her with a soft, pained sound and examined her injuries. For every mark he found he kissed every inch of it with no more pressure from his lips than a warm breath. His mind raced with images of what could have happened to her, to the torture she'd endured because of her sin in loving him. The sight of the bruises marring her golden flesh made him grow cold inside.

Before his icy rage could fill him, a hot tear dropped onto his shoulder, thawing his anger and replacing it with deep thanks. He pressed the side of his face to her belly and wrapped his arms around her hips, taking in deep breaths of her clean skin. With a soft murmur Rya began to run her fingers through his hair, her gentle touch soothing him. His love for her overwhelmed him and he wished he could tell her how much she meant to him, but he didn't have the words. Part of him wanted to ask her about the attack, but if he did, he knew his anger would overwhelm him. No, was better focus on the here and now, because he had Rya back in his arms, despite all odds, and he wasn't going to lose her again.

She loved him, without a doubt. He wanted to tell her that he loved her as well, that he was both her Master and slave, but she had enough to deal with right now. Once they were in Russia and he helped her ease into her new life, he would let her know that he couldn't let her go even if he wanted to. This crazy possessiveness was so unusual to him he had a hard time dealing with it. He wanted to put Rya in a gilded cage, to keep her safe, but she had a wild heart and confinement would kill her. So instead, he tried to bind her to him with pleasure, with his love, so that she would willingly come to him, and understand that he was strong enough to run with her, to live life at her side, to protect her always as they enjoyed everything the world had to offer.

"Tell me, *dorogaya*, what can I do to make you happy? I need to take this sadness from you, need to take care of you so you do not regret being my woman."

"Dimitri," she murmured in a soft voice that she seemed to reserve exclusively for him, "I will never regret my decision to come with you. The thought of waking up with you every morning...you have no idea how lost I was without you. It was like I'd been shown this amazing, wonderful world when I was with you, and once you left, I was thrown back into a mundane and dreary life. I thought about you all the time, wondering where you were, what you were doing. To say I was obsessed with you is a bit of an understatement."

While her words eased his tension, he worried that she didn't really know what she was getting herself into, that she had some romantic vision about what being his woman would be like. "You say this now, but what about when you are angry with me over the level of security that you will have to live with? What about when we have an argument that I am too overprotective, or you disapprove of my having to work long hours?"

"Then we deal with those things as they come up just like any couple deals with their problems."

He wanted to argue with her, but when she yawned he shook his head and stood, sweeping her up into his arms. "We will take nap."

"What about dinner?"

"I will call Ivan and ask him if it can be served a little later."

"I don't want to throw off their schedule," Rya murmured as he scooted her beneath the covers.

Already her eyelids were closing and he marveled at how soft her beauty was right now, how stunning. Bare of any makeup with her damp hair spread around her, his little Rya radiated a peacefulness that he wanted to wrap around himself like a blanket. Bending to give her a kiss, she made some kind of sleepy sound and he couldn't help but smile.

That smile dropped from his face as he moved across the room to retrieve his phone before slipping on a pair of pants and going out on the balcony. Watching the surf roll in, he began to place a series of calls to different people within his Bratva, making sure all would be ready for Rya's arrival. Before Dimitri left he'd made a couple very public comments about the fact that Rya was his woman. He also made it clear that she was also under the protection of those Bratvas allied with the Novikovs. Anyone who tried to harm Rya would be starting a war they could never win.

Dimitri could only hope the plans he'd put in place would be enough to keep her safe. He'd buried his mother and his sister, and Jessica and her unborn child. If he had to bury Rya as well he would soon follow her to the other side and hope that his version of hell wasn't spending eternity without her.

Rya leaned closer to Gia against the dinner table and they both burst into giggles at whatever they were talking about. Looking across the table to where Ivan was watching the women Dimitri met his eye and they shared an amused look. They'd finished a wonderful dinner made by Ivan's staff and the conversation had been easy. Gia and Rya seemed to have an instant rapport with each other and it eased his heart to see the women getting along so well. It would do Rya a world of good to have a friend in Moscow. Since they would be living on the same floor as Gia and Ivan, it made Gia the perfect choice for Rya's friend.

He just hadn't anticipated the attraction between his girl and Gia.

The women had split a bottle of white wine, and as they nibbled at their chocolate mousse, he caught an almost playful sexual tension between them. Ivan seemed to have picked up on it as well because he raised an eyebrow in Dimitri's direction and said in Russian, "Does Rya like women?"

"She does, but she tends to be sexually dominant with them."

Ivan chuckled. "Ahhh, that makes sense then."

"What do you mean?"

"Gia trained with a Domme who is similar to Rya in looks and personality. Your girl is exactly my woman's type. No wonder Gia has been flirting as much as she has."

The women looked over at them and giggled again. When Dimitri caught Rya's eye, she blushed and returned to whispering with Gia. He noticed the way Rya looked at the other woman from beneath her lashes, little heated glances that made his cock twitch. For her part, Gia seemed to be touching Rya often, seemingly innocent caresses that nonetheless had Rya's nipples stiffening and pressing against her top.

He turned his attention back to Ivan. "Are you open to letting them play together?"

"Yes, but you do not touch my Gia."

Dimitri gave Ivan an equally warning look. "And you do not touch my Rya."

Ivan held his gaze for a long moment, then his lips

twitched. "As you wish."

Not liking the full smirk that curved Ivan's mouth Dimitri grunted. "What?"

"Nothing." Ivan sobered then stood. "Come. We need to discuss your situation."

Dimitri stood and leaned over, giving Rya a kiss then said in English, "Ivan and I go talk business. Will you be all right?"

She beamed up at him and he was sure he grinned back like an idiot. "Okay. We'll be fine. Go do your manly man thing."

Gia giggled when Ivan leaned down and whispered to her. The only consolation Dimitri had for being so openly besotted with Rya was that Ivan was just as wrapped up in his fiancée. They left the blushing women and Dimitri followed Ivan through the house and up to the top floor where Ivan had his study. It amused Dimitri to see the similarities to Petrov's study in Ivan's house, but it made sense. Petrov was Ivan's uncle and a father figure to him. There were rumors that Petrov was grooming Ivan to head the Dubini family after he retired, but Dimitri wasn't sure Ivan would accept the position. His friend was a very successful businessman with an empire of his own to run. More importantly, Ivan had distanced himself from the Dubini Bratva, and Dimitri couldn't picture Gia living the life of a Bratva wife.

After pouring them both glasses of Iordanov Vodka, Dimitri took a seat in one of the oversized burgundy leather chairs near the bank of windows looking out over the moonlit ocean. The room had a barely lived in feel to it, but there were pictures of Ivan, Gia, and his family against the far wall along with an Impressionist painting of Moscow in the moonlight. A sudden bout of homesickness filled Dimitri as he studied the painting, and he wondered if Rya would find Russia as beautiful as he did. It was a very different world from America, and he hoped his free spirited woman could understand the more subdued ways of his people and appreciate them.

Ivan took a seat opposite him and crossed his leg before sipping his drink. "Petrov tells me you will be moving into his old penthouse in the building where Gia and I live."

Returning his attention to Ivan, Dimitri kept his face carefully blank. He counted Ivan among his closest friends, but this was business, and while it might be cordial, Dimitri never made the mistake of letting friendship interfere. Especially where Rya was concerned.

"We are. Will this be a problem?"

After a few tense moments, Ivan shook his head. "No. You are doing everything you can to ensure Rya's safety; Petrov has informed me that she is under his protection. While I do not think Rya will ever be truly safe, she will be as safe as any of our women are. It is the price we pay for the life we lead. Besides, it will be nice for Gia to be able to walk down the hall if she wants company."

"Does Gia know about your association with the Dubini family? Or about my Bratva?"

With a sigh Ivan nodded. "I told her about you and she figured it out about Petrov on her own."

"How?"

"Gia has her own business in Moscow restoring homes. When she had some issues with some workers not wanting to deal with an American, Petrov stepped in, or should I say some of his enforcers did. I'm not sure what exactly happened, but that night when I came home, Gia had already done some research. I answered her questions as much as I could, but she did not understand why I couldn't talk about it and it caused problems between us. Finally, Vera and Petrov spoke with her. I don't know what they said, but it calmed Gia down enough that she was no longer sleeping in the guest room."

Dimitri laughed. "You let her get away with that?"

Snorting, Ivan raised his glass at Dimitri. "Just wait. You will find out how stubborn these American women can be. And independent. Have you considered what Rya will do while she is in Russia?"

"Yes. She will stay at home and I will take care of her."

Ivan laughed. "Have you told her this?"

"What? Why would she not want to enjoy herself?"

Ivan tossed back a slug of his vodka, then laughed again. "Let me know when you tell her this. I want to be there to watch the fireworks."

"Are you saying she will not want to?"

"I'm saying that you should ask her instead of tell her. Learn from my mistakes."

Every woman Dimitri had been with would have been thrilled at the idea of staying home and being taken care of. He couldn't imagine why Rya wouldn't enjoy it but he had to admit that he'd never been with a woman like Rya before. Maybe Ivan was right. "I will consider it."

"Are you going to keep Maks on as her security?"

"Yes."

Ivan whistled. "And how does your brother feel about losing his favorite assassin?"

"He was the one who suggested it."

"Interesting." Running his finger around the rim of his glass, Ivan looked down into his drink with pursed lips. "Do you trust him with Rya?"

It took him a second to realize Ivan was talking about Maks, not Alex. "Of course. He would die to keep her safe."

"That is not what I mean. Maks has quite a...reputation with women."

Dimitri laughed. "Maks is also fond of his dick

staying attached to his body instead of cut off and fed to my dogs. Besides, Rya is loyal. She would not betray me."

"Do you plan on bringing Rya to our club?"

"Yes."

"Do you plan on sharing her?"

"Maybe, but that is between Rya and myself. Why do you ask?"

"I am curious if she would play well with Gia. While Gia and I have had other women join us and Gia has enjoyed it, none of them have clicked."

"What do you mean clicked? And I do not want you touching Rya."

Ivan shook his head. "I would not touch your woman. First, because I only want my Gia, and second, because my lovely fiancée would superglue my cock to my leg in my sleep if I did."

Both men laughed and Dimitri finished his drink. "What do you suggest?"

"Is your girl too injured to play tonight? I saw the bruising on her neck and she moved a little stiff."

The thought of Rya's injuries killed Dimitri's good mood. "She has some bruised ribs and throat, as well as a mild concussion, but other than that she is fine."

"Did she really kill that assassin?"

"Yes."

Ivan raised his glass in a small salute before taking a sip. "She is either very skilled or very lucky."

"I think a little of both. I'm sure Petrov told you about her background."

The corners of Ivan's lips curved upward. "He might have. But just because a woman is raised by killers does not make her a killer."

"No, it doesn't." He looked out the window and frowned. "Rya has a different view on death than most people. I would say she is more practical about it. Her father was killed by a drunk driver who got off on a technicality, but a month later, the man who killed her father was found dead on the side of the road. I believe her people extracted their own justice."

"It is good to know." Ivan sighed. "I fear that my Gia is not so practical. She does not understand or like violence or death. Her mother was murdered, yet she is happier with her mother's killer in jail than dead."

"That's not a bad thing. Gia has an innocence that we do not."

"Good way of putting it." Ivan gave him a small smile. "But my fiancée is not that innocent. She asked for my permission earlier to show Rya our dungeon."

Dimitri's cock twitched. "Really?"

"Yes. She asked me while I was fucking her. My Gia was in quite the mood after meeting your girl. Would you like to bet they are already there?"

Standing, Dimitri adjusted himself. "If they are not there already, they will be soon."

With a laugh Ivan stood as well and clapped Dimitri on the back. "It is good to see you happy, my old friend."

"I am always happy about two beautiful women playing together."

"Yes, but that is not what I meant. You deserve to be happy. I am glad you finally found a woman worth fighting for."

Chapter Twenty-Two

Rya sat back in the comfortable, oversized padded deck chair then took a sip of her wine before smiling at Gia. "Nice place you have here."

Laughing, Gia tucked her feet beneath her and turned to face Rya more fully. The elegant woman had changed from her green silk dress into a pair of worn jeans that fit her curvy butt perfectly along with a brown sweater that hung off of one shoulder. Right now she wore a thick cream shawl that set off the pearl and diamond studded gold choker wrapped around her graceful throat. A tiny gold medallion hung from the choker and Rya was pretty sure the piece of expensive jewelry was Gia's collar.

Tucking a stray strand of her honey brown hair behind her ear, Gia gestured out to the moonlit with her wine glass. "Trust me, this is all Ivan. I could never have afforded this on my own."

Rya tugged the blue shawl Gia loaned her around her shoulders. "It's still beautiful."

With a soft sigh Gia sat back. "It is. Ivan bought it so I could visit my family. I've been doing renovations on it for a little over a month now."

"Are you a local?"

"Kind of. I grew up in Atlanta but moved to Myrtle Beach after I graduated."

"What is it exactly that you do? I mean I know you're an architect, but your job sounds different from any architect I've known."

A smile of real pleasure curved Gia's full lips and Rya tried to reel in her libido. Just because she was attracted to the other woman didn't mean the feeling was reciprocated despite Gia's flirting. She could just be trying to be friendly. Plus neither Ivan nor Dimitri had given them permission to play and Rya really didn't want to start things off with Dimitri by going behind his back. That said, she really, really wanted to kiss Gia.

Setting her wine glass down, Gia pulled the shawl closer around her shoulders and turned to face Rya with a happy smile. "I restore old homes."

"Wow, really? That's so cool."

Excitement filled Gia's face. "Thank you. Right now I'm in the middle of restoring two town homes in Moscow for my future uncle...or would that be uncle-in-law? Either way, the town homes were built in the 1890s and they are amazingly beautiful, if totally neglected."

"So you have a job in Russia?"

"Oh yeah. Ivan would be thrilled if I would just stay home and laze around all day like a pampered house pet, but I'd go nuts."

"I hear you." She let out a soft sigh. "I have no idea what I'll do while I'm over there. I'd really like to continue my work as a hospice nurse, but I have no idea about what kind of license I would need, or if I'd have to learn Russian, or bunch of other shit."

"Have you talked to Dimitri about it?"

"Not yet. We've kind of had other stuff going on."

Gia was silent for a few moments, her unfocused gaze on the ocean. "Did you know I had no idea Ivan's uncle, Petrov, is some kind of super Russian mob boss?"

"He is?"

"Oh yeah. I thought he was just Uncle Petrov, a nice older man who seemed to view me as some kind of surrogate daughter. It's his town homes that I'm renovating."

"How did you find out?"

Gia laughed. "Well, I was having a disagreement with a local lumber supply company about some custom work I was having done. I needed to replace the bannister on the main staircase and wanted the original type of wood used. The company I contracted tried to give me inferior wood and they were such utter bastards about it. See, some people in Russia don't like foreigners, at all, and they get pissed when they think we're taking away jobs, and some guys don't like a woman doing what is traditionally considered a man's job, in this case, construction."

"Doesn't sound much different than the US."

"True. Well once I received my order from them and saw the shitty workmanship I decided to pay them a visit and those motherfuckers totally blew me off. They treated me like I was an idiot, pretended not to understand what I was saying, and kept telling me to make myself useful and go home and bake cookies. Cookies! I had a new translator with me that day, my usual girl was on vacation, and the poor guy had to carry me out of there before I tried to jump the counter and choke the asshole giving me such a hard time."

"Seriously?"

"Oh, yeah. I was pissed. The dick that owned the lumber company threatened to have me deported after I said some choice things about his mother." She grinned. "When I got home Ivan was there with his Uncle and I…uh, kind of flipped out and went on an epic rant. I think I scared them. Anyway, the next afternoon I got a very, very apologetic visit from the owner of the lumber company at the construction site along with a huge discount on my materials. The poor guy was terrified and asked me to please let him know if I needed anything else and to extend his most humble apologies to Petrov and Ivan. I couldn't figure out what the hell was going on so I asked

Ivan."

"What did he say?"

"He hemmed and hawed, but I think he realized that he couldn't hide it from me anymore. I'd been in Russia for over a month by this point and little things were starting to add up. I know this sounds dumb, but I honestly had no idea that Petrov ran the Dubini Bratva. I mean it's so far outside my reality that it never occurred to me that Petrov was anything other than a successful businessman, but once I thought about it, everything clicked into place." She pulled her shawl tighter as a brisk breeze rolled in off the ocean. "I think there's a lot of stuff I don't understand, but I do know that Ivan's more of a legitimate business man than a mobster. At least for now."

Trying to lighten the mood, Rya smiled at Gia. "Well, if it makes you feel better there is nothing legitimate about Dimitri."

Gia snickered. "I still can't be believe that Dimitri has fallen in love."

"What?"

"Oh, I don't mean that in a bad way. He's just never, ever had a serious girlfriend, at least from what I can tell. I thought he was just one of those guys that didn't do relationships."

Unease panged through Rya. "Does he have lots of girlfriends?"

Looking uncomfortable, Gia fiddled with her shawl. "You'd have to ask him that."

"So I take that as a yes."

"Please don't be upset. If it makes you feel any better I heard that Dimitri has publically declared that you are his woman."

"He did?"

"Yep. Ivan said Dimitri's been working hard these past few months to move heaven and earth to get you to Russia with him. I know I haven't seen Dimitri at the club since he came back from the States."

"Was he usually there a lot? It's okay, Gia. I know he's seen other women while we've been apart."

"I'm sorry. I shouldn't have said anything, but I don't think he's been with anyone. I mean he's been with Ilyena, but she just broke up with Alex and it was more of a friendship hanging out type thing."

At the mention of the woman that Dimitri was supposed to have been with at the lodge that night, Rya's hands clenched into fists, but she took a deep breath and tried to let her anger go. "No, seriously, it's okay. Things are complicated between us. Do you know about Dimitri's family?"

"Kind of. Alex, Dimitri's older brother, is a good friend and cousin of Ivan's as well, but he's scary so I haven't really talked with him much."

"What? You think Alex is scary? Really?" She had a guilty flash of arousal at the memory of the kinky scene she'd done with the handsome man. "I thought he was nice."

"You've met him?"

"Yeah, back at the lodge. He was really kind to me."

"He must like you because while he's been nothing but polite with me, he's a scary dude. He's got this cold serial killer stare thing going on when he's mad. And much like Dimitri, I've never heard of Alex having anything other than a casual girlfriend."

Rya bit her lip, wondering how much she could disclose to Gia. "Do you know about the Novikov Curse?"

"No, what is it?"

She told Gia about the long, sordid history of the Novikov family and by the time she was done tears streamed down Gia's cheeks.

"Rya, that's the saddest thing I've ever heard."

Before Rya knew it, Gia had come over to her oversized chair and grabbed her into a hug, making Rya wince. Gia released her and crouched before Rya's chair while patting her leg. "So that's why Dimitri was pretending you didn't exist. I mean I thought it was so crazy that he never said anything about you, then the next thing we know he's flown halfway around the world to rescue the woman he loves."

"He said he loves me?"

"Well, he didn't say it, but come on. Guys don't do this for girls they don't love. Why do you think you're going back to Russia with him if you think he doesn't love you?"

"Because someone found out about me and now I'm in danger. That's why I'm going back to Russia with him." She gestured to her neck. "A guy that was some kind of freelance killer for the Russian mafia tried to kidnap me."

"No shit. What happened?"

Rya's stomach clenched. "He...I killed him."

"Oh honey." Gia grabbed her hands and gave them a hard squeeze. "Good."

"What?"

"I'm glad you killed him. My mother was murdered, but I wish she'd had a gun so she could have killed the motherfucking drug addict before he took her life."

Gia's voice trembled on the last words and Rya scooted over, then pulled Gia over onto the oversized chair with her before giving the other woman a gentle hug. "I'm so sorry for your loss. My dad was killed by a drunk driver before I was born. But I have a great step-dad who's been just about the best dad I could ever want."

Returning her hug, Gia stroked her hair. "My dad died when I was a kid and my mom never remarried."

Leaning back enough so she could see Gia in the lights coming through the windows she smiled and brushed back a tear. "Damn, we're a hot mess, aren't we?"

Gia smiled back and wiped the tears from Rya's cheeks. "I'm glad you're coming to Russia. It will be really nice having someone there that I can talk to."

"You have no idea how relieved I am that you're not some über bitch. I'm terrified of going there, not knowing anyone. Knowing you really helps."

"Well, you haven't seen me when I'm PMSing," Gia said in a teasing voice, but Rya could tell Gia was happy about the compliment. "And don't be scared. Dimitri will take care of you, believe me. While our guys may be domineering, overbearing, über macho, controlling assholes, they're also amazingly sweet and protective. Just don't let him get away with too much, or next thing you know, he'll be deciding what kind of underwear you're allowed to wear and what you can eat for dinner."

Both women jumped as Ivan's deep voice came from behind them. "Controlling asshole?"

Gia swallowed hard then said, "I'm putting a damn bell on you so you can't sneak up on us."

Giggling, Rya turned in the chair so her back was to Gia's front and smiled. Dimitri was standing behind a very stern Ivan with a definite smirk. She fluttered her lashes at her man and gave him a beaming smile. "Hi, Masters."

Ivan snorted at Rya then looked over his shoulder at Dimitri. "You're in trouble."

"Best kind of trouble," Dimitri said and gave Rya a smile filled with such warmth that she sighed.

Gia whispered in her ear, "Oh yeah, he's got it bad for you."

"The feeling is entirely mutual," Rya whispered back and they laughed softly while the men watched them with dual suspicious looks.

Dimitri and Ivan said something in Russia before Ivan turned back to them with a wicked grin that made Rya's stomach clench while Gia whispered, "Oh fuck. We're in trouble."

"We?" Rya whispered back without taking her eyes off of the two Doms now watching them like a hungry bear and a wolf watching two tasty rabbits.

Ivan strode over to them and the aura of power and control rolling off of him made Rya's heart beat a little faster. He reached down and wrapped Gia's hair around his fist before looking at Rya. "Would you like to help me punish my mouthy little girl, Rya?"

Gia made a soft moan that sent a tingle of desire through Rya's body. She licked her lips and looked over at Dimitri. "Master? Would you like for me to help Master Ivan punish his girl?"

The pleased smile Dimitri gave her made everything inside Rya's heart go all warm and glowy. "It would please me very much to watch you help punish her."

Ivan pulled Gia up by her hair and Rya had to admit the contrast of Ivan's big body and Gia's slender frame was arousing. She wondered if she looked like that with Dimitri and her heart raced while she watched her Master slowly approach. Dimitri was in full-on predator mode now and she couldn't help a shiver of desire as he stopped right before her. With her face at the height of his cock she let out a little moaning purr of approval at the sight of his thick erection pressing against his pants. She wanted to lean forward, to nuzzle her lips against his dick, but she knew better than to move without his permission.

Ivan dragged Gia past them. "When you are ready, come down to the main floor. It's the second door to the left of the stairs with a keypad. The code is 7293."

"Understood," Dimitri said in that low, rumbling growl that he got when he was aroused.

He stroked his fingers through her hair, gently pulling out the tangles. "Are you okay with this, *zaika moya*? I will not be disappointed if you are not attracted to Gia."

Blushing, she leaned into his soft caress. "She is beautiful, Dimitri, and I like her a lot. Are you sure she wants to play with me?"

"Yes. Ivan said she finds you very attractive. Gia is pure submissive, but she was trained by both a Master and a Mistress."

"So I would be Topping her?"

"For my pleasure and Ivan's, yes, but you are submissive to me, always."

He pulled her head forward the slightest bit by her hair and she took a deep inhalation, scenting a faint hint of his musk mixing with the salty air. "And it would turn you on, Master?"

"Very much."

She hesitated, pulling back enough so she could look up at him. "Will you play with her?"

While she tried to keep her expression carefully neutral, she must not have done very well because the faint lines around his eyes crinkled as he gave her a small smile. "No, I will not touch her. You are the only woman I want to touch, little Rya. The things I feel with you, there is nothing like it."

"Thank you," she whispered and took his hand when he offered it to her. "I'm so glad I'm with you, Dimitri. I've been so lost without you."

He gently held her to his body, wrapping his arms around her as she rested her head on his heart. "I will take care of you, *dorogaya*. My life is devoted to your happiness. You are mine, my heart, my future."

She closed her eyes and basked in his open adoration, soaking up his reassurance and hugging him as tight as she could without disturbing her ribs. "I've fallen for you, so much that it scares me."

"Do not fear. I am here to catch you." He held out his hand. "Come here, *zaika moya*."

She placed her hand in his and couldn't help smiling up at him as he helped her out of her chair. "Have I told you yet that I missed you?"

He cradled her in his arms and nuzzled his face against hers. "I am completely addicted to you."

He held her tight as he walked through the house and she relaxed in his arms, contentment filling her as she examined his face while he carried her through the rooms. "Dimitri?"

"*Da?*"

"What will I be doing in Russia?"

He gave her an odd look then said, "What would you like to do?"

"I don't know. I do know I'd like to continue nursing, but I'm not sure how that will work."

"When we get to Moscow we can discuss it. I want you to be happy. I want you to wake up every morning never wanting to leave me because I will not let you leave. You are mine."

While it wasn't the heartfelt declaration of love she was looking for, his words still warmed her heart. "And you're mine. Speaking of which...do you...that is...um..."

"What are you asking me?"

"Can you please not have sex with Gia?"

He laughed, then gently placed her on her feet. "I told you. You are only woman I want, Rya. I mean that. I will not touch her or any other woman."

"I know you say that, but from what I've gathered you are quite...popular with women."

"It does not matter. I do not want them, only you."

"But for how long? What if you get bored with me?" She took a deep breath and let it out slowly.

"Look, Dimitri, I care about you a lot and I'm not trying to rush you into anything, but I can't stand the thought of you having sex with someone else. It hurts. I need to know if you're okay with that. Long term."

He was silent for a long moment, studying her before he said, "What about you? What if I wish to share you with another man?"

"Do you?"

He shrugged. "In the future I may. It is almost like bonding ritual to allow men I trust to give you pleasure. For many, many years I was third with couples so I could share their love, so I could be close to woman without endangering her. Was only way I can love. Now I want to share what we have with a few of my friends, to show them what is waiting for them when they find their woman. Is my way to show my love."

Ice filled her veins. "I see."

"That makes you angry?"

"Well, I'm not exactly happy to hear that the only way you can love a woman is if you share her with another man."

"No, that is wrong. Translation was bad. I mean I could only be affectionate with a woman if she belonged to another, if her heart was safely his. I never had a woman love me, just me. She always love her Master and was friend with me. You are only woman who I have ever had for my own, only woman who has my heart, ever."

She hugged him tight, rubbing her face against his chest. "Thank you."

With a gentle touch he rubbed her back. "I can only hope to someday win your heart as well, *zaika moya*. Please give me chance to show you how good things will be."

"Oh, Dimitri, don't you know? You already have

my heart."

He stiffened against her. "Do you mean it?"

"I wouldn't be here if you didn't." Standing up on her tip toes she threaded her fingers through his thick hair and tilted his head in her direction. "Kiss me."

The first gentle brush of his lips sent warmth flooding to her sex and she sighed against his mouth, caressing his tongue with her own as he slowly devoured her. A delicious, amazing rush of emotions filled her until she was smiling into the kiss, so happy she couldn't contain it so she tried to put her joy into her touch, to let him know what he made her feel, to try and share this pleasure with him. He responded eagerly, nibbling at her lips, his hands roaming her body and awakening her nerves.

By the time they came up for air she was panting and Dimitri's rock hard erection pressed into her body. When she wiggled against him he gave a pained laugh. "Come, Gia and Ivan are waiting for us."

"Are you okay with my Topping Gia with Ivan?"

"Okay?" He took her hand and rubbed it against his stiff cock. "More than okay. Is very sexy."

Giggling, she gave him a squeeze and followed him to the door with the keypad. After entering the code it slid open and Rya followed Dimitri into the dungeon. The lighting was low and it took her eyes a few moments to adjust to the room. The first thing she noticed was the gleam of chrome and she let out a little sigh of pleasure as she took in all the toys available to play with. This wasn't some tiny personal dungeon, but more like an adult playground.

The walls were a deep, almost blood-red color and the floors were made of smooth, dull black tiles. Sheer black cloth had been draped artfully from the ceiling, giving the feeling of being inside of some kind of exotic tent. Soft music came from hidden speakers and she shivered when Dimitri began to caress her back, the mournful violins in the song sending chills through her. The scent of leather and orange oil filled the air and she let her gaze wander until she found Ivan and Gia.

Gia's hair was twisted up into a bun and the other woman was completely nude while kneeling next to her Master with her head down, her hands resting on her spread thighs. Gold gleamed against Gia's dark, erect nipples and Rya smiled at the sight of those lovely piercings. For a moment jealousy intruded on her desire at the knowledge of Dimitri seeing Gia naked, but those thoughts were soon swept away by his lips rubbing against her ear, then his gentle licks that made her body warm beneath his caress.

"You have my permission to do whatever you wish with Gia, but no touching Ivan. Understood?"

"Yes, Master," she whispered, her gaze darting to Ivan who stood next to Gia with his shirt off wearing a pair of loose black pants.

He was definitely a good looking man, well-built and bulkier than Dimitri with a for sure scary, no-bullshit, look in his eyes. Between Dimitri and Ivan she was on testosterone overload and her clit throbbed with the need for her Master's touch. Ivan gave her a small smile that helped ease some of her apprehension before speaking to Dimitri in Russian.

Turning Rya to face him, Dimitri studied her. "I will watch at first. Ivan will help you discipline Gia, and if you do a good job I will fuck you."

"And if I don't?"

"Then I will put you in a chastity belt while I jack off on your tits and let Gia lick it off."

The image, at once arousing and irritating, had her lifting her chin. "What are my restrictions, Master?"

"Ivan said no hard humiliation, no bloodletting, and no giant dildos because he wants her pussy tight when he fucks her."

"Also," Ivan said from right behind Rya, "do not beat her ass too hard. We have a long flight back to Russia in a few days and I do not want her uncomfortable."

The feeling of being surrounded by the two Masters sent her hormones surging and she wanted to rub against Dimitri and climb him like a tree. "Yes, Sir."

Ivan snapped his fingers. "Gia, come here and help Dimitri undress Rya."

While Dimitri helped Rya out of her shirt, taking care not to upset her injuries, Gia lifted Rya's hair to the side and let out a soft gasp. "Holy shit, that's an awesome tattoo."

Smiling over her shoulder at Gia, Rya shifted her shoulders so the other woman could get the full effect. "Thank you."

Ivan frowned and looked at her back, then up at Dimitri. "The wolf has Dimitri's eyes."

Flushing, she nodded. "I call Dimitri *volk moy*, my wolf. I got the tattoo after we had to…be apart for awhile."

Gia sighed and stroked her fingers over the tattoo. "That is so romantic."

Ivan grunted. "Don't even think of it."

With a giggle Gia winked at Rya, then looked up at Ivan with an innocent expression. "Why, whatever do you mean, Master?"

"No tattoo," Ivan ran a finger over one of the diamond subdermal implants near the base of Rya's back. "But this, this is nice."

Gia knelt behind Rya and Dimitri unbuttoned and unzipped Rya's pants, pulling them over her hips so the top of her blue lace thong showed. He grasped Rya's ass in a firm grip and said, "Is very nice."

"Mmm, I agree," Gia whispered before she began

to gently lick at the lace patterned tattoo on Rya's lower back.

Even while surrounded by two very strong Masters, Rya's own dominance rose to the surface. She turned, grabbed Gia's hair and held her head back. "Did I give you permission to lick me?"

Gia practically melted in her grip and gave her big doe eyes. "No, Ma'am."

Looking up at Ivan, Rya had to fight a smile at his surprised look, then his slow, pleased smile. A lot of people didn't understand what being a switch meant for Rya, but she could at once be submissive in a scene and Dominant depending on who she was playing with. It wasn't an act or anything like that, instead she simply went with what her natural inclinations were. Both Dimitri and Ivan were so über dominant she couldn't be anything but submissive with them. But Gia was a submissive to her bones and that made Rya want to do very dirty things to her.

Stepping out of her pants, now clad only in her blue thong, she firmed her grip on Gia's hair and looked around the room, trying to decide what she wanted to play with. Her gaze went past the usual pleasure/pain devices until she came to an adjustable table with a small u-shaped head rest. Without another word she walked across the room, dragging Gia behind her by her hair. It was nice having Ivan with them because she knew he wouldn't allow Rya to do any real damage with Gia and that gave her the freedom to just go with it rather than worry about the usual first time playdate issues of going too far or not far enough with someone she was unfamiliar with.

"Up on the table, Gia, on your back."

Dimitri moved behind Rya and began to stroke her body while she helped Gia get comfortable on the table. After adjusting it to the level she needed, she rubbed her butt against Dimitri, groaning low in her throat. She looked up and Ivan was giving Dimitri a warning glare, but her Master only touched her, making her squirm against him while Gia watched them with dark, passion glazed eyes. When Dimitri pinched Rya's nipple, Gia gasped like it was her own. Rya grinned at Ivan, noting the way he responded to his woman's arousal. Biting her lip to hold back a moan as Dimitri continued to pinch and pull at her nipples, she leaned over and began to toy with Gia's piercings. Experimenting with the right amount of pressure, she soon had Gia whimpering and squirming on the table.

Ivan slapped Gia's inner thigh. "So little control. Be still."

Rya cried out as Dimitri bit the side of her neck, hard, before saying, "My patience is growing thin, *zaika moya*. I have been without you for too long. Punish your girl so I can fuck you."

A streak of naughtiness sizzled through Rya and she stepped away from her Dom with a teasing smile. "Yes, Master."

Moving over to Ivan, she motioned for him to lean down so she could whisper in his ear. "Can you adjust the table so that I can stand over Gia's face? I would like for her to eat me out while you flog her pussy and breasts, please."

Ivan gave a low chuckle that did naughty things to her girly bits. "My pleasure, little Mistress."

While Ivan lowered the table to the right height, Rya sauntered back over to Dimitri. His hunger for her practically vibrated off of him and she had to step carefully to keep her knees from going weak. Damn, he was by far the sexiest man she'd ever seen and he was all hers. Having him watch her like this, knowing her performance was turning him on, made her not only horny enough to consider jumping him, but it also made her feel pride to know she was pleasing her Master. Without thought she leaned down and kissed each of his now bare feet, the need to show her devotion to him, her submission to him overwhelming everything else.

He made a pleased sound that she felt all the way to her toes. "*Dorogaya*. Stand, take off your panties. Let me see my cunt."

With a racing heart she did as he asked and stood before him, fully nude. He closed the small distance between them and picked her up, stealing a kiss from her as he carried her over to Gia, then holding her by her hips, lowered her until her pussy was over the other woman's face. Gia moaned and her breath warmed Rya's soaking wet sex. Dimitri tried to back away, but Rya clung to him.

"Please, Master, kiss me."

He looked over her shoulder to where Ivan stood and said something in Russian. Ivan replied and Dimitri gave Rya a wicked smile. "There is price for my kiss."

"What is that, Master?"

"Ivan will flog you as well while Gia eats your pussy and I eat your mouth. I know how much you like to kiss me while you are taking your pleasure."

She bit her lower lip, tempted by the decadent scenario but apprehensive of having someone she didn't know flogging her. Lowering her voice to a whisper, trying to ignore how close her pussy was to Gia's mouth, she said, "Will he hurt me?"

"He is sadist, so yes, but not today. Today is for pleasure, not pain." He stroked her cheek with a gentle expression that made her love for him grow more than she'd thought possible. "You are mine, Rya, and I would not allow him to harm you."

Before she could respond Dimitri pushed her

down until her pussy made contact with Gia's lips. At the same time the soft, thick falls of a flogger glanced over her butt, no doubt striking Gia's breasts as well. The woman beneath her moaned and began to lick at Rya's sex, nibbling at her outer labia hard enough to sting. That bit of pain was instantly soothed away by Dimitri as he began to kiss Rya with such adoration that her mind couldn't keep track of any one thought. One moment she'd be thinking about how amazingly good Gia was at oral sex, then her thoughts would be diverted to the slight sting of the flogger, then the sensation of Dimitri's tongue stroking hers would take precedence.

Her arousal grew until she was grinding her slit against Gia's eager mouth and the moment the other woman began to suckle on her clit Rya came, hard.

She screamed against Dimitri's mouth and he seemed to try and eat the sound from her, sucking at her lips, licking the inside of her mouth, basically ravaging her until her legs shook. Gia grasped onto Rya's hips and continued to torment her overly sensitive clit, sending streaks of pleasure and pain through her as she tried to move away from the other woman's eager mouth. Dimitri growled and held her in place, making her take the overstimulation, making her endure the slap of the flogger, the edge of Gia's teeth, then her mind shut down until she was clinging to him and making incoherent sounds of both need and pain.

The craving to feel his skin overwhelmed her and she tore at his shirt, trying to get to his warmth beneath. With a muttered oath Dimitri broke their kiss long enough to remove his shirt, then unbuttoned his pants. He lifted her from Gia and Rya squirmed in his arms, trying to grasp his cock. With a low growl he gently set her into a sex swing and quickly strapped her ankles to the chains and cuffs dangling from overhead so that her legs were up in the air and spread wide while her body was cradled by the black leather swing.

After removing his pants he stalked to her, his erection swaying just the slightest bit with his stride.

"Please, Master," she cried out when he stroked her thighs. "Take me. Please."

Gia cried out from somewhere to her right in what sounded like a good orgasm, but Rya's attention was totally on Dimitri and his cock. She ached for him, needed that connection between them, and even though Gia had done a wonderful job giving her pleasure, nothing compared to the sensation of her Master owning her. Her clit throbbed to the beat of her heart and when he positioned himself at her entrance she shivered.

"Look at me," Dimitri said with a snarl.

She did as she was told, forcing her gaze to meet his as he thrust into her, fighting her body's natural reaction to clamp down while he forced her to accept him. Nothing felt as good as his shaft inside of her. She wiggled against him, trying to get more of him inside of her, but the sex swing held her immobile, totally under his control. Grasping the chains next to her head, Rya used that little bit of leverage to rub against him and she had to bite her lip in an effort to keep from coming, to ride that edge between almost having her release and the wonderfully terrible tension filling her.

Sweat stood out on Dimitri's face and chest and she wanted to lean up and lick it off, but he chose that moment to begin to slide in and out of her wet sex, stroking her until he found her g-spot. With her legs up in the air like this he managed to hit that pad of nerves just right, driving her out of her fucking mind with the need to come.

Using his thumb on her clit, he said, "Give me

your pleasure."

He pulled all the way out and she screamed out her orgasm, loving the intensity of her g-spot climax. The hot rush of her release poured out of her soaking Dimitri's cock as he shoved it into her again.

"So sexy," he said in a strained voice. "You will do that again for me. I love to watch you climax, is favorite thing in world."

He fucked her mercilessly, so hard and fast that she lost all control of her body, the orgasm blasting through her as she once again screamed out, clutching the chains and soaking Dimitri with her release. He rubbed his fingers over her pussy, then spread the wetness over her mound and up her belly before licking his fingers. "Sweet cunt, my sweet cunt."

She could only nod as he picked up the pace again, his jaw clenched, his gaze focused only on her. She was vaguely aware of Ivan and Gia playing near them, of the sounds of their enjoyment mixing with her own, but Dimitri was the center of her universe. He leaned over her and gripped the back of her neck, bringing her mouth to his so he could kiss her while fucking her hard and fast. Her pussy throbbed and she clenched on him, wanting to make her Master feel good, wanting to give him everything she had to offer.

He moaned against her lips and his thrusts became disjointed as he said, "You come with me. Wait."

Fire burned through her spine, flooding every nerve from her toes to the top of her head with pleasure until she was as tense as a statue beneath him, trying to fight off her orgasm.

"Can't...Master...going..."

He shuddered, "Come, *zaika moya*."

Two more thrusts and he roared out his release above her, sending her own climax blasting through her. She was hyperaware of his heat pouring into her, of the clank of the chains as the swing shook with their combined release, of how she was whispering his name in a broken voice. At this moment, she felt so alive that she couldn't help but cry as her emotions went out of control and all walls between her and Dimitri fell. Her heart opened to him and she clung to him, whispering how much he meant to her, how scared she'd been without him, and how much she loved him.

They were the only people in the universe, and when she slowly began to return to earth, she found that she was no longer in the dungeon, but in their bedroom. The lights were out but a full moon reflected off the ocean beyond the windows. Dimitri was curled around her to the point where every inch of her body that could be covered by his, was. She stirred against him and let out an exhausted laugh.

"Wow."

He was silent for a few moments, stroking her arms gently before he said, "Did you mean it?"

"Mean what?"

"Do you love me?"

Uncomfortable, but still buzzing from the overwhelming amount of hormones and endorphins spinning through her blood, she nodded. "I do."

"Say it."

"Say it?"

"Please, Rya, say it."

His voice held such uncertainty that she cuddled into him and whispered, "I love you, Dimitri Novikov."

The long sigh he let out would have been comical if she hadn't been waiting for him to say it back. "Thank you."

She waited, but he said nothing, only cuddling her. Hurt, she nodded and tried to get out of his arms. "I have to use the restroom."

He eased up his hold and rolled off the bed. "Come, I wash you."

"I can do it myself," she said with a bit of snap in her voice.

"Come."

Giving him a disgruntled look, she let him lead her to the blue and white bathroom. The bright lights stung her eyes and she muttered an apology before lowering them. "I will join you in a moment."

While she took care of business she managed to keep her tears at bay long enough to turn the shower on and step beneath its spray. Lifting her face to the oversized shower head she let the tears fall, but tried to muffle her cries. Okay, so Dimitri might be really fond of her, but he didn't love her. She could deal with that. Well no, actually she couldn't but she didn't have a choice. She was in love with a man who might not be capable of loving her back. On an intellectual level she knew that his fucked up childhood, and hell, his fucked up adult life might have made it extremely hard for him to allow himself to love anyone. She really had no right to be mad at him, but damn, it hurt.

The shower door opened but she ignored Dimitri as he joined her. She grabbed a bar of soap from the shelf in the shower and turned away, pretending to wash herself.

He tried to take the soap from her but she jerked her hand away. "I'm almost done."

"Rya? What is wrong?"

"Nothing."

He tried to get her to turn around and face him, but she managed to push away. "Just let me rinse off and the shower is all yours."

Frowning, he pulled her unwilling body against his. "What is wrong?"

"Nothing." She refused to look at him, instead focusing on the tile wall of the shower.

"Did I hurt you?"

She wanted to scream yes, but instead she gave him a stiff, "No."

"Do not lie."

"Fine. I don't want to talk about it."

He made a frustrated growling noise. "Tell me what is wrong."

"No."

"I will spank it out of you."

She shoved at his chest, but it was like trying to shove at a tree. "Just leave me alone, okay?"

"No, I will not leave you alone. You are mine, Rya. I will never leave you alone."

She shouted in anger, "Why the fuck do you want me? You don't love me. What's the point?"

Taking in a deep breath, he then grasped her wet hair and forced her to look at him. "You think I do not love you?"

Trying to keep her lower lip from trembling she shook her head. "Don't worry about it. I'll be fine. Just...just leave me alone. I need time to think."

He laughed. "You are foolish."

She wanted so badly to knee him in the nuts right now it wasn't even funny. "And you're an asshole."

That stopped his laughter and he glared at her. "You are not going anywhere. You are mine."

"I don't want to be yours," she yelled and tried to jerk his hand out of her hair. "I want you to want me because you love me, not because you want to *own* me."

"But I do want to own you. I want to keep every one of your smiles for myself, to be the source of all of your joy, to surround myself with you because you are my light, Rya. You are my warmth, my heart, my soul. I love you more than you can possibly imagine, foolish girl."

She stopped struggling and peered up at him through the water. "You love me?"

"I've been in love with you from the moment we met." He leaned down and placed a gentle kiss on her lips. "You are the first woman I have ever loved, and you will be the last. Why would you doubt that?"

"But you didn't say it back," she whispered against his mouth as her body melted into his.

He nipped her lips. "You do not remember me saying it back, but I did and I will as many times as you need to hear it to believe it. I love you, Rya DeLuca, and I will never let you go."

Chapter Twenty-Three

Rya took a deep breath and smiled at Dimitri as he helped her from the backseat of his navy blue Bentley three days later. She'd gained a nice tan from their time in South Carolina and sent a silent thank you to Gia for being such an awesome hostess. During the day she and Gia went shopping, or to a spa, then usually to a bar eating decadent appetizers and getting tipsy under the combined stares of their bodyguards. When they came home at night, the men would make them dinner, then take them down to the dungeon to play. It had been a very relaxing, indulgent few days and she was ever so grateful to Dimitri for giving them to her. Spending time with him like that, with his friends, was really, really nice. She could easily see herself being with Dimitri for the rest of her life and the notion didn't scare her like it should. That was proof that Dimitri had a magic touch that could make everything wonderful.

Damn, he'd fucked her stupid.

Giving herself a little mental shake to clear her mind of the arousing image of Dimitri fucking her, she took a deep breath of the chilly air and tugged her fox fur jacket closer around her. She'd felt odd wearing such a luxurious jacket until she realized a lot of women wore fur because it was cold as fuck in Moscow at the moment. They were somewhere near the Embassy district in the massive city. They finally arrived at the location of her new home after driving through the heavy traffic for what seemed like hours. Rya hadn't been sure what to expect, but this luxury high rise apartment building with a huge private park/garden wasn't it. This building looked like it belonged in some movie about the rich and famous and she stared for a moment at all the glass windows before giving the gate they'd just passed through a curious look. High cement walls topped with pointed black wrought iron enclosed the building and surrounding court yard. Cameras watched them as well as men dressed in black uniforms and wearing long coats patrolling the area. There were even a few guard dogs and she gave one of the obviously armed, sharp-eyed passing men a curious look before stepping closer to Dimitri.

In addition to the abundance of security, Maks was scanning the area like he expected an attack any second, and two more bodyguards that Dimitri had introduced to her stood a little bit away, their posture tense. Shifting on the high heels of her elegant black leather boots, Rya smiled up at Dimitri and tried to keep the stiffness out of her voice. "It's beautiful."

When Dimitri held her hand and gave her a gentle kiss she noticed a few of the people watching her look shocked. Dimitri had told her that news of her arrival had spread, but she'd still been surprised at the amount of attention they received. There had even been what amounted to the Russian version of the paparazzi waiting for them at the airport, but their bodyguards made quick work of the would-be photographer. Evidently, Russian laws didn't protect the paparazzi because the man's camera had been crushed while two police officers looked on and laughed. When she'd asked Dimitri about it he merely shrugged like it was no big deal.

He'd dressed her himself this morning, putting her in a lovely cream dress and pairing it with her sexy black boots. Then he'd put in the yellow diamond earrings and wrist cuffs. He said the view of her cleavage in that dress was sinful enough without adding diamonds. The look of pride in his gaze when he looked at her wearing the jewelry he gave her made butterflies take flight in her stomach.

Before she knew it Dimitri was leading her through the marble and bronze foyer of the apartment complex, pointing out the way to the gym, the spa, and a women's clothing boutique among the other shops on the main floor of the building where he had opened a line of credit in her name. There was even a bank, a small grocery store, and a gourmet restaurant leading her to believe that this apartment building was more like a luxury fortress than a simple place to live. He informed her that she had an appointment with the banker tomorrow to set up her own separate account with an undisclosed, probably obscene amount of money in it for her to play with.

She was surprised when they had to stop and get her fingerprints and retina scan done at the building's security office so she would be able to use the different biometric locks in order to access the building. Everyone she met treated her with a level of ass kissing that she'd never experienced before that made her very uncomfortable. The men and women were all elegant and professional, making her feel slightly out of place. She refused to be intimidated and kept in mind that just because they didn't smile at her didn't mean they hated her. However, Rya was pretty sure the hostess at the spa hated her. When Dimitri spoke to the hostess in English Rya had to hide a laugh at the way the woman's face fell when Dimitri said Rya was his girlfriend, his woman, and that she had his permission to do or buy anything she wanted. While she had no plans to go on any spending sprees, it was nice to know that she could now use her savings to pay off the mortgage she'd taken out on her grandparents' house to pay for college.

As they rode the elevator to their floor, she

absently stroked the lovely fur jacket and looked at their reflection in the polished brass doors of the elevator. Dimitri looked as good as ever in his dark suit and trench coat, but she appeared a little shell shocked. Her eyes were as big and round as dinner plates and her mouth was slightly parted. Giving herself a mental shake, she took a deep breath and let it out.

"So, this is where we live?"

"Yes. Do you like it? If not I have many other places where we could stay. Or I could buy new home for you."

The doors leading to the twelfth floor opened before she could respond. As they stepped out into the very modern black marble and chrome hallway she looked around with surprise. The hallway itself was very short and there were only two doors.

Dimitri moved over to the door to the right of the elevator and smiled. "Put thumb here please to make sure it work."

She did and the door slid open, revealing a breath taking circular foyer with Brazilian cherry wood floors and pale cream walls. Stepping inside, she turned in a slow circle, taking in the staircase leading to an upper level and the archways opening to different rooms. She was used to apartments being like the matchbox she'd shared with her roommate in college, not this palatial expanse of wealth and luxury. The faint scent of paint hung in the air and the place had a brand new feel to it.

"Holy shit. We live here?"

Laughing, Dimitri helped her out of her jacket and hung it up in a small closet off the foyer with his trenchcoat. "This is our home."

Something in the room to her right caught her eye and she wandered into what had to be a living room furnished in a surprisingly familiar manner. During the long flight over on Ivan's private jet, she'd spent a great deal of time with Gia looking through her design portfolio on the massive screen of the jet's entertainment system. At the time she'd thought she was just learning about interior design with Gia, but now she realized she'd actually been picking out furniture for her apartment. Dimitri had totally pulled the wool over her eyes and it touched her deeply that he somehow managed to make this happen, to give her new home her own personal stamp in the most amazing way. They'd spent the last day and a half in Paris, so when he was doing business while she was sightseeing with Gia and Ivan, he must have been setting this up.

What a wonderful, thoughtful man.

Rubbing her hand over the cream microsuede couch, she wandered over to the floor to ceiling windows looking out over Moscow. It was still early morning, Moscow time, and she stared in fascination at all the people moving about on the streets below. Dimitri joined her and wrapped his arms around her, resting his head on top of hers.

"Do you like it?"

"Dimitri, I'd be excited to live in a shack as long as you were with me, but I won't lie, this is pretty awesome."

He laughed, the first time she'd heard him do that since they landed in Russia, and hugged her close. "I am glad."

They stood there together, watching the world pass by at their feet, until her stomach growled. She'd nibbled on the plane ride from Paris, but her nerves had been wound too tight to eat much. Part of her had expected some kind of mafia war to break out the moment they touched down in the airport, but nothing had happened other than the photographer and she was slowly starting to relax. The insane security certainly helped. Dimitri was so paranoid that Maks and another bodyguard each had a room here in the palatial apartment. There was also a command center and a safe room on both floors. Dimitri was taking no chances with her safety and it kind of freaked her out.

The constant reminder that they would never be alone was sinking in and she was kind of bummed she wouldn't be able to ever relax in her home. Not that she was a nudist, but sometimes she like to lounge around naked. It was comfortable. But not something she'd do with a freaking bodyguard chilling nearby or cameras watching her. Urk. She would keep her exhibitionist tendencies to the bedroom, not in front of men trying to keep her alive. And Maks was scary; even though he was gorgeous, he was intense.

Tawny would love him.

The thought of her best friend made her sigh and Dimitri turned her around to face him. "Why sad?"

She blinked rapidly. "I'm sorry. I just miss my family, my friends. I've never been away from them for more than six months. And never so far. I mean…I'm sorry, ignore me. I'm jet lagged and just talking crazy."

"You are scared."

For a moment she thought about lying, then shook her head. "Yeah, I'm scared."

"Then it is my job to make sure you are no longer fearful."

Unable to help it, she snorted. "Just like that you'll make me not scared anymore?"

"Yes."

The utter confidence in his voice made something tingle low in her belly. Stupid hormones. "How?"

He ran his fingers through her hair and fisted his hand hard enough to make her scalp sting. "I am your

Master. It is privilege to care for you and to protect you. Trust me, Rya, no one will dare incur my wrath. It would be a slaughter and they understand that. I would destroy nations if you were harmed."

A cramp hit her stomach as she stared up at him, not sure if she was horrified or comforted. "Please, please don't kill any innocents, no more killing each other's women. Promise me."

He slowly shook his head. "Some would say there are no innocents."

"That's bullshit and you know it. Promise me you won't kill any innocent women or children whose only crime is being born into a war, or in my case loving their man."

Moving slowly, he held her hands in his and lifted them to his mouth, brushing his lips over her skin in a delicious stroke that tempted her to just let go and let Dimitri take care of her. He was so very, very good at bringing her pleasure and the idea of just being in his arms for the rest of the day sounded perfect. The thought of spending some time in subspace was beyond tempting; the ability to lose herself in him was a drug she craved. She wanted to surround herself with his will, to do whatever he wanted because she trusted him.

He loved her.

"Master?"

Heat flared in his gaze but his face was expressionless as he said, "Yes?"

"Will you please take care of me?"

Closing his eyes, Dimitri knelt before her and rubbed his face against her breasts. "*Dorogaya*, I live to take care of you. Is my greatest pleasure. We do not need words to understand each other's souls, only us, touching, caressing, loving each other."

She sifted her fingers through his hair, loving the way the sunlight brought out the deep auburn highlights. "Are we alone? I mean can I get naked right now without worrying about someone seeing me?"

"You want privacy, yes?"

"I do."

"One moment."

He took out his cellphone and said a few things in Russian before hanging up. "We will not be disturbed and cameras are off here. Show me your beautiful body. Show me what is mine."

It was easy to slide out of the pretty cream dress he'd provided her with. When the frilly pink lace bra and panty set she bought in Paris came into view he growled. "Wait. I did not know you picked this to wear beneath. Keep it on."

Basking in his open approval, she stretched and gave him a little pout. "You sure you don't want me naked?"

"Do not move."

She froze with her hands above her head, pressed to the glass while she basically dared him to fuck her. With her boots still on, she tipped her ass up just the slightest bit and Dimitri sucked in his breath through his teeth. Instead of shedding his clothing and taking her, he took a step back and crossed his arms with a stern look. "I realize we have not begun any formal training, but I want you to know that in my home I demand a different level of control in the bedroom. I've never loved anyone before you and the level of control that I will need from you may be trying at times. I ask for your patience, because right now I fear that you will be taken from me if I let my guard down for one second. I need your submission to keep me sane."

His raw honesty tore at her and she approached him slowly before sinking to her knees and kissing his feet softly before sitting up on her heels. "Yes,

Master. I'm yours. I trust you."

"I want to see my mark, stand up, turn around, take off bra and put hands on glass."

She did as he commanded, her gaze once again turning to the view beyond the windows, "Master, can they see us?"

"Do you think I will let another covet what is mine?"

She laughed and shimmied her bra off. "No. I do not think you would allow that."

"My girl is smart." He stepped up behind her and lifted her hands up, placing her palms flat on the window. "The glass is specially treated so we can see out, but no one can see in. It even blocks infrared heat signatures and can jam any radio frequency."

"Wow," she whispered, her skin prickling as he lightly stroked his nails down her back.

"When I first saw this wolf," Dimitri said softly, "I saw for the first time what I look like to you. I am humbled."

Realizing he was tracing the tattoo design with his nails she smiled. "I felt so lost after I got back. So alone. I needed something, some kind of mark that wouldn't fade that would reflect what had happened between us. It made me feel better to know my wolf was protecting my back."

He sucked in a quick breath. "I am so sorry you got hurt, Rya."

"No, no, don't be silly." She looked over her shoulder at him. "Are we going to fuck or what?"

His eyes grew wide before his shock was replaced with a smirk. "Such a bad girl, topping from the bottom."

The urge to stick her tongue out was huge, but before she could he gave her a sharp slap on her butt that left her gasping. "Holy hell. That hurt."

"Bad girls don't get nice spankings, little Rya. Bad

girls get punished."

Her ever kinky libido ramped up at his dirty talk. "What if I'm only a little bit bad?"

His reply came in the form of a hard slap against her ass that gave a satisfying crack before the pain heated her butt. "Shit."

"Mmmmm, such a lovely ass. You have no idea how good it feels to rub up against all of your softness." He pressed his groin to her and she moaned aloud at the feeling of his bare cock pressing against her slit.

"Please, Master," she whispered and tried to hold as still as possible.

"Look at how well you behave when you want something," he said in a chiding voice, keeping his cock poised at her entrance but not moving. "So eager to please, for now."

He smacked her ass, hard three times in a row and by the third strike she screamed.

"What, *zaika moya*, is too hard? You were begging for my punishment, I merely obliged."

When he rubbed his hand on her bottom she hissed, "Hurts."

"Then let me make it feel better."

He knelt behind her and began to lick her bottom, his beard brushing painfully against her burning skin. Damn he had big hands, that shit hurt. When he started to lick right next to her pussy she locked her body in place, wanting so bad to move enough to encourage his mouth on her wet sex. As if sensing her thoughts his tongue teased along one side of her labia, a soft stroke that had her going up on her tip toes.

Dimitri smacked her ass and she sank down again, crying out as he slid his tongue into her pussy and licked.

He pulled back and she almost fell before he

pulled her down onto the thick, ultra soft carpet. His gaze locked with hers and he licked his lips slowly, her arousal still gleaming on his skin. As she watched he cleaned his face with his thumb, eating every bit of her cream that he could. By the time he was done she was one good thigh press away from climaxing. Holy hell, he destroyed her with pleasure.

Laying back, Dimitri smiled up at her. "Come, straddle my face."

Biting back a moan of anticipation, she shifted around until Dimitri was happy with the way her pussy pressed against his mouth. She had to brace her hands against the window because Dimitri was on a mission to make her come. She knew this wasn't going to be a slow build up the moment he began to suck her clit while shoving two fingers into her pussy. Intense arousal hit her and she cried out, shamelessly grinding her sex against his eager mouth. The brush of his beard on her waxed labia was just unbelievable.

Then he began to scoop up her arousal and spread it on her anus and she lost it, shuddering over him while he licked at her clit with exquisitely gentle strokes that allowed him to eat her through her entire orgasm without jerking away because she had become too sensitive.

He rolled her over until she was on her hands and knees. Not satisfied with her positioning, he roughly rearranged her so that her shoulders rested on the carpet with her ass tilted up to him. He made a pleased sound when she was finally properly arched in a position he liked. Without so much as a word he leaned over and began to press his cock into her, stroking her pussy as he kept filling her. When he was all the way in, she felt possessed on every level and abandoned herself to him.

Dimitri set a languid pace and she rolled her hips into his, losing herself in his gaze and smiling as happiness bordering on bliss filled her. No doubt her spanking had added to this lovely sexual buzz, but it was Dimitri who did this to her, who was here with her, who said he loved her. He toyed with her breasts, squeezing them and toying with her nipples. "I love your tits."

"I love your everything," she said with a wide smile.

His pace increased and his eyes darkened until they were the color of storm clouds. "*Ya lyublyu tyebya fsyem syertsem.*"

Lifting her hips slightly, he began to massage her pussy with his free hand, making the most delicious sensations unfurled inside of her. Then he began to tug at her clit, pinching and pulling it until she tensed against him. "Master, may I come?"

"You may."

He released her clit as soon as the first contraction hit and began to fuck her hard and deep. She arched beneath him, striving to catch her breath as pleasure overtook her to the point where only her heartbeat let her know she was still alive. As the first crest broke, she sucked in a desperate breath of air and moaned. His hard body rubbed against hers and she loved the contrast between them, loved his thick muscles and the smell of his cologne and musk mixing together. Dimitri flipped her over with a low growl. Wrapping her legs around his waist she urged him to take her harder and he obliged.

Her back burned slightly on the rug as he pounded into her. When he began to suckle her nipple she lost it, crying out and shaking as he jerked his hips and joined her, his orgasm drawing growls from him that vibrated against her breast between his lips. Instead of releasing her breast, he continued to toy with her nipple while he slowly softened inside of her. By the time he moved she was languid with pleasure and sprawled out on the soft carpet. With a chuckle he picked her up and she nuzzled into his chest.

"I love you."

He laughed again and began to climb some stairs. "I love you too, *zaika moya*."

"No, I mean I *really* love you. Like the forever kind."

He didn't say anything until they reached what she assumed was his bedroom. The entire room was done in white, silver, and navy, giving it a very modern, clean feeling. It was as awesome in person as it had been in the pictures, and she let out a happy sigh. "See, how cool is this? I mean really, Dimitri, you are totally spoiling me. I had no idea you were buying everything I picked out. You're so damn sneaky."

He set her down on the navy blue silk comforter that had tiny silver threads woven through it, making it slightly iridescent yet incredibly soft. "Anything you want, I will get it for you."

Laughing, she pulled him down onto the stainless steel canopy bed with her. Long deep blue velvet curtains hung from the canopy and they could be drawn closed, sealing them in darkness inside. Eager to see what that looked like, she rolled out from under Dimitri and bounced around the massive bed, pulling the drapes of the canopy closed. By the time she was done they were lost in almost total darkness.

"Wow, she said then giggled. "This is an amazing bed."

From somewhere to her left she felt the mattress shift, and a second later she was tumbling through the darkness with Dimitri on top of her. Before she could push him off he slid into her with a sigh. The man had an eternal hard-on...then again she was always wet around him so she couldn't really talk. He nuzzled her lips as he said, "I will be gentle because I do not want your pussy too sore to fuck, but right now I am too greedy for you. I cannot help it, you feel perfect around me. That you are here, in my bed...is too good to be true. Like a dream."

"Oh, I'm very real." She wiggled against him with a happy sigh. "You feel so good inside of me."

He fucked her slowly to orgasm and as she coasted down she was sure that there was no price she wouldn't pay for the privilege of being in his arms.

Chapter Twenty-Four

Guilt tried to intrude on Rya's extreme joy at getting outside of the building she'd been stuck in for over a solid week. Her bodyguard, Maks, had finally let his guard down a bit and while he was in the bathroom, he used to pee with the door open, but for once, he closed it, she'd taken that opportunity to don her heels and slip out the door. On the way out she'd grabbed the lovely mink coat Dimitri had provided her with. He explained that it was his mother's and her heart had melted at the warm look in his eyes when she put it on. The jacket was pure decadence and she loved rubbing her fingers over it.

Or at least she did on the one occasion she'd been outside since she arrived.

It had only been for about ten minutes, long enough for Rya to get into Dimitri's car so they could go have dinner at Alex's house. She was going absolutely stir crazy but Dimitri wasn't letting her out of his sight. Oh, he'd provided her with every kind of entertainment and luxury available, but she needed to go outside before she suffocated. She felt weird when Gia went to work while she was forced to stay in the apartment.

When Dimitri was home she could care less, but when she was alone she was...lonely. And homesick. Talking to her bodyguards and enlisting them to start to teach her Russian helped keep her mind busy, but they were all stern and professional. Usually it was just her chatting to herself while they grunted or laughed every once in a while. Maks talked to her more than any of the others and she felt bad for betraying him, but desperate to get some fresh air.

So when the doors to the elevator opened she slipped inside and let out a sigh of relief. As she descended her heart raced and she looked forward to exploring the enclosed, guarded grounds of the building. There was a lovely pond she could see from the apartment that was kept ice-free by constantly flowing water. At night, the lovely fountain in the center was illuminated by LED lights and she loved to watch the shifting colors.

She just wanted to breathe fresh air, and for a few moments, feel like the world wasn't closing in on her.

The doors opened and she did a quick scan around the lobby. The only other tenant there was Mrs. Landry from three floors above. She was an American ex-pat, the widowed wife of an American diplomat who chose to stay in Russia after her husband's death. She was a little crazy and had nine small, yippy dogs, but Rya liked her. Especially right now when one of her dogs was taking a crap on the pristine marble floor of the foyer. That provided the distraction Rya needed to walk down the hallway leading to the fountain. She passed the spa on the left, and the bar on the right, before exiting the massive glass doors to the garden.

It was colder than she expected for this time of year, and she instantly regretted not having boots. The pathway was swept clean of any snow, but walking around in high heels in this weather was not smart. She gathered her coat around herself and turned her face to the sun, letting out a deep sigh. If someone had told her how much she would chafe from being confined indoors a month ago she'd have laughed at them. But now she realized she needed her freedom, at least more than she had now. She loved Dimitri and knew her situation was serious, but this building had crazy good security…and she had bodyguards.

At the thought of security, she quickened her step, knowing Maks would find her, and when he did, he would be pissed, and so would Dimitri. So, she wasn't going to waste her precious time out here worrying. Better to apologize than ask permission.

The sound of the fountain lured her further into the garden and she tried to imagine what it would look like in the spring. There were rose bushes everywhere and she imagined this place smelled divine in the summer; she looked forward to sitting in one of the grassy areas and reading.

Her thoughts were so preoccupied with the vivid image of a warm summer's day she didn't notice she wasn't alone.

She'd reached the pond by this point and stood on the edge of the concrete, loving the sparkle of the snow around the water. This green space was a little slice of heaven in the middle of Moscow, a natural place where she could reconnect with the earth. It sounded stupid, but she was a country girl at heart and she missed the solitude of her home. But when she imagined being her with Dimitri, holding his hand while they strolled the gardens, she couldn't help but smile.

"Ms. DeLuca?"

She turned to find a matronly looking woman in what appeared to be a white fox jacket and a pair of sturdy brown boots. Her English was very good and Rya wondered if she was yet another ex-pat. The woman reached into her purse and pulled out an envelope and a small, black velvet box.

"Yes?"

"I have something for you from Mr. Novikov."

Happiness filled her soul and she wondered how the hell Dimitri knew she was out here. Hell, all Maks had to do was call security and they could probably find her with the zillion cameras they had everywhere. Rya took a step forward and accepted the envelope and box. Her hands shook with the cold and the other woman made a tsking sound.

"What are you doing here without gloves? Silly woman, you could lose your fingers. Your bodyguards need to take better care of you."

"What?"

"Come, you need to get inside. If you want to be out into the Russian winter you must dress for it." She made an odd clucking sound. "I need to have a talk with Dimitri about taking care of his woman."

Rya found herself being escorted inside like an errant child as the woman switched to Russian while she continued to scold Rya.

Right before they reached the doors the woman said in a low voice, "I'm very happy to see Dimitri with someone. To know that he's finally given himself permission to love? It does my heart good."

Blinking at the other woman, Rya said, "Who are you?"

"My name is Gerta. I was Dimitri's nanny."

Rya turned to study the woman closer, but her examination was interrupted by a really, really angry male voice directed at her. "Where the fuck have you been?"

It was said in a calm, even tone but Rya's blood froze in her veins.

It was Maks.

And he was angry.

The woman next to Rya spoke quickly in Russian while Rya looked at her cute black patent leather high heels and tried to think of a way out of this. They had a little red bow on the back that she adored, but right now she wished she was wearing sneakers because she had a feeling her day was about to go downhill. The idea of running away was becoming very appealing. She wasn't sure what she expected to happen, but Maks sounding like he was going to kill someone was not a good sign. Even though she knew Maks would never hurt her, he sounded fucking scary, all cold and rage-filled whispers in Russian that made the hair on the back of her neck stand up.

While they argued she opened the letter and frowned in confusion.

Dear Ms. DeLuca,
Forgive me for contacting you like this, but I'm afraid my son refuses to have anything to do with me. My name is Jorg Novikov, and I am Dimitri's father. I would like to extend my welcome to you and invite you to my home, along with my son. As you may know, my health is not very good and I need to see my son before I die. I'm asking you, as a father, to convince Dimitri to bring you to meet me. I mean you no harm, Rya, this I swear. As a sign of my goodwill I would like to give a gift. This ring has been in the Novikov family for generations. If you come to the manor you will see portraits of Dimitri's ancestors wearing it. I would like for you to have it. If anyone ever bothers you, show them that ring and let them know they will answer to me.

The signature was in Cyrillic and she was aware of Maks and Dimitri's old nanny's gaze on her as she put the note into her pocket then opened the black ring box. Inside was a heavy gold woman's ring with cluster of rubies set in gold. It looked old and as she took it out of the box Maks made a choked sound.

"Rya, you need to come upstairs, now."

She started to protest, but Maks was done. He grabbed her arm and escorted her, in a most undignified manner, across the lobby. People stared and whispered, making her cheeks flame as they waited for the elevator. She shoved the ring box into her pocket then freed her arm from Maks' grip.

"What the *hell* is wrong with you?"

He turned his arctic stare on her and she was pretty sure she shrunk a couple inches beneath the weight of his gaze. She was wrong. He wasn't angry. He was furious.

Instead of shouting at her, his gaze grew as fathomless as that of a shark. "That ring in your hand? It was Dimitri's mother's favorite ring. Only one person could have given you that, and if Dimitri's father contacted you behind Dimitri's back, Dimitri is going to lose his mind. And so is Alex, so if I give you advice, it is this. Shut up and take your punishment for scaring the men in your life to death with your foolish carelessness."

Her sense of self-preservation told her to shut the hell up, and for once, she did.

By the time they reached the apartment she was really regretting her decision to sneak out, but a small part of her was also pissed at being returned to her apartment like some errant child.

"Maks, I don't want to go in there."

He ignored her and opened the door, then grabbed her by the arm and marched her in.

She'd been expecting Dimitri and Alex to be here and ready to yell at her like her step-dad would have done, but instead the foyer was empty. When her gaze landed on Alex standing in the doorway leading to the formal sitting area she took a step back against the closed door. Oh boy, he was mad. Really mad. Wondering just how much trouble she was in, she smiled at Alex.

"Hi."

His nostrils flared and he said in a soft voice, "Where were you?"

"Um, I wanted to go for a walk around the fountain."

"And why did you not take your bodyguard?"

"Well...." She dropped her gaze, not liking the dead look in his eyes that made her stomach clench. "Dimitri didn't want me leaving the building, so I didn't think Maks would let me. I just wanted to go outside."

"So, you are saying you willingly disobeyed my brother, put yourself in danger, and you did this all because you wanted to go outside?"

"Gets worse," Maks said in a tight voice from behind her and she winced.

Maks told his story, and at the mention of Alex and Dimitri's father contacting her Alex went arctic and she swore the temperature of the room dropped by twenty degrees. If she thought he was mad before, the icy rage that was reflected in his eyes for a brief moment before his expression shut down scared the piss out of her.

Trying to mitigate the damage, she whispered, "Alex, I'm sorry."

With three swift strides he crossed the room then put hand over her mouth and said, "Go to your room."

Normally, she would have told him to fuck off, but glad for the chance to escape Alex's anger she went up the stairs in record time and into the bedroom she shared with Dimitri.

As soon as she entered she chucked her heels off and threw her jacket into the corner. Her stomach cramped up and she moved to her bed, grabbing Dimitri's pillow and holding it close before she began to cry. This was so fucked up. All she had done was go outside. Well, okay, so she should have taken Maks, but they were all overreacting. The only thing that had happened was that Dimitri's nanny had given her a ring from his father. That wasn't exactly terrible.

She lied to herself, trying to deal with her fear as

best she could. A few minutes later another man's voice roared from downstairs and she clutched the pillow harder. That was a bad, bad sound.

Oh fuck, Dimitri was home.

She curled up into a ball and hoped he wouldn't be too mad at her.

When the door opened, she flinched and tucked her head down, waiting for the yelling to begin.

Instead, Maks said in an unexpectedly gentle voice, "Rya, you need to come downstairs. Dimitri and Alex wish to speak to you."

She whimpered and he made a soft, shushing sound.

"Rya, you must face them."

To her humiliation her voice came out shaky as she said, "I'm afraid."

"Why? He loves you beyond reason, but you must be punished for what you've done. He will tolerate almost anything from you, but putting yourself in danger like that...is very selfish. If anything had happened to you he would have never forgiven himself. I would never forgive myself either. It is my job, my privilege to keep you alive, but I cannot do that when you do something like this."

Guilt began to chase away her fear and she sat up in bed. "Okay."

He helped her off the bed and she followed meekly behind him as he led her to Dimitri's study. The closer they got to where Dimitri was waiting the more her breathing increased until she was panting.

"Calm," Maks said in a low voice when they got to the door.

She wanted to tell him to fuck off, but he opened the door and she followed him in, keeping her eyes firmly on the floor. Nervously lacing her fingers together, she waited for someone to say something, but there was only tension-laden silence. Taking a step further into the room, she dared to dart a glance up and really wished she hadn't.

Alex and Dimitri stood right next to each other, about two paces in front of her, watching her with the combined fury of two angry gods. She studied their faces, looking for some kind of compassion, but she may as well have been looking at robots. Nothing came through and her lower lip trembled as Dimitri stared at her with complete dispassion.

"Kneel," Alex said in a dead voice.

She did so without hesitation, going into the slave position with her forehead touching the ground, her arms stretched out before her, and her butt resting back on her heels. It was the most humbling position possible from her, a way to use her body to show her how sorry she was. No one said anything for a moment and she pressed her hands to the carpet so they couldn't see her fingers trembling. Adrenaline flooded her bloodstream and she really, really wanted to run away from the terrible anger directed at her.

Someone moved next to her then Alex said, "Sit up and look at me."

She did as he asked, flinching when her gaze met his. "Yes, Sir."

"Do you have any idea what you did?"

He didn't even give her time to answer, instead tearing into her and giving her a lecture that was so scathing that by the time he was done she was nearly hysterical with tears. Her soul had been shredded by his harsh words, and worse yet, Dimitri hadn't interrupted Alex even once. In fact, Dimitri was sitting behind his desk doing paperwork, totally ignoring her. That only made her cry harder and she tried to apologize again, only to have Alex cut her off.

"I am very disappointed in you. All the things our men do to keep you safe, the constant danger they put themselves in, and you run off. Worse yet, we find you with a messenger from our father? You have no idea how lucky you are that you aren't either dead, or being tortured and gang raped right now."

"Please, Alex, please...I didn't mean any harm."

He crouched before her and surprised her when he pulled her into a hug. "I know you did not, because you are an innocent and would see nothing wrong with going for a walk like a normal woman. But you are no longer living in that world. You belong to us now, and the laws you used to live by no longer apply. If anything had happened to you...it would be like losing the sun again."

The raw pain in his voice reached her through her own messed up emotions and she hugged him tight. She was such a selfish bitch, never even considering what kind of trigger her going missing would be for Alex. There was no question in her mind that he was trying to achieve some kind of absolution to his dead wife by keeping Rya alive. During her brief time in Russia they'd had become friends and she'd scared the hell out of him. That didn't mean she appreciated being lectured, but at least he was giving her a chance to earn his forgiveness.

Alex abruptly released her and stood. "I think you do not understand how badly my father could hurt you. He will not spare you because you are a woman, be assured of that. After all, he tortured his own sons."

Dimitri stood and moved around to the front of his desk and began to take off his suit jacket, then his shirt as well. Alex followed and she soon found herself staring at their bared torsos...their scar-covered bare torsos. As she watched, they cataloged one by one the injuries received at the hands of their father. There were scars across their backs in a pattern of what she thought might be belt marks, as though they had been whipped raw in spots when they were children, long, thin knife scars where salt had been rubbed into the wounds to 'toughen them up'. They pointed to each and every wound and told her in detail how they had received it from different beatings and torture at the hands of their father, an endless list of atrocities stamped into their flesh. She wanted so much to comfort Dimitri and Alex, but she was rooted to the spot by her guilt over making them relive their terrifying past. Dimitri's were the worst by far, but Alex had a large patch of scarred skin on his torso from where he'd had a clothes iron pressed onto his stomach, punishment for losing two girls he'd been ordered to kidnap. Rya's stomach threatened to empty as she stared at that shiny scar, imagining the pain he'd endured.

She said in a choked sob, "Please, please Dimitri. Don't make me hear anymore, you or Alex. My heart is breaking for what you endured and your father is a monster. If he were here right now I'd gut him myself, but he isn't and I'm so sorry I scared you."

Without a word Dimitri put his clothes back on, no longer making any eye contact with her. Alex thawed the slightest bit and slipped his shirt back on, hiding the proof of his father's insanity. "What my father did to us, he would do to you if it benefited him in any way. Except with you it would be worse because you are a woman. My father has special tortures for females."

Her stomach lurched and she placed a hand over her mouth. A hard tremble went through her before a male thigh pressed against her cheek. Without looking she clung to that leg, only realizing when she smelled the fabric that it wasn't Dimitri. Her Master had returned to his seat behind his desk while Alex gently stroked her hair.

"We will not let that happen, little Rya. But you have to help us to protect you."

She released his leg and tried to wipe her tears away. "I understand."

"Good," Alex stepped a pace back, then looked behind her to Maks. "Now you owe your bodyguard an apology. If anything had happened to you Maks' life would be forfeit."

"I'm so sorry," she cried out, then yelped when Maks hauled her up by her hair, leading her over to the couch before he placed her hands onto the back, bending her over so her butt was in the air. "What are you doing? Dimitri?"

Her Master didn't look up, but his jaw clenched and she dropped her head in defeat. After Alex's lecture combined with the knowledge of the torture they'd had to endure made her feel like shit for sneaking away like some spoiled teenager. Without a doubt she hurt the man she loved, deeply, and she wanted to make up for it. Her pride was gone at this point, and at the first burning smack of Maks' hand against her bottom, she cried out.

After ten swats she was trying to dance away from Maks' hand, but he wasn't allowing it.

Dimitri finally looked up and said in English in a bored tone, "You have my permission to spank her bare-assed."

She tried to catch her Master's gaze, but he returned to staring at the papers on his desk, leaving her alone to face her punishment. When Maks lifted her dress and slid her panties down, she didn't resist, instead lifting her feet so he could toss her underwear over to the side. Even though her pussy and ass were bare to the room, there was nothing sexual about it. She'd never been spanked as a punishment before, and she hated how cold, how impersonal it felt. There was no reassurance, no sense that Maks was enjoying this, just anger and pain.

The next slap hurt, really hurt, and she bit her lip,

trying to keep from screaming. She could do this; she would do this. Whatever she had to endure to get Dimitri to forgive her she would do. Her poor Master must have lost his mind when he found out she'd snuck off and she could only imagine all the terrible things he'd thought before she'd been found. Then to find out that his paranoia was justified, that she had been instantly approached by someone that could be considered an enemy, it made her hate herself.

An especially hard slap caught her just right and she bit her lower lip, tasting blood as she choked on a scream.

The brush of her dress being lowered over her abused ass made her suck in a breath.

Dimitri said in a low voice, "Go kneel in the corner facing the wall."

She stumbled over to the nearest corner, kneeling as he'd said and whimpering in discomfort as her tender ass rested on her heels. Her breath came in hitches and she was a heartbeat away from hysterical tears again. Being ignored by Dimitri was the worst; she hated it even more than Alex's lecture and Maks' spanking. At the memory of the look of disappointment in Alex's eyes renewed tears fell and she sucked at her wounded lower lip.

The men behind her talked for a long time in Russian and her mind began to drift, exhaustion pulling at her. She rested her forehead against the wall, the pins and needles in her legs having long ago faded to numbness. Her ass still hurt, but it was a distant pain and she closed her eyes, her breathing becoming more even as she drifted into darkness.

Warmth surrounded her and Rya moaned softly as her sore ass rested on something scratchy. She shifted, turning over on her front and found her cheek resting on a damp, solid chest. Slowly opening her eyes, she found herself in the massive bathtub in Dimitri's bathroom, surrounded by candles and held by her Master. It took a moment for her mind to fully surface from her sleep, but when it did she pushed up out of his arms.

Dimitri made a hushing noise and pulled her back against him, brushing his lips over her temple. "Shhh, easy *zaika moya*."

"I'm so sorry," she whispered and blinked as new tears burned her eyes.

"I know you are." He ran a soothing hand down her back. "You must promise me you'll never do that again. Swear it."

"I swear it." She threw her arms around his neck and hugged him, burying her face against his neck. "I'm so, so sorry, it was selfish and…"

"Rya, it is over. You took your punishment. There will be no more." She cried with relief and slowly relaxed as he continued to pet her. "But why did you do it? Do I not give you everything you need? What can I do to make you happy here?"

"No, no you give me everything I need, I just…I'm used to being alone, to doing whatever I want whenever I want without answering to anyone. I've never been trapped like this before."

"You feel trapped?"

"Yes, but it's not your fault and I'm trying to deal with it."

"I make you feel trapped?"

The hurt in his voice made her lean up and look him in the eyes. "No, no. You never make me feel trapped. This situation does, but you, never. You could lock me up in a room with you for a hundred years and I would never feel trapped. I love you."

He pulled her close and rained kisses on her face. "When I heard that my father had contacted you…Rya you have no idea how badly things could have gone."

"Yeah I do," she said in a shaky voice. "You made sure to tell me, in great detail."

"I am sorry we scared you, but is true. My father, he has potential to do terrible things. I cannot trust him around you."

"That woman that he sent, was that really your nanny?"

"*Da*. I think is his way of showing he meant no harm, my nanny is the gentlest woman in the world, but I will never take you to meet my father."

"Why? Do you really think he'd torture me?"

"If he thought it would benefit him, absolutely." She started to protest and he placed his finger over her lips. "Please, believe me. You never want to get drawn into his schemes. Everything from him has a price, including the ring he gave you."

Searching his face, she then nodded. "I believe you."

Dimitri got a fierce look in his eyes, "I would die without you. When I hear you missing I lost my mind imagining the things that were done to me, the pain I endured, being done to you. Let me love you, Rya, so I can make you feel good with my body when words fail me."

Wanting to soothe the fear, the desperation coming off of him, she leaned in and gave Dimitri a long, gentle kiss that had him at once softening and stiffening against him. He lifted her so that he could suck at her nipples, laving the hard tips then biting them hard enough to sting. She ran her fingers through his hair, encouraging him to bite her harder in a soft whisper, urging him to make her hurt. Oddly enough she still felt like she hadn't paid the price she owed him for scaring the crap out of him and when he bit the mound of her breast almost hard enough to draw blood she screamed and rubbed her pussy against his shaft.

He tilted his hips just enough to push into her and she came undone around him, shivering and crying out his name when he roughly pinched her nipples. His touch was cruel and she loved it, loved every bit of pain he drew from her because the sensation of his thick dick filling her was nothing but pleasure. While he continued to torture her nipples she rode him hard, the water splashing over the sides of the tub. Right before she was ready to come he lifted her off of him and out of the tub.

As soon as he was out he pushed her down so she was on her hands and knees, then knelt behind her and covered her body with his. The feel of him curving over her back, caging her in, surrounding her with his damp warmth, was heaven. He guided his shaft to her entrance and slowly pushed in until she was impossibly full, arching her back to try and alleviate the discomfort of being stuffed with cock. He shifted his hips, just the slightest bit, and she moaned at the sensation of his dick pressing from a new angle.

Delicious chills raced through her as he began to move, her breasts swaying against the rug, her ass smarting from having his weight thrusting against it. She embraced the pain, let it sink into her and moved her hips back to match his strokes. Dimitri leaned up and grasped her hips.

"That's it. Fuck me."

She needed no more encouragement, throwing her hips back at him as she rocked back and forth on her hands and knees, bright ribbons of ecstasy wrapping around her body. He reached beneath her hips and began to tug at her clit. It felt good, really good, and she sank all the way back to the root of his cock, gasping as he brought her closer to orgasm.

"Give it to me," he growled. "I want your

pleasure."

Her pussy clamped down on him and Dimitri had to struggle to pull back, fighting her inner muscles in a way that caused her release to explode in her. As soon as she began to come he started to fuck her hard, really hard. Her whole body convulsed while he thrust into her, gripping her hips firm enough to hurt, that discomfort easily swept away by the contractions tearing through her, rendering her useless. Dimitri wasn't satisfied and he fucked her to orgasm two more times before he finally took his own release, roaring out behind her in a way that made her smile.

When he collapsed on top of her she could barely breathe, and didn't give one shit about it. Dimitri's breath was heavy on the back of her neck, and the occasional aftershock twitched through her nervous system, making one of her arms or legs jerk. He pulled out of her and warm fluid trickled out of her pussy, their combined release saturating the folds of her well-used sex.

She was completely limp when Dimitri carried her back to their bedroom and barely awake when he set her on the mattress. He spread her legs and lay between them, then began to clean himself from her pussy with long sweeps of his talented tongue. Her sex throbbed and even though she felt like it should be impossible, he roused her all over again until she was grinding herself against his face.

"Love this," he whispered before kissing her clit. "Love the taste of me on you. Don't leave me, Rya. Please."

It took a great deal of effort, but she managed to lift her arm enough to run her fingers through his hair. "I'll never leave you, Dimitri. I love you, I will always love you, and that will never change."

He took her again, this time slow and gentle, and

before her final orgasm of the night was even complete she found herself passing out into an exhausted totally satisfied sleep.

Chapter Twenty-Five

Six weeks later

Rya sucked in a quick breath and let it out slowly, counting to ten and trying her hardest not to verbally tear Dimitri's stubborn head off in front of Maks. Her chief bodyguard watched her square off with Dimitri with a highly amused expression, well, highly amused for Maks. The man almost never actually changed his facial features, he always looked arrogant and bored, but after studying him for three weeks, she understood that he was one of those people who hated to reveal anything about themselves. While he was good at masking his emotions, he couldn't hide the occasional flash of humor or warmth that went through his pale green eyes. Like right now. His gaze sparkled with mirth and the faint lines around his mouth deepened while he watched as Rya threw a fit of epic proportions.

Smoothing her hands down her cardinal red silk dress she took a deep breath and looked up at Dimitri. "I've been out in public with you six times and nothing happened. I can't stay in this building all day, every day. Don't get me wrong, this place is beyond awesome, I mean I totally dig everything that you've given me, but I can't be trapped here. I need to get certified in nursing, take classes, do everything that I have to do so I can work in Russia. I need to do my job, it's...it is so important to me and I know that I am here for a purpose, aside from loving you. I feel like I've gone crazy. I need to ground myself in my work. It keeps me sane and you can't be here with me every day, Dimitri. You have an evil empire to run and I hate being stuck inside when you're not here."

Maks was no longer laughing, instead giving her a surprisingly encouraging look as if to tell her she was doing well.

With a long sigh Dimitri rubbed his face and she could see how much the idea of her leaving the apartment without him terrified him. She took a step forward and laid her hands on his chest, stroking the soft material of his pale blue dress shirt. "Honey, I know how much you want to keep me safe. I'm not stupid and I won't be easily caught. And I've been so good. Please. Your men are the best and they'll keep me alive. Maks is pretty fond of his dick, as are most of the women in Moscow, so he would be most upset if something happened to me and you gelded him."

Now, Maks didn't look so encouraging. In fact, he looked like he wanted to take her over his lap and spank her. Dimitri actually allowed Maks to spank the hell out of her two weeks ago when she gave a homeless man some money in Moscow while she waited for Dimitri to finish speaking to an associate outside of the restaurant where they'd just had dinner. The homeless man had been panhandling nearby, and she approached him without thought, moving out of the protective shelter of the restaurant's awning and crossing the street to where he sat on the frozen concrete in just a coat. She had no idea how dangerous that was and ignored Maks, right up to the point where they were suddenly mobbed by homeless people wanting money. When they got home Dimitri allowed Maks to spank her ass while he lectured her on taking her safety more seriously.

It was a lesson she hadn't forgotten and didn't want to repeat.

"Is too soon, Rya."

"When will it not be too soon? Do the women of

the other Bratvas live like this? Were they born never to be allowed to live? It must have driven them crazy. If I ever meet any women of the Boldin Bratva I'm going to give them a hug because this fucking sucks."

"You want to leave me?" Dimitri asked in a cold voice.

That was so the wrong thing for him to say to her at this point. Dimitri was a master at manipulating people, and over the past six weeks she'd clued into some of his tactics, like using guilt to try and get her to do what he wanted. Though she had to admit, he did seem honestly worried that she was going to leave him at the drop of a hat. They really had to work on Dimitri's trust issues before he worried himself into an early grave.

"Listen, buster," Maks winced at her bitchy tone and she ignored him as she continued to lay into Dimitri. "You are stuck with me. Am I clear? You brought me over here, made me fall in love with you, and I gave up my entire world to be with you. I'm not walking out in a huff anytime soon. I'll beat *your* ass before I let that happen. We're in this for the long haul and I expect you to fight just as hard for us as I do."

Dimitri gave her a smile filled with love and pride. "You are so fierce. It is sexy."

Maks said something in Russian that had Dimitri laughing. When she cupped her Master's cock and gave him a small squeeze he stopped. "You think I'm cute, do you?"

"No," he said with a slow smile. "I think you are adorable."

She squeezed him, hard and he liked it, the kinky bastard. "You know, there are people out there that fear me. I've seen how your bodyguards get all scared around me. Maks is the only one who doesn't look at me as if he's terrified of me."

Maks burst out laughing and she mentally gave herself a pat on the back. Getting Maks to laugh was hard, but worth it. The guy had a great laugh. Dimitri made a growling noise that made her instantly wet. Hell. They'd had sex so much that he had her well-trained to be ready for him at a moment's notice. That dark heat she loved so much had entered his gaze and she knew he was going to make her do something in front of Maks. Part of her found the idea hot, but another part of her was kind of uneasy about doing anything in front of the strawberry blonde bodyguard. There was something almost fragile about Maks' friendship with her and she didn't want to hurt him.

Dimitri bent down to whisper something to her, but she cut him off before he could speak. "Master, please don't make me do anything in front of Maks that would make him unhappy. He's my friend and I don't want him to hurt."

Gripping her ass possessively, the expensive silk making her feel naked beneath his touch, he smiled. "Such a good heart. Rest assured, *zaika moya*, I would never be that cruel. I know what it feels like for Maks to be alone. Is terrible. I want to give him something to think about. Something beautiful. Remind him he is alive."

"Well, when you put it that way..." she frowned up at him. "Wait, you're not making this about sex. You, Sir, need to learn to express yourself in some manner other than fucking me mindless. I need to go back to school. To at least leave the house."

Dimitri stroked her cheek and she moaned softly, cursing herself for being so damn weak around him. "Tomorrow, why don't you go shopping with Gia? She will be selecting things for her business and asked if you would like to join her. I believe she will be looking at antique pieces tomorrow. You go with her and buy things for our home. Things that make you feel good. I want you to be happy here, Rya, more than anything. So against my best judgment I will let you go, but I ask that you please be careful."

Making a soothing noise she eased down to her knees before him and swiftly unbuckled his belt using only her mouth. Next she made quick work of the button of his pants, then pulled down the zipper with her teeth. With a soft oath Dimitri jerked his black boxer briefs down and freed himself for her. Okay, so maybe she was a bit of a hypocrite about saying Dimitri used sex instead of words to display his emotions, but sometimes the only way to properly thank a man was to suck his dick. Crude, but true. He was hard, thick, and deliciously warm against her lips as she kissed the slit of his cock. She adored giving him oral pleasure, loved to bring him such gratification and joy. Turning him on aroused her greatly, and the naughty knowledge that Maks was watching them only added to her need to drink Dimitri down.

With a low groan her Master began to fuck her mouth and she relaxed her throat, taking him easily now that he'd shown her how to let him throat fuck her. Every once in a while she'd still gag, but he seemed to like those noises and it always made his dick twitch. She laced her hands behind her back, allowing him to use only her mouth as he wished. Sometimes he liked to do that, only fuck her mouth, not allowing her to touch him and somehow making her even more eager to please him. At this moment in time she existed only for her Master, and his soft praise for her efforts made her feel completely satisfied.

"That's it, *zaika moya*, suck it how I like it. Open your mouth for me, wide, good girl. Now seal your lips around my cock and *suck*."

She did as he commanded and almost right away he began to come in her mouth. She swallowed every trace of him and sucked harder, trying to drain him dry. Dimitri tensed and let out a sound that was a raw mixture of pain and pleasure. "Enough."

Panting, she released him with a kiss and wiggled on her heels, her pussy soaking wet and her thong sticking uncomfortably to her body. Hell, her inner thighs were wet and there was no way either man could miss her nipples sticking out through the silk of her top. She could smell her arousal in the air and knew without a doubt that Maks could as well. Dimitri tucked himself away and smiled down at her.

"I have to go out for a bit."

"What? Will you be back soon?"

"No. And you will not orgasm until you return safely from shopping with Gia tomorrow."

"What?" He gave her a stern look and she clenched her hands into fists and tried to swallow her anger. "Yes, Master."

Both men chuckled and Dimitri crouched before her. He cupped the back of her neck and brought their foreheads together. "If you mouth off to me in front of Maks I will make you suck his cock. You may, of course, safeword out, but if you keep being brat, I will give you something better to do with your tongue. Am I clear?"

"Crystal clear," she whispered.

"You will be good?"

"I'll be good."

"Promise?"

"Yes, Master." She gave him an impulsive kiss. "I only want your cock."

He chuckled. "Charming, but will not get you out of your punishment if you continue to misbehave."

Abruptly he stood and offered her a hand up. She took it and wrapped her arms around him, cuddling close as he hugged her back. "I love you so much. Thank you."

"*Dorogaya*, I will do anything for you. Even if it drives me crazy, I do it."

She sighed and wiped away a tear. "Thank you."

Dimitri grumbled and glanced at his watch. "I wish I could stay, but I must leave."

Her heart rate accelerated as she thought about the man she loved leaving the safety of their luxurious fortress. "Be safe, please."

He caressed her face. "The way you feel? That worry for me? Is how I feel at the thought of you leaving my sight. Is not good, is it?"

"No, it's not good." She sighed and took a step back. "Okay. Go do your super villain stuff. Have fun storming the castle."

Laughing, he nodded to Maks before giving her another brief kiss. "Adorable."

She scowled at him as he left, but as soon as the door closed her shoulders slumped.

To her surprise Maks spoke up. "Your love for him is real."

She narrowed her eyes at him. "Excuse me?"

He shrugged, his thin lips pursed. "At first, I was not sure. I have never seen Dimitri happy with a woman before. It was very odd for me to see him so openly love someone. Trust me when I say that his love for you is just as real. I know he has probably not told you this, but Dimitri and Alex saved my life. I was born and raised in a brothel owned by another Bratva. Was bad and I ran away when I was eight. When Alex found me eating garbage in an alley near one of his father's businesses he took pity on me and saved me from a terrible fate. Together with Dimitri they made sure I got an education, that I was safe and warm. I swore then that I would give my life for either of them, and now I extend that vow to you. It is my privilege to guard you, Rya DeLuca, because you are a good woman. You have no idea how rare that is in my world. No idea of the filth that clings to those of us that do terrible things."

That was the most she'd ever heard Maks speak at once and she stared at him for a long moment. "Thank you."

Giving her one of his rare smiles, he inclined his head in her direction. "You are welcome."

Toeing off her heels, she made her way to the kitchen. It was a little after lunch and she was hungry. The kitchen had a fantastic view of Moscow and she loved the almost French Country feel to the space. It was exactly what she wanted, but it felt kind of sterile. Perhaps tomorrow at the market she'd find something to bring some life to the space, maybe some baskets to put on top of the tall cabinets, or some whimsical glass work to place on the window sill over the sink. The need to put her stamp on the home filled her and she realized that she was allowing herself to put down roots.

Glancing over at Maks, she lifted her chin. "You hungry?"

His lips twitched and he nodded. "I could eat."

"How about some grilled cheese?"

"Whatever you are making, I will eat. Especially if you bake. You bake very, very well."

She laughed at the hungry gleam in his eyes. "Okay, I get the hint. I'll make more of the cookies that you like."

"The snickerdoodles?"

"Yes." She laughed as she buttered the bread, liking how exotic everything sounded when said in a Russian accent. "Who would have thought the scariest men in the world had such sweet tooths. I make at least six dozen cookies a week but you guys go through them before they're even cool from the oven."

"Yes," Maks said in a quiet voice that struck her as odd, then winked. "We cannot wait to eat you."

She shook a piece of cheese at him. "No flirting. I know you can't help it, you flirt with anything female, but you will not use your wiles on me, Mr. Maks. I've seen your trail of broken hearts."

He blinked at her in surprise. "What?"

Turning on flame beneath the pan she'd taken out, she looked over her shoulder at him. "You think I don't know how to do searches on the Internet? Hello, I've got nothing better to do most of the day than to do research and I've seen some pictures of you with your women that made me blush. PDA much?"

"PDA?"

"Public Display of Affection. It means like kissing in public. Or in your case, getting a blow job in an alley from three cute blondes at once. No wonder you were too distracted to notice you were being filmed."

"I knew I was being filmed. Was part of...job to make sure of it." To her surprise he actually blushed. "Those women, they do not matter. They were nothing but tools to use to get to my target."

"Is that supposed to be endearing? Are you proud that you treat sex like some kind of casual function?"

His cheeks heated even redder and he took a deep breath. "It is bad, I know. I never make a promise to keep any woman I am with. They know I am only good for one night."

She shook her head and flipped the sandwiches, the comforting smell of grilled cheese easing her heart. "Look, it's none of my business, but you do know the difference between fucking and making love, right? Have you ever made love?"

"No."

Giving him an arch look she said, "No?"

"No. When I make love to a woman she will be the only woman I ever make love with. When I find her I will not leave her or let her leave me."

"And you'll know after one night if she's the woman?"

"Absolutely."

"Wow." She flipped his sandwich on to a plate and slid it down the pale granite counter to him. "That's...different."

"Tell me, did you not know after your first night with Dimitri that he was the one you were meant to be with?"

She took a bite of her sandwich, hoping he didn't notice the way her cheeks heated. "Maybe."

"Maybe?" He snorted.

"Fine, okay. I knew he was something special right away."

"I have never had that feeling for a woman. Why lie to her and pretend she may be the one if I don't believe it?"

"You sure you're giving these women a chance? I mean one night isn't much."

"Ah, one night having sex. I will usually date a woman for a bit before I go to bed with her."

"You are one busy boy, aren't you?"

He shrugged. "When time allows."

"Am I putting a dent in your social calendar?"

Shaking his head, he gave her one of his barely there smiles. "Yes, but I will survive."

"So do you think I'm stupid for wanting to leave? I mean, at least I'm safe here."

"I think it hurts your soul to be trapped. You need to be free, even if it is dangerous. But don't worry, little rabbit, your wolf has his pack protecting you."

The smile he gave her was downright predatory and she tried to ignore the tingle of arousal. "Well, okay then. I'm going to go do...stuff."

With his laughter echoing behind her Rya went up to her bedroom and slammed the door behind her, pissed off at Dimitri for doing orgasm denial with her because right now she was dripping wet and horny. The banter with Maks did nothing to cool her down. She was embarrassed that she was now having naughty thoughts about sucking him off. Damn Dimitri! He knew exactly how to manipulate her. He was like a mad sexual genius, able to push her boundaries with little to no resistance on her part. She wasn't sure if that thought was more arousing or scary and vowed that next time she got Dimitri in bed it would be time for a little payback.

Rya was in seventh heaven the next day wandering through a massive climate-controlled warehouse on the western edge of Moscow filled with all kinds of antique furniture. They were looking through a private estate collection but she felt as if she was walking through a museum. Everywhere she glanced there were pieces of European furniture from the seventeenth and eighteenth centuries mixed with assorted odds and ends. Gia's two bodyguards were walking ahead with her while Rya trailed behind, listening to the tall, imposing Russian woman in charge of the estate sale rattle off details about the pieces they were looking at in clipped English. Maks and Chen, Rya's bodyguards for the day, constantly scanned the room in a most disconcerting manner, reminding her of how vulnerable she was. For the entire ride over in their armored motorcade, between Ivan and Dimitri's paranoia about their safety she was surprised they didn't take a tank, she'd been worried that any second they'd be attacked by some crazy rival Bratva, but the trip had been boringly normal. Well, as boring as traffic ever got in Moscow.

She was starting to debate the wisdom of being

here when her gaze landed on the most beautiful writing desk she'd ever seen. With a soft sigh she walked over to the desk and examined the detailed inlay work and the beautiful flowing lines of the desk. The front was shut and she looked over her shoulder to the sales woman. "Does it open?"

"Oh yes. It is a mechanical desk, with many surprises. Watch."

The woman proceeded to show Rya all the different secret drawers and hiding places, ingenious little spots where no one would think to look for a message. It was such an astonishing piece of furniture and she gently stroked the curve of the desk, admiring the mother of pearl and onyx inlay. "How much is it?"

Before the woman could respond Maks interrupted them in Russian. She glared at him, but he ignored her and pulled the saleswoman over to the side. A few moments later the woman left, beaming as Rya glared at Maks and Chen accompanied the saleswoman to the office at the back of the warehouse. "What did you just do?"

"Dimitri ordered me to buy what you like. You love that desk don't you? I can see in your eyes when you look at it."

"Yes," she admitted in what even she knew was a sullen voice. Giving herself a mental shake, she said, "Do I even want to know the price?"

"No, you do not. Be happy that you are rescuing a beautiful piece of art from someone who would not appreciate it. You love it, there is no greater compliment to a craftsman than that."

She crossed her arms and gave him a searching look. "You sound like you know what you're talking about. Do you make furniture?"

He laughed and shook his head. "No, I make guns, sniper rifles to be exact. Is not art, but I still like to see them go to people who appreciate them."

Ahead of them, Gia called out, "Rya, come here."

She gave Maks an exasperated look. "I'm not done talking to you about Dimitri buying me random things. I want to decide what I want, Maks, not you or Dimitri."

Maks ignored her, looking over his shoulder to see where Chen and the saleswoman had disappeared to. With an exasperated sigh, Rya walked over to where Gia stood next to a massive wood cabinet surrounded by rolled up carpets in the back corner of the room. As she approached she noticed something odd about Gia and it was only when she was close enough to see her clearly that she noticed Gia was trembling. Rya's heart raced as she looked for Gia's bodyguards and found they had disappeared.

Gia shook her head and whispered, "Rya, run."

Someone swore from beside the cabinet and Rya moved forward enough to see two men with guns pointed at her and Gia. "Fuck."

The men stepped out and the older one with a heavy face and scarred knuckles gave her a quick up and down look. "You are Rya DeLuca."

She considered lying, but his friend had his gun trained on Gia. "I am. You don't want her. I'm Rya."

The men stepped carefully around Gia. "You will come with us. Ms. Lopez will not be hurt if you cooperate."

Panic roared through her and before she could totally freak out Maks said, "Don't touch her. She is under protection of many Bratvas."

The man with the gun on Gia said something in rapid fire Russian and argued with Maks for a few moments before the older man next to Rya spoke up in English. "Ms. DeLuca, you will not be hurt if you come with us. I promise. Someone wishes to speak with you and then you will be returned, unharmed, to

Dimitri. If you fight us, people will be hurt."

"Who wants to see me?"

"Mr. Novikov. He said to remind you of the ring, even if you do not wear it."

She took a step back and came up against Maks. He settled his hands lightly on her shoulders. Shit, Dimitri's father wanted to meet her. She wasn't sure if she was relieved or even more terrified. Maks held her shoulders tight, rubbing his thumbs on her arms, and that helped her get ahold of herself. Okay, they were going to take her, that was a given. She wouldn't risk Gia and Maks' lives, they were too precious. Still, she'd try to stall as long as she could.

Looking up at Maks, she whispered, "Tell Dimitri I'm sorry."

"What?"

Before he could stop her she moved away from him and to the older man's side. "Where are you going to take me?"

The man glared down at her, but his gun was no longer pointing at anyone. She looked up at him, letting him know that she wasn't fucking around. Hopefully, if she could get them to stand around and talk, it would give Maks or Chen, wherever he was, time to figure out how to get them out of this mess. "I can either go with you willingly, or you can fight me. I'm guessing that you have orders not to harm me, or Gia, because right about now you should have smacked us around a bit to get us to do what you want. So let's stop messing around. Tell me where I'm going and I might go with you. Don't tell me and I'll make you fight me."

The older man laughed at her and she swallowed hard, hoping she hadn't overplayed her hand. When he reached out and grabbed her by her hair she screamed and drew back her arm. Maks yelled out for her to stop, but before she could second guess herself she caught the man under his chin with an upper cut that hurt the fuck out of her hand, but sent the bigger man stumbling back. She hissed and shook her fist out, but looked over at the man with his gun to Gia's head, trying to figure out how to distract him long enough for Maks to take him out.

"Let go of her!"

The man said something to Maks in Russian. He responded with obvious anger and the two men argued for a solid minute before she took a step between them, ready to settle this shit.

Unfortunately, she'd forgotten about the older man and a piece of cloth with some kind of stinky fumes on it was placed over her face, she realized her little gamble to stay here as long as possible had backfired. She struggled, and the last thing she remembered was someone hitting her on the side of her head, hard.

Chapter Twenty-Six

Rya batted away at something annoying hovering around her nose. She managed to finally shove it away and opened her eyes, but the world was blurry. Taking another deep breath, she forced her scattered thoughts to come together and tried to remember where she was and why her face hurt. This time she was able to focus and found a grim faced man in his late thirties dressed in a tuxedo bent over her. He had deep hazel green eyes and dark red hair with a flushed complexion. Tattoos showed all over his hands and she sucked in a quick breath. She was in so much trouble.

The man gave her an anxious look. "Are you okay?"

His English had a heavy Irish accent to it instead of Russian and she stared at him in surprise. "Yes, who are you?"

"First let me apologize for the lengths we had to go to in order to arrange this meeting, but it is very important and Dimitri is stubborn. My name is Peter and I promise you, we mean you no harm."

She glanced around surprised to find herself in a luxurious fairy tale princess bedroom that looked like it hadn't been used in a while. A musty smell hung in the air, the scent of a room that was cleaned, but not lived in. After sitting up, she looked around further and gaped at the beauty surrounding her. Everywhere she looked there was exquisite furniture, elegant watercolor paintings, and lovely blown glass art. Without a doubt this room was meant for a woman. Not only was it done in shades of pink, but it was very comfortable—in the way only a woman would enjoy.

Mystified as to where the hell she was, she rubbed her head where she'd been hit. "Where am I?"

"Has Dimitri spoken about his father, Jorg?"

At the mention of Dimitri's dad her stomach clenched. "Maybe."

"You're a bad liar," he said with a chuckle.

"Look, just tell me why I'm here. Dimitri is going to lose his damn mind and I don't want him getting hurt."

"I happen to agree with you. It is refreshing not to deal with hysterics. You're here because Dimitri's father wishes to meet you. He's been trying to see you since you arrived in Russia, but Dimitri has forbidden it."

"And this surprises you how?"

"His father is dying."

"And?"

He grinned at her. "You are a ruthless little thing aren't you? No wonder Dimitri loves you so much."

"Um...thanks?"

"Please, come meet Jorg, Dimitri's father. It is his most desperate wish that his sons find happiness before he dies. Dimitri has been quite...adamant about not seeing his father, but it is vital that he comes here. I'm afraid that we have to use you as bait in order to make that happen."

"Awesome." She carefully slid off the other side of the bed and groaned as her head ached. "Can I get some Tylenol or something for my head? He really clocked me good."

Peter stood and came quickly to her side. She flinched when he reached for her, but he made a soothing, almost humming noise. "Easy now. I just want to make sure you don't need a doctor."

"And if I did, you'd take me to one?"

Peter grinned. "I might at that. Look, the sooner you talk to the old man the sooner you'll be returned to Dimitri, unharmed. Trust me when I say I'm not among Jorg's greatest fans, but you don't want him for an enemy. Keep that in mind."

After being led to an old fashioned kitchen that was well cared for, she sipped at her cup of tea as she took what she hoped was aspirin. While she had no idea what kind of building she was in, it felt like a castle. Everything was lush, opulent, and over-the-top expensive, yet tasteful with a sense of great age. She certainly felt out of place in her modest navy suede skirt and matching jacket with a turquoise blue silk blouse beneath. At least she wore comfortable black leather boots. This morning she'd thought she looked put together in this outfit, now she wished she'd worn a pair of jeans or maybe a suit of armor.

She set her tea cup aside and followed Peter when he led her past a group of maids who looked to be in their late fifties and sixties. The women spoke in excited whispers as they passed. Rya kept her eyes forward and tried to pretend that this was all normal, that she was used to being abducted by her boyfriend's dad.

No biggie.

Even before she reached the rooms where Dimitri's father was staying she knew she was approaching a sickroom. The familiar smells that she associated with her hospice tinged the air and she took a deep breath then let it out slowly, chagrined that the hospital odors relaxed her. She didn't associate hospitals with bad things and she spent so much time there that this almost smelled like home to her.

Before Peter opened the door to room, he looked over at her and all humor was gone from his face. He held her gaze and said in a low voice, "You will be respectful to Mr. Novikov. Do you understand me? If you love Dimitri you will do nothing to upset his father. He is lucid most of the time, but every once in a while he slips and when he does his temper flares. You will not fight with him. It would be a big mistake and complicate matters."

"I understand. Go in, make nice, get the fuck out of here. Got it."

He made a frustrated noise and opened the door. "Lucky for you Mr. Novikov has a similar taste in spirited women as his sons. He may enjoy your candor. Just don't be stupid."

Rya lifted her chin and strolled into the room, stunned by what lay on the other side of the door. The room itself was massive, with at least thirteen-foot ceilings and art covering every inch of wall space. And not just any art, wonderful paintings done in a variety of styles. She gazed around the room in awe, her eyes unable to focus on one object, overwhelmed by the splendor. After a long moment her gaze trailed over to the massive cream marble fireplace against the far wall and the very utilitarian hospital bed near it. A withered man watched her from the bed and as she stared into his sunken eyes he smiled at her. He was completely bald, even his eyebrows and eyelashes were gone, and she sucked in a soft breath at the obvious signs of the cancer ravaging his body.

He said in surprisingly good English, "You look like my first wife."

She looked over to Peter for guidance but he seemed as baffled as she was. "Thank you. Was she Alex's mother?"

"Come closer, little rabbit. That is what my son calls you, yes?"

She flushed and nodded, trying to keep in mind that this was a terrible man who had done dreadful things despite the fact that he was obviously on death's door. "It is."

"And what do you call him?"

"My wolf."

He cackled with delight, then coughed heavily and brought his oxygen mask to his face. In reaching for it he almost knocked over the picture of a beautiful toddler dressed in a bright jumper with red gold curls and the Novikov gunmetal grey eyes. With a trembling hand he straightened the picture before turning to look at her again. "Yes, I have heard that you have brought out the predator in my Dimitri. He has become most savage in his defense of you."

Unsure what to say, she kept her silence. There was a gleam in Mr. Novikov's eyes she didn't like, that small hint of insanity she was used to seeing in her older patients as dementia set in. Things had the potential to go really, really bad; she had to be smart and keep her temper. "Why am I here, Mr. Novikov? What do you want from me?"

Okay, maybe that wasn't exactly super polite, but she hadn't told him to fuck off.

Mr. Novikov smiled at her, his gums had receded in an alarming manner. "You are here because I need some answers from you."

Her heart raced and she pressed her hands to her skirt to try and hide their shaking. "What are they?"

"Did you really kill the man who tried to kidnap you?"

"I did."

He lowered the oxygen mask and slowly nodded. "How did it feel?"

"What?"

"When you killed him, how did it feel?"

"I'm not talking about this."

He cackled. "Yes, you are. You will answer my questions, little rabbit, or I will not let you go. I won't hurt you, but I will keep you in a cage until your wolf comes to rescue you."

She gingerly rubbed the tender bump on the side of her head. "Yeah, sorry if I don't believe you thanks to this nice goose egg on my skull. Since I've already been hurt, forgive me if I doubt that you care about what happens to me as long as you get your way."

Anger suffused his face, turning his skeletal features into something horrifying. "You have been harmed?"

Peter stepped up behind her. "Looks like Veldor hit her on the temple to knock her out."

"What?"

Mr. Novikov began to scream in Russian and she stared in shock as he seemed to fill with energy, a brief hint of the man he'd once been shining through the shell of his fading body. Peter began to rush her out of the room but Mr. Novikov roared, "Stop!"

They both froze and exchanged a fearful expression before turning back to the madman on his death bed. His chest heaved and sweat made his sallow skin shine. He pointed at her with one trembling finger. "You have my protection, Rya. The Novikov Bratva will protect you, all of us and those loyal to us. You have my word."

With that, he slumped back into the bed and grabbed his oxygen mask. A couple of older women in medical garb came in and Rya watched them tend to their patient for a moment before Peter hauled her out of the room. His phone rang and he answered it in Russian. After a minute of conversation, he was pale as snow and by the time they reached the hallway they were practically running. She was able to keep up in her boots but by the time Peter slowed down she was out of breath as he ended his call.

"What the hell is going on?"

Peter looked at her, really looked at her, then slowly smiled. "Mr. Novikov likes you."

"That's a good thing? He seemed pretty pissed

when we left."

"He was angry that Veldor harmed you. Mr. Novikov knows this will enrage Dimitri and he may never give Mr. Novikov a chance to make amends."

"All of this was because Dimitri's dad wants to apologize to him?" She shook her head and followed Peter through the mansion, taking in rooms where the furniture was covered with drop cloths. "Where are we?"

"The Novikov family estate." Peter glanced over at her. "Once Mr. Novikov dies, this estate goes to Dimitri and Alex. If I was a betting man, I believe Dimitri will want to live at the summer home on the estate."

"What?" She glanced around and took in the massive space. "Is this the summer home?"

"No, this is the winter home." He stopped and pulled his phone out. "One moment."

While he spoke in Russian she wandered down the hallway, looking at the different portraits on the walls. They seemed to be of the same man as he aged, starting out with a portrait where he was an infant in a bassinet fit for a king, all the way there where he stared out of the painting in full armor, the lines around his face deep, but his gaze was still fierce. She lingered there, seeing hints of Dimitri in the man's features.

She was jerked from her examination of the portrait when Peter grabbed her arm. "Can you run?"

"Why?"

"Because Dimitri is about to shoot his way onto the compound and I need you to stop the bloodshed."

"Fuck, give me your phone and call Dimitri."

He handed it to her as they walked swiftly through the home and it went to voicemail. Pissed, she called it again, and again. By the time she called him for the fourth time Dimitri picked up and shouted something in Russian.

"Ouch, that was my fucking ear you just blasted," she yelled into the phone. "Damn."

"Rya?"

"Yes, it's me, I'm fine. Stop whatever crazy Rambo bullshit you're about to do."

He sounded frantic in a way she'd never heard before as he said, "Why do you sound out of breath? Have you been harmed?"

"I'm out of breath because I'm running through your ungodly huge family mansion trying to get outside before you start shooting. And I'm in boots that were not made for running, so if you could just not kill anyone until I get there, that would be sweet."

"You are okay," he said with an audible sigh of relief. "Give phone to Peter."

She did and Peter slowed down to a walk, nodding and speaking rapidly in Russian before handing the phone back to Rya. "Hello?"

"Stay with me, talk to me. I need to hear your voice as I come into this place that I swore I would never return to."

"Okay, well, um I bought a desk today. Or maybe you bought it. Either way, I got you a new desk."

"Tell me about it."

She rattled through the details of the desk trying to remember what the sales lady had said about it while Peter led her to a gracious library with beautiful green and burgundy carpets and cream walls accented in gold. A fire burned in the fireplace and the whole room had a wonderful feel to it. Above the fireplace hung a picture of a woman with her hair piled atop her head wearing a sumptuous old fashioned gold dress. She had pale blonde hair and what must be the signature Novikov eyes, silver rimmed in black, captured by an artist hundreds of years ago.

Turning look at the picture, Rya said, "Dimitri, does everyone in your family have your grey eyes?"

"Why you ask?"

"Well, I've seen a bunch of portraits here and it's kind of eerie to see so many people with your eyes."

"You are in library, right? So you see image of blonde woman above the fireplace."

She smiled. "Yep. She's beautiful."

"Is my great, great, great, great aunt Anastasia. She was the third daughter and ran off to join convent when she found out she was betrothed to a man much older than her. He went after her and they ended up falling in love, but not before he had to kidnap her from her convent."

"Wow, your family history is amazing." She sighed, imagining the smiling woman in the picture being taken from her safe, virginal bed at the convent. If Dimitri's ancestors were anything like him, she never stood a chance.

The door across the room opened and Dimitri stormed in. She threw Peter his phone and ran across the room to Dimitri, jumping up into his arms as she began to cry. All the pent up fear and anger came pouring out as he held her tight and she tried to keep from sobbing while she clung to him. He was here and as long as he was holding her she was safe.

"Are you hurt? Why you cry?"

"No, no I'm okay." She kissed his cheek. "You're here, I'm okay. I was just scared."

"*Zaika moya*, I am so sorry you were frightened. Is inexcusable."

"I'm okay, really I am. Just...just hold me for a minute, okay. Give me a second to get my shit together."

He cradled her to his chest and she sighed, snuggling close. "Thank you."

"Your woman is very brave," Peter said in a low

voice from across the room. "I'm sorry it had to be like this Dimitri."

"What are you doing here?" Dimitri snarled in English. "Does Alex know you are here?"

Peter replied in Russian and the more he spoke the tenser Dimitri got.

Her man said something Russian that sounded menacing. She reached up and cupped his cheek. "Hey, please don't be mad at Peter. He kept me safe."

Dimitri frowned and turned her head to the side, examining her temple before sucking in a harsh breath. When he spoke his voice vibrated with rage. "Who did that to you?"

Peter spoke up and Veldor's name was said a few times. Instead of freaking out, Dimitri quieted and nodded a few times before looking back at her. "He will not bother you again."

The final way he said that kind of scared her, but she had enough to deal with at the moment. "Can we leave, please?"

"Not yet. I must speak with my father or he will keep taking you until I do." He cupped her chin and lifted her face to his. "Do you want to wait here while I talk to my father, or do you want to come with me?"

Though the idea of going anywhere near that crazy old bastard frightened her, she reached out and took his hand. "With you. Always with you.

Chapter Twenty-Seven

Dimitri strode down the hallway of his father's wing. Things hadn't changed much in the four years since he'd been here last and he wondered if his blood still stained the floors in one of the basement holding rooms. A fine layer of dust seemed to have settled over everything and he wondered if his father even had the rooms freshened anymore, of if they were rotting away just like their current owner. Dimitri's mother had taken pride in keeping the Novikov homes updated and cared for and it would have hurt her heart to see their current state of neglect.

The only solace he could offer himself was that these walls would be standing long after his father was in the ground.

Rya jerked to a halt behind him and he turned back, finding her staring out the window. "Holy shit."

Wondering what had caught her attention, he saw that her gaze rested on the Summer Home sitting on the edge of the lake. It was a beautiful palace, constructed in the 1700s with fanciful towers and balconies designed to catch the cool breeze from the big lake. Great sweeping dual stair cases flanked the front entrance and an elaborate fountain, now dormant for the season, sat between the stairs. Only a few lights burned on the main floor, illuminating a few squares of glass in the slowly falling dusk.

"What is that?" Rya asked with wonder in her voice.

He ran his finger down her cheek, avoiding the bruise spreading over her temple and on the side of her face. "The Summer Home. When that bastard dies it will belong to us. I would like to live there for at least part of the year. It is a beautiful home with much history and where we lived when my mother was alive. I have many happy memories of my mother and sister there."

She bit her lower lip and looked up at him. He could tell by her expression that this idea did not please her. "Dimitri…"

"No, we will talk about this later. Come."

He held her hand again and led her back to his father's room, his nose scrunching as the stink of death reached him. For a moment he stood before the closed doors, his heart racing as he tried to get his mind into the right place for dealing with his father. At one time Dimitri had worshiped his father, had thought he was a great man, but now his gut churned at the thought of seeing the monster who had so casually ordered his torture in the very home he'd grown up in all because he tried to keep two innocent young girls from dying.

Rya squeezed his hand, hard. "You don't need to do this."

He looked over at her, studying her face, her beautiful golden eyes and let out a pent up breath. "Yes I do. I do this for us."

She tried to protest, but he'd already opened the door. Normally, they would have been locked, but without a doubt his father knew he was coming. Not only because Peter would have called ahead, but because he would have been seen on the surveillance system set up throughout the home. As Dimitri stepped into what had once been his step-mother's suite a pang of sorrow hit him. Though he'd never met Alex's mother, both he and his brother had spent a lot of time in this room, reading her books, looking at the pictures of her family, and basically helping

Alex feel some connection to his mother.

The heavy indigo blue brocade curtains had been drawn over the windows and a fire blazed in the hearth, but the rest of the room was dimly lit. He looked all around the open space, noting how many of his father's favorite pieces of art had been crammed into the room, but he didn't see Olga, Alex's mother's picture hanging over the mantle and briefly wondered if his father loved the Monet that currently hung there more than he loved his first wife.

People milled around, nurses, bodyguards, and a group of his father's advisors. He looked at them first, silently letting them know that they would pay for their part in taking his woman. While he wasn't foolish enough to wage war on his father, the men standing at his side and looming over his sickbed like vultures waiting to swoop in for the kill would know his wrath. One of the vultures in particular, Gravel, made him want to stride across the room and snap the old man's neck. Gravel was one of his father's most trusted enforcers, a cruel man who only respected those with a greater propensity for violence than even Jorg possessed. Four years ago, Gravel was the one who'd been in charge of torturing Dimitri for information on the Boldin twins and Dimitri owed him much suffering.

Gravel looked away and nervously licked his thick lips.

When Dimitri finally looked into his father's eyes he was surprised at the open joy he saw there and shocked at how bad Jorg looked. The last time Dimitri had seen his father two years ago he was ill, but still robust. Now the cancer that was slowly killing Jorg had almost won and Dimitri could see death hovering around the wizened old man. It took him a moment to process the changes, but once he was in control of himself and had pushed away the annoying pity that tried to take residence in his heart, he stared directly into his father's eyes.

"If you ever touch Rya again I will end you."

Everyone gasped, but Jorg gave that horrible, cackling laugh that Dimitri hated so much. In Russian Jorg said, "Good. I love that bloodthirsty streak you've developed. But do not worry, she is under my protection."

Baffled, Dimitri stared at his father and drew Rya closer to him, aware of her confused look but too focused on what was being said to reassure her. "Your protection? Why would you do that?"

"You mean why would I give Rya my protection, and not Jessica?" He sneered at Dimitri.

"Yes."

"Because Jessica was too weak, too gentle for the life of a Bratva leader's wife. She would have been quickly killed. I was saving her."

Striving to control his anger, Dimitri said in a low voice, "Saving her? She was killed anyway. Maybe if she had your protection she would still live and you would be able to love your granddaughter instead of visiting their empty grave."

Jorg laughed and Dimitri had to grip his hands into fists to keep from launching himself at his father. How dare he mock Alex's pain at the loss of Jessica. "You are so arrogant, so sure of yourself. How I wish I could see your face when you learn the truth."

Confused by his father's rambling, and concerned by his father's increasing struggles to draw a breath, he shook his head. "You aren't making any sense."

Smiling at him, Jorg put his oxygen mask over his face and his voice came out distorted as he said, "I know you, Dimitri. I know how you think, how you will react. I know your heart."

Dimitri kept silent, striving to hold his father's increasingly intense gaze. "You know nothing about me."

His father flapped his skeletal hand in his direction, the white tape holding the IV in place a sharp contrast against the dark age spots littering his skin. "I know what I need to know. I chose you, Dimitri, to head the Novikov Bratva when I die. You are my chosen heir."

Conversation erupted through the room and Dimitri's father smiled at him. He dragged a deep breath into his lungs, willing himself to keep standing upright. No, this was wrong. Alex should inherit, not him. He tried to form the words to reject his father's offer, but his mind couldn't comprehend what had just happened.

Jorg gave the room an imperious look. "Leave us, except for you, Peter-and your rabbit can stay, Dimitri. I rather like her."

By the time the room emptied Dimitri had regained control of himself. "Why? Why me? You hate me."

"I do not hate you. You are my son. You will always be my son, but I did not pick you because of any affection I might feel for you. Dimitri, you have proved yourself to be the man I believe can lead the Novikov Bratva with strength after I die."

"But what about Alex?"

"What about Alex? He will take over my public business, will run my corporations and be the public face of our enterprise." For a moment his father's eyes dimmed and sorrow etched his face. "I want Alex to have what he wants most in the world, a normal life for his wife and child."

Dimitri frowned at Peter, who slowly shook his head. "Father, Jessica is dead."

For a long moment his father stared at him, then nodded. "I forget these things."

Peter cleared his throat. "Dimitri, if you will come

with me, there are some things we must discuss, alone."

He tightened his hold on Rya and said in English, "She does not leave my side. Whatever you say to me can be said in front of her."

"That is mistake," his father said in English then switched to Russian. "Do not burden her with the evil of our lives. She is a strong woman, but kind. It is your job as her husband to protect your wife, to keep her safe."

"We're not married."

His father laughed, but this time it was a deep chuckle that reminded Dimitri of when he'd been a child and his father had laughed like that all the time. "You will be, and you will keep her safe and break this curse, this plague that took my wives and my daughter from me,"

When his father's voice broke on the last word Rya made a soft sound and whispered, "Is he all right?"

Looking down at his woman, Dimitri nodded. "Do not worry, *dorogaya*."

"I have something for you, little rabbit," his father said suddenly and began to dig around the blanket over his lap. "Come here."

Chapter Twenty-Eight

Rya stared at Dimitri's father, not trusting him a bit, but approached his side of the bed anyway. If he tried anything she could probably snap his bones like a twig. "What is it, Mr. Novikov?"

He pulled out a worn gold velvet case about the size of a book from beneath the blankets. "I want you to have this. It belonged to Dimitri's mother, and has been in her family for generations. They were to go to my daughter, but she died a long time ago. I want you to have it."

His hands trembled as he handed her the box and when she opened it she found a gorgeous rose gold necklace and earring set studded with hundreds of apple green gems that sparkled like nothing she'd ever seen. The necklace and earrings were done with floral patterns of the gold woven around the stones and even if she didn't hold the old fashioned box in her hands she would have known this jewelry was antique.

Looking up at Mr. Novikov, then back down at the magnificent jewelry she shook her head. "I can't take this."

"You will take." His stern tone allowed no argument. Still, she looked over at Dimitri who nodded with an unreadable look on his face before she took the box.

"It is very beautiful. Thank you."

Peter moved from around Mr. Novikov's bed and said in English, "Dimitri, we must discuss business. Please, time is of the most importance."

"I will not leave Rya alone."

When Dimitri gave her a worried look she smiled

and hugged the soft velvet case close to her chest. "Go ahead. I'll wait for you in the library."

"Actually," Mr. Novikov said in a strong voice so at odds with his frail figure that she did a double take, "I would like Rya to stay with me."

"No." Dimitri said and moved to Rya's side, sliding a possessive hand over her shoulder.

Mr. Novikov made a tsking noise. "I will not harm her or tell her anything that would make her feel less for you. I promise."

"You promise many things and they are all lies," her man growled and the tension thickened between them until Rya found herself clinging to Dimitri.

"Leave us," his father demanded and Rya inwardly groaned, knowing there was no way in hell Dimitri was leaving her alone with his father now. Eager to get the hell out of here, she leaned forward and said, "Dimitri, please go talk to Peter by the fireplace. That should give you the privacy you need and I'll let your father say his piece then we will leave."

"I do not want him harming you," Dimitri said in a voice so low it was almost a growl.

She winked at him. "*Volk moy*, there is nothing that he could say that would make me leave your side."

Dimitri and his father argued in Russian before Dimitri stalked to the other side of the room. Mr. Novikov looked up at Peter. "Go talk to my son. Get the documents signed, now."

Peter stared at Mr. Novikov with open animosity. "Then you will do it? You will tell me where they are?"

"Then I will fulfill my promise to you."

When Mr. Novikov turned his attention back to Rya she could see how much this had drained him and her gaze skittered over to the medical equipment that was showing an increasingly weak heartbeat.

Without thought she said, "What are you ill with?"

"Cancer," he said with a grim look. "When I was young man I was exposed to massive amounts of radiation from Chernobyl."

"The nuclear power plant that blew up back in the eighties?"

"Yes. The place I lived, Kiev, was in direct line for fallout. I was in parade, a celebration held on May first in old Soviet Union. While I was marching with the rest of the people we were being slowly poisoned by radiation falling from the sky like invisible rain. Many, many people got sick and died in the weeks that followed."

"Wow," she said in a soft voice and slowly shook her head. "No one told you about the accident? Or that there might be an issue?"

He rested back into the pillows mounded behind him, his breathing labored. "No, no one told us. Our government hides many things from its people. They are more corrupt than even the worst Bratva. Never forget that, little rabbit. But I do not have much time. I must know some things that you have answers to."

She glanced over at Dimitri and found him talking with Peter in hushed tones over by the fireplace. "What is it?"

"Is true you died?"

"What? I mean yes, but how did you know?"

He gave her a look that made her feel foolish. "Come, Rya, you must know I would have you researched."

"Right. Well, if you did then you know that technically I did die."

"I am not interested in your death, I want to know what you saw after."

This didn't surprise her in the least. In her experience as a hospice nurse she'd had this conversation many, many times with her patients and it allowed her to get into a different mindset, to stop thinking like Rya the freaked out woman and like Rya the nurse. "What do you want to know? I'll answer you as best I can, but I would like to remind you that this is just my experience and that my memories may not even be correct."

"What was it like?"

She told him her story and watched him carefully as she did, looking to see if her words gave him peace or unsettled him. That's the way it usually went. People were either comforted by her story, or scared of it. In Mr. Novikov's case, fear seemed to be his response. After she finished he watched her for a few moments, swallowing convulsively before he said in a low whisper, "I would like to think that my wives and my daughter are waiting for me, but what if they are not happy to see me?"

"Were you cruel to them?"

"To my women, no...to their sons...I did what I had to in order to make them strong men, but I hurt them in ways that now shame me."

She tilted her head. "If they really are waiting for you, then perhaps now would be the time to try and settle any wrongs you've done against your sons. While you still have a breath in your body it isn't too late."

He leaned back and closed his eyes, his lips trembling as if he was speaking but there were no sounds coming out. Not sure if he was sleeping or not, she took a step away and looked over to Dimitri who was signing a thick stack of documents. After he finished the last one he glanced in her direction then over to his father and back to her again. "Ready to leave?"

"Yes, please."

He came over and took her hand. "You have made me so proud today, *zaika moya*. Now, let me take care of you."

Holding the box to her chest, she looked over at where Dimitri's father lay sleeping and nodded. "Do you want to say goodbye?"

Dimitri's expression grew cold and he shook his head. "We said our goodbyes years ago."

She wanted to argue with him, to urge him to find some kind of closure, but she also knew the hard truth that just because someone was dying, it didn't make them a saint. Dimitri's father had made his life hell and even though he'd been nice to her, she hated him for everything that he'd done to her man, hated him for continuing this stupid feud that threatened her life, and hated him for making Dimitri the head of the Novikov family. While it was a great honor, or at least an honor among thieves, all she could think about was the fact that the price of loving Dimitri had just grown exponentially and she didn't know if she could pay it without losing her soul in the process.

When they reached their apartment later that night she let out a sigh of relief, all the tension draining out of her. Maks was waiting for them and she winced when she saw the bruises on his face. One of his eyes had almost swollen shut and it looked like it really hurt.

"Maks," she said in a rough whisper. "What happened to you?"

Dimitri growled and swept her up into his arms. "He failed you."

Oh, that pissed her off. All this crap that she'd been through today, how well she'd managed to keep her shit together, and Dimitri had the balls to say that Maks *failed*?

"Um, excuse me. Let me tell you something. I've had a shit day. A really, really, really crazy shitty one. There were only a few bright points in this day. One of them being Maks doing everything he could to save me even when I made it impossible for him to do that. I went with your father's men, kind of willingly."

Maks stared at her like she'd lost her mind, and she realized she might have fucked up when Dimitri growled.

It was a very, very scary sound and she tensed up, then tried to wiggle away. The moment she shifted his grip on her tightened and when she looked up at him she flinched. Yep, she'd said something that really pissed him off. And he looked almost scared. That didn't bode well for her.

Trying to alleviate the damage she patted Dimitri's chest. "But I'm fine, I'm here, and we're all good. Let's go make love."

Without looking away from her, Dimitri said, "Bring food and vodka to my room in an hour."

For some reason, she'd lost all control of her mouth. "What? An hour? We're going to be done by then? Man, I was hoping for a little more loving than that."

His jaw clenched, but then the anger seemed to flow from him and he smiled down at her. "You are begging for it."

"Begging for what?" Her pulse raced and she bit her lip with excitement as he smiled down at her.

"For my whip. You will get what you need, *zaika moya*. I will make it all go away, but you will accept how I do it."

"Yes, Master."

Maks snickered, and she was sure for a second there that Dimitri was going to drop her and beat the bodyguard's already beat ass. She sank her nails into Dimitri and he shuddered hard, turning his glare on her. "Please, I need you."

Looking into her eyes, he studied her face. "I am yours. You know this. Take what you need, *dorogaya.*"

After that she didn't care where they were, or how they got here. The only thing she wanted was to be in their bedroom as quickly as possible. She began to tremble and Dimitri took her upstairs, yelling something over his shoulder in Russian before moving quickly to their room. The minute he stepped inside he dropped her and began to shred her dress from her body after kicking the door shut. She was mad for him, dying for his touch, needing to rub herself against him and breathe in deep. He'd come for her, he'd saved her. He loved her and she loved him so much. Words couldn't begin to describe her need for him.

Once her dress had been reduced to tatters, Dimitri stepped back and began to take his own clothes off in a way that had her squirming. Every inch of skin that he revealed as his suit came off was sinful. There was just something about a man without a shirt on but still wearing his dress pants that did it for her. She really wanted to go down on him, but right now, Dimitri wasn't showing much restraint. Seeing his fear for her reflected in his touch as he caressed her face made her tears slip free.

Dimitri made a low, almost cooing noise as he kissed her tears away. "None of this. You deserve joy, not tears. Please stop crying, *zaika moya*, is breaking my heart."

"I love you," she whispered and stepped into his arms, adoring the way her touch gentled him. Slowly the tension left his body as she stroked him, letting him know with her caress how much she adored him. The energy between them had always been insane, but tonight it was off the charts because of all the volatile emotions built up between them.

"I need to own you," he whispered and her whole body flushed with heat.

"Please."

He eased her over to the bed and laid her back among the sheets that smelled like them. She loved that smell, loved the scent of their dreams mixing together in the fabric. It was such a visceral thing and she turned her head into the pillow, inhaling Dimitri's scent. She still wore his cologne and every time he was near her he would dip his head down to sniff at the back of her neck with a satisfied grunt. It never failed to make him want to fuck her and mark her as his.

Reaching beneath the bed, he pulled out the Velcro restraints and she grinned at him. He knew she loved these, they were soft enough that she didn't have to worry about rubbing her wrist raw if she wanted to struggle a bit but strong enough to keep her in place. And she could unhook them herself if she felt anxious. Her man really did think of everything when it came to her pleasure. It was like he memorized everything she liked and kept trying to improve on it. He'd definitely spoiled her. There would never be anyone who could make her feel the way he did.

"Master," she whispered as he finished strapping down her arms.

He smiled down at her and sat back on his haunches between her spread legs. His gaze went from her pussy, to her tits, to her eyes, then her mouth, then back to her eyes. His impressive pectoral muscles flexed and his abdominals put on a hell of a show as he leaned forward. "The most beautiful woman in the world is my woman."

Damn, he was always saying things like this that made her blush. But, she'd gotten better at accepting the fact that he worshiped her. And she loved every minute of it. "Thank you, Master."

He moved down so that his forearms bracketed

her head and his body pressed against hers, covering almost every inch. His heat radiated into her and she took a deep breath, relaxation flowing through her. He was here, and he would keep her safe because he loved her. Never in her life had she imagined being in love would feel like this, this all-consuming, but now she understood what people meant by forever love. She would love this man until the day she died.

Dimitri took a deep breath and allowed himself to sink further down onto Rya, the softness of her body cradling him as he fought the panic filling him as he thought of how close she'd come to dying. The terrible things he'd imagined happening to her dominated his thoughts and he took a deep breath, trying to dispel the thoughts of pain and suffering. If anything had happened to her...

She jerked at her bonds and wiggled a bit beneath him, the sensation making his balls draw up tight. "Feeling needy?"

She frowned up at him and he couldn't help but grin back. He loved it when she was begging for discipline, trying to get him to lose his temper and punish her. Silly girl. She had no idea what she was inviting on herself.

"Yes, Master," she said and licked her lower lip, her pupils hugely dilated. He gave her nipple a hard pinch and they darkened further.

So responsive.

So his.

Leaning back, he quickly shed his pants and underwear, then knelt between her thighs and began to jerk himself off. He needed to take the edge off or he'd give in and fuck her. The sight of her bound before him like this, with that fucking bruise shadowing the side of her face, made him savage. It was either cum or run the risk of accidentally hurting her.

She licked her lips and watched him. "Can I help you with that, Master?"

"No."

That made her pout and he wanted to put his cock in her smart little mouth. She was so good at sucking dick that he almost forgave her for being such a brat, almost. An idea came to him and he must have smiled because Rya was giving him a very worried look. "Master?"

"This is what will happen. I will come on you. Wherever my seed lands, I will paint your body with the aphrodisiac oil that Alex used on you at the lodge."

A hint of guilt moved across her expression and he bit his lip to keep from laughing. She was an exhibitionist, she'd enjoyed being with Alex with Dimitri's permission, and he did not understand why she felt guilty for enjoying it. He'd certainly enjoyed watching it, up to the point where Alex looked like he was going to fuck her.

Then he'd had to step in.

The thought of anyone but him fucking Rya made him suddenly furious. He bit her neck, sucking it hard as he marked her there, wanting to leave a bruise that everyone could see saying she was his. He grasped her breast and began to torment her nipple with sharp nips while rubbing himself against her stomach as he jacked off. It took only a few moments before he climaxed and marked her left breast and her pussy along with a bit of her stomach with his seed. She whimpered as he rubbed his cock through her folds, saturating her with his fluids.

"Mine. This body is mine; this pussy, is my pussy. You are my woman."

He reached down to the foot of the bed where he'd hidden the oil. After pulling the bottle out she cursed and her whole body tensed, but he liked the anticipation gleaming in her amber eyes. So beautiful, like autumn leaves in the bright sun. She licked her lips and watched him roll the vial on his palm. "Shit, you really do have it."

"Oh yes." His cock began to harden again as he gently shook the mixture. "More precious than gold, but I love what it does to you. How it makes your pussy so hot and wet for me. How you beg for my cock, how it drives you crazy."

Her gaze stayed fastened on the small vial as he began to uncap it. "You don't need that to make me crazy."

"I know. But I like playing with you, Rya. I will always want to try new things with you, to see if I can find new ways to bring you pleasure. I am your Master and I will always take care of you."

Her lower lip quivered and she looked unbearably vulnerable and cute as she said, "Thank you. I need you so much. I don't think I could survive without you."

"Shush, *lyubimaya*, you make me ache for you." He quickly wet the tip of his finger with the oil before smoothing it over her entire left breast. She startled and glared at him even as her nipple hardened beneath his palm. He would never get enough of her lush curves.

"How much of that are you going to use?"

"As much as I want. Do I need to gag you? Can you not control your mouth?"

That pissed her off and he loved it. Loved the snap of fire in her gaze, the curl to her lips that said if she wasn't tied down she'd be wrestling with him. But, if she really wanted out all she had to do was undo those straps, so she was here, submitting to his will so beautifully despite her sassy mouth. She was still too far inside her own head so he would have to start to break her down, get her past her emotions.

With this in mind he got a rubber gag that had a small dildo on the inside of the mouth part. He coated that protrusion with the oil, then held it up for her. Rya gave him a good glare, but she opened her mouth and even gave the dildo a little tease with her lips that made him want to fuck her in the worst way. "Bad girl. Soon you will feel the need to suck that fake cock in your mouth. You are not allowed to suck it. Do you understand? If you do I will not let you swallow my seed."

She nodded and whined a bit as he coated his finger with the oil, then began to mix it with his cum on her pussy. Rubbing it through her folds, he imagined what it would feel like when he fucked her, all oiled up with the aphrodisiac. He'd never used this much on a woman before because he would take her until they both couldn't move. That would mean he would have to take care of her, see her for longer than he wanted, so he'd never bothered. But with Rya...he wanted to keep her in his bed forever. She belonged here.

After oiling her down to his satisfaction, he sat back and poured some oil into his palm and capped the bottle before fisting himself. At the sensation of the oil coating his dick like liquid silk he let out a harsh groan. Despite coming less than five minutes ago, he was ready to go again after three strokes of his dick. Forcing his eyes opened, he slowed his moves and watched as Rya's body continued to heat. When he looked up to her face and saw her desperate gaze, he could only smile at her distress.

For a moment she looked angry, then she arched her back with a groan and mumbled around the loose gag. "Please, Master, touch me."

Running just the tips of his fingers over the swell of her breasts, he marveled at how quickly her pussy became saturated with her arousal. It hung thick and heavy on those perfect pussy lips, mixing with his seed and the oil, and he wanted to take a taste, but needed to be inside of her. He lined himself up with her opening, then sank in, tweaking her nipples and gritting his teeth when she began to climax around his cock, squeezing him incredibly tight as he strained not to join her without having even fully penetrated her yet.

Pausing halfway in, he panted as he watched her beautiful golden eyes open up. Then she smiled at him and it was like the sun warming his skin. He took the gag off and she licked her lips before saying, "Thank you, Master."

"We are not done yet, *zaika moya*."

"Thank God," she whispered, then began to undo her wrists, "because I need to touch you, Dimitri. I need to love you. Please, Master, let me love you."

"Anything you need, Rya. You know that. Come here. I am yours."

She crawled into his arms and gently pushed him back before straddling his hips. He moaned deep in his throat as she ground herself against him without any shame, creating one of the most sensual images he'd ever had the privilege of seeing. Watching his woman pleasure herself with his body was the ultimate voyeurism. She placed her small hands on his chest and he watched with absolute pleasure as Rya began to rub herself on him, chasing her release. He was tempted to help her, but decided to sit back and let his submissive entertain him.

Rya tossed her hair over her shoulder and smiled down at him. "Have I told you how much I love your cock?"

"You might have. A time or two."

"Well I do." She shuddered and he thought she might climax, but she managed to hold herself back.

"So good."

"Fuck yourself with it. Take my cock and shove it in that pretty cunt."

She grasped him in her delicate fist and held him to her entrance before slowly descending on him. As she came down she arched her back until her head was almost between his knees. He sat up on his elbows to watch as she took him and the sight of her pussy spread by his shaft made him groan. Beautiful. Perfect.

But he wanted to fuck, not play.

"Up, Rya."

She lifted herself back up with her stomach muscles and smiled at him. "Perfect."

Hearing her echo his thoughts made him smile even as he said, "Fuck me. Now."

Shifting her hips, she began to ride him and he watched her breasts bounce with her movements, loving the way she whispered his name. Her exquisitely soft, oiled cunt gripped him with her every move and he began to softly stroke her body, to ease her enough so that she would enjoy the buildup. Responding like she'd been made for him, Rya purred low in her throat and arched her back, then dug her fingers into the muscles at the top of his abdomen as she swayed. He thumbed her nipples, then leaned up and took one in his mouth. She must have enjoyed the new angle because she came with a harsh cry, slowing her movements until she barely stirred against him.

He savored the feeling of being connected to her for as long as he could before the urge to fuck wiped away all thoughts of nice and gentle.

Lifting her by her hips, he lay fully back and fucked himself with her wet body, loving how her gaze sought his before she lay against him, her breasts cushioned on his chest while she nibbled and sucked at his neck. "Mmmm, you feel so good inside of me, Master. So thick and hard. You make me come so much."

Her dirty talk made his balls draw up tight and as he went over he bit the other side of her neck, leaving a big mark there as well. His little Rya jerked against him as she climaxed in his arms, her pussy milking him for his seed. He wished that right now he was getting her pregnant, that they were making a baby together. The need to see her swollen with his child, to hold her while she nursed their baby filled him and he held her close, their bodies slippery with sweat.

After a long time, during which he was pretty sure she slept at least a little bit, she stirred against him and stretched with his hard cock still hard inside of her. "I need a shower, our bed needs new sheets, and I'm hungry."

He laughed and moved her off of him, both of them wincing at the motion. Evidently, he'd been a little too arduous with his woman's body. "Go, get in the shower. I will have the bedding changed while we clean."

She smiled at him and rolled off the bed, her fine ass swaying as she walked. He wanted to grab her and throw her back on the bed. If her pussy was sore maybe he would fuck her ass. Looking back over her shoulder at him, she winked. "I'll be waiting for you."

As soon as the water turned on he called the housekeeper and requested new sheets, then called the kitchen and asked that Maks be sent up with their meal. Pausing to grab something from the drawer next to the bed, he made his way across their room to the master bath. Normally, he would have had a maid bring their meal up, but by having Maks do it Dimitri was signaling to the other man his forgiveness.

Steam filled the bathroom and when he opened the smoked glass door of the immense shower he found Rya standing beneath the main showerhead with her face tilted upwards. The turquoise green marble with its hints of deep bronze brought out the olive tones in her skin and with her hair wet like this it fell all the way to the top rise of her perfect ass. He filled his hands with her breasts as he stood beneath the spray. When she opened her eyes and smiled at him he couldn't think of a time in his life when he'd been happier than at this moment.

He placed a gentle kiss on her swollen lips and smiled. "Let me wash you."

Used to his need, almost a compulsion really, to care for her, she closed her eyes and let him go about his routine, first washing and conditioning her hair before washing her body. Though he took the opportunity to enjoy her, he didn't make the cleansing overtly sexual. He wanted to give her all kinds of pleasure, to let her know on every level that he loved her. Rya was his sunshine and he would do everything he could to keep her in his life forever.

Kneeling before her, he began to soap up her hand. "Rya?"

She brushed the water off her face before looking down at him with sleepy, content eyes. "Yes?"

Taking a deep breath, he held up the ring he'd been hiding in the soap dish while he washed her. It was an antique three carat yellow diamond surrounded by two rows of rose cut white diamonds and flanked on either side by perfectly matched white diamond baguettes. On the day he'd returned to the United States to bring her home he'd bought the ring and had been waiting ever since, letting Rya get used to him and hopefully grow to love Russia enough to say yes. He didn't want her to feel trapped here, ever, but he couldn't wait any longer.

"Rya, will you marry me?"

Her hands shook as she cupped her fingers over

her lips. "What?"

Nerves tried to make him move off his knees, but he steeled himself. "I wish to marry you, Rya. To make you my wife. To let the world know that my heart belongs to you and you belong to me."

"Dimitri..."

The hesitation in her voice was like a fist to his heart. "You do not want me?"

"No, no I want you. I just...it's been a long day. I can barely stand let alone think."

"What is there to think of? You love me, you marry me."

She slowly shook her head. "I do love you, but we need to talk about what my future with you would be like, especially now that you're the leader of the Novikov Bratva."

"I will give the responsibility to Alex if you want me to." The little muffled pained noise she made worried him and he stood, holding her close. "Shhh, is no time limit. Think about it."

Shaking her head, she clung to him. "I want to say yes, but I'm scared."

"I'm sorry I failed in protecting you, *zaika moya*."

"That's not what I'm worried about. What if you die and I'm left alone? How am I supposed to live without you? You're my heart, Dimitri."

"*Lyubimaya*, please marry me. I would die without you as well."

She leaned back in his arms and studied his face. Such sorrow filled her gaze that he feared she was going to leave him, but when she smiled all the jagged holes in his heart filled with her light. "Yes, Dimitri Novikov, I will marry you. But, I want a big wedding with my friends and family here."

He would have given her a wedding on the moon at this point if that is what she wanted. Before she could change her mind he slipped the yellow diamond onto her ring finger and let out a harsh sigh. "Mine."

She began to giggle, then outright laugh. "Mine? How about I love you."

"Is what mine means. You are mine, I never wanted anything more. You are the love of my life, Rya, and I am unbelievably blessed to have you."

Standing up on her tiptoes, he obligingly tilted his head down so he could kiss her. "Rya Marie Novikov, my wife."

Kissing him lightly, she bounced back on her toes, making her breasts move in a most distracting manner. "I have to go call my Mom. And Tawny, and my cousins, and..."

He picked her up and positioned her so that her pussy ground against his abdominals. "Later."

She tilted her head back beneath the shower, the water making her gorgeous body gleam. As he shifted her so he could slip gently into her sex, she shivered lightly and whispered, "Later. Love me, Dimitri."

"Always, *zaika moya*."

Epilogue

Peter Clery strained to keep his expression blank as he stared at the dying monster before him. If he had a camera, he would take pictures of the mighty Jorg Novikov laid low by old age and illness, then sell them to all those people who prayed for his death and make millions. Even as his body literally rotted around him, Jorg's cold, grey eyes still projected enormous power.

The last of Jorg's henchmen left the room, leaving Peter alone with the bastard. He took one step forward from his position before the fireplace. He kept his gaze fastened on Jorg's face and did not glance at the framed portrait of the beautiful little three-and-a-half-year-old girl once again placed on the nightstand next to Jorg. That picture had vanished when Dimitri still lived here, but served as an effective muzzle on Peter, keeping him from telling Dimitri what he was really doing here.

"I've done what you asked and brought Dimitri to you," Peter said in a low voice. "Now where is she?"

Jorg chuckled, the sound raising the hair on Peter's arms. "Well done, Peter. Ever my loyal hound. You always were the best at finding a way to make the impossible happen."

Anger tightened Peter's stomach and he reminded himself that the bastard was the only one who could give him the information he needed, so he swallowed his wounded pride and decided to humor the old man because Peter needed the information the old man had before he died or changed his mind. A secret so astonishing Peter had scarcely believed it could be true until he'd seen a tantalizing hint of proof in the pictures of a little girl who shouldn't exist.

With a shaking, age-spotted hand Jorg reached beneath the edge of his pillow and pulled out a thick manila envelope. "Here."

Expecting some kind of trick, Peter was surprised when he went through the envelope and it contained exactly what he needed. "Thank you."

"Don't you want to know why?"

Actually, he did, but more than that, he wanted to go find his last living relatives. "Our business here is finished."

"It is not done until *I* say it is done!"

The medical monitors went crazy for a moment as Jorg surged upright in his bed.

Peter would have been happy to see the old fuck die right now, but he didn't need or want the complications of being present when that happened. "Why did you do it, Jorg? You know he loved her more than anything in the world."

Collapsing back against the pillows, Jorg clawed for his oxygen mask and brought it to his face, taking deep breaths and closing his eyes. Peter was almost sure he was asleep before Jorg said in a low voice, distorted by the mask, "Find her. Bring her to Russia."

"No fucking way."

"You will do this, or I will have the lovely April taken from you."

Peter struggled to contain his rage, a picture of his adopted daughter's smiling face flashing through his mind. There was no question Jorg would do as he said, or that his orders would be carried out—even after his death. Hating the evil bastard with every fiber of his being, Peter nodded.

"I will bring her back to Russia."

"Both of them."

"Both of them."

Peter pulled a picture out of the envelope, eagerly

scanning the woman's features. It had been taken while she was unaware, crouching down next to her daughter as they fed ducks at some pond, their deep auburn hair so like his own blazing in the sunlight. She was looking away from the camera, but his heart stopped as he scanned the delicate features of a face he thought he'd never see again. A grown woman, she still looked like an elfin princess, but the past four years had matured her, the last of the baby fat melting away and revealing the high cheekbones and tilted eyes that were the genetic stamp of the Clery family.

God she looked like his sister.

An ache lanced through his heart and he traced his fingertip over the picture, as if he could somehow touch them both by doing this. He'd failed her, in the worst way possible, and even now he had a hard time believing that his deepest wish had come true. It was both a miracle and a curse. He wouldn't fail her this time so that meant he had to somehow save her from the machinations of the monster lying in bed before him.

"What are your plans for her in Russia?"

"She is a very smart woman, a forensic accountant. You will hire her to go through the financial records of the Pobeda Corporation. There is true fraud there and much corruption. It is where Alex will have to start his work when he becomes CEO. Make her an offer she cannot refuse, but she cannot know it's you who makes that offer. Do not let her know who you are until she is in Russia."

Looking up from the picture, Peter sneered at Jorg. "I'm flying to America as soon as I leave here to see her."

Jorg actually chuckled. "That would be a mistake. She hates you, Peter."

"What?"

"You never told her who you really are, what you really do. Your betrayal, your lies, hurt her just as much as Alex's and she wants nothing to do with you. She fears you, and my son. She will run fast and far the moment she gets wind of you."

The urge to choke Jorg, to end his miserable life filled Peter. "What did you do?"

"What I had to do in order to protect her."

"You twisted bastard."

Ignoring Peter, Jorg reached for the portrait next of the little girl next to his bed and rested it on the bed so he could see it as he spoke. "You will put her in the same building as Dimitri and Ivan. She is currently working for a prestigious accounting firm in Chicago, make sure she is fired and her name is ruined. As you know, she has no family and she has no man in her life. Leave her nothing to return to in the United States."

"Why? After all you've done to her, why bring her more pain?"

"When Alex sees her he will not let her go, but she will run from him the first chance she has. There must be nowhere for her to flee to, no options but to let Alex win her heart back. While I am fond of her, I'm doing this for Alex. This is my final gift to him."

Stunned, Peter stared at Jorg, unable to believe that he was doing something to try and make amends to his son without any personal motivation. "If you gave a shit about Alex, you would have done this years ago. Why? Why now?"

Jorg closed his eyes and let out a long sigh. "I am dying; it is no secret. When I do, if my wives are waiting for me I do not want them to hate me."

This Peter believed. Even now, at the end of his life, Jorg was a selfish fuck who thought of himself before everyone else. Of course, he wasn't doing this for Alex. He was doing this to ease his own guilt.

"Is there anything else, or are we done?"

Jorg didn't even bother to open his eyes. "We are finished."

Without another word Peter left, his mind filled with plans on how he would bring his niece, Jessica, and her daughter, Tatiana, back from the dead.

Bonus Chapter
A Glimpse into Ivan andGia's Happily Ever After

Gia Lopez glanced over her shoulder at her fiancé and gave him a teasing smile. She was in a good mood tonight, overjoyed that her best friend in Russia, Rya, was off of whatever crazy ass hit list she'd been on. Ever since Rya had gotten engaged she'd been able to get out of the house without incident, but Gia knew how hard it had been for her friend to leave, paranoid about someone wanting to hurt her everywhere she went. When Rya said she was afraid she was going to turn into one of those people that never left the house, Gia decided it was time to organize a field trip to help ease her friend's fears.

In this case, a field trip to Gia and Ivan's home BDSM Club in Russia with Dimitri and Rya.

Glancing over at Rya, Gia took in another good look at Rya's outfit. Or what passed for an outfit. Dimitri, in his usual outrageous manner, had dressed Rya in a lovely, but plain see-through peach shift. Then he'd covered her in diamonds, including her collar which was a lovely platinum choker with a large, square shaped yellow diamond in the center. Tantalizing glimpses of more jewelry beneath the thin dress made Gia wonder what kind of amazing body jewelry Dimitri had put Rya in. Even without the diamonds Rya radiated sultry elegance, but Gia could tell she was nervous.

Shoot, Gia had been terrified her first night here, but after playing at the Club dozens of times since she'd become engaged to Ivan, she now entered the large building with a sense of anticipation. Ivan's flare for the dramatic came out when they played in public and she couldn't wait to let her Master have his wicked way with her. Well, hopefully her Master and Rya. Though Rya was completely submissive to the men, she topped Gia with ease and Gia had to admit, she loved it. Ivan never crossed the line, never touched the other woman in a sexual way, and the same thing went for Dimitri.

But with her and Rya? They tended to be all over each other.

Slipping her hand into Rya's, she gave the other woman a gentle squeeze. Rya glanced over at her and her golden eyes shimmered with hidden laughter as she winked at Gia. Inwardly sighing, Gia glanced down at her floor length crimson gown. They'd just come from some party at Ivan's Uncle Petrov's house. She thought it had been to celebrate Dimitri's engagement, but she felt like there was a lot she was missing. Something big had happened with Dimitri and she'd seen Petrov having lots of in depth conversations with Alex. She'd been learning Russia, so she got hints here and there of what was being said, but everyone spoke so fast and she was having trouble learning the language as quickly as she wanted.

But, she knew enough to hear those envious bitches gossiping about Rya as they passed through the Club. Fuck them. There were some very angry women here tonight, wanting to see the woman that had so perfectly captured Dimitri's heart. He worshiped Rya, loved her to death, and even though he rarely let it show in public, because that's just how most Russian men were, she'd caught private glimpses of them together and knew without a doubt Dimitri was pussy whipped. Not that she could blame him. Rya was a catch.

As they neared the area of the Club where her group hung out, she burst out laughing. She and Ivan's friend, Master Karl, stood there with a bottle of vodka and two glasses. As usual he looked like a dashing pirate with his black leather pants and white poet's shirt.

"Oh shit," Gia whispered to Rya. "Meet the welcoming committee. Hope you like vodka."

Rya giggled, the happy sound making everyone around her smile, though some people scowled as soon as they realized they were smiling. Fucking bitches. Without a doubt the one thing Gia hated about playing here was all the women that had fucked Ivan in the past. Oh, it was all before they met, but she was very possessive of him. So possessive, in fact, she'd done something last week while he was away on business, a physical proof of his ownership of her. Tonight was his first back in town and so far she'd managed to hide her surprise.

He was going to flip out, but she hoped he wouldn't lock her up in a cage all night as punishment.

While she greeted her friends, air kissing some, hugging others, she turned to watch Rya lift a glass with Karl. Holding the other man's gaze she calmly drank her vodka and Gia had to laugh. Petrov had come over one evening and taught Rya and Gia how to drink vodka. He'd been very serious about it, but by the end of the night Rya and Gia were wasted and snorting with laughter until their sides ached. Petrov had just watched them, highly amused at their drunken antics, and Ivan had just stood there and shook his head after he came down at three a.m. to tell them to shut the hell up. Dimitri had been out of town on business and when that happened Gia always invited Rya over. She knew the other woman hated being alone, and god knew, she and Ivan had the room for a sleepover. They had six empty bedrooms at their place and even though Ivan had already picked out what room they would use as a future nursery, they still had a room specially set up for Rya with her own alarm system.

Watching Rya finish her drink and wink at Karl, Gia had to laugh. Catrin, dressed tonight in a flowing baby blue sheer dress, stepped up and gave Gia a quick hug. "How is she?"

"Good," Gia whispered back. "Have you already done damage control?"

"You mean have I told every pissy cunt here that if they mess with Rya I'll have their tongues cut out? Yes."

The scary thing was that Gia wasn't sure if Catrin was kidding or not. To Gia's surprise, she'd found over the months that beneath that cultured, sometimes silly persona that Catrin portrayed, she was wicked smart and ruthless. Not in a bad way, just in a very…protective manner. She didn't like anyone messing with her friends and she made her allegiances very clear. Gia was certainly grateful to have her as a friend and the fact that Catrin adored Rya made things much easier.

"Haters gonna hate," Gia sighed and Catrin giggled.

"Indeed. Are you playing tonight?"

She flushed and looked down. "If Ivan allows me."

"What do you mean?"

"I…I did a bad thing." She sighed, shaking her head but unable to hide her smile. "He is going to kill me when he sees it."

Catrin's pale blue eyes widened. "What did you do?"

Before she could answer Ivan's delicious energy burned against her back. He was in a mood tonight, possessive and very touchy. Not that she minded. She loved it when he was hungry for her like this because she wanted him just as bad. Even after almost eight months together she wanted him more every day.

Ivan slipped his arms around her, pressing her to his body, letting her feel his erection. "Come, my Gia. I want to play with my pussy."

Her brain began to shut down just the slightest bit and she softened against him. "Yes, Master."

When he began to lead her to the dungeon area with the toys she bit her lower lip. Okay, maybe he'd go to one of the more shadowy areas. Someplace where she might be able to position herself so he couldn't see her surprise. When he stopped before a massive, flat padded table with restraint fastenings all around the edge, she groaned. Nope, she was fucked, in every sense of the word.

Rya stood on the other side of the table and Ivan positioned Gia so she could watch Dimitri slowly undress Rya. The other woman's hair hung in waves all the way to her hips, and when Dimitri lifted all that glorious hair off Rya's back, her wolf tattoo appeared. It was beautiful, a work of art, but Gia still found it kind of eerie to see Dimitri's silver eyes staring back at her out of a wolf tattoo. A rope of diamonds hung down Rya's back, and at the base a little yellow diamond heart hung perfectly between her two lower back diamond dimple implants. Rya was so curvy, so full figured and Gia loved it. Another rope of diamonds encircled Rya's waist and highlighted the woman's exquisite curves.

Ivan pressed against her, his bare skin warm against her, and whispered in her ear, "I enjoy it when you watch her. You get this soft look in your eyes, a gentle expression that is almost innocent, but very arousing. Looking at her gives you pleasure, and I love that about you."

She arched into him, her body already wet and

aching for his cock. "Please, Master, use me."

"I plan on it, *moya sladkaya lubov*."

Across from them Dimitri was now nude and she took a second to admire his thickly muscled body. He was so much bigger than Rya, and for a moment, she wondered if that was how Ivan looked against her, like a predator about to eat his prey. A hot shiver raced through her and Ivan began to kiss the side of her neck.

His accent thickened, deepened as he whispered against her skin, "Do you have something to tell me, my Gia?"

For a moment she froze, freaked out that he might know about her surprise, but that was impossible. She'd been super careful and Rya's bodyguards had covered for her. They promised they wouldn't tell Ivan. Trying to hide her nervousness, she shrugged. "Not really."

"Not really?" He bit her, hard. "Last chance. Do not lie to me."

Fuck, when he put it like that she had to answer him honestly. Asshole knew just how to manipulate her. "How did you find out? Did you see it?"

"See what?"

Irritated that her surprise had been ruined, she snapped, "Take off my dress."

"I had planned on it. But now you will get a spanking for acting like a sullen child."

An angry noise escaped her and Ivan laughed, the bastard. He loved driving her crazy, and if she was being honest with herself, she loved it as well. There was something about challenging him, and having Ivan always keep control that flat out did it for her.

He moved her so she was up on her hands and knees with her ass facing him. The table was, of course, at the perfect level for fucking. On the other side, Dimitri put Rya up in a pose that mirrored

Gia's. They were almost close enough to touch and Gia took a deep breath of Rya's rich and cool scent. Whatever perfume she wore was unusual, but it smelled wonderful on her. Leaning forward, Rya rubbed her nose against Gia's and got a smack on her ass from her Master. "Behave, *zaika moya*."

Gia froze as Ivan grabbed her by her hair and turned her head so she could see that he was holding a pair of wickedly sharp silver scissors. They gleamed in the low lighting and as some hard bass music poured through the sound system of the club, he said, "Stay very still."

She nodded, then let her head drop, assuming a relaxed position she'd learned in yoga that would allow him to cut the dress off of her with the least amount of risk possible. Her Master liked to tease her, but he would never hurt her. Much. Then again, she liked owie pleasure, pain that aroused her, made her body sing. He began cutting at the bottom of the dress and snipped it to right where the dress met the lower curve of her ass.

With a low growl he came up unto the table behind her, his bare cock rubbing against her bottom. She moaned and pressed back into him, her empty pussy clamping down, leaving her feeling unfilled and aching. A bit of wetness from the tip of his cock rubbed against her ass and she sucked in a hard breath when he grabbed her dress and tore it from her body in two quick jerks. A moment later he swore softly and traced his fingertips over her lower back with a reverent touch.

When he didn't say anything, just continued to trace the elaborate Cyrillic script of his name, she bit her lip and looked over her shoulder at him. "Do you like it?"

"I love it, *printsessa*." He gave her ass a brisk slap. "But I told you not to get any tattoos."

"And I told you that you can't tell me what to do."

As soon as the words fell from her lips she winced while Rya laughed, the bitch.

When Rya heard Gia call her a bitch she laughed harder until Dimitri smacked her ass. "Is this funny to you, little Rya? To see your friend mouth off?"

Smirking at her friend's suddenly pale face, she had to hold back a giggle as Rya said in a meek voice, "No, Master."

The men conversed in Russian and Gia had to look away from Rya before they started giggling again. When she did that she noticed Alex watching them from a couch nearby, his hand buried in the hair of two submissives giving him a blow job. His gaze was entirely focused on Rya and Dimitri. Instead of looking aroused, Alex seemed melancholy despite the fact that he had two women sucking on his dick. Gia was worried about him, he'd been in a deep funk since Rya had been taken by his father. Ivan said that for Alex, watching Dimitri with Rya and seeing how obviously happy and in love they were reminded Alex of how alone he was. She wondered if Alex would finally move on from Jessica's death and hoped that for his sake he would. When Alex wasn't busy being a super scary mobster he was actually a very kind man.

She glanced over at Dimitri to see if he'd noticed, but he was entirely absorbed in looking through his toy bag. Gia wanted to look over her shoulder to see if Ivan had seen the brief anguish in Alex's gaze, but she didn't want to draw Dimitri's attention to his brother's distress. When she looked again Alex was now watching her with heavily hooded eyes that made her clit tingle. While the sight of Dimitri and Rya together obviously hurt him, his gaze on her was an entirely different matter. Now he looked, hot, hungry, and aroused as he slipped one hand each into the hair of the women servicing him and gave Gia a small, feral smile that sent a delicious shiver through her.

Damn, that man was potent.

Turning her attention back to Rya, she licked her lips and let all the dirty things she wanted to do to the other woman fill her gaze. Almost right away the curvy brunette groaned and thrust her ass back towards Dimitri. He laughed and looked over to Gia. "What are you doing to my woman?"

"Nothing," Gia said too quickly, inwardly wincing at the guilty sound of her voice.

Ivan had evidently picked up on it because a moment later he smacked her ass, hard. "Bad girl. Move onto your back, with your thighs over Rya's legs. I want it so your pussies are across from each other, only inches apart."

The men helped them into the position they wanted and Gia's skin hummed with the energy of the people watching them. They had a nice little crowd right now and she grinned when she noticed Nico fucking Catrin on a nearby St. Andrew's cross. Then her gaze went back to Alex and the way he gritted his teeth as he stared at them was incredibly sexy. He looked like he was in pain, yet his cock appeared excruciatingly hard as the two submissives worked him over with their mouths.

Ivan hopped up onto the table next to her on her left side, while Dimitri lay next to Rya on the right side. The women's thighs rested on each other and she couldn't help but feel how close that put their pussies. When she noticed that Ivan had a double dildo all she could do was grin. He caught her smile and shook his head. "Such a naughty girl."

She startled a moment later when Dimitri began to rub something cold and slick on her anus. "Hey!"

"Shush," Ivan scolded her. "Do not shame me and

make me gag you for your lack of self-control."

His words fell on deaf ears because when she looked up and watched Dimitri rub the lube into her ass with one hand Rya's with the other, she was pretty sure she had a small climax.

Dimitri slid his thumb in her ass and she groaned deep in her throat, the noise joining with Rya's soft sigh. Ivan tapped her lips with his cock and she opened up for him, greedily sucking on his hard length and delighting in the taste of her Master. When Dimitri slid two fingers into her ass she hissed, the pain a little more intense now. Ivan helped to distract her by shoving his dick down her throat, forcing her to relax her gag reflex and take him. The guttural noises he made when he was all the way down her throat had her clit throbbing, begging to be touched.

Her body tried to grip down on Dimitri's fingers as he withdrew them, but the next thing she knew the head of the dildo was pressing against her bottom. She opened her eyes and released Ivan from her mouth, leaned up on her elbows, watching as Ivan carefully adjusted the women's bodies while he slowly slid the dildo into their bottoms. Rya was leaning back against Dimitri, her eyes glassy while he whispered into her ear, the pink flash of his tongue as he licked her skin highly erotic. Ivan made a low, almost humming noise then he rubbed Rya's clit. A little flare of jealousy caught Gia by surprise, until she noticed that Rya's face was scrunched down in discomfort.

Ivan began to move the dildo between them and Gia's arms refused to hold her anymore. She lay back on the table and stretched her arms over her head, enjoying the decadent sensation of her Master pleasuring her and of Rya's eager movements. The other woman cried out and Gia was pretty sure she was about to come, but then Ivan stopped.

Gia sucked in a huge breath of air when, a moment later, Ivan began to lick her pussy and suck on her clit. He must have been on his knees next to her by the angle of his mouth, and when she looked up she found Dimitri's head moving next to Ivan's, obviously eating Rya's pussy like Ivan was eating hers. She made a choked whimper as her body tightened, and her bottom clamped down on the dildo. Ivan's slick, warm tongue rubbed against her clit with expert skill and she strained to keep from coming.

"Master, may I come?"

Ivan lifted his head long enough to say, "Not yet."

She screamed and clawed at the table, trying to hold back, to not go over. He kept fucking her and by the time he said, "Give me my pleasure," she was about to pass out from holding her breath for too long. Sucking in a huge gasp of air she let it out in a shout as her climax tore through her, enhanced by Ivan's attention to her pussy and the fact that a second later Rya screamed out her orgasm as well. Energy seemed to flow between all four of them and Gia arched up, trying to rub herself against Ivan. She rubbed her hand over his head. "Please, Master, I need your cock."

He chuckled against her overly sensitive clit, then kissed her. "My pleasure."

Ivan pushed back from Gia's sweet pussy and licked his lips, watching as Dimitri carefully removed the double dildo before wrapping it in a towel and setting it at the edge of the table. His friend was nude and slick with sweat, and obviously very aroused. Not that Ivan was in much better shape. His dick ached to be inside his girl and the pleased smile she was giving him made his life all the sweeter. He could still barely believe that she was his and the thought of their upcoming wedding made his heart nearly burst with joy.

Not caring that they were in the middle of a BDSM Club, he picked Gia up and sat back on his heels. He positioned her on his lap and bit his lower lip when she gripped his cock and placed him at her entrance. The first few inches of his cock slid into her and he had to stop, holding her suspended above him with his face buried against her small, beautiful breasts. Shifting her just a bit, he nuzzled at her nipple and licked the gold barbell piercing it, loving the way her cunt clamped down on him. Unable to resist, he gave her a few more inches of his cock and grinned when she wiggled against him. He loved how she was always needy for him, always so eager to have him inside of her.

He worked himself in deeper, and deeper still, until she sat fully against him and cried out.

Movement came from his left and he watched as Dimitri moved Rya around so he could mount her from behind. The sight of his friend's cock sliding between Rya's juicy cunt lips had his own erection jerking inside of Gia. His woman licked at his neck and he closed his eyes, losing himself in her. With soft, sexy moans Gia rocked against him, their movements in perfect synch. While he loved the wild, crazy sex they'd had when they first met, nothing could match the intensity of their love making now. It was by far the best feeling in the Universe and he was totally addicted to loving his woman.

Gia captured his lips in a long, deep kiss that had him moving faster against her, his hips thrusting into her welcoming body while she chanted his name. Satisfaction surged through him as he gently touched her lower back. Yes, he'd hated the thought of her defiling her perfect skin with a tattoo, but now that he saw how it looked on her he decided he would let the tattoo artist live.

She pulled back enough to look into his eyes and gave him a sultry smile. "I love you, Master."

"I love you, my Gia."

They whispered these words against each other's lips, wanting to keep this intimacy to themselves. He gripped a handful of her butt and began to fuck her harder, the tight glove of her sex rubbing him just the right way. Being inside of her felt so damn good he never wanted it to end, but he was swiftly approaching the point of no return. As the fire began at the base of his spine he groaned, his senses fully opening to Gia as he whispered, "Come with me."

She ground her pelvis against his, massaging his cock with her inner muscles, then cried out as she began to climax. Gia's body rippled around him and he let out a growl of his own as he began to come inside of her, fill her body with his essence. She continued to writhe against him, her pussy contracting sharply and making him grit his teeth at the pain from being over sensitive. It wasn't unusual for Gia to have another orgasm after he came so he bit his lip while she ground herself against him, her release running over his lap as she gave herself a g-spot orgasm.

The way she shivered against him was delicious torture and he wrapped his arms around her, opening his eyes when someone threw a blanket over them. He looked up to find Dimitri smiling at him before he picked up Rya, already wrapped up in a blanket and looking like she'd fallen asleep.

Ivan couldn't help but laugh. Once Rya was asleep she was done for the night. He'd often come down to find her sleeping on his couch after he and Gia had gone to bed when Rya had spent the night. Rya didn't sleep well without Dimitri and Ivan had grown to care about the woman. She was funny, kind, and yet a dangerous female. But she obviously cared about Gia and made her happy, so that was good enough for him. His woman let so few people close to her that it did his heart good to see her friendship with Rya continue to grow.

Moving off the table, he put on his pants then wrapped Gia up in the blanket and lifted her into his arms. She smiled at him with total adoration as she stared up at him and while he carried her to where their circle of friends were waiting, he couldn't help but feel like the luckiest man in the world and prayed that no matter what troubles the future bought, their love would be strong enough to withstand it.

Ann Mayburn

A Thank you from Fated Desires

Thank you so much for reading **Dimitri's Forbidden Submissive**! The Submissive's Wish series is one of our favorites and we're glad you had a chance to read it. We do hope if you liked this, that you would please leave a review from where you purchased this or on another platform. Not only does a review spread the word to other readers, they let us know if you'd like to see more stories like this from us. Ann loves to hear from readers and talks to them when she can. You can reach her through her website and through her Facebook and Twitter accounts. You guys are the reason we get to do what we do and we thank you.

If you are looking for more stories like these, you don't have to wait much longer! Ann is cooking up new works in this series and a few others. Also, we have a few new authors coming that will be sure to whet your appetite.

If you'd like to know more about Fated Desires, check out our website or email us at admin@FatedDesires.com.

You can always find out more about the upcoming titles from Fated Desires by signing up for our MAILING LIST.

About the Author

With over thirty published books, Ann is Queen of the Castle to her wonderful husband and three sons in the mountains of West Virginia. In her past lives she's been an Import Broker, a Communications Specialist, a US Navy Civilian Contractor, a Bartender/Waitress, and an actor at the Michigan Renaissance Festival. She also spent a summer touring with the Grateful Dead-though she will deny to her children that it ever happened.

From a young age she's been fascinated by myths and fairytales, and the romance that was often the center of the story. As Ann grew older and her hormones kicked in, she discovered trashy romance novels. Great at first, but she soon grew tired of the endless stories with a big wonderful emotional buildup to really short and crappy sex. Never a big fan of purple prose, throbbing spears of fleshy pleasure and wet honey pots make her giggle, she sought out books that gave the sex scenes in the story just as much detail and plot as everything else-without using cringe worthy euphemisms. This led her to the wonderful world of Erotic Romance, and she's never looked back.

Now Ann spends her days trying to tune out cartoons playing in the background to get into her 'sexy space' and has accepted that her Muse has a severe case of ADD.

Ann loves to talk with her fans, as long as they realize she's weird and that sarcasm doesn't translate well via text.

Also from this Author
Now Available

Submissive's Wish
Ivan's Captive Submissive
Dimitri's Forbidden Submissive

The Chosen
Cursed
Blessed
Dreamer

Coming Soon

Iron Horse MC
Exquisite Trouble

Bondmates
Casey's Warriors

Other Titles
The Dark Fates Anthology

Made in the USA
Middletown, DE
23 November 2015